THE BURNS ENIGMA
THE FIRE SALAMANDER CHRONICLES BOOK FIVE

N. M. THORN

N.M. THORN

THE BURNS ENIGMA

THE FIRE SALAMANDER CHRONICLES • BOOK FIVE

The Burns Enigma

By N.M. Thorn

Copyright © 2020 by N.M. Thorn. All rights reserved.

nmthornauthor@gmail.com

This is a work of fiction. Any resemblance to actual persons living or dead, businesses, events, or locales is purely coincidental. Reproduction in whole or part of this publication without express written consent is strictly prohibited.

Cover art design by www.originalbookcoverdesigns.com

Edited by Spirit Editorial

PROLOGUE

* * *

September, 1942
Karelia, Russia. An unnamed hill 264.9

THE GROUND SHUDDERED from continuous explosions. Each blast ripped chunks of dirt, rocks, and moss as though they were pieces of dead flesh. The broken trees cried thick clear tears of sap, mourning all those who fell in this battle that seemed to have no end.

The ruckus of automatic weapons and gunshots bounced from tree to tree in an infinite earsplitting echo. Harsh shouts of commands, and the moans of the wounded and the dying blended into a terrible pandemonium that unfolded over a tiny, unnamed hill, 264.9. The stench of gunpowder and the reek of blood dominated the scent of the summer forest, the odor of damp moss, and the decaying smell of deadly swamps.

A cartridge, spat out by the lightweight Finnish mortar 81 Krh/42, exploded nearby, spreading pieces of rocks and dirt across the plateau. Starving and exhausted, a small partisan brigade was completely surrounded, and even though they held the elevated position, their situation wasn't favorable. Dead on their feet, people could barely move without falling, let alone fight in this deadly confrontation. And from the last telegram they received a few days ago, they understood that neither help nor supplies were coming.

They had no choice—they had to break free or they were all doomed to die either of starvation, or from the non-stop bombing of overwhelming enemy forces.

As the night slowly descended upon the battered plateau, a small group of soldiers started their way down the hillside, taking the southwest direction, away from the fight and the sharp cliff on the north. After the continuous cacophony of the battle, the silence on the southern slope felt unnatural, almost jarring. The leader of the group turned sharply to the east, heading toward a small hill behind enemy lines, and Aleksey stilled, throwing one last look back. From here, he could see the bright flares of explosions and thin, shiny lines of tracer bullets cutting through the darkness from every angle.

The group moved stealthily, following the edge of a swamp, unnoticed. Everything seemed to be working out well—too well even, but something was bothering Aleksey and he couldn't put his finger on what it was.

He had joined the partisans, almost from the first day of the war, when the German army invaded the Soviet Union on July 1941, following the plan of Operation Barbarossa. So, he wasn't new to war, battles and death. However, there was something here, in this shadow-infested forest that set his nerves on edge, making his hairs stand on end.

It didn't take them long to place the mines and since their path seemed to be unobstructed, the group took an east-bound route through muddy land. Walking single file, they moved slowly through the dangerous marshlands, carefully choosing their every step, probing the unstable surface of the swamp with long branches and make-shift staffs.

Walking last, Aleksey kept swiveling his head from left to right. Staring into the darkness, he couldn't get rid of the feeling that someone was watching him, and an expectation of upcoming trouble settled heavily in his heart. He didn't notice when the man in front of him halted, and he almost ran into him, stopping in the last second.

The wind picked up, showering them with leaves, breaking off small dry branches. Suddenly, it seemed like the temperature dropped by a few degrees, and Aleksey shivered, rubbing his arms with his hands. The forest came to life, and the swamp bubbled up right next to his feet. With his nerves stretched to the limit, Aleksey tensed, his stiff fingers squeezing the SVT-40 rifle so hard that his knuckles turned white.

Nevertheless, he managed to stay still and silent, staring into the darkness ahead without blinking. Somehow, the air got thicker, and he had a hard time filling his lungs with oxygen, his chest shuddering with short breaths. An unusual wave of heat rose within him, traveling through his body toward his hands, and cold sweat beaded his forehead.

Like through a wall, he heard people speaking in loud, grated voices, but his mind couldn't process the words. Every sound blended into a sickening dull mush in his ears. A heartbeat later, the buzzing white noise was shattered by the harsh barks of gunshots. Like on autopilot, he dropped to the ground, feeling the icy, putrid swamp water drenching his uniform, chilling him to the bone. But it wasn't the cold that bothered him. For some strange reason, the touch of this muddy liquid to his body was painful, burning his skin as if he were on fire.

He grunted, shifting uncomfortably in a puddle of foul muck, searching for a drier spot unsuccessfully. As the pain intensified, the noise of the unfolding battle dimmed down in his mind overwhelmed by the torment his existence had become. He pushed off the ground, struggling to get away from the water and its fetid stench, but only sunk deeper.

Unable to tolerate the agony any longer, Aleksey dropped his rifle, squeezed his head with his hands and howled, his tortured voice traveling far through the forest. All the other sounds ceased completely, and the darkness swallowed him whole.

* * *

"So, this is it? He is... Well... not much to look at..."

An unfamiliar female voice sounded somewhere above, getting louder and then fading off in his frazzled mind. As he felt a sharp jab to his ribs, Aleksey cracked his eyelids open and blinked a few times. Everything was dark and blurry, but a single bright orange spot hung somewhere right above him. Distorted, swaying shadows moved behind it, but he couldn't make out what they were. Waves of warmth spread around the small shining shape, filling him with hope and solace, and the only thing he wanted was to touch it, bring it closer.

He blinked a few more times and attempted to raise his arm, but it felt too sore and heavy, and he dropped it powerlessly. With surprise, he realized that he no longer lay in the mushy mud of the swamp. The ground beneath him was firm and he could feel small rocks digging into his back.

"Are you sure this worthless maggot is the man we are looking for?" asked the female voice again, unmistakable tones of disgust lacing her every word.

A pair of strong hands grabbed his shoulders, yanking him into a sitting position. He moaned as a sharp jolt of pain rushed through him and leaned forward, trying to find a position he could hold on his own.

"Allow me to demonstrate, my lady," said the gruff male voice.

Someone pushed him lightly on his shoulder, almost unbalancing him, and he sensed a gentle brush of warm air against his skin. Slowly, Aleksey opened his eyes and squinted at the brilliant orange light just inches from his face. With a painful grunt, he was finally able to lift his arm and rub his eyes. As his vision started to clear, he realized that the orange light was produced by fire. A small playful flame danced in the hand of a large man dressed in a black SS officer uniform, doing him no harm.

What the hell? Aleksey tried to distance himself from the stranger but couldn't move and just closed his eyes, turning his face to the side.

The man squatted next to him, regarding him with icy contempt.

"You," he said with a hard German accent, seizing Aleksey's chin and forcing him to look up. "Tell me, this little *das feuer*... I mean, fire... Does it make you feel better, soldier?"

He brought the fire closer to him, slowly moving it over the exposed skin of his face and neck. Aleksey didn't answer, so the man squeezed his face harder, his nails, too long for a male, digging deep into his skin, drawing a few drops of blood.

"I asked you a simple question, soldier," he hissed through his clenched teeth. "I'm not asking you to betray your comrades. All I want to know is if the closeness of the fire makes you feel better." He let go of his chin and then backhanded him, sending him flying to the hard, rocky ground.

Aleksey moaned, the copper taste of blood quickly filling his mouth. He coughed, splattering scarlet liquid on his chin, and propped himself up on his elbows, realizing with a shock that the SS Officer was right—the close presence of this little flame made him feel a little better, stronger even. Ignoring the ringing in his ears and the white spots dancing in his vision, he pushed himself up into a sitting position again.

"Yes, it does... but I don't understand how..." His voice trailed off. "Where am I?"

He checked his surroundings, not recognizing the place. He sat next to the edge of a small body of water—most likely a lake—surrounded by strange rock formations. Giant boulders stood supported by a few smaller stones, and it was amazing that such an unnatural contraption could be balanced at all. Next to every group of rocks, there was a tree, warped and twisted to such a terrifying degree that it was hard to imagine how it could grow like this in the first place.

The Officer snickered and squeezed his fingers into a fist, extinguishing the flame. He got up, straightening his pants, and threw a quick glance at his companion. A tall blonde woman stood behind him with her hands on her shapely hips. Also dressed in a black SS uniform, she exuded a vibe of arrogance, her mere presence making Aleksey's blood run cold. Her gloved hand rested on the pommel of a sword, which only high-ranking officers were allowed to carry. She gave the man a barely visible nod and he turned back to Aleksey.

"As far as I recall," he started, sarcasm dripping out, "locals gave this place quite a remarkable name. They call it Vottovaara, which in normal language means '*No Trespassing*.'"

He guffawed, slapping his hips with his hands, and threw a glance back at the woman as if he needed her support. She didn't respond to him. Her face, too hard to be called beautiful, remained cold and emotionless.

"Vottovaara..." Aleksey breathed out. His brigade could be a kilometer or two away. So close, yet so far away.

"Yes, it is Mount Vottovaara." The woman approached him and lowered down to one knee. She took her gloves off and gently ran her fingertips over his cheeks. Then she looked at the man over her shoulder, her eyebrows forming high black arches. "But I barely sense any fire in him. Are you sure he is the one?"

The man chuckled. "Yes, my lady. I'm quite certain."

He whispered something that sounded like gibberish, and a bright ball of fire materialized in his hand. The flames crackled, sending bright sparks into the dark sky, and Aleksey held his breath, his eyes wide.

That's impossible... It can't be...

"You see, these rare creatures of fire are always born human," the man continued his explanation, his fingers making the fireball spin in his palm. "They can live their entire miserable human life and never discover that they were meant for greatness..." His voice trailed away for a moment. "Never ascend to their power and immortality."

The Officer moved his hand with the fire from left to right, and Aleksey couldn't help but follow his movement.

I don't understand... What is he talking about? The thoughts in his head rushed in every direction and he couldn't stop their wild stampede.

"To get him where we need him to be, all we have to do is help him discover who he is." The man lowered down to his knees, a sinister snarl curving his thin lips. "Would you like to do the honor, my lady?" he asked, extending his hand with the fireball to her.

The woman chuckled, and her soft laughter sounded scarier and more dangerous than the most terrifying threat. Muttering something under her breath, she took over the fire and glanced at the man.

"Hold him," she whispered, and a sinister dark glow ignited in the bottom of her eyes, her bright red lips stretching into a semblance of a smile.

As the man seized Aleksey's arms, twisting them behind his back to immobilize him, she thrust the fireball through his chest.

They will burn me... I'll die...

For a split second, the wild thought lingered in his mind.

The next moment, a pain, unlike anything he had ever experienced before, made his body arch and thrash in the man's hands, wiping his mind blank.

Time slowed down.

All sounds seized.

He screamed, not recognizing his own voice.

The woman laughed and uttered a few words that meant nothing to him. Another ball of fire materialized in her hand. Her eyes focused on his as she pushed it through his chest again. Another howl erupted from his lips, his vocal cords tearing. She didn't wait for him to relax and manifested another fireball. He pushed against the hold of the SS Officer restraining him, and the man fell back.

With a low growl, Aleksey rose to his feet. Breathing heavily, he looked down and realized that his entire body was engulfed in scorching flames. At first, his uniform ignited around his neck, but a few minutes later the fire devoured it all, leaving him completely naked.

Slowly, the fire subsided, and just a few small flames were still dancing on his arms and shoulders. He stood frozen in place, his mind unable to process how it was possible. While his clothes had burned to ashes, he felt no pain and his skin didn't even blister. On the contrary, he felt stronger and more energized than he had felt in days.

The woman laughed, displaying a perfect set of white teeth, and a predatory gleam ignited in her eyes. Approaching him, she placed her hand over his heart, unfazed by the closeness of the fire, and a malevolent happiness transformed her hard features. He stared down at her, his flaming arms spread wide, his unclothed chest rising and falling with heavy breaths. Everything inside him screamed, FIGHT! Run for your life! But he couldn't make a move.

"Now I see you..." she whispered absentmindedly. "There you are..."

She laughed again and touched his forehead with two fingers, whispering something in the same weird language he couldn't recognize. As the world twirled around him into a tornado of sounds, flashes of light and a plethora of strange smells, his knees buckled. The SS Officer caught him and lowered him down to the rocky ground of Mount Vottovaara. With his fading mind, he registered just a few more words, before the darkness finally surrounded him.

"You're coming with us, Child of Fire…"

CHAPTER 1

~ ZANE BURNS, A.K.A. GUNZ ~

Somewhere in the United States...
Probably...
Date—unknown...

The room was absolutely white. Except for unblemished white walls, polished white tiled floor and white ceiling, there was nothing else in this room—no furniture, not even a mattress on the floor. A small area in the back was separated for personal needs by a low white wall. Long white light panels were embedded into the ceiling all around the perimeter.

The lights never went off, not even at night, and since there were no windows or a clock, it was impossible to count time. Gunz sat on the hard floor, resting his back against the wall as he stared at his reflection in a one-way mirror at the other end of the room. If not for his dark hair, he would be invisible against the white wall in the white medical scrubs he was wearing.

He got up, pushing off the floor, and swayed slightly. Since he'd been brought here and locked up in this room, he hadn't been able to take a deep breath as the air in this chamber of torture was infused with halon, a low-toxicity fire extinguishing agent. There was enough oxygen here to keep him from dying a human death, but his fire was suppressed, and he experienced a constant nagging pain accompanied by lightheadedness and fatigue.

Despite feeling weak and unsteady, he assumed the initial stance of Koryo—a Taekwondo pattern Aidan had taught him a while ago—and closed his eyes, focusing on his breathing, as shallow and uneven as it was.

The loud clank of the lock made him flinch. He opened his eyes and stared at a small window in the entrance door as a guard knocked on it with his baton.

"Inmate 802313," he said dryly. "You've been summoned."

Gunz sighed. Usually that meant nothing but trouble for him. Approaching the entrance, he pushed his hands through the window, allowing the guard to lock the handcuffs on his wrists. The restraints were just the human variety type, and normally something like this wouldn't keep him restrained for longer than a few minutes.

Here, however, everything was different. Magic detectors and heat detectors were installed in his cell and as soon as the magical energy field around him spiked up even a little, or if his body temperature went up by a few degrees, a large doze of halon was released, incapacitating him, leaving him curled up on the floor screaming in pain. The muscle weakness was so debilitating that he had to wonder if it was only the fire suppressants that made him feel this way, or if there was some powerful dark magic in play too. In this facility, he was disabled as a Fire Salamander, as a wizard, and as a man.

The guard opened the door and seized his shoulder, yanking him roughly out of the room. As a reaction to the sharp movement, everything around him spun and his stomach heaved. He leaned forward, bracing himself with his handcuffed hands against the wall, and rested his forehead against his elbow.

The guard pulled him away from the wall, shoving him farther ahead. "Keep moving, inmate," he said icily, adding an extra push into Gunz's back, which almost sent him flying to the floor.

Gunz glanced back at the man, shaking his head. In this hellhole, all guards wore strange helmets, covering their faces. All he could see was a pair of blue eyes, staring at him with icy contempt. He walked the already familiar path along the well-lit corridor and stopped in front of a door with a name plate on it stating, "Dr. Roger Harris".

The guard knocked and once he heard a loud buzzing, pushed the door open. He grabbed Gunz by the back of his neck, forcing him inside the room.

"He's all yours, Doc," he said, pushing Gunz toward the table.

Gunz grunted as he lost his balance and fell forward, hitting his forehead on the edge of the desk. The room flipped upside down as he dropped to the floor. With his blurry vision he saw the guard leave and close the door. Then he felt someone's hands grabbing him under his armpits, pulling him up gently. Doctor Harris helped him sit down and walked around the desk to his own chair.

Gunz leaned back in his chair and closed his eyes, taking a few deep breaths to fill his lungs with clean air. When he opened his eyes again, he saw Doctor Harris observing him with interest.

"Feeling better, Mr. Burns?" he asked.

Gunz nodded, staring at the doctor with a deadpan expression. It wasn't their first meeting, and every time he was in this room, the good doctor tried to take his mind apart, block by block, as if it were nothing but a bunch of Legos. He hated these sessions and couldn't understand their purpose. Everything here was designed to torture him, and he still couldn't figure why. It seemed like whoever held him captive was torturing him for the sake of torture.

"I'm fine, Doctor," said Gunz, his voice raspy from constant coughing.

"Great, great." The doctor rubbed his hands together, an expression of delight on his face. "So, Mr. Burns... or should I call you Gunz? Or maybe Fire Salamander?" he asked, arching his eyebrows at Gunz.

Gunz tensed—that was the first time the good doctor let it slip that he knew his nickname and his true nature. But he suppressed his emotions and smiled lazily.

"No, you should not," he replied. "Only my friends can call me that, and you're not one of them."

"Aw, Mr. Burns." The man leaned back in his chair, making a steeple of his fingers. "I was just trying to be nice. There is no need to be so offensive. Not just yet, but I'll give you the opportunity to fight once we're done here."

That's something new, thought Gunz, cringing inwardly.

Since Gunz didn't say anything, the doctor continued, "So, Mr. Burns, what do you think about your stay here?"

"Your five-star accommodations could do with a good interior decorator," replied Gunz, sarcasm clear in his every word.

"And why is that?" asked the doctor.

"I'm not the biggest fan of the color white," replied Gunz, an uneven smirk curving his lips. "Besides, sleeping on a cold floor with lights on doesn't promote a healthy living environment."

"Are you suffering from sleep deprivation, Mr. Burns?"

"No, Doctor Harris, I suffer from infinite boredom," he replied dryly. "I don't even have reading privileges. Come to think of it, I didn't even get my phone call when I was brought here, which is a violation of my rights."

"You mean it's a violation of *human* rights, Mr. Burns," replied Harris with a sugary smile. "We both know, you're not human. Legally, there is no human rights violation here."

Gunz grunted, clenching his teeth to stop himself from saying anything that would trigger painful consequences.

"I see," purred the doctor, observing his reaction. "How does it make you feel?"

"Hmm," hummed Gunz. "How does it make me feel? Good question. Well... Like strangling you with these very handcuffs, for one." He lifted his chained arms with a cold smile, his fingers clenched into tight fists.

"I see." The doctor nodded, calmly observing him like he would any lab rat. Then he cocked his head and smiled as if Gunz didn't just threaten his life. "Do you read a lot?"

"I used to," replied Gunz with an indifferent shrug. "Until you threw me in this hellhole, that is."

"Hellhole? Hardly." The doctor laughed. "So, Mr. Burns, if I give you reading privileges, which book would you like to read?"

Gunz smirked. "Infernal Justice."

"Interesting choice," mumbled Doctor Harris, writing something in his notepad. "Why did you choose this particular book?"

Gunz raised his eyes at him, his jaw set. "Because I would prefer Infernal Justice to that of the Destiny Council."

For a moment, Doctor Harris stared at him mortified but quickly pulled himself together and his lips stretched into a forced smile, the corners of his mouth twitching a little.

"I have no idea what this Destiny Council is. Never heard of it," he said frostily, putting his notepad away. "Our session is over for today, Mr. Burns. I will make sure you receive the book you requested. In the meantime"—he pushed a button on the intercom—"your guard will escort you to the training facility. You're cleared for training."

He grabbed a piece of paper with his name printed at the top and quickly wrote something on it. Gunz heard the door open but didn't turn around. Doctor Harris waved his hand at the guard and once he approached the desk, he offered him the paper.

"He's cleared to begin training," he said coldly, pointing at Gunz. "You can escort him there now and give my note to the Commander."

The guard grabbed Gunz's shoulder and yanked him up to his feet. A low growl rumbled in Gunz's chest as he jerked his shoulder out of the guard's grip. He stood staring at the man who'd been abusing and torturing him for the last—he had no idea how long—and his chest rose and fell with heavy breaths as he struggled to suppress his fire.

"Mr. Burns," hissed the doctor, "you would do well to cool down. Literally. If you don't want to trigger the fire suppressant system in my office, that is." He pointed at the magic and heat detectors on the wall. "In a minute, you will be in the training facility where you can safely let out some steam."

He quickly walked around the desk and put his hand on Gunz's shoulder. Gunz snapped around, death staring from his eyes. But then he took a deep breath and relaxed his tense shoulders.

The doctor glowered at the guard. "Can you *please* take him to the training facility without insulting or abusing him?" he hissed, throwing his hands up.

"Yes, sir," replied the guard, but his voice carried through his displeasure.

It seems like this man has something against me personally, thought Gunz as he headed toward the door.

* * *

THE TRAINING FACILITY looked like a high school gymnasium equipped with all kinds of martial arts training equipment. Gunz looked around, taking in his surroundings. About fifteen men were already training there and even without using his other sight, he could sense that except for one man, none of them were human.

Gunz stood barefoot on the hardwood floor, not in a rush to make a move. The guard who brought him here approached the man who was the only human in the room and gave him the letter from Doctor Harris. The man stopped what he was doing and took the letter, dismissing the guard with a quick flick of his wrist.

Once the guard was gone, the man approached Gunz. Standing no more than a foot away, he stared down at him, a vibe of arrogance exuding from his every pore. He glanced at the paper in his hand again and smirked.

"So, you are that infamous Zane Burns I've heard so much about," he said, his voice raspy like the voice of a man who started smoking in his early teens. He gave him one more once-over and laughed, slapping himself on his thighs. "Nothing much to see, is there?" He glanced at the rest of his team that gathered behind him. Then he switched his attention back to Gunz. "So, boy, show me what you're good for."

Gunz met his mocking gaze calmly. Then he sighed and sat down on the floor, crossing his legs. The man looked back at his crew and snickered.

"Do we have a little rebellion on our hands?" he asked snidely and flicked his fingers at one of his fighters.

A man separated from the crowd, stepping forward. He was tall, no less than six-foot-eight, and had long white hair flowing freely down his back and shoulders. His eyes were angled and shone with an electric green light like that of a feral feline. Despite his size and considerable bulk, he moved with the grace of a dancer and his chiseled features didn't betray his emotions as he glanced down at Gunz.

"Lucan," said the man, "help him to his feet. Our new friend needs assistance."

Lucan closed the distance between them in one step and

easily lifted Gunz to his feet as though he weighed nothing. When he bent down, Gunz caught the sight of Lucan's pointed ear. *He's an elf,* he thought, shivers running down his back. *How did they break him?*

Elves possessed powerful magic only they could wield, but in the realm of humans, they were quite rare and capturing them was practically impossible, whereas breaking one into submission was unheard of. Yet, as Gunz stood slightly swaying, he had no doubt he was staring at an elf.

"Lucan," said the commander, "would you like to try out our new recruit and have a quick sparring match with him?"

Lucan's leaf green eyes darted to Gunz, and he shook his head.

"And why not?" asked the commander.

"He's a Fire Salamander," replied the elf, his voice as void of emotions as his face.

"Don't be scared, Lucan." The commander snickered. "Here, he is just a little man. He can't use his magic or his element unless he wants to get a nice dose of fire suppressant."

"My apologies, Commander Moore," said the elf, crossing his massive arms behind his back. "As a man he is too small. Even without me using my magic, it won't be a fight but cold-blooded murder. I'll kill him before the fight ever begins. There is no honor in that."

"You dare to disobey a direct order, elf?" hissed the Commander, heat rising from his thick neck to his bulldog-like face. "Who gives a damn about your honor?"

The elf froze, his angled eyes widened in unmistakable fear. Gunz smirked and sat back on the floor with his legs crossed.

"I'm not fighting for you," he said flatly. In other circumstances, he would probably be burning with anger, but right now, he could barely speak. "You are starving me, torturing me with sleep deprivation, abusing me physically and poisoning me with halon. How the hell do you expect me to be able to move, let alone fight an elf who is almost a foot and a half taller than me?"

"First of all, we are not poisoning you with halon. The fire suppressant we use is not halon but halotron—works just as well and environmentally friendly," grumbled the Commander sarcastically, anger almost palpable around him. "We're all about a green earth here, you know. Second, you're going to do as I command. You have no choice."

"We all have a choice," replied Gunz quietly, his eyes sliding over the faces of the fighters, "and I already made mine."

The commander approached him and swung his arm, punching him in his jaw. Gunz cried out as he fell to the side, his weakened body not complying with the demands of his mind. His mouth filled with blood and he spat on the floor, pushing himself back up into a sitting position.

"We'll see about that," hissed the commander, turning toward the elf. "Lucan, since he already made up his mind, now the choice is yours. Who is going to be punished today, you or him?"

"Me," said Lucan, dropping his head, his long hair falling over his face and chest. "I refuse to fight a man who is not in his best shape."

"Fine," growled the commander, distaste curving his lips. He turned to his team and waved his hand. Two more men stepped forward, their eyes glowing with a scarlet light, putting on display their vampiric nature.

Naturally, elves had pale, white skin, but as soon as the undead monsters approached Lucan, his face became ashen, bordering on blue. Nevertheless, he didn't make a move when they put their hands on his shoulders. The vampires pushed him down to his knees, and to Gunz's shock, the elf didn't fight them even when they stripped his thin shirt off. One of the vamps tilted Lucan's head to the side, exposing his jugular, and his fangs expanded.

Lucan froze in place, his eyes wide, his lips slightly parted as his chest shuddered with short breaths. Gunz shook his head, clenching his jaw. *I am so going to regret this,* he thought as he got up to his feet and raised his hand.

"Hey, Commander Moore," he said as loud as he could, "stop it. I'll spar with your elf."

The vampires let go of Lucan, waiting for the next order. The commander nodded with a cold smirk, and both vamps walked back, joining the others. Lucan got up and approached Gunz, his heavy green gaze boring into him.

"Follow me," he said quietly, directing him to the mats in the center of the training room.

Gunz stepped on the soft mats, bowing, but then smirked and bit his lip. Showing respect to the dojang was so deeply rooted in him that he was doing it automatically. For a moment, his memory flashed back to his training sessions at Aidan's school and his soul bled as he thought of his friends.

At least they are safe, he thought, regarding Lucan calmly as the elf took a position facing him. *Now that I'm blacklisted by the Destiny Council, they're safer away from me.*

Lucan stepped closer, placing his hand on Gunz's shoulder. "Thank you for taking the punishment for me," he whispered so only Gunz could hear him. "I'm deeply sorry, Salamander, but you will probably regret your decision."

Gunz looked straight ahead, his gaze landing on the firm squares of the elf's stomach. As he slowly raised his eyes up, he felt like he was staring at a high-rise.

"I think I already do… Jesus, man, what did they feed you when you were a kid? You're as tall as Kal…" He scratched the back of his head, a lopsided grin crossing his face. "Do you worst?"

The elf squeezed Gunz's shoulder, and he sensed a wave of elven magic surging through him. It felt like an adrenalin shot—his heart sped up and everything inside him came to life. He shuddered from the unexpected sensation, struggling to keep his fire under control. As his gaze fell on the magic and heat detectors under the ceiling, he wondered why the magic detectors didn't sense the elven magic, but he couldn't even get in touch with the Dark Codex in his mind without triggering them.

"Better?" asked Lucan quietly, and Gunz gave him a barely visible nod. The elf laughed coldly and asked loudly, "Are you ready for pain?"

Gunz smirked and quickly drove his arms up, sending his body into a backflip while he whipped his right leg, kicking the elf lightly under his chin. He didn't intend for this kick to be hard, but rather wanted to show Lucan that despite the height difference he wasn't an easy prey.

"Jumpy little lizard, aren't you?" asked Lucan, rubbing his chin as excitement lit up his cat-eyes. "I'm still going to destroy you."

"Like I said—do you worst."

Lucan stepped back into a guarding stance, and for the first time a true smile changed his cold features.

"Fire Salamander—go!" growled the elf, turning his hip as he threw his entire body into a powerful hook.

CHAPTER 2

~ AIDAN ~

Ft. Lauderdale, Florida

Aidan paced the living room of Tessa's apartment, feeling like a caged animal—angry and helpless. With Zane's and Yaroslav's sudden disappearance, he was on edge. He had called Jim a few times in the past week, but the FBI agent hadn't returned his calls, which was quite unusual. Akira had locked herself in the *EverSafe* building and was accepting no one. He had tried calling, visiting and even summoning her, but to no avail and all this left a bad taste in his mouth.

Besides that, Angel and Uri were still MIA, and Aidan had no idea what to do about it. Every day, Tessa kept telling him that she felt Angel's distress, and every day he looked for a way to trace his location, having nothing to show for it. Svyatobor had come back a few days ago, but his story was so vague that Aidan decided not to ask any questions and leave the god of Nature alone. He knew nothing about Angel and Uri either.

As a last resort, he had summoned Kal and Mrak Delar, but to his shock neither the Fire Elemental nor the Master of Power knew anything, nor could they sense Zane's presence. Both left a few hours later extremely distressed, promising him that if they found anything, they would let him know right away. After that, no matter how many times he tried, Kal wouldn't answer his summoning calls.

Aidan stopped pacing and pulled his phone out. Opening the list of his recent calls, he dialed Jim's phone number again. After a few beeps, the call was forwarded to voicemail.

"Screw that," grumbled Aidan and snapped his fingers.

He teleported into the main area in front of Jim's office. A few members of Jim's team who were there gasped, jumping aside as he materialized in the narrow space between desks. Aidan ignored them, clenching his teeth, but everything was playing on his nerves. Disregarding the FBI agents, he made his way to the door of Jim's office and knocked.

"Come in!"

Aidan recognized Jim's voice and frowned. *What the hell is going on? If Jim has been working all this time, why didn't he answer any of my calls?*

He swung the door open and walked inside, slamming it shut behind him more forcefully than he intended. Jim jumped to his feet, and for a split-second his eyes widened.

"Aidan—," he started and snapped his jaws shut as he caught Aidan's furious gaze, shining with the light of his magic.

"Shut up!" growled Aidan and waved his hand, muttering a spell. "*Oprimenta Amnia.*"

The yellow glow of the spell encapsulated the office and Aidan took a ragged breath, struggling to suppress his boiling rage unsuccessfully. The walls trembled, and pens rolled off the desk, falling to the floor. Jim took a step back, running into a chair.

Aidan planted his fists on the desk, leaning forward heavily. "Are you screening my calls, Agent Andrews?" he asked in a low growl.

Jim frowned and met Aidan's eyes without blinking.

"Yes, I am," he replied dryly. "I can't be talking to you, Aidan. I can't even be seen in your company."

Aidan slammed his hand on the desk and a deep fracture marred its polished surface.

"Why, Jim?" he whispered, swallowing as pain shredded his insides. "Why? Zane is your friend too. At least I believed he was more than just another FBI asset to you. Don't you care to find out where he is and what happened to him?"

Jim pressed his lips into a straight line, a muscle twitching in his jaw, and stepped closer, only his desk separating him from the furious god of the Otherworld.

"Don't you dare talk to me like this, Mr. McGrath!" he hissed. "You know nothing! Don't even presume that—"

"Then tell me!" yelled Aidan, and the walls of the office trembled again. "I'm going crazy! Tessa is back with the Guardians, and the Archmage blocked my access to their HQ. He said it's a temporary precaution and I'll be able to enter soon, but something tells me it's not true. Akira doesn't want to see anyone. Zane and Yaroslav have gone missing on the same day. Angel and Uri have disappeared a while ago. And on top of all that, you are screening my calls? Goddammit, Jim! What is wrong with you? We're supposed to be friends!"

For a moment, Aidan's appearance changed as the god of the Otherworld in him took over, fueled by his anger and pain.

"Control your power, Aodh mac Lir!" hissed Jim. "No one should know that you are here!"

"Why?"

The walls of the office trembled, and Aidan raised his hands, closing his eyes. He took a few deep breaths and was finally able to suppress his anger and get his magic under control. Powerlessly, he lowered himself into a chair, dropping his hands to his lap.

Jim sighed, visibly relieved, pulled his chair closer, and also sat down.

"Aidan, I need you to keep your power under control," he warned, frowning. "Here is what I know. Zane was charged with the premeditated murder of Hazel Wells and Sophia Porter."

"Excuse me?" Aidan stared at Jim with his mouth open. "I know the names, he told me the story... It was a powerful demon. Zane didn't..."

"I know he didn't, but that's what he is charged with," replied Jim, shaking his head. "I've been ordered to stand down if I want to keep my job. I'm on probation, Aidan. I am sorry, but I can't help you and I can't get involved in what's going on with Zane."

"What the hell is going on?" mumbled Aidan, rubbing his forehead, feeling cold sweat under his fingers. He remembered the story as if Gunz had told it to him just yesterday. Two teenagers had been targeted by a powerful ancient demon. Gunz had been able to save the boy. But before he vanquished the demon, the monster had killed the girl and the boy's mother.

"I have no idea, and by the way, Peyton is also missing. I haven't heard from her since that meeting in the Otherworld." Jim leaned forward, closer to Aidan. "I hope you can figure it out, Aidan. You're the last man standing. The rest of us are either gone or controlled." He turned away, a deep wrinkle cutting through his forehead, but then turned back and whispered so quietly that Aidan practically had to read his lips. "Aidan, Zane's neighbors told me that when he was arrested, the entire neighborhood was blocked, and his house was surrounded by police and firefighters with a few fire engines parked upfront."

"Firefighters?" muttered Aidan. "Doesn't sound like a standard police procedure to me."

"No, it's not," replied Jim. "I think whoever took him, knew his true nature. But here is the worst part. He has never been transferred to any jail or prison facility that I know of. There has never been a trial or any kind of legal proceedings. His name is nowhere in the system. Something is not right with all this."

Aidan got up, feeling like his entire world just dissolved into ashes around him.

"Thank you, Jim," he said, his mouth dry.

"Find him, Aidan," whispered Jim, his eyes veiled with sadness. "Bring Zane home. I'll do what I can on my side, but I have to be extremely careful and discreet, or I may end up losing everything, including my freedom. And something tells me, we won't be able to find out anything through the official channels."

"You're absolutely right. The official channels are not the way to go about it," replied Aidan with a bitter smirk on his lips. "I'll do everything I can."

He rubbed his forehead, feeling a slow headache building up behind his eyes. He held out his hand to Jim for a handshake, and as the agent squeezed it, the headache intensified to a new level, eliciting a cry of pain from him.

"Aidan!" Jim was by his side in a heartbeat, supporting him.

"Summoning call," Aidan managed to say, panting, cold sweat running down his face and neck. "Got to go... Guardians... *Incanto Comlium...*"

As the yellow light of his cloaking spell dissipated, Aidan snapped his finger and vanished from Jim's office.

* * *

A MOMENT LATER, he manifested in front of the gates into the Guardians Headquarters. Almost falling, he grabbed the pendant and swiped it over the security monitor, muttering an opening spell. The gate didn't move. Aidan moaned, searched the screen for an intercom button, and pressed it.

"This is Aidan McGrath," he said, barely able to move his lips. "I'm here. Please let me in and stop the summoning call."

"Please hold, Mr. McGrath," said a pleasant female voice. "Someone will be with you momentarily."

She hung up the phone, but the constant pain of the summoning call didn't get any better.

"Dammit!" yelled Aidan, slamming his hand on the screen of the security monitor. The screen blinked a few times and went dark as a large web of fractures crossed it.

Aidan dropped to his knees, wrapping his arms around his head. Instead of getting better, the pain suddenly intensified, and he was on the verge of fainting when he felt someone shaking his shoulder. With an effort, he unlocked his arms and lifted his face, barely able to see.

"Mr. McGrath!"

He heard a familiar voice and focused on it.

"Jamie…" he exhaled as he recognized the young guard who was always kind to him.

"Mr. McGrath," Jamie groaned, straining to help Aidan to his feet. Aidan stood up, leaning heavily on the young guard's shoulder. "Aidan, can you understand me?"

"Yes… can you tell them to stop?" mumbled Aidan, his eyes watering from pain.

"I can't, sorry… I was sent here to bring you in," continued Jamie, a sound of urgency and fear in his voice. "But I can't do it to you. The entire HQ is surrounded by some kind of spell that's supposed to render you powerless. I have no idea what their plans for you are, but it must be something serious since it takes twenty witches and mages to sustain this spell. You need to leave, Aidan. Run…"

"Oh… God…" moaned Aidan. "But if you come back alone… they will punish you… Jamie, I can't do it to you…"

Jamie smirked. "It's okay. I'll tell them you sensed the trap and punched me out. Can you punch me?" he asked, doubt in his eyes.

Aidan screamed, spreading his arms wide. Gathering all the power he could, he transformed into his godly form and ripped the chain with the pendant off his neck. A blinding white light exploded around him, and Jamie backed away, raising his arm to protect his eyes. The headache of the summoning call burned out, leaving him tired and angry.

He stuffed the broken chain into his pocket and a sad smile transformed his face.

"I owe you, Jamie Coldwell," he said quietly, his voice trembling with emotions. "I'll never forget what you did for me today. I'm sure the spike in the magical energy field I just created was felt in the HQ and the Guardians will be here in a moment. So, I am very sorry for what I am about to do."

Before Jamie could say anything, Aidan swung his fist and punched him in the jaw. The young guard yelped and dropped down unconscious. Aidan glanced at him, remorse twisting his soul. Still having a hard time processing everything that just happened, he snapped his fingers and vanished.

AIDAN MATERIALIZED on the steps of a large house. As soon as he appeared, a sound of alarm howled through the property, and a few men with automatic weapons—most likely security guards or bodyguards—rushed out the front door, pointing their guns at him. One of the guards wasn't armed with mundane weapons, but the energy of his magic was prominent enough for Aidan to sense it right away.

Clever bastard. Aidan smirked—the head of the Russian mob had wizards among his bodyguards. He raised his hands peacefully.

"I come in peace," he said, stifling his laughter while cringing inwardly at how cliché this statement sounded. "Please let Mr. Karpenko know that Aidan McGrath is here to see him."

The wizard gave a barely visible nod at one of the guards and he rushed back into the house. A few minutes later, Anatoly Karpenko, the head of the Russian mob in South Florida, appeared on the steps. He stared at Aidan, and a shadow of fear crossed his features, but this happened so fast that Aidan wasn't sure if it wasn't a figment of his imagination.

Anatoly plastered a dutiful smile on his face and gestured at the door. "Mr. McGrath, what an honor. Please come in." He frowned at his guards and they lowered their weapons, stepping out of the way.

As Aidan walked upstairs, closely followed by Anatoly Karpenko, he thought back to his first meeting with the mobster. The last time he was in this house was because Anatoly blackmailed Gunz by holding his friends imprisoned. Since Gunz held his side of the deal, Aidan had come here to make sure that Anatoly would release his friends.

He sighed. Their last meeting hadn't been pleasant, and he was sure that the mobster had a long memory. However, in the given circumstances, Aidan had no choice. Anatoly was well-connected in the human circles as well as in the supernatural, and if anyone stood a chance of digging out any information on Gunz's whereabouts, it was the infamous mobster. It was unsettling to think how easily this devious and conniving man could slither his way into places that normal people— mundane or touched by the World of Magic—didn't even know existed.

Anatoly opened the door into his office and gestured for Aidan to come in. Nothing had changed since Aidan's last visit. The windows were shaded by heavy burgundy panels, and the large space was illuminated by a beautiful crystal chandelier. Anatoly walked around the desk and lowered himself into a massive leather armchair with a grunt.

As Aidan moved a chair and sat down, Anatoly leaned forward slightly, clasping his hands on top of the desk.

"So, Mr. McGrath," he said, his cold eyes drilling into Aidan. "I'm sure you are here not because you wanted to say hello."

Aidan smirked. "No, Mr. Karpenko," he said quietly, putting all his power of will into concealing his aversion toward this man. "I'm here because I need your help."

"You don't say!" exclaimed Anatoly, his eyebrows rising. "And what can a modest human such as myself do for a mighty god? Do tell."

Aidan winced. If a year ago someone had told him that he would be sitting in Anatoly Karpenko's office, asking for his help, he would punch this person out. But here he was.

"Zane Burns is missing," replied Aidan, calmly meeting Anatoly's sarcastic gaze, even though everything inside him was twisting with anger and pain. "I need your help to find him."

"Tsk, tsk, tsk." Anatoly clicked his tongue, leaning back in his chair. "How about Agent Andrews? I am sure the FBI has great resources at hand. Besides, Mr. Burns is an FBI consultant."

"Mr. Karpenko," said Aidan flatly, "if the FBI could help me, I wouldn't be here, would I? Trust me, you are my last resort."

Anatoly laughed. "I'm sure I am. So, what happened to Mr. Burns?" He pulled a small white handkerchief out of his pocket and touched the corners of his eyes.

Aidan gave Anatoly a quick overview of the events surrounding Gunz's disappearance and everything he found out from Jim. Anatoly listened without interrupting him and as Aidan continued, his frown got deeper.

"Dammit," muttered Anatoly, shaking his head. "I know it's hard for you to believe, but I actually like Mr. Burns."

"What are you saying, Anatoly?" asked Aidan, unease spreading through him. "Can you help me locate him?"

"Everything you just told me has the distinct stench of supernatural bullshit," said Anatoly, his fingers playing with a pen absentmindedly. "From my experience, I can see that you are in danger yourself, Mr. McGrath. As powerful as you are, there is always a bigger fish, if you know what I mean."

"I know," said Aidan. "This is why I need to disappear. At least for a short while. Agent Andrews is right—I am the last man standing. So, it is up to me to unravel this mess."

Anatoly got up, gesturing at Aidan to remain seated and walked out of the office. He came back a few minutes later with a new iPhone in his hand. He offered the device to Aidan.

"Take this phone, Mr. McGrath," he said, as Aidan took the device, twirling it in his hands uncomfortably. "I'll get in touch with you as soon as I learn anything about Mr. Burns' whereabouts. Usually, I work fast, so hopefully, I am not going to make you wait too long."

Aidan got up, placing the phone in his pocket, and regarded Anatoly with a heavy gaze.

"I'm sure you're not going to be doing it out of the goodness of your heart, Mr. Karpenko," he said, an uneven smirk curving his lips. "What is it going to cost me?"

Anatoly smiled—the cold eyes of a snake were warmer than his eyes, and the snarl of a wolf observing its prey was friendlier than his smile.

"I'm a businessman, Mr. McGrath, and as far as I know, a 'thank you' cannot be deposited into a bank account," he said dryly. "But I am also a man of honor and I have my own moral code. You and Zane Burns saved my daughter's life. So, yes, I will help you locate Mr. Burns and yes, you're still going to owe me a favor."

Aidan clenched his teeth, shoving his screaming intuition to the back of his mind. "It's a deal, Mr. Karpenko," he said softly. "You help me find Zane and I'll owe you a favor."

He shook Anatoly's hand, small hairs rising on the back of his neck at the touch of this man's cold skin to his, and then snapped his fingers, teleporting out of the mobster's office.

CHAPTER 3

~ AIDAN ~

Aidan materialized in the middle of nowhere, surrounded by nothing but dry patches of grass and tall Saguaro cacti. It was late afternoon, but the sun shone brightly in the cloudless sky, beating at the dry ground mercilessly.

Despite the fact that as far as he could see there was no human presence around, Aidan knew exactly where he was and why he chose to be here. He needed a place where no one would think of looking for him, so he could regroup and think through his next step while waiting for Anatoly's call. Even though the Otherworld had always been his safe haven, if the Guardians decided to look for him, it would be the first place they would go. Besides, there was no cell service in Gwyn's kingdom, and he was hoping to hear from Anatoly soon.

A while ago, he had helped a local pack, and the Alpha swore his loyalty to him. No one knew about that and no one would think about looking for him here, in the middle of the Sonoran Desert. The pack owned a small ranch house and a considerable size real estate, living off their land and making a few extra bucks by fixing heavy machinery. Their ranch was located away from any populated area and that also worked well for Aidan.

Besides, after their fight with the dark soul of Rasputin, he sent Theron, the weretiger, to live with the pack. At first Theron tried to assist Aidan, working in his martial arts school, but soon Aidan realized that the weretiger was a little too rough and wasn't good teacher-material. Hawk, on the other hand, didn't mind an extra set of hands on his ranch and since Theron had nowhere else to go, it was a good arrangement for both parties. Now, Aidan hoped that the weretiger would join him, in case he needed a capable fighter.

He didn't teleport directly inside the ranch but a few hundred yards away. He wanted to give himself a few minutes to think about how to explain everything to the Alpha. Hawk was an honorable man and keeping him in the dark didn't feel like the right thing to do. On the other hand, in the given situation, the less he knew, the safer he would be.

Deep in his thoughts, Aidan didn't notice when he approached the main gate into the pack's property. He moved his arm in a wide arch and smiled, recognizing his own wards and protection spells he had placed around the perimeter of the ranch a while ago. He opened the gate and walked inside, knowing that his presence wouldn't trigger any alarms.

Nothing had changed since he was here the last time. The property was well taken care of and the house shone with a fresh coat of paint. Metallic clanks and the hiss of an air compressor announced that someone was busy working in the machine shop. Instead of going into the house, Aidan circled around it and headed in the direction of the sound.

He halted in the doorway and for a few minutes observed Hawk and Theron working on a large engine. They looked so normal and so peaceful that he started doubting if he made the right decision by coming here. Sooner or later, the Guardians would find him, no matter how well he shadowed his own magical signature, and trouble would follow. He sighed, hoping that Anatoly would find Gunz before the Guardians found him.

Hawk turned around and noticed Aidan. He dropped the wrench he was holding and lowered down to one knee, pressing his fist to his chest over his heart. Theron followed him, but a wide grin split the weretiger's face.

"My lord," Hawk said, sincere happiness reflected in his golden-yellow eyes.

"Please don't kneel," said Aidan. He walked up to Hawk and offered his hand. "And the name is Aidan, if you remember."

Hawk smiled, crow's feet spreading around his eyes, making his face look softer. He rose and took Aidan's hand, squeezing it in a firm handshake.

"Come on, Theron. After everything we've been through together, I thought we were done with the formalities." Aidan smiled down at the weretiger.

Theron got up, shifting from foot to foot. "Yes, my lord… um… Master McGrath—"

"Just Aidan, Theron." Aidan sighed, reminded how awkward Theron could be at times.

"Sorry… Aidan. Are Gunz and Yaroslav here with you?" Theron asked.

"No," replied Aidan, sobering up. "That is why I am here."

Hawk glanced around, quickly checking his shop and then waved his hand toward the house.

"Let's talk inside the house," he proposed, wiping oil from his hands with a piece of rag. "We're pretty much done for today, anyway."

Aidan followed Hawk into the house through a semi-dark hallway and into the kitchen. All four burners of the stove were occupied, and a young woman was chopping something on a wooden cutting board, handling a large kitchen knife with the skill of a five-star restaurant chef. As soon as they walked in, she turned around, placing her fist to her chest, greeting the Alpha. But as her eyes halted on Aidan, her small puffy lips opened up a little and her golden eyes rounded.

"Aidan, this is Ruby, my daughter," Hawk introduced, notes of fatherly pride in his voice.

"Aidan?" Ruby whispered breathlessly, staring at Aidan in awe. "As in *the Aidan*, Father? The young god who saved us all?"

Hawk nodded and Ruby lowered to her knees, bowing to Aidan, a blush coloring her face in a tender pink shade. "My lord, please forgive my lack of manners. I had no idea who you were. You look just like any regular young man." She gasped, clasping both hands to her mouth. "Oh… I shouldn't have said that… sorry…"

"It's okay, Ruby." Aidan threw a reproachful gaze at Hawk and helped Ruby to her feet. "Please don't kneel before me. You don't have to do it and I am not that young." He chuckled.

Ruby flushed brighter and glanced at her father, expecting a command.

"Ruby, can you please get us something to eat?" Hawk asked softly. "Theron and I are starving, and I'm sure Aidan can do with a good dinner, too."

At the thought of food, Aidan's stomach twisted, and he remembered that he hadn't had anything to eat since last night. He sat down, thanking Hawk for his hospitality. Ruby rushed around the kitchen like a little tornado, quickly serving dinner for three. When she was done, she bowed to Aidan and was about to leave the room when Hawk grabbed her hand, stopping her.

"Ruby, do me a favor," he said. "You know how kids are, especially girls." He sighed. "They always find at least a few creative ways to eavesdrop when they are curious about something."

Ruby giggled, pressing her hand to her mouth, and at that moment, she looked like a little girl herself.

"I'll keep all the children away—boys and girls," she said with a sly wink. "I still remember how to be creative myself."

"Yes, please," said Hawk with a smile. "Aidan, Theron and I need to have a serious conversation that requires privacy."

It took over an hour for Aidan to tell everything that happened since the attack of the followers of Chaos, about the pollution of the Land of Dreams and some of what followed after. Making a quick decision, Aidan also mentioned that the Guardians were after him, and he needed a safe place to hide for a few days, at least until he would get a call from the Russian mobster.

When he finished, both Hawk and Theron remained silent for a short while. Then Hawk frowned, his expression becoming harder.

"Aidan, my home is your home," he said, slightly leaning forward. "You have my protection for as long as you need it. If you need strong fighters, we'll stand and fight by your side, but I think I should get my kids away from here. At least until we know it's safe for them to come back."

"Thank you," said Aidan, but then shook his head. "A simple thank you is not enough, and I'll find a way to repay your loyalty and kindness when this mess is over. I am working hard to suppress my energy signature, but it doesn't mean that a powerful mage won't be able to locate me. I just want you—"

"I know," Hawk interrupted him, raising his hand. "I'm old and experienced enough to understand the risk, but everything I said still stands, god of the Otherworld. You have the protection and support of my pack."

* * *

THREE DAYS PASSED since Aidan knocked on the door of the Arizona pack. During this time, he tried to help Hawk in his shop or do any kind of work around the property. Not knowing what was going on with his friends and with Tessa was driving him crazy, and keeping himself busy was the only way to keep his sanity.

Sitting on the fence, he watched the sunset, staring into the endless desert sky. There wasn't a cloud anywhere in view, but as the sun was slowly moving down, the air became considerably colder and fresher.

Aidan put his hand into his pocket and pulled the Guardians' pendant out. He placed a complicated enchantment on it, just to make sure that it wouldn't give out his location. However, his main concern was how his disobedience would affect Tessa's situation. By ripping the chain off and ignoring the summoning call, he broke his oath. Breaking an oath always had severe consequences, but he didn't care how it would impact him. Tessa's wellbeing was his only worry.

A loud shrill of the cell phone startled him and he almost dropped the pendant. He pulled Anatoly's phone out of his pocket and answered the call, getting ready for bad news.

"Mr. McGrath?" asked Anatoly. "Are you alone? Can we talk?"

Aidan jumped off the fence and slowly headed into the desert. "Yes, Mr. Karpenko. What did you find out?"

Fifteen minutes later, he hung up the phone, and silently stared into the sky, colored in red and purple shades of the Arizona sunset. Then he slowly sat down on the ground and closed his eyes, pressing his hand over his mouth. For a few minutes, he remained silent, trying to wrap his mind around everything the mobster just told him.

Then he clicked the home button of the phone and as the screen lit up, dialed Tessa's phone number.

CHAPTER 4

~ TESSA ~

Tessa turned the page of the *Modern Witchcraft and Wizardry* book and stared at the small print covering it. Her eyes moved from left to right, but her brain didn't process anything she was reading. Her mind kept circling back to Aidan and every time it happened, she couldn't get rid of an overpowering feeling of dread.

Something wasn't right. A few days had passed since she came back to the Guardians HQ and she still hadn't heard from Aidan. That was unlike him, and she couldn't believe that he would forget to call her or got too busy for a quick hello.

She closed the book and put it away. Then she grabbed her phone from the nightstand and checked notifications. There were no missed calls. Opening her favorite contacts list, she pressed the dial button next to Aidan's name and held her breath. The call went straight to voicemail. She frowned, staring at the screen. It sounded almost as if Aidan's phone was shut down, or he was in an area with no cell services available.

A sudden wave of cold spread through her and she sucked in a sharp breath, wondering what it was. For a split second, she attributed it to her worrying about Aidan, but as the second wave—colder and more powerful—assailed her, she realized that it had nothing to do with her emotional state.

While the strange wave wasn't pleasant, it felt familiar, and she knew exactly what it reminded her of. She closed her eyes, allowing the reaper in her to take the wheel. When the third wave enveloped her, she was ready and could see it—the energy of death softly tugging at her subconscious. She cleared her mind, listening to the whispers.

Tessa slipped off the bed and quickly put her sneakers on. It wasn't past curfew yet, but the sun had gone down already, and she knew the hallways of the Witches' Wing would be dark and empty. She opened the door, peeked outside and once satisfied that no one was watching, tiptoed her way toward the stairs.

She took the stairs, jumping two steps at the time, all the way until she reached the roof access door. Halting with her hand on the handle, she took a few deep breaths and pushed the door open. As she walked out onto the rooftop, the fresh evening air enveloped her, carrying over the soft rustling of the wind and loud screams of night birds. Tessa closed her eyes again, focusing on the whispers and blocking the rest of the background noise.

"What are you saying?" she mumbled, walking to the edge of the roof.

Leaning over the railing, she glanced down and gasped. From here, she could see that the entire building of the Guardians HQ was surrounded by a massive crowd of dark hooded people.

Reapers.

She didn't try to count, there were just too many of them. Their heads were upturned, and even though she couldn't see their faces, she could swear they stared directly at her. The whispering became louder and more agitated, but she still couldn't make out their words.

"Please," she yelled, desperation making her voice break on

high tones. "I don't understand anything you are saying. I need all of you to shut up!"

She didn't think the Reapers would listen to her, but they did. The whispers ceased all at once, but now, the surrounding silence was creepier than their freaky whispers. The creep-factor also increased by the fact that every single reaper was silently pointing up in her direction. Tessa swallowed, feeling the small hairs rise on her arms. She looked around but could see nothing special.

"What are you pointing at?" she asked, reaching out to the reapers not only with her words but with her mind as well. "Can one of you come here, to the roof, and talk to me?"

The reapers lowered their arms and one of them stepped forward, removing the hood. It was a tall woman with dark skin and bushy, black hair. She made a wide arch with her hand and her soft whisper reached Tessa's mind. As the woman kept chanting, a shining dome encapsulating the entire building of the Guardians HQ became visible for a split second, and Tessa held her breath.

"Therasia," said the woman, and even though her voice was still just a soft murmur, Tessa could more or less understand her. "Death must ride again. Find him... There must be four... always four..."

She waved her hand again, and all the reapers vanished before Tessa could ask anything else.

"Dammit!" she yelled into the darkness, slamming her hand on the railing. "Why must all these beings of magic be so friggin' cryptic. What the hell is that even supposed to mean—there must be four... It's like some crazy Hollywood movie."

She stopped talking, breathing hard. "Force... field. This is why Aidan is not calling and I can't get hold of him." The image of a shining dome of magic blocking the building, which the reapers had showed her, materialized in her mind, and she bit her lip, frowning. "Something is not right, and I'm going to find out what it is even if it's the last thing I do."

Tessa ran across the rooftop, zoomed down the stairs, and bolted straight into the Mages' Wing. She came to a halt in front of Missi's room and drummed on the door impatiently. Missi opened almost immediately and frowned, her steel eyes blazing from under her straight black eyebrows.

"You look like you ran a mile," she hissed as she walked out on the hallway, closing the door behind her. She wrapped her robe tighter, hugging herself with her arms. "What's up?"

Tessa pursed her lips, giving Missi a quick once-over. "Go get dressed and do it quick," she said in a no-nonsense tone. "I need to show you something. It's important."

"It's important," Missi huffed, rolling her eyes. "I think these words should be engraved on the gates to Hell." She sighed, shaking her head. "Wait for me here. I'll be right back."

She took no more than five minutes, but to Tessa it felt like five hours. She kept circling the hallway, nervously wringing her hands. As soon as Missi came out, Tessa grabbed her hand and ran toward the stairs, pulling Missi along. They made it to the rooftop in one breath and Tessa pushed the door open.

When they stopped at the railing, Missi stared at her with reproach. "What are we doing on the roof?" She glanced down and backed away from the edge, sweat shining on her forehead. "I don't enjoy heights, you know."

"Missi, look at this," hissed Tessa, waving her hand around to reveal the glow of the magical dome. "The Guardians HQ is blocked by some kind of magic."

Missi lowered her eyes and her face turned a shade paler. "I know that, Tessa," she said softly. "I was one of the mages who cast this spell. I'm not supposed to talk to you about it."

"Why, Missi? What's going on?" asked Tessa, the feeling of dread intensifying tenfold. "I need to know. I just had a bunch of reapers talking nonsense to me. Why can't you tell me straight what's going on?"

"Because it's about Aidan."

A soft male voice answered her question, and Tessa spun around to see the young guard, Jamie Coldwell, standing in front of her. A large bruise decorated his jaw, and he looked guilty, remorseful even.

He glanced at Missi and asked, "Do you want to tell her the truth or should I?"

"James Coldwell, you will keep your mouth shut," growled Missi, taking a step closer to the guard.

"No, Missi, I won't," he objected softly. "I like Aidan and I respect him. He's a good, honorable man and what the Guardians wanted to do to him was…" His voice trailed off and he looked away. "Just inhumane."

"So, it was you," whispered Missi, her eyes widened. "You warned him. If the Destiny Council and the Guardians find out—"

"By helping Aidan, I forfeited my life. You think I don't know? I know and I don't care," replied Jamie calmly. "And if given the chance, I would do the same exact thing again. And you, Missi, you know what you have to do now, right?"

She nodded and stamped her foot, throwing her hands in the air. "I hate you both," she mumbled. "Why couldn't I have a normal charge. Not a crossbreed between a god of Thunder and a reaper." She sighed. "Fine, let's do it. As soon as I start chanting, get ready to run, Tessa. The Guardians will sense the spike of magical energy on the roof, and we'll have just a few seconds to make an exit."

Tessa squealed and threw her arms around Missi's neck. "Yay! I knew you'd do it for me." Then she turned to the young guard. "Jamie, thank you. I owe you one."

"No, you don't," he replied, rubbing his bruised jaw. "Say

hello to Aidan. I better leave now. I don't want the Guardians to find me at the crime scene a second time."

Missi waited until Jamie left and gave him a few minutes to get as far away from here as he could. Then she channeled her magic and extended her arm up, weaving a complex enchantment, softly pronouncing the words of the Dragon tongue. A ray of blinding white light escaped her hand, impacting the dome at its apex. The entire magical barrier lit up and responded to Missi's assault with an angry buzz, but nothing happened. Missi grunted, intensifying the flow of her magic, but the dome just glowed brighter and started to vibrate.

Missi dropped her arm, staring at Tessa with wide eyes.

"I can't break it," she panted, pressing her hand to her chest. "Their combined magic is stronger than that of a single mage."

"I don't think, it's stronger than the magic of a god though," muttered Tessa, channeling her power.

She closed her eyes and outstretched her arm. She wasn't casting a spell. She just thought of the Axe of Perun and the weapon materialized in her hand. She flicked her eyebrow at Missi, who stared at her with her mouth open.

"I've been working out. You know, those thirty-day challenges?" she explained with a sly wink, twirling the deadly weapon in her hand as if it were nothing but a training escrima stick. "Works like a charm. You should see my abs."

A loud noise coming from the stairs reached her ears, setting Tessa's mind back to reality. She raised her arm up, pointing the Axe at the top of the dome. The roof trembled under her feet and lightning spliced the ultramarine sky, cutting through the magical barrier as though it was nothing more than a piece of paper. With a thunderous bang—or maybe it was real thunder—the dome collapsed. At the same time, the entrance door burst open and Archmage Allerton, accompanied by a few high-level mages, rushed toward them, shouting some spells.

"Time to go," yelled Tessa.

Grabbing Missi's hand, she snapped her fingers, and they both vanished from the roof.

* * *

"Where are we?" asked Missi, twirling around.

"Chicago Botanical Gardens," replied Tessa tiredly, lowering herself down on a bench. She placed the Axe across her lap, her fingers tracing the shape of the golden inlays. "Aidan brought me here one time… seems like forever ago." All the excitement of their escape, the use of her power and the constant feeling of dread made her weary with exhaustion.

"Who taught you how to teleport?" asked Missi, sitting down next to her.

Tessa glanced at the young mage, but quickly averted her eyes.

"No one," she replied quietly. "I had a suspicion that the Guardians weren't teaching me all I needed to know about my powers, so I kinda"—she threw a guilty look at Missi—"broke into the forbidden section of the library again. Like I said, I've been working out."

"You're crazy, girl." Missi chuckled.

Tessa shrugged and leaned forward, hiding her face in her hands. She felt Missi's hand on her knee and smiled.

"Sorry, Missi," she said, lowering her hands. "I got you in trouble again."

"I was in trouble the first time I laid my eyes on you," Missi objected, readjusting the hair clip that held all her long braids in a single thick ponytail. "Nothing new. Well, this time the Guardians are not going to expel you. You're going to spend the rest of your life in their confinement chambers. Just keep in mind—you owe me. So when it happens, I am taking the top bunk."

They laughed, but their laugher absent of mirth died down quickly.

"Where to now?" asked Missi, surveying the dark park. "We can't sit here forever."

Before Tessa could reply, the loud ring of her phone interrupted their conversation. Tessa pulled the phone out and a wave of warmth expanded in her chest as she saw the picture of Aidan on the screen.

"Aidan," she answered the phone breathlessly. She got up, placing the Axe on the bench. "Where are you—"

He interrupted her, speaking fast and with the kind of urgency she had never heard from him before. A few minutes later, Tessa hung up the phone and looked at Missi, biting her lip.

"Missi, Zane and Yaroslav are missing under suspicious circumstances, and Aidan is being chased all over the realm by human and supernatural forces alike. He needs our help. I know where to go," she said, taking Missi's hand into hers, "but the question is… are you with me?"

"You really have to ask?" Missi raised her eyebrows, her eyes glowing silver against her dark skin.

"Yes, I do," Tessa said seriously. "Give me your Guardians' pendant." She took her own chain with the pendant off and grabbed the Axe of Perun with her other hand.

Missi raised her eyes, staring at her flabbergasted, but reached into her pocket and unhooked the pendant from her keychain, offering it to her. Tessa took both pendants and walked toward the lake. She touched the enchanted jewelry, whispering a quick spell, and hurled them into the water. Mixed feelings—remorse and defiance—surged through her as she heard the splash and watched the pendants sink into the dark lake.

Then she put her hand on Missi's shoulder and snapped her fingers, leaving the midnight garden behind.

CHAPTER 5

~ ZANE BURNS, A.K.A. GUNZ ~

The next few days turned into a continuous blur of agonizing nightmares. Every morning started with a therapy session with Doctor Harris. His drilling, invasive questions drove him insane, and it took Gunz all his self-control not to jump over the desk and strangle this man who arrogantly thought he had the right to rip his soul apart and torture him psychologically.

He was like the Josef Mengele of psychology, running experiments on him to see how much mental anguish he could take before his self-control started to waver. After each session, Gunz felt like he was lobotomized with an icepick. With his soul torn and bleeding, he had been escorted to the training facility where Commander Moore made sure that the bleeding on the inside was matched by the bleeding on the outside.

Remembering the kindness Gunz showed him on his first day, Lucan tried to help him as much as he could. And any moment when no one was looking, he gave Gunz an energy boost, using his elven magic. While it helped him a little, no amount of magic could give him the physical strength he needed to fight effectively against Commander Moore's team that was comprised of powerful supernatural beings.

Each of them was tall, strong and a well-trained fighter. On top of it, they could all use their magical energy freely. Gunz, on the other hand, had to fight as a man—even less than a human, because with his magic suppressed and his elemental power drained, he felt weak and lightheaded all the time. Besides that, he barely received any food and water, so constant hunger and thirst made him even weaker.

If before fighting ten regular vampires on the streets of his city had never presented a problem for him, now a single vamp could bring him down to his knees in less than a minute, and Commander Moore never stopped his vampiric team members when they sank their fangs into Gunz's neck, adding blood loss to the list of his other problems.

However, neither the therapy sessions from hell, nor the body-crashing training with the Commander and his team could compare to what he had to endure after he was sent to his cell. As soon as he was thrown back into the room, a doze of halotron was released in the air, suppressing his fire and leaving him thrashing and screaming on the cold floor.

His guard—always the same man—waited for the fire suppressant to do its job, observing Gunz through a one-way mirror. He enjoyed watching him helpless and in pain and he made sure Gunz knew it. Wondering who this man was and why he took personal pleasure in abusing him, Gunz tried talking to him, but those attempts earned him nothing but more pain and humiliation. The guard released his anger by kicking him while he was most vulnerable or drenching him with icy water.

Even with his fire and magic suppressed, Gunz still healed faster than any human and that was the only thing that allowed him to get up in the morning and start this vicious cycle again. Most of the time, he wasn't sure if his fast self-healing was a blessing or a curse, and often wondered what would happen if one morning he wasn't able to get up and walk.

* * *

Gunz barely made it to his cell, and when the guard pushed him in through the door, locking it behind him, he felt something close to relief. He made it to the far end of the room and slid down to the floor. Sitting with his back against the wall, he shielded his face with his arms, bracing himself as much for the exposure to the fire suppressant as to the assault of the guard.

Nothing happened. Instead, he heard the man snicker, his laughter filled with mockery and repugnance.

"I trained you well, fire-worm," said the guard through the small window in the door. "Well, you got lucky. Tonight, I have an order to leave you alone and let you heal. So, enjoy it while you can."

He left but came back a few minutes later and pushed a tray with some food and water through the small opening at the bottom of the door. It slid across the floor, spilling some water. The guard snickered again and shut the opening.

For a while, Gunz just sat by the wall, unable to move, his forehead resting atop his bent arms. When he was sure that the guard hadn't lied, he got up and pulled the tray closer. As hungry as he was, he wasn't sure he could keep any food in his stomach. Nevertheless, he knew he needed at least some nourishment, so he nibbled on some bread and drank the water.

Then he curled on the floor and closed his eyes. His body, bleeding and sore, didn't appreciate the hardness of the tiles, but that was all he had. Trying not to think about anything, he started to count in his mind. Eventually, he drifted to sleep, lingering on the border with consciousness, waking up from the tiniest sound.

He woke up with a start a few hours later and saw the guard

standing over him, tapping the baton on the palm of his left hand. Gunz grunted and sat upright, raising his arms protectively. The guard smirked and shook his head.

"I would love to play a little, fire-pet, but right now we have no time for it," he said, throwing a plastic bag with some clean clothes next to him. "Take the bag and follow me."

With a painful grunt, Gunz got up, grabbed the bag and headed out the door after the man. As he followed him along the chain of hallways, he wondered what kind of new, elaborate torture these people had come up with this time. To his surprise, the guard took him into a large shower room with a few stalls along the wall.

"You have ten minutes," said the man frostily. Lowering himself down on one of the chairs, he stretched his legs, placing his baton across his lap. "What are you waiting for, fire-worm? Take any stall and get on with it."

Without waiting for extra encouragement from the guard, Gunz walked into a stall and opened the water. As he expected, the water was cold, and its touch to his skin resonated with extra pain through his already tortured body. Looking up, he noticed the heat and magic detectors installed in the shower room. Even here, he couldn't relax and let go.

Despite the coldness of the water, it was pleasant to wash all the dirt and blood off, so he ignored the discomfort, scrubbing his skin vigorously. He came out of the shower before the ten minutes ran out and grabbed a folded towel from a shelf, quickly drying himself off. The guard watched his every move, his narrow eyes suggesting a smirk invisible under his helmet.

"With all the welts and bruises, your body looks like a map," rasped the man, tilting his head slightly. "Does it hurt to sleep on a hard floor with all these..." He waved his baton, pointing at him.

Gunz didn't reply. Throwing the used towel in a laundry basket, he reached for the plastic bag with the clothing, but the guard moved it away. Gunz sighed and stilled, staring at him reproachfully.

"You didn't answer my question, reptile," growled the guard. "You know I don't take disobedience well."

Gunz sighed, lowering his eyes. "Yes, of course it hurts," he said quietly, feeling exposed and defenseless, inside and out. "Is that what you wanted to hear? That I'm in constant pain? Yes, I am... every moment of the day and night."

"Good," hissed the guard, rising, and pushed the bag to Gunz's feet. "I'll make sure to add a few more landmarks to this map of yours later on tonight, lizard. So, you have something to look forward to. Get dressed. It's not like you have anything to show anyway."

Gunz opened the bag and saw a black tactical uniform, completed with combat boots. He got dressed quickly and squatted, lacing his boots. All this time, the guard stood, silently observing him.

"Let's go," he said finally, pulling Gunz to his feet, and pushed him toward the exit.

Gunz let him walk out first and then followed him all the way to the training facility. Commander Moore and his team were there already, seemingly waiting for him. While all of them were dressed in the same black uniforms, each member of the team was armed differently.

Gunz spotted Lucan right away, his long bluish-white hair stark against the blackness of his outfit. The elf had a quiver with arrows and a giant black bow strapped to his back. Besides that, a long dagger was sheathed at his belt. He gave Gunz a hardly visible nod, greeting him.

The Commander dismissed the guard and came closer to Gunz, giving him a quick once-over, his every move exuding mockery. Then he looked over Gunz's head at one of his soldiers and raised his eyebrow without saying a word. A moment later, a purebred werewolf approached them, offering a black box to the Commander. He took it and turned to Gunz.

"Well, we're almost ready to depart," he announced, staring down at him with a crooked smirk. "You cleaned up nicely, but I believe your makeover needs one last touch, Burns."

"Where are we going?" asked Gunz and immediately regretted as the Commander took his thick leather glove off and slapped him across his face.

"You will go where I tell you to go," he growled, invading his personal space, splattering saliva with every word. "You will do what I tell you to do and you will remain silent doing it. Am I clear, Burns?"

"Yes, sir," replied Gunz, averting his eyes, his jaw set.

The Commander turned the box around and opened it. Inside there was a strange contraption that looked like a gas mask. It wasn't hard to guess what it was, and Gunz took a step back involuntarily, raising his hands.

"Sir, please, you don't have to do it," he said quietly, his eyes glued to the gas mask. "If you make me breathe halotron, you will disable me as a fighter."

"Don't you think I know that?" the Commander huffed, rolling his eyes. "This is why this mask is just a precaution. In case you decide to get smart with me, I can activate the fire suppressant at any time. It has the mundane and magical detection systems installed, so if you try to teleport or open your portal, I'll know before you make your move. Behave, and the halotron will never be released. Got it, soldier?"

"Yes, sir," replied Gunz, his voice hoarse.

"Now, stop wasting my time and bite down." The Commander pressed the gas mask over Gunz's face and locked it with a harness over his head. Then he grabbed his shoulder and pulled him toward the closet at the other end of the room. He opened the closet and gestured for Gunz to approach.

"Choose your weapon and do try to remember what I said about behaving."

Gunz approached the closet and stared at its contents with interest. The closet was filled with weapons—anything from modern firearms to ancient swords and throwing knives. His gaze stopped on a small red Swiss army knife and he held his breath, unable to believe his eyes. As he moved his hand over it, the familiar touch of the magical energy emitted by the weapon caressed his skin. It wasn't just any Swiss army knife. It was *his* sword.

He glanced at the Commander over his shoulder, and the man nodded to him, gesturing to hurry up. With a trembling hand, he took his knife and put it in his pocket, then he turned back to the Commander and gave him a thumbs up.

"That's all you want?" asked Commander Moore, his eyebrows rising. "Just a tiny pocketknife?"

Gunz nodded.

For a moment the Commander stared at him flabbergasted, but then shrugged. "You're a glutton for punishment, boy," he muttered. "We're about to fight a giant nest of vamps. Are you sure you don't want anything... um... bigger?"

Gunz shook his head and touched his chest, making a gesture as if he was casting a spell, and then held up his index finger, indicating number one.

"I see, all you want is this knife and one-time use of your magic. Am I correct?" asked the Commander with a smirk.

Gunz nodded, touching the gas mask over his face.

"Fine, you got it," replied the commander. Then he looked at the team and shouted, "Let's get moving, boys!"

Two men moved forward, holding small vials with a shimmering blue liquid inside. Gunz didn't need to guess—these men were wizards and they were getting ready to open a portal. As if to prove his point, one of them pulled a heavy dark curtain aside, exposing a large pentagram painted on the wall.

They smashed the vials against the pentagram, chanting a spell, and as the liquid spilled, splattering the wall, a huge rotating vortex of a portal opened inside the training facility. Watching the men jumping through the portal one after another, Gunz had no doubt that it wasn't a first time for them.

"Let's rock 'n' roll, Salamander," growled the Commander and pushed him through the portal.

CHAPTER 6

~ ZANE BURNS, A.K.A. GUNZ ~

Gunz walked out of the portal and took a deep breath. The familiar touch of humidity to his skin and the close presence of water left no doubt—he was in Florida. Even through the thick gas mask he could feel the freshness of the night air unpolluted by the fire suppressants. He closed his eyes and rolled his shoulders, slowly moving his head from left to right. He felt his element surging through him, restoring some of his strength, and he exhaled, instantly feeling better.

Lucan put his hand on Gunz's shoulder, looking down at him. "Control your fire, Burns," he whispered. "You don't want Moore to activate your mask."

Gunz took another breath, getting in control of his element, and observed the area. As his eyes halted on the building across the road from him, dizziness assailed him as if he got thrown into a room filled with halon.

The Shadow Grove... Please, God, don't let it be this building...

Commander Moore waved his hand at the complex ahead and said, "Our target is The Shadow Grove—just another nest of some dirty vamps. You know the drill. We must work quickly and soundlessly. Get in, kill them all, get out. After we're done, there should be nothing undead moving. Am I clear?"

Gunz stared at the building in horror. Every apartment in this small, secluded complex belonged to Akira Ida's company. Every single tenant of *The Shadow Grove*, human or undead, worked for *EverSafe Security*. He couldn't even imagine going inside and killing the vampires and upirs who lived in peace with humans, fighting for the safety of the city, whenever they asked for their help. He had fought side by side with many of them. He knew how they looked. He knew their names...

Moore is after Akira's organization. No, the Destiny Council is after her... But why?

Gunz was positive that this facility and the entire organization reported to the Destiny Council. Since the Scarlet Queen was good for South Florida, keeping her subjects under strict control and the city streets safe for humans, why would the Destiny Council order eradication of her entire organization?

The way the supernatural organizations worked was similar to medieval throne inheritance rules. The thrones were never empty, and if one ruler was gone, another one would come to power almost immediately. Basically speaking—the king is dead, long live the king situation. If Akira was killed or dismissed as one of the supernatural rulers, no doubt someone would take her place. And the new demonic ruler might not be as kind to human population as she was.

Before he could stop himself, Gunz stepped in front of the Commander and pointed at the building, a desperate question in his widened eyes. Moore frowned at him and put his hands on his hips, pursing his lips.

"What now, Burns?" he asked irritably.

Gunz pointed at the building and shook his head no, cutting his hand through the air. Then he looked back at the building and shook his head again.

"Are you refusing to comply with my command?" asked Moore, stepping closer, unconcealed threat in his every move.

Gunz shook his head vigorously, his eyes pleading with the man in charge. With one hand, the Commander seized the mask and upturned Gunz's head so he couldn't look anywhere but at him.

"Listen to me, little reptile," hissed Moore, jerking Gunz's head higher at such an angle that something cracked in his spine. "You will do what I say, when I say it. No questions asked." He turned toward the elf and growled. "Lucan, come here!"

As soon as the elf approached, he stared up at him, his chest moving with heavy breaths, a calculating look on his face. Gunz followed the direction of his gaze and shuddered inwardly. He grabbed the Commander's hand and shook his head again.

"Your hand, elf," hissed Moore. He seized Lucan's arm and locked a cuff over his left wrist. Then he took Gunz's arm and locked the other side of the handcuffs over his right wrist. "Lucan, you will make sure he fights and does his job. Am I clear?"

"Yes, Commander," replied Lucan, sounding calm, but his handcuffed hand clenched into a fist.

"Now you, Burns," said the Commander, turning to Gunz. "In case you didn't know—elves and vampires don't get along. A vampire would do anything to taste his blood." He pushed Lucan on his chest. "If you slow him down or refuse to fight by his side, they will drain him. Even though it's not going to kill him, he's not going to enjoy it."

Gunz glanced at Lucan, but the elf had his best version of a poker face on and there was no way of telling how he felt about it. Gunz threw his hands in the air, forgetting that the elf was attached to him. Then sighed and touched his chest, holding his index finger up.

"Oh?" Moore's lips curved into a snarl that was supposed to be a smirk. "You're asking for the single use of your magic?"

Gunz nodded.

"Does it mean you are ready to comply with my commands?"

Anger spiked the fire within him, and he groaned, struggling to keep it under control. He glanced around, realizing that he was surrounded by a group of powerful supernatural beings who were loyal to the Commander. Fighting them in his current condition wasn't the greatest of ideas as he would get restrained or killed faster than he could say Fire. Clenching his teeth on the mouth grip of the gas mask, he nodded.

"Fine," Moore said, pulling a small box out of his pocket. Pressing some buttons on the box, he turned the mask's magic and heat detectors off. "Do what you need to do and do it quickly. I wasted too much of my time arguing with you already."

Gunz reached into his pocket and produced his Swiss army knife. Touching it with his fingers, he channeled some of his fire through it, in his mind calling his sword's name. A heartbeat later, the tiny knife was gone, replaced by a beautiful medieval sword. The members of the team shifted closer to him, ready to spring into action if he got any wrong ideas.

"You don't say! I thought I'd seen it all, but you magic freaks always find a way to surprise me." Commander Moore clapped his hands and laughed. Quickly, he restored all the mask's settings and put the box back into his pocket. "Now, off you go and you better show me you know how to put that thing to good use."

Lucan touched Gunz's shoulder and pointed at the gates into the apartment building. They were opened, and a guard hung through the broken window of the guardhouse. Blood was streaming down from his throat, cut by a knife or sword, and his horror filled, dead eyes stared into the midnight sky.

As they crossed inside the complex, Lucan dropped his bow

with an expression of regret on his face and unsheathed his dagger. This move didn't surprise Gunz. The elf couldn't use his bow and arrows with only one hand available. Walking softly, he swung to the right, pulling Gunz with him. He stopped in front of one of the apartments and brought his dagger up, ready for action. As Gunz glanced around, he realized that every member of the team was in place, waiting for a command.

There was nothing complicated about Moore's plan of attack. The Commander counted on the element of surprise. What Gunz couldn't understand was why the vampires and upirs, sensitive by nature, hadn't heard them approach. He remembered the time he spent in training with Akira or with Yaroslav —they could hear his heartbeat way before he could see them or detect their vampiric energy signature. Something wasn't right.

Gunz twirled around as far as his right arm attached to Lucan would allow him but didn't notice anything suspicious. Since he couldn't use his magic even to open his other sight or channel his elemental power to expand his Salamander senses, he couldn't see the flow of magical energy around the area.

A bright ball of light rose up in the sky, shone there for a moment, and then dissipated. No doubt it was the signal everyone was waiting for. Lucan kicked the door of the apartment he was standing in front of and it flew off its hinges with a thunderous bang. At the same time, the rest of the team did the same.

In a split-second, the silence of the night was replaced with ear-splitting pandemonium and the calmness turned into chaos. As soon as the vampires and upirs realized they were under attack, they reacted with the viciousness and speed of their species. Without his power and magic, Gunz couldn't see them move, but Lucan's dagger worked with a speed and precision he had never seen in a fight before.

"You don't need to kill them, but try not to slow me down,

Burns," whispered Lucan, making his way through the apartment complex that now looked like some eerie battlefield where there were no dead bodies but only piles of ash.

A few times, Gunz got attacked and he had no choice but to put his sword to use. He didn't recognize the vampires he had to kill, but that didn't make him feel any better. As he moved through the area, he kept surveying it, terrified of the idea of finding Yaroslav or Akira here. Even though he knew neither Akira nor Yaroslav lived here, he was worried that someone would alert them, or they would sense the distress in their ranks.

That was another thing that raised a red flag in his mind. Why did no one in this complex sound a silent alarm or got in touch with Akira? If someone did, surely the Scarlet Queen would have arrived here in a heartbeat with reinforcements and that would have been the end of Commander Moore and his team.

He had no time to think about it as Lucan got attacked by a few vamps at the same time. The massive elf moved quickly, pushing his attackers to the wall of the building, decapitating them with one swing of his long dagger.

Holding his sword in his left hand, Gunz was as dangerous as he would be if he used his right hand, but he was no match to Lucan. Fast, powerful and silent, the elf moved like Death itself, leaving piles of ashes in his wake. Soon, they stood knee-deep in ash, and Lucan's dagger rested at the neck of a young woman. She stood barefoot in a silk night slip with her back pressed against the wall, bloody tears sliding down her pale cheeks, her long fangs expanded.

Gunz glanced at her and everything inside him twisted with painful recognition. She was the youthful-looking vampire-secretary he had seen so many times when he came to visit Akira at *EverSafe*. Despite the gas mask and all the blood and dirt covering his face, she recognized him too, because she stretched her arm to him, pleading for her life.

Gunz took her hand and turned to Lucan. He couldn't say anything, but he was hoping that his eyes conveyed the message clear enough. A low growl rumbled in the elf's chest as he looked around, lowering his dagger.

"Look, Burns," he whispered, pointing up at the roof. "She can't escape, and we can't let her go. Their magic will keep her inside the complex anyway and if the Commander sees you showing mercy, he'll punish us both."

Gunz followed the direction he was pointing at and saw the two wizards he'd seen earlier standing on the rooftop of the building. Holding their arms up, they wielded their magic, and finally Gunz started to understand why Akira didn't sense that her vampires were in distress, and why the vampires and upirs hadn't detected their approach. The wizards blocked the entire building, breaking the psychic links between the vampires and concealing the approach of their team.

Gunz felt a heavy hand on his shoulder and flinched, spinning around. Commander Moore stood next to him, twirling a massive wooden stake in his hand. Covered in ash, blood and dirt, he looked like a death omen himself. He grabbed Gunz's right hand and thrust the stake into it with an arrogant smirk on his face.

"Do it, Burns," he ordered, pointing at the vampire. "I want to see this stake in the dead heart of this creature."

Gunz raised his eyes, meeting the Commander's cold stare and shook his head, silently pleading with him.

"Hold on, Commander," said Lucan peacefully. "You've been talking for a while about getting a female fighter for our team. Let's take her. She's an old vampire, means fast and strong. We can train her."

"Nice try, elf. Not this one." Moore chuckled, shaking his

head, and then turned to Gunz. "You have an order, soldier. Do it!"

Gunz bowed his head, ready to drop the stake and submit to whatever punishment was coming, but Lucan grabbed his fist with his hand and drove the stake Gunz was holding through the vampire's heart. For a moment, she still stood, staring at Gunz, the last scarlet tear running down her face, her mouth open in shock, and then her body disintegrated, gray ashes soundlessly falling at his feet.

"Dammit, Lucan!" Moore roared, fury coloring his bulldog face in a terrifying shade of magenta. He swung his arm and slammed his massive fist into Lucan's face. The elf grunted and swayed, but didn't fall, pressing his right hand to his jaw.

Gunz looked at the man in front of him, then his gaze traveled around, darting from one cold, indifferent face to the next, and finally stopped on the pile of ashes in front of him. Flames of anger fueled by grief and despair shot through him, and he could no longer control it.

The fire broke through, engulfing his entire body in flames and he screamed with his jaws locked around the mouth grip of the mask. While every member of his team jumped aside, Moore didn't move. With a diabolical laughter, he slammed his hand on his jacket pocket, activating the device he had there.

Gunz choked, inhaling a large dose of fire suppressant, and collapsed, pulling Lucan with him. His body curved into a ball and his muscles tensed to the point where he thought his bones would snap. He thought he was screaming but wasn't sure his jaws ever unlocked.

With his entire world twisted into a giant vortex filled with undiluted agony, he felt a twitch of magic in his mind, a soft ping of the Dark Codex. Unintentionally, he reached for it, triggering the magic detectors in his mask. The second dose of halotron filled his lungs, suffocating him. With his fading mind, he clutched to his life, somehow still remembering that if he died a human death, he would take hundreds, if not thousands, of human lives with him.

Don't die...

The ground beneath his back shook and swum, and he felt someone's arms lifting him. With effort, he cracked his eyelids open, but his vision was distorted and blurry. Right above him, he saw a pair of green eyes glowing like two large emerald stars.

"*Yaroslav... Aidan...*" he called to his friends but found an empty void in the place where their physic bond had existed before.

* * *

When Gunz regained consciousness, he found himself lying on the floor of the training facility. The mask was gone, but the weakness and soreness of his body was overwhelming and when he tried to sit up, he couldn't. With horror, he noticed that he was absolutely naked. With painful clarity, he recalled everything that happened at the *Shadow Grove* and cringed inwardly as sadness and remorse hollowed him out. He remembered partially losing control of his power and the fire breaking free, which explained why he was naked, considering that the clothes the Commander had provided weren't fire-proof.

Lucan... What did they do to him?

He strained to lift his head and saw Lucan kneeling behind the Commander. His head was bowed low and the mass of his bluish hair, matted with blood and sweat, fell over his face and chest. His hands were handcuffed in front of him. The elf was as still as a statue, but at least he was keeping an upright position, which told Gunz that he was okay. For now.

Commander Moore was talking to a guard and once Gunz heard his voice, he shivered as if an icy breeze swept through the facility. The voice belonged to *his* guard, the man who had abused and tortured him for days.

"...you can take him now," said the Commander, unusual sadness in his voice. "I am going to have a talk with the boss and Doctor Harris. Yes, they were right. He has fighting skills that are beyond that of a regular man or even a supernatural being, but his spirit cannot be broken. God knows I tried... He will never obey."

"Let me do my job," said the guard, his voice harsh and cold. "I'll break him."

Moore huffed and shook his head. "Doubt it. To break a man like this you would have to wipe out everything he is," he muttered, throwing a glance at Gunz, but avoiding his eyes. "I really wish I could have this man on my side—strong, amazing fighter, and loyal. You don't meet too many of his kind nowadays." He sighed, rubbing his forehead. "But I know it's not going to happen. So, I'm done. You can take him now and do as you please with him. I can bet you anything, you're not going to break him."

The guard approached Gunz and lifted him easily, throwing him over his shoulder. Gunz closed his eyes, mentally getting ready to what was to come. The walk to his cell seemed to be endless and when the guard dumped him on the hard floor unceremoniously, this little bit of extra pain made him lose his breath.

The man walked out of the room and released a dose of halotron. Gunz curved into a ball, but had no strength to scream, which didn't satisfy the guard. He walked back into the room and pushed on his shoulders, forcing him to lie on his back. Feeling exposed and vulnerable, Gunz jerked his hands down, trying to cover himself. The guard snickered coldly and squatted next to him, throwing his arms apart.

"I will break you, you know," he said, his bright, blue eyes crinkling through the opening of his helmet as if he was smiling. His fingers slid over Gunz's face, down to his chest, pushing into every bruise and cut he found. "I will see you squirming and begging for your worthless life, even though I know you are an immortal Fire Salamander."

"Why?" whispered Gunz. "Why do you torture me? Why is it so important to you?"

"Really? You still don't recognize me?" The guard rose, staring down at him with abhorrence.

"I don't know you...," whispered Gunz, his vocal cords giving up on him.

The man pulled his leg in a heavy combat boot back and slammed it into his side. His ribs cracked and Gunz cried out, his body curving of its own accord. The guard kicked him a few more times on his chest and stomach, and all Gunz could do was pull his knees up and cover his head with his arms.

"Don't worry," the guard said, breathing heavily. "I'll reintroduce myself in a moment. After all, I want you to say my name when you're begging me for mercy."

Never... I'll die first... Gunz coughed, spitting some blood on the white tiles of the floor.

The guard grabbed his arm and jerked it, turning him on his stomach. Gunz moved his head to the side and with horror watched him pull his belt out all the way. As he did that, his slightly wide pants slid half-way down his narrow hips, but he made no move to pull them up. Instead, he folded the belt in half, leaving the heavy metal buckle out of his hand. Then he took a deep breath and removed his helmet. Wincing from the lack of oxygen in the room, he stared down at Gunz with a malevolent smirk.

"Do you recognize me now, fire-worm?" he hissed. Raising his arm, he struck Gunz's exposed back with his belt, making sure that the belt buckle and the metal spikes ripped his skin to shreds as he pulled it across.

As much as Gunz promised himself not to give this man the satisfaction of hearing him scream, in his condition, he couldn't control the pain. He howled as the pain turned him inside out, his fingers scratching at the slippery tiles spasmodically. The guard stepped back and cocked his head, a one-sided smirk on his face.

When Gunz regained his breathing, he frowned, feeling the pain contorting his face. "I do...," he croaked. "Liam... Porter... why..."

Liam howled in rage so deep that his entire body shook. He put his helmet back on and took a deep breath.

"You killed her!" he yelled. "You killed Hazel. You killed the woman I loved. And my mother's death is also your doing! You! Killed! Every! Person! I had ever loved!"

Liam kept shouting, striking his back and his legs with the belt with each word. Gunz screamed each time his skin ripped apart, but he could no longer move. A moment later, Liam stopped. Breathing laboriously, he flexed his right arm, staring at Gunz sprawled motionless in the puddle of his own blood. Then he took one knee next to him and seized his hair, pulling his head up.

"Beg me for forgiveness, asshole," he hissed.

"Hazel... I'm sorry, but I'm glad... you can't see... what he's become...," whispered Gunz, his lips barely moving. "You will never hear me begging—"

Liam howled again and connected his fist with Gunz's face. For a moment, everything went dark, but the pain of the lashes brought him right back as Liam kept working on him with his belt, rhythmically raising it up and lowering it down.

Suddenly Liam stopped and lowered his arm. He laughed maniacally, his blue eyes glowing with anger bordering with insanity.

"I'll take everything from you, just like you took everything from me but with interest," he hissed, his fingers fumbling with the bloodied belt.

Gunz followed the movement of his hands and fear ripped through him, panic making his already frazzled mind foggier.

"No...," he moaned.

"Oh, yes," roared Liam, kicking him in the stomach.

A strained howl escaped Gunz's lips as he tried to move away from him, his fingers clawing at the cold, slippery floor. Liam watched his struggles, his eyes gleaming with sadistic pleasure as he moved a step closer to him.

"After I am done with you today—," he started but didn't get a chance to finish his statement.

With a thunderous bang, the one-sided mirror exploded inside the room, showering both of them with splinters of glass. A tall man vaulted through the broken mirror and kicked Liam under his helmet, sending him flying across the cell.

At the same time, the door flew off its hinges and three women walked inside the room.

CHAPTER 7

~ ZANE BURNS, A.K.A. GUNZ ~

Without halting, the man stepped over Gunz and covered the distance between him and Liam in a couple of giant steps. He dropped to one knee, ripped Liam's helmet off and kept punching him with admirable persistence. With an agonizing effort, Gunz turned his head to the side and watched as Liam's blood splattered all over the white wall and floor.

"Lucan, stop...," he whispered. "Enough..."

Even though he didn't think the infuriated elf could hear him, Lucan got up and stilled, curiosity reflected in his cat-like eyes. Gunz felt a touch to his injured back and sucked in a sharp breath, turning his head.

"Tessa... how did you find me?" he whispered, barely moving his swollen lips. He was too tired to be surprised, too weak to wonder how they managed to break through the tight security of the Destiny Council compound.

"Aidan did," replied Tessa, her voice uncharacteristically hoarse. "Long story and you probably won't believe it. Anyway, we're here to take you... Well, not home, but to a safe location, okay?"

"Okay," he managed to say, his eyes stopping on two more familiar faces.

Missi and Karma stood behind Tessa, looking mortified as they stared at him. Gunz smirked and swallowed, suppressing the nausea.

"That bad?" he asked, his voice flat and emotionless.

"I've seen worse," replied Karma, squatting next to him. "I've seen you worse, if you remember our promenade through the Dark Nav."

"We don't have time for a trip down memory lane," Missi cut in. "We must leave now, before it's too late."

Gunz glanced at Lucan, who still stood by the wall, his bloodied fists dangling by his sides.

"We must take Lucan with us, Missi," he croaked, jerking his chin slightly toward the elf. "I owe him… a lot…"

Tessa got up and measured Lucan with her eyes, tilting her head a little. "Hey, you, giant," she said, gesturing at him.

"Are you talking to me, my lady?" asked Lucan, notes of shock in his deep voice, and Gunz stiffened, choking on pain, awaiting Tessa's reaction.

"My lady?" huffed Tessa, planting her feet wide. "Yeah, I am talking to you, since you are the only jumbo-size moron in this room. What are you waiting for?" She stamped her foot. "Take your shirt off and cover him." She glanced at Gunz and winked. "His shirt should cover you from head to toe, right?"

Lucan pressed his hand to his lips to stifle his laughter, humorous twinkles dancing in his eyes, but pulled his shirt over his head and covered Gunz's back. As he did that, Gunz noticed that the elf winced, and a shadow of pain crossed his features.

"Lucan," he demanded quietly, "show me your back."

"It's okay. I'll be fine," muttered Lucan.

He squatted next to Gunz and lifted him with a strenuous grunt. Gunz cried out and his head tilted backward as he had no strength to keep it up.

"Try not to scream," mumbled Lucan, his white eyebrows gathering over his eyes as he stared at Gunz with concern. Then he turned to Tessa, Missi, and Karma, inclining his head in a light bow.

"Let's go," said Missi, heading toward the door, "we have a portal waiting for us and it's not going to wait forever."

Karma whispered a spell, conjuring a shiny blue orb. For a moment, it lingered in the air above her, then soundlessly started gliding away. Following the orb, they walked through the maze of hallways, and every step Lucan took resonated with a spike of pain in Gunz's back. All he could do was bite his lip and suppress his screams. Luckily, the portal wasn't far away, and they made it all the way without any adventures. Lucan stopped in front of the rotating vortex and smiled, the relief on his face making him look younger.

"I can't believe I'm finally free," he whispered more to himself than to Gunz and stepped through the portal.

As soon as they walked out of the portal, Gunz took a deep breath and moaned. The air was clean and cold, unfamiliar scents and sounds invading his senses. He tried to lift his head, but his body was completely out of order, and he gave up. Lucan noticed his struggle and gently readjusted his position, allowing Gunz to rest his head against his chest.

"Where are we?" asked Gunz weakly, staring at a large ranch house surrounded by a white fence.

"Aidan will tell you everything," replied Missi, touching his hand. "We're almost there."

They headed toward the house, but before they reached it, the door swung open and Aidan walked out on the porch. He halted for a moment, staring at Gunz, a painful line etched between his brows, but then quickly covered the distance between them. He stopped in front of Lucan, his eyes never leaving Gunz's, and shook his head.

"What kind of trouble did you get yourself into this time, Fire Gecko?" he asked lightly, but his voice shook, betraying his emotions.

Gunz didn't reply and bit his lip, staring over Aidan's shoulder into the darkness of the night.

"My lord," said Lucan, addressing Aidan. "I would bow to you, but my hands are busy. Burns needs to heal himself, unless you can heal him…"

"You don't need to bow to me, elf," replied Aidan. "And no, I don't have healing power, but I know a place where he can safely revert into his natural state and heal himself. I'll take it from here."

"Wow! He's an elf?" murmured Tessa and giggled. "I don't think I have a big enough shelf to put him on."

"Aw, I'll find a shelf for him any time, not only for Christmas," purred Missi, winking at Lucan.

Lucan started at them with his mouth open, but Aidan nudged him on his shoulder, chuckling.

"Ignore them," he said, gently taking Gunz off Lucan's hands. "They'll poke jokes at you any time you give them an opportunity."

As soon as Aidan took Gunz, Lucan kneeled, lowering his head. "My lord," he said to Aidan. "I'm Lucan, the last of the Elzara clan."

Gunz grunted and sighed. "The last?" he whispered and closed his eyes.

"Lucan, don't kneel," said Aidan, sounding impatient. "Thank you for helping my friend. If you choose to stay with us, I'll be honored to have you on my team." Then he turned to Karma and jerked his chin toward the elf. "Karma, I need you to tend to his back, please. I think, he had his fair share of flogging too."

Without waiting for Karma's response, Aidan snapped his fingers and vanished from the ranch.

THEY MANIFESTED in the middle of empty land, covered in dry grass and spiky cacti. Aidan threw Lucan's shirt to the ground, gently lowered Gunz on top of it, and squatted next to him. Gunz glanced at his friend and averted his eyes. He was naked, hurt and helpless, but that wasn't the worst. Inside, he felt hollow. There was no desire to fight, to live, to know anything. He just wanted silence with no one around. Lying on his torn back was pure agony, but he didn't even want to heal.

Aidan touched his shoulder, sympathy in his blue eyes.

"Gunz, look at me," he said quietly. Sitting down on the ground next to him, he rested his arms atop his bent knees. "I need you to revert and heal yourself."

Gunz raised his eyes at Aidan and visibly cringed. The sympathy in his friend's gaze—he didn't want it. He didn't want anything.

"Is Yaroslav here?" he asked, his lips not moving.

Aidan shook his head. "After we returned from the Land of Dreams, I lost all three of you—Yaroslav, Peyton and you," he said, pulling a dry blade of grass out of the desert sand. "Angel and Uri are also missing, and Svyatobor is not quite himself." He pulled another blade of grass out, rolling it between his fingers, and stared at Gunz. "Please, Zane, heal yourself. Revert. I need you, my friend."

Gunz turned away from him and grunted as his back responded with a jolt of pain.

"I can't," he croaked. "And I don't want..." He couldn't speak—words stuck in his sore throat.

"You know, it took me forever to find you," said Aidan as if he hadn't heard Gunz's words. "No one could—FBI, Kal, the Ancient Master... They all had tried and failed miserably."

Gunz glanced at his friend, wondering where he was going with it. Aidan met his eyes and smirked darkly.

"You're not gonna believe it, but it was Anatoly Karpenko who found you and gave me the plan of that facility you were imprisoned in. We had to open a portal blindly, based on that plan. It was a risk, but the girls were willing to take it to get you out," continued Aidan, staring somewhere into the nothingness of the desert. "Anyway, now I owe Anatoly Karpenko." He laughed bitterly. "I broke my oath to the Guardians, and I owe a favor to the Russian mobster. How much worse can it get?"

"Aidan, I—" His voice broke off, and he looked away.

Aidan took his chin with his fingers and gently forced Gunz to look at him. "I'm so sorry, my friend," he said, his voice distant and hollow.

Before Gunz could say anything to stop him, Aidan manifested a giant fireball and thrust it through Gunz's chest. Gunz cried out, his body arched for a moment and then fell back to the ground limply.

"Revert, Gunz," yelled Aidan. "Heal your body and I promise you'll have all the time you need to heal your soul."

Gunz stared at Aidan in shock, feeling his own element surging through him. Aidan didn't wait for him to respond and pushed another fireball through his chest. And another... and one more...

Even though Aidan was trying to help him, after everything he had gone through and everything he had been forced to do against his will, Aidan's actions felt invasive and aggressive. Anger rushed through him, igniting the fire within, and he screamed. Liquid flames gathered in his eyes, threatening to spill as he partially reverted into the natural state of the Fire Salamander.

A weak wave of elemental energy spread around him, and

for a moment, his body got enveloped into scorching flames, forcing Aidan to raise his arms, shielding his face. He let go a few seconds later and lay limply on the ground with his eyes closed.

Gunz felt Aidan check his back to make sure all the wounds were healed, but he didn't open his eyes. Aidan lifted him and a soft click followed as his friend snapped his fingers, teleporting them back to the ranch.

He heard a door being shut and cracked his eyelids open. Aidan stood inside a small room, still holding him in his arms. An older man he had never met before stood next to them and even in his condition, Gunz could detect the distinct energy signature of the purebred werewolf in him.

"Hawk, can I use your bath, please?" asked Aidan. "I need to take care of..."

Aidan's voice disappeared into the darkness of his frazzled mind. The next thing he felt was a touch of hot water to his body. Someone was gently running a luffa over his shoulder and chest, washing off all the dirt, blood, and ashes. He opened his eyes, expecting to find Aidan, but it was Karma. She was out of her tactical gear and wore a soft pink bath robe with yellow ducks printed all over it.

She smiled at him without stopping what she was doing, and to his relief, she didn't say or ask anything. Embarrassment coiled in his chest at the thought that she was washing him like he was a child, but he couldn't bring himself to protest and closed his eyes, turning away from her.

As darkness surrounded him, he let go, finding a temporary relief in oblivion.

* * *

GUNZ OPENED his eyes and stared at a white ceiling. The absolute whiteness above him made him shudder and cower closer to the wall. For a few minutes, he lay on his side in a fetal position unable to think clearly. As the panic slowly gave in and his mind started to clear, he opened his eyes again, realizing that not everything around him was white.

On the contrary, the room was full of colors. Colorful window treatments were competing in vibrant colors with the blanket he was covered with. A bookshelf was overflowing with colorful books, and the walls had pink wallpaper with a floral design.

Gunz pushed himself up on his elbows and looked around. At the foot of his bed, Aidan was sitting in an armchair with his legs stretched out. The god of the Otherworld was asleep, but the deep gray shadows under his eyes and his lips set in a straight line showed just how exhausted he was. Gunz wanted to wake him up and tell him to leave. He didn't need a babysitter, but instead, he dropped on his back and pulled his blanket over his head.

The next time Gunz opened his eyes, he thought he saw Lucan in his room. The elf stood by the window, daylight throwing playful flares of shimmering light on his long white hair. Gunz turned to his side and shrunk closer to the wall, wrapping his arms around his head, and closed his eyes again.

He didn't know how long he was out this time, but when he carefully pulled the blanket down and looked around, the room was finally empty, and he was alone. He sat up and lowered his feet to the floor, flexing his shoulders. The reality where nothing and no one was hurting him, where nobody was trying to dissect his mind, and the air was clean, felt like a shock to his system. He got up and looked down, noticing that he had pajama pants on. He didn't remember putting them on and tried not to think about it. On a chair next to his bed, he noticed a set of clean clothes.

He didn't bother getting dressed but walked to the window and pulled the flowery curtain aside. Sun was blasting from the perfectly blue sky and his eyes, unaccustomed to bright light, started to water. He dropped the curtain and turned his back to the window, rubbing his eyes.

It was probably the sound that was too loud for his stretched nerves or maybe the fact that he still couldn't see clearly, but when someone walked into his room, shutting the door with a loud thud, it sent him over the edge. As a knee-jerk reaction, he slid down to the floor. Trying to take as little space as he could, he pressed his back against the wall and raised his arms, shielding his head.

It wasn't fear. What he felt was a lot more terrifying and debilitating than fear itself. It was the expectation of something awful to happen, the unknown that promised nothing but more torment, the dread of being completely defenseless against what was coming.

Gunz felt a light touch to his arms and his body shuddered, a painful groan escaping his tightly pressed lips. But then he heard a soothing unfamiliar voice, felt someone gently stroking his shoulder, and he finally opened his eyes. In front of him, he saw an older man, his magical energy signature screaming purebred werewolf. Gunz remembered him.

"Hawk," he whispered his name, slowly lowering his arms, his moves painfully stiff.

Hawk smiled, sadness in his golden eyes. "That's okay, son," he said, patting him on his shoulder. "You're safe here. No one will hurt you in my house."

Gunz nodded silently, heat rising to his cheeks. He took Hawk's hand and got up, wrapping his arms around himself awkwardly.

Hawk picked up the clothing from the chair and offered them to Gunz. "It's my son's," he explained. "He's a little taller than you, but it should still fit you."

"Thank you," replied Gunz, avoiding Hawk's eyes.

Hawk sighed, frowning. "What's your name, son?" he asked,

carefully touching Gunz's shoulder. Gunz flinched, unintentionally taking a step back.

"Zane," he replied, staring down at the clothes he was holding. "Zane Burns."

"Well, Zane," continued Hawk as if he didn't notice his reaction, "if you are not otherwise engaged, I was wondering if you could help me with something."

Gunz looked up and for the first time truly met Hawk's golden eyes.

"Me?" he asked incredulously. "What can I do for you, sir?"

"You're a Child of Fire, aren't you?" asked the Alpha. Gunz nodded. "I have an old smithy here, on my land, but for whatever reason, no one seems to be able to restart the forge. So, I was wondering if you would be kind enough to try?"

"Yes, sir," replied Gunz. "Of course, I'll do what I can." He took a step toward the door, but then halted and smiled shyly. "I think I should get dressed first."

"Good idea," agreed Hawk, hiding a smile.

* * *

A FEW MINUTES LATER, Hawk walked Gunz out of the house and led him through the property toward a small smithy. On their way, they didn't meet anyone, and when Hawk opened the squeaky old door into a dark hut, Gunz sighed with relief—there was no one there. He wasn't sure he was ready to face his friends, but he was positively sure he didn't want to answer any questions about what had happened to him.

He moved his hand in a wide arc and the air lit up with faint traces of fire energy. A tiny smile quirked up the corners of his mouth as he turned to Hawk, and flames slowly rose in his eyes.

"I can do it," he said airily. "Just give me a few minutes and I will bring back the fire to your smithy."

Hawk nodded, warmth lighting up his weather-beaten face

as he observed Gunz. Then he slapped his hands on his thighs. "Oh, dammit, I forgot to offer you something to eat. You're probably hungry. I should have fed you before dragging you here."

Gunz shook his head. "Thank you, Hawk, but I don't need food. I just need to be..." His voice trailed off as he stared at the anvil and the heavy hammer on top of it.

"Alone," Hawk finished his statement. "I understand. I'll see you later."

Gunz didn't notice when Hawk turned around and left. He approached the cold forge and put his hand over it, listening to the whispers of the flames within him. Then he got up and closed his eyes, surrendering to the Almighty Fire. Slowly he dissolved into his element, allowing it to take him over and block everything that wasn't burning.

He didn't channel the Fire magic as he would normally do. Instead, he willed his element to do what he wanted. The red wave of elemental fire swept through the smithy, bringing everything to life, changing it and reshaping it to his desire. The magical energy field spiked around him as he tapped into it without a conscious thought. It wasn't him wielding the fire—it was him being it.

Gunz took a piece of metal and put it on the anvil. He placed his hand over it, and a heartbeat later, the metal lit up with an orange-red light. He took the massive hammer and swung it with his full might, crashing it down.

The metal sang and a powerful wave of elemental fire energy spread around him. For a moment, Gunz stood still, staring into the fire. Then he tilted his head back and screamed, placing all the pain accumulated in his soul in one gut-wrenching howl.

CHAPTER 8

~ AIDAN ~

Aidan sat on the fence, staring into the desert absently. It'd been a week since Tessa, Missi and Karma brought Gunz back. Neither Karma nor Missi had ever seen the facility he was held in before, and Lucan didn't know anything about it either. The elf wasn't sure how long he spent in captivity, but he was positive it was counted in years.

Aidan sighed, wishing he could talk to his friend, but Gunz drifted in and out of sleep, and Missi was right when she suggested letting him sleep for as long as he needed to recover. Aidan wasn't sure what had been done to Gunz in that place, but it seemed like his soul had suffered damages a lot worse than his body had.

He thought back to the way Gunz's body had looked when Lucan brought him over and shuddered. But it was the look in his eyes—haunted, empty and lifeless—that truly troubled him.

A sound of laughter and loud clunks of metal hitting metal reached his ears and he turned around. In a wide empty space in front of the house, Missi, Tessa and Karma were attacking Lucan. They were obviously playing, but even though all three were using their swords and their magic, the giant elf had no problem deflecting their attacks.

Fluid like liquid mercury, he moved gracefully, his footwork light and fast despite his size and weight. Watching Lucan, Aidan had to wonder how powerful that organization had to be to capture the elf in the first place, let alone break him into submission.

Abruptly, Lucan came to a sharp halt and waved his hand, erecting a power shield between himself and the young women, stopping them in their tracks. His body tensed, smile gone from his face, and when Aidan opened his other sight, he saw a soft glim of elven magic surrounding him.

As if feeling Aidan's gaze on him, Lucan met his eyes and raised his hand with the sword, pointing at something at the other end of the pack's property. Before he could see what had alerted the elf, Aidan felt a wave of fire energy spreading through him and held his breath. It wasn't strong enough to travel far, but it was an undiluted elemental wave, purifying fire included.

He jumped off the fence and scanned the area with his other sight. At the far end, he noticed a small hut. The entire building seemed to be engulfed in fire energy and every few minutes, a new elemental blast spread around it, every next one more powerful than previous.

"Gunz," he whispered, a feeling of dread coiling in the pit of his stomach. He waved at Lucan and the women to follow and ran toward the hut.

A few yards away from the hut, he found Hawk. The Alpha stood with his hand pressed over his mouth, a troubled expression on his face. When Aidan approached him, he just shook his head and sighed.

"What is this building?" asked Aidan, but he didn't need Hawk's answer. He already knew it. It was a blacksmith's hut, and it looked like a carbon copy of Kal's smithy in Kendral.

"It used to be a tiny smithy," mumbled Hawk, scratching the back of his head, "but it never looked like that…"

"Fire Almighty," whispered Aidan, cold sweat covering his forehead. "He's reshaping reality using his element."

"What?" asked Hawk.

"Zane is there, right?" asked Aidan.

"Yes," replied Hawk. "I took him there. I'm not a doctor, but even I can see that your friend is suffering from serious PTSD. I don't know what those people had done to him, but he is in more pain than he's willing to admit, and I thought being close to his element would help him clear his mind."

As the next wave of elemental power spread around, more powerful than before, Aidan grunted, raising his hand at Lucan and the girls to stay behind. Carefully, he approached the smithy and opened the door.

Gunz was inside, working with a giant hammer like it was a child's toy. When Aidan walked in, for a brief moment, the Fire Salamander stopped what he was doing, looked at him impassively as if he couldn't see him, then returned to his work.

Aidan froze in place, staring at his friend in awe. It was Gunz, but it wasn't him. The man with the hammer was tall—as tall as Kal. He had the face and body of his friend, but his hair was long, running down his back and shoulders like a flaming river, and when his scorching gaze fell upon him, there was no recognition in his eyes.

"Gunz!" yelled Aidan, fighting the heat. "You need to stop, my friend. You are not controlling your elemental power. Soon, your elemental blasts will reach the towns around the ranch. You'll kill thousands of humans."

Gunz lowered the hammer and glanced at Aidan, his face void of emotions, and then returned back to work.

"Dammit!" yelled Aidan, punching the air.

He channeled his power and erected a shield around the smithy, endeavoring to contain the elemental blasts, but to his horror, the next wave of energy disintegrated his shield as if it was nothing.

"Lucan! Tessa!" he shouted, breathing hard. "I need help. Lucan, perhaps your elven magic will be strong enough to contain the elemental fire. Tessa, add your powers into the mix."

Standing a few feet away from the smithy, all three of them channeled their magic and power at the same time, manifesting a powerful shield. While their shield was able to contain the next wave, Aidan knew that if the elemental blasts would get any stronger, their shield would fail. Besides, even the three of them together wouldn't be able to sustain such a powerful shield for much longer.

"Aidan, you need help," said Hawk quietly. "Zane needs help. Summon his Father. Call someone who can control the fire."

"Kal hasn't replied to my summons since Gunz disappeared," muttered Aidan, straining to hold his shield.

As the next wave spread around the smithy, knocking Lucan and Tessa off their feet, Aidan's magic collapsed, and the thunderous bang echoed through the desert. Aidan cursed and drew a glowing white rune in the air, summoning Gwyn ap Nudd.

As the communication window opened up in midair, Aidan waved his hand, maneuvering it so his mentor could see what was going on inside the hut.

"No...," Gwyn breathed out. "When did this start?"

"Maybe ten-fifteen minutes ago," said Aidan, panic flooding him at the look of fear on Gwyn's face.

"What happened to him? Something has had to provoke this change," yelled Gwyn ap Nudd, slamming his hand against the surface of the window. "Never mind that! Call Kal. Call Mrak Delar. Call anyone who can control fire!"

"Kal doesn't reply to my summons!" shouted Aidan, feeling more desperate by the moment.

"What are you? Born yesterday? Use the forbidden summons!" roared Gwyn ap Nudd, his face ashen with fear.

"Summon Mrak Delar and the Master of Kendral. You don't understand the gravity of this situation. If they can't contain his state, you will have a cemetery on your hands in a few minutes! Thousands will be dead."

Aidan hated using the forbidden summons, but the fear and urgency in his mentor's words left him no choice. He closed the communication window and muttered the summoning spell, calling to Kal. A moment later, a flaming curtain opened up and Kal staggered through it. Falling to his knees, he squeezed his head with his hands, his fingers digging into the mass of his flaming hair.

"Aidan," he groaned, "stop the summoning call… or I swear… I will strangle you with my bare hands."

"Incanto Comlium," muttered Aidan, pointing at the hut before Kal had a chance to follow through on his threat.

Kal got up and as soon as his eyes fell on Gunz, a strangled scream escaped his lips and he darted into the hut. He crossed the threshold and yelled, "Cease!"

Neither Gunz nor the fire energy inside the hut responded to his command. Kal gasped and twirled around. Anger and fear blended into one explosive mix and the fire energy around the Fire Elemental spiked up, adding to an already heavy presence of his element in the area. Using the fire, he drew a flaming rune in the air and slammed his hand over it.

"Master Mrak Delar, I summon thee," he hissed through clenched teeth. Then he drew one more rune identical to the first one. "Master Alliandr, I summon thee."

Two men appeared next to Kal a moment later. Both tall with long black hair and obsidian eyes, they looked like brothers. They stilled, their eyes slowly coloring red as the presence of the elemental fire overwhelmed their senses.

Aidan had heard enough stories about Master Alliandr—the young Master of Kendral. He was known as one of the youngest and most magically gifted Masters of Power who had ever sat on the throne of Kendral. His complicated relationship with Mrak Delar, and the way he came to power was the stuff of legends. However, until now, Aidan had never met him in person.

Mrak Delar turned around and took a sharp breath, staring at Gunz with wide eyes. He ran into the smithy, and ignoring the heat, placed his hands on Gunz's shoulder, trying to suppress his fire to no avail.

"Mrak, stop," yelled Kal, "you can't bring him back like that. Right now, he is stronger than any of us, but maybe not than all of us together. We must syphon the fire out of this hut and when he gets a little weaker, we'll see what we can do to help him."

Mrak Delar came out of the hut and stared heavily at Aidan.

"What's going on here, Aidan?" he asked through gritted teeth. "Gunz dropped his humanity, and I want to know what triggered the change? If we stand a tiny chance of bringing him back, I must know what pushed him to this extreme."

"I don't know! I wish I knew," yelled Aidan, throwing his hands in the air. "He was injured. Severely. He was abused physically. That's all I know. He wouldn't talk to me or to anyone for that matter."

"It's not the physical abuse that pushed him over the edge, my lords," said Hawk, bowing to both Masters of Power and the Fire Elemental.

"What do you know, wolf?" asked Kal, approaching him.

"I know nothing," replied Hawk, rising. "He wouldn't talk to me either. But I saw the look in your boy's eyes and there was no life there. I have seen eyes like this before. I don't know what was done to him, but whatever it was, it damaged his soul and destroyed his spirit."

As the next wave of elemental fire spread through the area, Kal gasped and spread his arms, partially absorbing it.

"Let's do it," he said to both Masters of Power. "Let's bring him back." Then he turned to Aidan, pointing at the hut. "Aidan, conjure the strongest shield you can muster around yourself and go inside. Gunz will get weak quickly, and I don't want him to be alone when it happens."

Kal took his position, digging his feet into the ground, and channeled his element. Spreading his arms wide, he absorbed the next wave and then brought his hands together. As he clapped, a tight wall of elemental energy surrounded the hut, leaving Aidan inside the circle.

Mrak Delar and the Master of Kendral stepped on either side of Kal and placed their hands on the wall. Their eyes lit up with a bright red light as they started to chant, the sound of their voices just as alike as their appearance. Aidan conjured a shield around himself and looked back before crossing into the smithy.

He could see that whatever Kal and the two Masters were doing didn't come easy to them. Their arms got wrapped into tight ropes of muscles, and their faces were strained as if they were lifting a heavy weight. Nevertheless, whatever they were doing seemed to be working and the amount of fire energy within the circle started to drop.

Aidan took a deep breath, bracing for the heat, and walked inside. Gunz stopped working and turned toward him, his flaming eyes settling on him.

"Zane... my friend...," said Aidan, carefully approaching him.

Gunz lowered his arms and swayed slightly. His fingers unlocked, and he dropped the hammer. Slowly, the flames wrapping around his body dissipated, and Aidan saw that his clothes were gone, burnt by the fire. As his appearance began to change, Gunz's flaming hair disappeared and he returned to his normal height.

"Aidan," whispered Gunz, finally recognizing him.

His knees buckled and he would have fallen if Aidan didn't

catch him. Aidan lowered him gently to the ground, took his shirt off and wrapped it around Gunz's hips.

"Please leave," Gunz whispered, turning away. He pushed himself up with his arms and sat up, resting his back against the anvil. "I'm begging you... Please, Aidan... I can't..."

Kal walked into the hut and kneeled next to Gunz, putting his hand on his shoulder, but Gunz flinched and shied away from his touch. Kal looked up at Aidan and then turned to Mrak Delar and the Master of Kendral. Both were staring at Gunz with an identical expression of horror imprinted on their faces.

"Gunz," said Mrak Delar softly, approaching him.

"Mrak, please...," whispered Gunz, raising his hand to cover his face. "I need to... I have to..." He bit his lip and a tear of liquid fire slipped from his eye. He wiped it, running his fingers over his face. "I'll be all right. Do me a kindness... and leave..."

Aidan stared down at his friend, unable to recognize the strong man he once was in this destroyed person with haunted eyes and pained expression on his face. Everything inside him twisted in one agonizing jolt as sorrow and anger swirled through him.

But before anyone could say anything else, Tessa strolled into the hut. She stopped between Gunz and the rest of them and put her hands on her hips. For a moment, her eyes moved from one face to the next. Then she raised her hand and pointed at the exit.

"All of you, out!" she yelled, stamping her foot.

"Tessa—," started Aidan warningly, throwing an apologetic glance at the Master of Kendral, but Alliandr just smiled and bowed to Tessa lightly.

"I do not dare to disobey, my lady," he said softly, then turned to Kal. "I believe Gunz is in good hands now. Great Salamander, if you no longer need me here, I must go back to Kendral." He snapped his fingers and vanished.

Tessa raised her eyebrows, glowering at the rest of them. "Why are you all still here?" she asked, throwing her hands up.

"Mrak, we should have a word," said Kal.

He turned around and walked out of the hut, pulling Mrak Delar with him. Aidan headed toward the exit but changed his mind and lowered himself to the ground, resting his back against the doorway. Tessa huffed but didn't kick him out.

She approached Gunz and for a moment stood over him. He raised his eyes at her but turned away without saying anything. She sat down next to him with her back against the anvil, then grabbed him under his armpits and pulled him closer, resting his back against her chest. Before he could resist, she wrapped one arm around his chest and the other across his throat, placing her head atop his.

He tried to throw her arms off, but she just squeezed him tighter. Aidan watched the silent feeble fight his friend put up, everything inside him painfully numb. Suddenly, Gunz stopped fighting her embrace. His fingers wrapped around her delicate wrists, digging so deep into her skin that Aidan had no doubt, he was hurting her. Tessa didn't try to loosen his grip. Instead, she kissed the top of his head, her fingers gently stroking his skin.

"It's okay, Zane," she whispered into his hair, gently rocking back and forth, as if he were a child who needed comforting. "It's okay... I'm here... We are all here for you..."

Gunz's face tensed. He threw his head back, pushing against her shoulder, and screamed, a sharp howl filled with so much anguish and despair that it didn't sound like it was produced by human vocal cords. He bit his lip as tears—pure liquid fire—slipped from his eyes, running down his pale cheeks, and his entire body shuddered. She held him, gently caressing him and murmuring something into his hair, despite his flaming tears burning her skin into blisters.

Aidan wasn't sure how long they sat like this. Little by little,

Gunz's fiery tears were replaced by clear human ones. When he finally relaxed against Tessa's chest and closed his eyes, she waved her hand at Aidan to approach.

He squatted next to Gunz and as his friend raised his bloodshot eyes at him, Aidan smiled softly, even though inside he wanted to scream and curse and break something, or someone who had done this to him.

"Aidan, I am sorry," said Gunz, his voice barely above a whisper. "I have no idea what happened. I just needed for this"—he pressed his hand over his heart—"to stop. I wanted to stop feeling…" His voice faltered, and he fell silent. "Can you take me home?"

"Not yet," replied Aidan, lowering his knee down and seizing Gunz's hand to help him sit upright. "I'll tell you all the details when you feel a little more… um… yourself. Just take my word for it. Hawk's house is the safest place for all of us to be right now."

"I understand," muttered Gunz, bowing his head. He released Tessa's hands and gasped, noticing fresh bruises shaped like his fingerprints and ugly blisters of burns.

"Gunz, I am not asking you to tell me any details," said Aidan, carefully choosing his every word, "but do you know who this underground facility belongs to? Who tortured you?"

Gunz smirked, looking away. "I thought you knew," he said quietly. "Didn't Anatoly tell you?"

"Yes, I know who owns the facility," replied Aidan. "But considering my source of information, I want to hear it from you."

Gunz glanced at him, a bitter uneven smirk twisting his lips. "The Destiny Council."

CHAPTER 9

~ ZANE BURNS, A.K.A. GUNZ ~

"Can you get up on your own? Can you walk?" asked Aidan. There was no mockery or sarcasm in his voice, no pity or sympathy. Aidan was just asking if he needed help, but a wave of embarrassment flushed through Gunz, making his ears burn.

"I can walk. I think...," he answered but didn't move. Aidan raised his eyebrows and offered his hand, but Gunz just shook his head, averting his eyes. "I'm naked."

"So?"

"Tessa is here," he whispered without raising his eyes.

Aidan turned around and saw Tessa still standing by the entrance into the hut. He cocked his head, staring at her reproachfully. She flashed a quick grin at him and walked out. Gunz got up but swayed a little and had to grab the anvil. Then he picked up Aidan's shirt, ripped it lengthwise and wrapped it around his hips.

"My favorite shirt." Aidan sighed, but his eyes twinkled with humor.

"You'll survive," muttered Gunz, slowly moving toward the exit.

He felt exhausted, drained, and it had nothing to do with his overuse of magic. He wasn't ready to face Kal, and he definitely didn't want to face Mrak Delar. He halted in the doorway, bracing himself against the wall with his arm and bowed his head, his other arm hanging limply by his side.

"Zane, look at me," said Aidan. He didn't touch him, but Gunz flinched, raising his hand instinctively. Aidan sighed and continued, "I know it's not easy, but I need you, man... pull yourself together. Please."

Gunz pushed himself off the wall and fixed up his makeshift loincloth. "I will, Aidan," he said quietly, "I just need more time."

"Time is one thing I can't give you, my friend," replied Aidan, staring toward the house, his eyes slightly foggy as if he was looking into some invisible crystal ball. "We have a huge problem on our hands, and I need you back—powerful and strong."

"Don't we always have problems?" asked Gunz dryly, walking like on autopilot, dry grass poking at the soles of his bare feet. "I already forgot when I had a restful night and a day when I didn't bleed."

"Zane—"

"That's right, Aidan," Gunz growled, throwing a scorching gaze at his friend. "We all bleed on a daily basis for this realm and for the World of Magic. And how does the Destiny Council repay me for all I've done?" He stopped, his chest rising and falling with ragged breaths, flames playing in his eyes. "They had me beaten into a bloody pulp day after day after goddamn day. They allowed some psycho to dissect my mind, wiping his feet on my soul like it was his personal doormat."

"Zane..." Aidan reached for his shoulder, but Gunz shrunk back, shaking his head.

"Aidan, they forced me to kill Akira's vampires," he whispered. "Remember her vampire-secretary that looked like a fifteen-year-old girl?" Aidan nodded, staring at his friend, a muscle twitching in his jaw. Gunz bit his lip, deep wrinkle etched between his eyebrows. "I drove a wooden stake through her heart... I watched her body disintegrate into ashes while she was still pleading with me for her life."

"I'm sorry—"

"They destroyed me, Aidan, they—" He cut himself off and pressed his hand to his chest as a painful tightness settled there. Then he just resumed walking toward the house. "I don't want to talk about it. But I am done bleeding for the Destiny Council. They can go and fuck themselves." He waved his hand, picking up his pace.

"Zane, stop!" yelled Aidan, desperation in his voice. "It's not about the Destiny Council anymore. Screw them and the horse they rode in on! I couldn't care less about them. It's about Death!"

"Death? Life?" Gunz threw his hands up. "I don't give a damn. Every single day I spent in the care of the Destiny Council, I prayed for Death and he didn't come! I am so done with it all, Aidan. Kal got it right! I am done living under the constant pressure of keeping my power under control. I am done bleeding and I am done fighting! I am going back to Kendral!"

Gunz stopped on the porch ready to knock when the door opened and Kal walked outside, his body breathing with heat. He seized Gunz's shoulder and pulled him closer. Gunz hissed like in pain and struggled against Kal's grip.

Kal let go, staring at him with his burning eyes. "You're not going to Kendral, my son," he said calmly. "You're needed here."

"You can't force me," objected Gunz, anger boiling up in him.

"You know I can," said Kal, folding his arms over his chest.

"Not anymore," growled Gunz, getting in touch with the Dark Codex, and his eyes lit up with a blinding white light.

"Stop it! Both of you!" Mrak Delar stepped between Gunz and Kal, holding his hands up. "Gunz, disconnect!" He turned to

Kal. "Great Salamander, don't try to control him. This is not what he needs right now."

Gunz let go of his magic and lowered himself down on the porch, hiding his face in his hands. Mrak squatted in front of him, searching his eyes.

"Gunz, Gwyn never told me what happened during my trial," he said quietly. "What did you do? Why is the Destiny Council punishing you?"

Gunz lowered his hands and glanced down at the Master of Power.

"I did what I had to do," he replied flatly and switched his attention to Aidan. "Since it seems that the rule of freewill no longer applies to me, Aidan, go ahead and enlighten me. What can I do to help Death?"

Before Aidan could say anything, Mrak Delar rose and gave him a warning stare. "It's getting late," he interjected calmly, waiving his hand toward the setting sun. "I suggest we all take a good night's rest and regroup early in the morning."

No one objected, leaving Gunz and Mrak Delar on the porch. The Master of Power got up and disappeared into the house. He came back a few minutes later, carrying a bottle of vodka and two shot glasses. Sitting down next to Gunz, he placed the glasses on the porch between them and filled them to the brim.

Offering one to Gunz, he smiled sadly. "I know you need it," he said, taking the second glass. "I also know that this evening could be your last opportunity to let go and relax."

Gunz took the glass and inhaled the burning scent of alcohol. Mrak was right, but to just begin mending this agonizing rip in his soul, he would probably need to take a swim in vodka.

"But you don't drink, Mrak," he said, observing the Master of Power holding the glass in his fingers. "You never do."

"I like my mind clear," muttered Mrak Delar, his obsidian

eyes carefully scanning Gunz. "I believe I can make an exception today though. I think I actually need it, too."

Gunz touched his shot glass with his, a melodious clunk of crystal ringing in the silence of the evening.

"For friendship," he said quietly and downed it in one gulp without flinching.

Mrak smiled and followed suit. Placing the empty shot glass on the porch, he refilled them.

"Do you remember when we met for the first time, Gunz?" he asked softly, his index finger tracing the outer rim of the glass absently. "Do you remember the way I looked at the time?"

Gunz nodded and smirked. "Sometimes I want to forget the way you looked then," he said, his fingers wrapping tighter around the shot glass. "You were like a beat-up dog, spending most of your time on your knees in the darkest corner you could find and flinching from every sound."

"Yes," Mrak breathed out, his eyes fogging up with sadness. "Perfect description. I felt like a beat-up cornered animal. Oleg was unconscious, and you and your friend Sasha were the only people who showed me some kindness at the time. You actually trusted me…" His voice disappeared into the night.

"I remember." Gunz raised his glass and clinked it with Mrak's. "I've always trusted you, Mrak, and I swear I always will… no matter what."

"For trust," said Mrak Delar airily. Swallowing vodka, he shuddered and laughed. "It's liquid fire. This is why you like it so much, Fire Gecko."

Gunz chuckled softly and drank the second shot, closing his eyes as he enjoyed the heat spreading through him.

"It helps me forget and let go a little," he whispered, opening his eyes to meet Mrak's dark gaze.

Mrak's smile faded away slowly, and he sighed. "The way you look right now, my friend, you painfully remind me of that terrible time in my life," he said. "You look broken on the inside and on the outside... And knowing what drove me into that kind of condition, I'm terrified to even think what has been done to you."

"Please don't ask..."

"I wasn't going to," said Mrak Delar, leaning forward to rest his elbows on his knees. "I don't think I want to know. I just wanted to tell you that I'm here if you ever need me. For anything. To share a drink or to raise a sword."

He looked sideways and Gunz smiled. "I know that, Mrak. I guess everyone knows that. Kal told me that when I'm in trouble and need help, I always call you."

Mrak Delar filled the third shot glass and got up, holding it tightly in his fist. "I think that's the way Oleg and you drink the third shot?" he asked, looking at Gunz with curiosity.

Gunz nodded, rising. He touched Mrak's fist with his and drank the vodka in silence. When he was done, he picked up the bottle from the porch and exhaled. "For the fallen... for my Angie..."

Unwanted tears burned somewhere behind his eyes and he grunted, turning away. He swayed a little as dizziness assailed him, grabbing the railing, and felt Mrak's hand squeezing his arm above his elbow.

"I'm okay—"

"You're anything but okay," objected Mrak Delar, squeezing his arm tighter. "And I understand it more than anyone else in this house. This is why it is so hard for me to ask you..." He swallowed, blackness flooding his eyes—a sure sign of his turmoiled emotions.

"Aidan already did, Mrak," replied Gunz, staring into the desert where the large orange moon hung right above the endless horizon.

"Maybe he did, I don't know," objected Mrak Delar, tugging at his arm to turn him around. "I'm not a Celtic god. I am a

Master of Power and here is the thing, Gunz. The darkness is rising from beneath—"

"Not the first time—"

"A kind of evil that I have never felt in my life, which is not as long as Gwyn's or Kal's of course. Yet both of them agreed with me," he continued, his voice harsh and raspy. "Whatever it is, it's tipping the balance of the universe toward darkness."

"Let the Destiny Council fight it." Gunz turned away from Mrak, staring at the bright disk of the moon. "I am done... nothing left to give."

Mrak Delar grunted, shaking his head.

"I expected this answer," he said. "It's not about them, Gunz. It's about me. The battle between darkness and the light is coming. The kind of battle we haven't seen in ages, and I fully intend to stand and fight on the side of light, and so will Aidan and Kal and Gwyn ap Nudd. Even the Master of Kendral will leave his realm to join us. But I need you, Gunz. Not because you are a Great Fire Salamander and the Codex, but because I need my friend, whom I trust unconditionally, to stand by my side. So, here I am, asking you—would you raise your sword for me, Gunz?"

Gunz stared up at his friend, thousands of thoughts swirling through his mind. Then he shook his head, leaning back against the railing. "I don't even have my sword anymore. Even that was taken away from me..." He brought the bottle to his lips, taking another gulp of vodka. "The Destiny Council has it."

"They had it," agreed Mrak Delar. His eyes got lighter and his lips twitched in a sad smile as he reached into his pocket and produced the Swiss army knife.

"But how..." Gunz took the knife and touched it with his fingers, manifesting his sword. A light red glow surrounded the weapon as he channeled some of his fire energy through it, and something snapped within him, warmth expanding in his chest.

"Lucan retrieved it—your new biggest fan. That rescue elf of yours is a giant." Mrak chuckled. "I don't know how you did it, but he would do anything for you. To earn the loyalty of an elf is not easy, but I'm not surprised you've done it." He tapped Gunz on his shoulder and gave him an arched stare. "So, now that you do have your sword, would you stand and fight by my side?"

Gunz raised his sword, caressing the intricate design on the blade with his fingers. Lowering the tip of the blade down to the floor, he placed it between himself and the Master of Power.

"For you, Mrak? To my last breath," he said firmly. "I swear."

CHAPTER 10

~ TESSA ~

Tessa woke up with a start and propped herself on her elbow. A clock was showing past one in the morning and the room was semi-dark. The bright disk of the full moon shone through the window. Somewhere in the distance, a low howl pierced the silence and a few more answered its call. She glanced down at Aidan and smiled. In his sleep, he looked so young and so normal, relaxed and calm like there was not a trouble in the world.

She sat up, pulling her knees to her chest, wondering what had woken her up. Tenderly, she brushed his cheek with her fingers, feeling the roughness of his golden stubble against her skin. He sighed, turning his head to the side, and his lips parted, just asking to be kissed.

Kissing the tips of her fingers, she gently touched his lips. "I love you, my ancient god," she whispered, warmth expanding in her chest.

Tessa was ready to lie down and snuggle to his shoulder when she felt a soft touch to her mind. She could barely detect it, but she knew it was there. Sharpening her senses, she slipped off the bed, trying not to wake Aidan, and tiptoed to the window. Through the wide space between the curtains, she saw the white fence surrounding the property. But as far as she could see, there was nothing or no one else there.

She turned around, ready to climb back into the bed, when she felt that soft tug at her mind again, and this time it was stronger. She pulled her boots on and grabbed her jacket on her way to the door. Soundlessly, she ran through the silent house and walked out on the porch. Putting her jacket on, she wrapped her arms around herself as the cold night air enveloped her. A freshness of the desert with its dusty scent mixed in with the odor of earth and grass invaded her senses, and she inhaled deeply, the last traces of sleep gone now.

Soft whispers sounded in her mind as she headed toward the fence. The closer she got there, the louder the whispers became, and Tessa had no problem recognizing their energy signature.

Reapers.

The entire property of the ranch was surrounded by powerful protection spells and wards which Aidan had placed himself a while ago. When they all gathered here, hiding from the Guardians, he had to readjust them to allow everyone to go in and out without the need to deactivate the wards. Keeping that in mind, Tessa wondered if she couldn't hear the reapers clearly because of the protective magic.

As she approached the gates, she noticed two dark silhouettes by the fence. Tessa narrowed her eyes and recognized Missi and Karma. Sitting under the cover of a blanket, both leaned their backs against the wooden rails, looking comfortable and calm. They talked softly about something that most likely wasn't related to the current situation since their faces were relaxed and their eyes shone with laughter. They were so engrossed in their conversation that they didn't notice Tessa's approach.

"Missi? Karma? What are you doing here?" Tessa asked, observing both witches with interest.

Missi pushed the blanket off and got up. For a moment, she looked slightly uncomfortable, but then cleared her throat and folded her arms over her chest, exuding the authority of a Guardian Mage.

"Tessa, what are you doing here this late? And alone." She threw a quick look at her wristwatch.

"I can ask you the same question," huffed Tessa, raising her eyebrow.

"Couldn't sleep. Just wanted to clear my mind," said Missi. Her skin, the color of dark chocolate, had a barely noticeable blush, and her large gray eyes darted to Karma and then went back to Tessa. "Karma didn't want me to go alone. With everything that's going on lately, none of us should be wandering alone at night." She gave Tessa a pointed stare.

Tessa shrugged indifferently and opened the gates, ready to walk outside the protective circle, but Missi stopped her.

"Tessa, you can't go outside the warded area," she said, holding her arm. "It's not safe. Besides, someone from the Guardians Order may detect your energy signature."

Tessa shrugged and pointed into the darkness of the desert where at least fifty reapers were standing, shoulder to shoulder.

"I think if the Guardians Order is searching for me, they would find them first," she said, observing the reapers with interest.

"Who are you talking about?" asked Missi and Karma at the same time. Karma got up and turned around, surveying the area as her hand went down to the dagger sheathed at her belt.

"Them... Reapers. I can't see them clearly, but I know what they are," whispered Tessa. "There are so many of them right by the gates, and they are calling me. I must talk to them, Missi. It's important."

"Wait. We'll go with you." Missi channeled her magic and whispered a spell, *"Latentius revelare."*

The air shimmered with a soft glow of Missi's magic and the reapers materialized in front of them, their shapes becoming clear, even though still not quite corporeal. Tessa opened the gates and walked outside the circle of protective magic. As Missi and Karma followed her, she heard the thin sound of a dagger being unsheathed and smirked, thinking about Karma trying to use a blade against the messengers of death.

"Are you sure they are reapers?" asked Karma, observing the dark-hooded figures with doubt. "Where are their scythes?"

"Do you see me walking around with a scythe?" Tessa huffed with a half-shrug. "I'm also a part reaper."

"Well, no," mused Karma, mischievous twinkles dancing in her eyes. "I see you walking around with a giant double-edged battle axe and the Celtic Otherworld's very own Cerberus on a short leash."

For a moment Tessa stared at Missi, trying to process what she had just said, but then put her hands on her hips and frowned. "Aidan is not some three-headed dog. Don't you dare—"

"Aw, I'm sorry," sang Karma. "He is a slightly defective Cerberus—some heads are missing."

"Ugh," grumbled Tessa, "why am I wasting my time talking to you at all."

She turned toward the reapers, greeting them with a wave of her hand. A tall figure separated from the crowd and approached her, lowering their hood. Tessa recognized the same female reaper she had been talking to on the roof of the Guardians HQ a few days ago. However, her image was slightly different. She looked drained, her shape coming in and out of focus, becoming translucent at times.

"Greetings, Therasia," she whispered, a sad smile touching

her pale lips. "I'm sorry to be the bearer of bad news, but you need to rush."

"Can you please speak plainly?" Tessa asked, desperation ringing in her voice as a feeling of dread spiked to the next level within her. "What's going on?"

"He is getting weaker," whispered the woman, stretching her translucent hand toward Tessa. "And as he weakens, so do we. You are not a full reaper, but you should sense it too. The weakness is overwhelming. Soon, we won't be able to guard the veil... the veil will collapse... and the world will... ahhhhh..." She exhaled and swayed with the night breeze.

Tessa shivered, chills running down her spine. "What do I do? Where do I look for him?"

All the reapers whispered at the same time, and she couldn't understand a word they were saying.

"Death must ride again. Find him... There must be four... once more..." The reapers shimmered, the energy of death spreading around them like a wave, and a moment later, they were gone.

"Not again...," mumbled Tessa, turning toward Missi and Karma.

"Well, that sounded pretty scary," muttered Karma. "The veil will collapse? That can't be anything good."

"No, it's not," said Missi urgently, waving toward the house. "I think we should wake all of them up. They must know what's going on."

Tessa nodded, starting on her way to the house. An image of a sleeping Aidan flashed through her mind. He was so tired. He needed to get at least some rest. And Zane too. She had never seen the Fire Salamander so indifferent and drained of life. He wasn't the Zane she knew—a strong man and a powerful being of magic, he was always a pure force of nature. She thought back to that moment when they opened the door into his cell and what that horrible man was doing to him, and shivers ran down her back, raising goose bumps on her arms.

They all needed a break. They barely had a few days to breathe after the fight for the City of Gold and now this? She sighed, shaking her head.

"So much for a good night's rest," she muttered, pushing the door open.

CHAPTER 11

~ ZANE BURNS, A.K.A. GUNZ ~

Gunz heard someone approaching the door and his body tensed, his mind instantly awake. His hand snaked under his pillow and his fingers wrapped around his knife, ready to turn it into a sword at the first sign of trouble. He expanded his Salamander senses and relaxed.

Aidan. The god of the Otherworld stood outside his door, and the shuffling sound of him shifting from foot to foot reached Gunz's ears. Gunz sighed. So much for the good night's rest Mrak had promised. *Dammit... Here you go again.*

"Aidan," he yelled, sitting up on the bed, "come in already."

The door opened with a high-pitched squeak, and Aidan walked inside. His shirt was unbuttoned, and he looked more tired than he had before, if it were only possible.

"Sorry, man," he said, his voice sounding raspy as if he had just woken up. "The peace is over. The war council has assembled in the kitchen and they're not willing to discuss anything without you present."

Gunz grunted and got up. Grabbing the new set of clothes Hawk had provided, he cast a spell making them fireproof. Then he got dressed quickly and put his knife into the pocket of his jeans. Following Aidan to the kitchen, he couldn't help but feel resentment. Not toward his friends, but toward doing anything related to the Destiny Council and their shady ways. He was positive—whatever was going on right now, they were involved someway, somehow.

He walked into the kitchen and halted, leaning his shoulder against the doorway. Everyone was there, including Hawk and Theron. The weretiger smiled at Gunz, greeting him with a wave of his hand. Karma and Missi perched on top of the granite countertop, and Tessa walked up to Aidan, wrapping her arm around his waist.

Kal, Mrak Delar and Hawk sat at the table, and Lucan stood behind the Master of Power with his arms crossed behind his back as if he was still at the Destiny Council prison, facing Commander Moore.

"Well, that's a lot of power for one tiny farmhouse," muttered Gunz. His eyes stopped on Mrak Delar, and he raised his eyebrows. "So, what's going on?"

Kal turned to Tessa and nodded at her. In so many words, she told everyone about both of her encounters with the reapers and the warning they had given her.

"Like I said earlier," said Aidan, putting his hands on Tessa's shoulders, "we must find Angel. Judging by the message from the reapers, we don't have much time to do it."

"My lord, I assume this person you're calling Angel is Death himself?" asked Hawk. Aidan nodded. "Then I don't understand. I've never heard of anyone who could imprison Death."

Mrak Delar chuckled darkly, shaking his head. "Just a few months ago, I held Angel captive," he said quietly, throwing a guilty look at Aidan and Gunz. "So, if I know how to do it, there can be other old ones privy to this ancient knowledge."

"Like Skiper-Zmey or the likes of him, for example," offered Kal. "Don't forget, it's not only that they're holding Death captive, they are also concealing his energy signature to such a degree that even the reapers can't find him."

"So, what you're saying is that there is no way to find him," concluded Gunz. "If reapers can't sense him, we stand no chance." He rubbed the back of his neck, moving his head from left to right as exhaustion settled in his shoulders like a heavy load.

"There is always a way," said Lucan, his voice emotionless. "We just don't know it yet. If there is darkness, there is always a light to balance the scale. Such are the ways of magic."

Everyone fell silent for a moment, then Kal shook his head. "I am the oldest here," he said quietly. "If I don't know, I doubt anyone would. There is a reason that everything to do with death and creation is hidden from us and only a very few are privy to this knowledge."

Missi slipped off the counter and looked around the room, a light smile gracing her face. "But we do know someone who has access to knowledge. Hidden knowledge included."

Gunz met Missi's bright gray eyes and a deep shudder ran through his body.

"No," he said, raising both hands. "If you're planning to summon someone from the Wardens Order, do it without me. I'm done with the Destiny Council and their flunkies."

Before he finished his statement, Tessa turned toward him, stepping into his personal space. "Flunkies, eh?" she asked, pushing him on his chest with her finger. "So, just because Missi and I are Guardians, we're no longer in your circle of trust, firetwat?"

Anger swept through him and small flames broke through his skin, dancing on his shoulders. Gunz grunted, suppressing the fire within, but his fingers wrapped around Tessa's wrist, squeezing it, before he could stop himself.

"I doubt..." His voice broke, and he took a deep breath. "I doubt either of you will remain a part of the Guardians Order if they find you're here... And by summoning a representative of the Destiny Council, Tessa, you are taking the chance of losing Aidan or submitting him to the same torture I went through."

Tessa gasped, staring at him horrified. As understanding shadowed her features, her eyes darted to Aidan's chest, where she didn't find the chain with the Guardian's pendant. She paled, her lips whispering his name soundlessly.

Aidan put his hand on Gunz's shoulder, leaning down to him. "Let her go, Zane," he said softly, but there were iron tones in his voice. "You're burning her."

Gunz let go off Tessa and took a step back, raising his hands in resignation. Kal turned in his seat to face Aidan and frowned.

"Where is that cursed chain, Aidan," he asked, his voice filled with danger. "Did you break your oath, boy?"

"I had no choice," replied Aidan, meeting Kal's heavy gaze calmly. "They used the forbidden summons to get me into their trap. That was the only way I could escape, and after my conversation with Agent Andrews, I knew I was the only one who could find Zane and help him. So, I did what had to do."

"Dammit!" shouted Kal, rising, and the energy of fire spread around him, turning the room into a semblance of a sauna. "Why didn't you summon me? Or Gwyn?"

"Because you haven't been answering your summons lately!" yelled Aidan, taking a step closer to the Fire Elemental. "Because I was in so much pain I was on the verge of fainting and I had no time to think! Because Zane was missing and Yaroslav... and Angel—" He cut himself off and chewed on his lip, slowly getting in control of his emotions. "Like I said, I did what I had to do. When I found out where Zane was, I realized that I couldn't show up in a facility run by the Destiny Council myself, triggering all the *'broken oath'* alarms. I knew Mrak Delar wouldn't be welcome there either, so I called Tessa and Missi, and then summoned Karma. We got lucky that Lucan decided to break Gunz free at the same time. You know the rest."

"Fire Almighty," whispered Kal, lowering himself down into his chair heavily. "We're in more trouble than I realized originally." He slammed his palm on the table, making it slide with a loud screech. "I hate human realms. This is exactly why I don't want to have anything to do with their affairs."

Mrak Delar turned to Gunz. "How about not the Wardens Order, but just one Warden?" he asked, regarding everyone in the room calmly. "I believe there is one member of the Wardens Order we can all trust."

"Raoul de Beaumont," muttered Aidan, reaching for his cell phone. He pulled it out and searched through the contact list.

"He's still a Warden, loyal to his Order and to the Destiny Council," said Gunz quietly, shaking his head. "I believe we're taking a chance by contacting him, but go ahead, Aidan, call him."

Aidan dialed the number, putting the phone on speaker. After a few long beeps, Raoul answered the call.

"Aidan?" he asked sleepily. Something knocked and shuffled, and then Raoul came back online, sounding a lot more alert. "Aidan, what's going on? Why do we have—"

"Raoul," interrupted Aidan, "remember Friday the thirteenth."

For a moment, everything died out on the other side of the line, and a loud squeak, followed by a soft thud announced that the Warden shut a door. Raoul cleared his throat and spoke a little louder. "Aidan, where are you? What in the Lord's name is going on?"

"Raoul, I can't explain everything over the phone, and I don't think I should," replied Aidan, throwing a quick glance at Gunz. "We need your help. It's important."

"Christ Almighty!" hissed Raoul, his words accompanied by a loud bang as he probably slammed his fist into something wooden. "Do you know what you are asking me to do? You're asking me to betray my Order, *Monsieur* McGrath! Every

Warden has orders to find you and Zane Burns and deliver both of you to any of the Destiny Council's locations in this realm. Don't tell me where you are. I don't want to know."

Raoul's French accent got heavier with every word he said, a sure sign of how nervous he was. Gunz tapped on Aidan's shoulder and took the phone from his hand.

"Raoul," he said, cringing at how hoarse and deep his voice sounded. "This is Zane Burns. Why did the Destiny Council issue an order for Aidan's and my arrest?"

"As far as Aidan, the explanation was simple," replied Raoul after a short pause. "They said he broke his oath. With you, however, there was no explanation given, Zane. So, I don't know."

"You have known all of us for years, Raoul," continued Gunz. "You know that none of us would do anything to jeopardize the safety of the human realm or expose the World of Magic."

"Yes, but—"

"Raoul, we are asking for your help not for personal gain, but for—" His voice cut off, and he swallowed hard, fighting the desire to hang up and be as far away from this room as he possibly could. "Forget what the Destiny Council said or didn't say. I'm asking you to remember Friday the thirteenth and tell me, would you help us, Raoul *le Bel*?"

For a moment, the line went silent and Gunz threw a gaze at Aidan, bitterness reshaping his lips into a crooked smirk.

"I'll do it, *mon ami*," said Raoul, his voice barely a whisper. "How can I find you?"

Mrak Delar got up and took over the phone. "Raoul, this is Master Mrak Delar," he said, holding the phone with his fingers with such caution as if he were expecting it to bite him. "Where are you right now?"

"In front of the Church by the Sea," replied Raoul.

"Go behind the Church and wait for me at the edge of the

forest. I'll see you in a minute." Mrak gave the phone to Aidan and raised his hand, ready to teleport.

"Are you sure it's a good idea for you to teleport there?" asked Aidan, stopping him. "The Wardens can trace the residue of your magical energy."

"Aidan, we just got a sworn Warden involved into this mess," the Ancient Master objected, chuckling darkly. "If the Destiny Council decides to find us, all they need to do is tap into Raoul's mark—that pendant that all Wardens and Guardians are wearing. So, don't trouble yourself with small things like my magical energy residue."

He smirked and snapped his fingers, vanishing from the room.

Mrak Delar returned a few minutes later with Raoul de Beaumont. The Warden observed the room and his eyes widened. His gaze lingered a moment too long on Lucan, his eyebrows slowly rising, but he didn't ask anything. Instead, he bowed to everyone, greeting them respectfully. Then he approached Gunz and pinned him with his steady gaze as if he were trying to read his soul.

Turning back to face Kal and Mrak, he jerked his thumb in Gunz's direction. "If you don't mind, my lords," he said, "I would like to have a word with the young Salamander before we begin."

Kal and Mrak exchanged a look of surprise but they had no objections. Gunz moved aside, allowing Raoul to leave the kitchen and directed him to the porch. As soon as he closed the door, Raoul turned to him.

"Zane, do you have the Dark Codex?" he asked, his voice breaking with tension. "You swore that when everything was over, you would deliver the book to the Wardens."

"I have it," confirmed Gunz, touching his forehead.

He connected with the Dark Codex in his mind and his eyes lit up with the bright energy of its magic. Raoul gasped, stretching his hand to him, but Gunz shied away from his touch, raising his hand to stop him.

"I am the Codex," he continued, meeting the Warden's shocked gaze. "The person who hid the book within my mind, told me that only the Grand Master of Wardens can retrieve it, but I didn't get a chance to get in touch with you. As soon as I arrived home, the Destiny Council had me arrested." He looked away. As his chest got tighter and an unusual numbness spread through his left arm, he sighed and shook his head. "I'm sorry, Raoul, but at the moment, I don't trust the Destiny Council or the Wardens, so I will keep the Dark Codex until we know what's going on."

"Lord save us all," whispered the Warden, crossing himself. "How is that possible? You are not a god. How were you able to merge with the Codex?"

"I have no idea. I'm a Great Fire Salamander? Perhaps that was enough to complete the merging process." Gunz shrugged. "I wasn't the one who performed the spell. The Codex accepted me, and it allowed me to use its power. I guess it's another mystery I need to solve, but in the meantime, with everything that's going on, I have a feeling I may need its magic. My oath to you still stands, Raoul. As soon as we clear things out, I will give the Dark Codex to the Wardens."

The Warden nodded, but his eyes were unfocused as if he was deep in his thoughts. "Don't rush, Zane," he said after a short pause. "Something tells me, the Dark Codex is as safe as it can be at the moment." He lowered his eyes, staring at his hands —the calloused hands of a trained warrior. "Who else knows?"

"Kal, Mrak, and Gwyn ap Nudd," replied Gunz, unease squeezing his soul into its iron grip. "Possibly the Destiny Keeper. But I'm not sure."

"Oh, crap...," breathed out Raoul. "Well, let's hope that if he still didn't tell anything to the Destiny Council, he'll keep his mouth shut. He is a wise man, and he's not a stranger to breaking rules—for the greater good, of course."

Gunz chuckled humorously. "After my performance at the Destiny Trial, the Council may suspect something anyway," he said. "I don't give a rat's ass what they think."

"Zane, don't talk like this," whispered Raoul, glancing around. "You have no idea what they can do to you—"

"Actually, I have a pretty good idea. Tried their hospitality on my own skin," growled Gunz and opened the door, motioning for the Warden to get inside.

* * *

AFTER AIDAN EXPLAINED everything to the Warden, Raoul sat quiet for a while, his fingers fidgeting with the heavy cross on his chest.

"I don't have this kind of knowledge in my head," he said at length, giving Aidan a troubled stare.

"How about the Wardens Library?" asked Kal.

Raoul winced at the sound of the Great Salamander's voice and his eyes widened for a split second. "Yes, the Wardens Library has enough information about Death and how to locate him, my lord." He inclined his head respectfully. "I can access the library from here, but if I do so, I will project my location."

"Do it." Kal shrugged his massive shoulders, his hard face showing no emotions. "This location is warded and protected against any intrusion, magical or mundane. The wards and protective spells were placed by a god, a Master of Power and the Fire Elemental. I assure you it can withhold a month-long siege by all the Guardians mages. Let them try."

Raoul squeezed the cross in his right hand and a soft white light radiated around him as he connected with the Wardens

Library. He stared into space, his eyes milky white and unmoving. For a while he just stood motionless and quiet, and it seemed that even his chest stopped moving.

Gunz made a move toward him, but Kal raised his hand, stopping him. A few minutes later, Raoul's eyes got back to their normal blue color, and he gasped for air like a person who had to hold his breath underwater.

"I have the knowledge you seek," he said once he could speak again, a light smile touching his lips. "There is one way to find Death." He cleared his throat, and the smile vanished. "But I'm not sure that when you find out how, you'll choose to do so."

"Why?" asked Gunz, chills running down his back.

"Does the word *Apocalypse* ring a bell?" asked Raoul.

His last words got swallowed by an earsplitting noise as all the wards and protection spell got activated at once.

CHAPTER 12

~ ZANE BURNS, A.K.A. GUNZ ~

Gunz darted outside and froze in the doorway, observing an enormous dome of pure magical energy encapsulating Hawk's property. He directed his power toward his eyes to enhance his vision. Right outside the dome, a chain of people stood with their arms spread wide, and as far as Gunz could see, they had the area surrounded.

They channeled their magic, chanting something in even, monotonous voices, and their whispers rose into the dark sky, becoming a continuous white noise. As they kept weaving their magic, a powerful blast of energy escaped their hands, impacting the dome. Glowing with eye-watering white light, the wards responded to the assault with a loud buzz.

"Just as I expected. They traced my location and followed me here."

Raoul's voice, tense and husky, sounded somewhere on Gunz's left, and he looked in his direction. The Warden stood clad in his ancient armor with a long sword in his hands. Hawk and Theron halted beside him, and the air shimmered around them as they started to transform into their animal forms. A heartbeat later, Theron's long, orange tail wrapped around

Gunz's feet as he stepped in front of him, and a low dangerous growl rumbled in the tiger's chest.

Aidan transformed into his godly form and stood with his icy sword at the ready, shielding Tessa with his body. Karma halted by his side with a dagger in her hand, pushing Missi back.

"The wards will hold," said Kal nonchalantly. There wasn't any doubt in his voice as he watched the next attack that made the wards buzz and vibrate. "Having said that, I think we should show the Destiny Council that if they continue attacking us, we're not going to hold back either."

"I second that," muttered Mrak Delar, and his eyes flooded with darkness as he channeled his power. "Let's show them that two can play this game." He laughed, his dark hair fanning out around his face, his bottomless eyes sparkling with the excitement of the upcoming fight.

Lucan didn't say anything. Stepping softly on the ground, as supple as a wild animal, he made his way toward the center of the protected area. Stopping there, he spread his arms, throwing his head back. He started to chant, and his voice, deep but soft, rolled through the desert like a lethal war song. While his language couldn't have been translated by magic just like Dragon tongue, goose bumps ran down Gunz's skin from the sheer power of elven magic.

He opened his other sight and stared at Lucan with reverence. The elf's entire body shimmered with the bluish glow of his magical energy, and as he continued chanting, a powerful blast spread around him, reinforcing the protective dome with elven magic.

Lucan turned around, and a smile, dark and dangerous, changed his features.

"The Destiny Council can never break these wards," he hissed and made a gesture with his arm which Gunz didn't understand, but Kal and Mrak Delar exchanged a look and burst out laughing.

Kal turned around, and his thin lips stretched into a cold smirk that usually promised nothing good to his enemies.

"Aidan, put your sword away. I need you to take everyone inside. There will be no fighting tonight. You and the Ancient Master will shield the house while my son and I will show these... Guardians"—he waved his hand dismissively, disdain reflected on his face—"what it means to play with fire." He growled the last words, and smoldering flames ignited in his eyes.

Kal approached Gunz, putting his hand on his shoulder.

"Ready?" he asked, and Gunz shuddered as uncontrollable fury hastened through him.

"I thought you'd never ask," he roared, rising to the same height as his mentor, his body dissolving into flames.

Kal spoke to him, and it was unlike anything Gunz had ever experienced before. The Great Salamander looked straight into his eyes, and his fire energy invaded all of Gunz's senses at once. He didn't hear his words—he absorbed the ideas Kal was transmitting. He accepted his silent communication with his mind, with his skin and body, with his entire being.

They both channeled the elemental fire, entwining it with their magic, and moved their arms up above their heads, gathering as much energy as they could. As they brought their hands together, a bright circle of flames materialized outside the dome of protective magic, rising between the fence and the circle of Guardian witches.

The tight line of people fell apart as they darted back, raising their hands to shield their faces from the unbearable heat. They stopped chanting and a thick silence blanketed the area, the crackling of fire being the only sound breaking through it.

"It's not over, Father," hissed Gunz. He channeled more fire energy, rising higher in the air, pulling Kal with him. *"One more time..."*

For a split second, Kal's eyes widened as he accepted Gunz's message, but then he nodded. They spread their arms, commanding their element and a second circle of fire erupted behind the chain of witches, blocking all their ways in and out. The Guardians screamed—some in fear, some in fruitless attempts to control the fire. But with the Fire Elemental and the Great Fire Salamander present, the element would obey no one but them.

"What do you want to do next, my child?" Kal transmitted a question, staring at the panicking Guardians flouncing between two circles of flames.

"I'll send a thank-you card to the Destiny Council."

Lowering down to the ground, Gunz closed his eyes, opening himself to the Dark Codex. As powerful magic rushed through him, he grunted, stifling a cry of pain, and opened his eyes. With his chest shuddering with heavy breaths, he screamed and dropped to one knee, punching the ground with his fist.

A heavy rumble of an earthquake spread around him and both circles of fire responded to Gunz's command, burning hotter and moving a few inches closer together. The panicked screams of fear, pleas, and shrieks of pain blended into a mighty commotion, but Gunz was oblivious to it. He rose in the air and observed the witches coldly.

As the anger and pain surged through him, clouding his mind, he extended his arm, squeezed his hand into a tight fist and twisted it. The fire rose higher, dark smoke curling above the dome of protective magic, and the stench of burnt flesh permeated the air.

"Let them go, my boy... They are just soldiers, doing as they have been commanded by their masters. It's not them you want. I think your message was loud and clear."

Kal's words broke into his frazzled mind, and Gunz shuddered but nodded, clenching his teeth so hard they squeaked. Slowly, he turned in the air and pointed at the witches. They responded with screams of fear.

"Look at me, Guardians," he shouted. His voice infused with fire echoed through the desert. "I'm Zane Burns, the Great Fire Salamander. LOOK! AT! ME!"

The commotion beneath ceased and every single witch and mage raised their heads, staring at Gunz with horror.

"Now that I have your attention," he continued, slowly getting in control of his anger. "Tonight, I am letting you leave with your lives, but I have a message to your superiors, and I want you to deliver it to them word for word." He took a short pause, observing the transfixed Guardians. "My friends and I are here to defend the realm of humans, fighting on the side of light. The Destiny Council should either support us or get the hell out of our way! Next time you come after me or my friends, I swear, I'll reduce you to ashes and I'm not going to stop until you are all dead, including your masters!"

He waved his hand, extinguishing the fire circles, and watched the Guardians as they took off into the dark desert. Then he slowly lowered himself to the ground and sat down, pulling his knees to his chest. His body, engulfed in flames, was still trembling with rage. Kal sat next to him and touched his shoulder.

"Fire Salamander, down," the Great Salamander said softly, commanding all fire to cease.

Gunz moaned and let go, for the first time submitting willingly to Kal's control. Then he lay down on his back, folded his hands over his stomach and stared into the endless sky, dotted by millions of stars.

"We need to go back into the house, my son," said Kal, gently patting his shoulder. "Our time is limited. We need to free Death and restore the balance before the veil collapses."

"I know…"

"You may rise…" Kal got up, releasing his control, and offered him his hand. Gunz took it unwillingly. He rose to his feet, and headed toward the house, moving his legs slowly as though they were filled with lead. He stopped on the porch, ready to open the door, and regarded his mentor calmly.

"When all this is over, I'm going back to Kendral with you, Father," he said, and it wasn't a question. He wasn't asking for permission, just stating the fact. "I'm done…"

"We'll see." Kal smirked sadly. "Talk to me after all this is over."

Gunz pushed the door and walked inside the house, heading straight for the kitchen.

* * *

As soon as they crossed the threshold, everyone who was sitting got up, and those who were standing turned toward them, staring at them with an anxious expectation.

"What?" asked Gunz, slightly unnerved by all the attention. "Didn't we have something to discuss? Brining Death to life or something like that."

"I assume our friends from the Guardians Order have retired? In one piece, preferably?" Mrak Delar asked, raising his eyebrows, but his face reflected no objection to whatever the answer to his question would be.

"They left, alive and well," replied Kal icily as he sat down on a chair, propping his elbow on the table. "While I'm sure they will come back with reinforcements, I hope we'll have enough time to decide what to do next." He switched his attention to Raoul, tapping his fingers on the tabletop impatiently. "So, Raoul, how can we find Death and why should we concern ourselves with the Apocalypse?"

The Warden got up and looked around the room, his eyes moving from one face to the next.

"Because, in the situation when the reapers can't detect Death, there is only one way to find him," he said after a short pause. "By letting the Four Horsemen ride again."

"Now I understand the message," whispered Tessa more to herself than to the others in the room. "The reapers said that Death must ride again and there must be four."

"Four Horsemen?" repeated Gunz in disbelief, rubbing his forehead. "As in the Four Horseman of the Apocalypse? Jeez, when Angel said he was one of the horsemen, I thought he was joking."

"Everything is real," muttered Aidan with a sigh, throwing a reproachful glance at Gunz, and slammed his hand on the wall. "I wish Uri was with us. He knew all this Heaven-and-Hell stuff better than any of us."

"I understand it well enough, Aidan," said Raoul with a half-shrug, but then frowned and added, "But I wouldn't mind an Archangel being with us when we invoke the power of Four."

"So, to find Death and restore the balance, we have to bring around the Apocalypse?" asked Hawk. The corners of his lips lifted a little, but his mirthless smile didn't light up his sad eyes. "Don't you think it defeats the purpose? What's the point of preserving the balance and keeping the veil intact if we'll destroy everything anyway?"

"Hawk has a point," said Aidan. "If we let the Four Horsemen ride again, wouldn't it mean we have to break four seals out of seven?"

With a short shake of his head, Raoul smirked, unease shadowing his features. "The first four seals are already broken. They have been broken for a while, *mon ami*," he explained, leaning back in his chair. "If we want to survive what's coming, we must find the three other Horsemen and bring them together. Only then can we find Death. The trick is to have all this done fast enough and without breaking the last three seals."

"Piece of cake," muttered Gunz with a light shrug. "And all that, we have to do with the Destiny Council's sword hanging over our heads, without Yaroslav, Uri and Angel by our side, and before the veil collapses. Sounds like another Monday morning to me."

"Well, if that were all our problems, I would agree with you, son," said Kal, glancing at Gunz sideways. "Unfortunately, no one knows where to find the Horsemen and since the world is not ending, I'm positive, each of them is playing their little games in different parts of the human realm."

"If you give me a few hours, I can locate them," said Raoul, rising, but then adjusted his chainmail and added with a vibe of discomfort lingering around him, "Well, I won't be able to give you their exact location, but I'll be able to point you in the right direction."

"All that sounds like so much fun," said Karma, yawning and stretching, "but until the Warden is ready to give us some kind of direction, I'm going to bed."

Missi also got up, placing her hand on the counter. Even though she didn't say anything, her hooded eyes and her pale lips pressed together tightly showed just how tired the young mage was.

"I agree with Karma. Let's regroup in the morning then," suggested Mrak Delar, rising, his face gray with weariness. "I know we're in a rush, but if we collapse from exhaustion, it won't help anyone. Besides, Raoul needs a few hours anyway." He clasped his hands behind his back and flexed his shoulders, stretching them.

* * *

Gunz managed to get to his room and dropped onto the bed

without undressing. He turned on his back, folding his hands over his stomach, and closed his eyes with a deep sigh. At least now he didn't need to put the ring on to sleep. Since he had merged with the Dark Codex, the magic of this powerful artifact guarded his mind from any external intrusions. Sometimes, he felt the dark shadow of Zmey's presence lingering on the outskirts of his dreams, but so far, the Lord of Chaos couldn't break in.

Even though he felt drained physically and magically, he couldn't sleep. In his mind, he kept going over everything that had happened to him from the moment he was arrested to the attack of the Guardians. But no matter how much time he spent thinking about it, he couldn't understand the Destiny Council's motives. Why would they do it to him while he'd been nothing but loyal to them, always fighting on the side of light, despite the personal scarifies he had to make.

It wasn't only that they tried to break him and keep him locked up in their facility, they tried to capture Aidan as well. And if Tessa, Missi and Karma hadn't freed him, what would they do next? Would they stop after disabling him and Aidan, or would they go after someone more powerful, like Mrak Delar or Kal, or Gwyn ap Nudd.

And why? They were supposed to be working on the same side. Was their behavior connected with Angel's disappearance in any way?

He rubbed his face and moaned, turning to his side, pulling a pillow under his cheek. There were no answers to all that, and he had no idea what he would have to face come morning.

Just another Monday...

CHAPTER 13

~ YAROSLAV ~

The Crimson Creek Casino was located away from the promenading crowd of tourists, the glamour and noise of the Las Vegas Strip, and the light-extravaganza of Fremont Street. Not many locals knew about its location and those who did know, kept away from it. It wasn't like the Casino had a bad reputation, but a powerful turn-away spell placed on the area around the building made all humans wish to be as far away from it as possible.

Even if some crazy tourists lost their way and wound up in front of the casino that looked like a medieval castle, they would suddenly feel an overwhelming fear and the only thing they wanted was to run until they were back on the Strip.

The Crimson Creek Casino was owned by Santiago del Castillo, an old vampire with a history longer than he would like to admit. At least a thousand years old, he kept moving up the corporate ladder of demonic organizations, and about a century ago, he had taken over all vampire affairs in the state of Nevada, proclaiming himself King.

Through his long life, he had owned quite a few businesses, but *the Crimson Creek Casino* was one of his favorites. It wasn't his only business, but he enjoyed running it as much as spending time there, watching his visitors donating their cash to his noble cause of moneymaking every time they deposited quarters into his slot machines or blew on the dice before rolling them on his craps tables.

The house always won, and the members of the Nevada supernatural community were as addicted to gambling and good times as any human. So, while the supernatural easy-money-seekers were ravaging their pockets for one more dime, Santiago relaxed in his luxurious office, observing the casino floor through the state-of-the-art security equipment with a cat-like smirk on his sensual lips.

While the King of Nevada wasn't as strict as the Scarlet Queen when it came to relations between vampires and humans, he had made his Casino an official sanctuary. By announcing that neither supernatural nor mundane blood could be shed within the walls of his establishment, Santiago del Castillo made it a safe place for different clans of Nevada's supernatural community to relax and have some fun.

Yaroslav approached the tall iron doors of *the Crimson Creek Casino,* raising his eyes at the light display above his head. It had been a few decades since he gambled the last time and even longer since he had the pleasure of meeting with the King of Nevada.

Unfortunately, their last meeting wasn't what one would call a friendly reunion. While Yaroslav didn't hold a grudge, he wasn't sure if Santiago was on the same page with him. Nevertheless, he had no choice—besides the Spaniard himself, the only person who could help him worked here, in this glamorous establishment. He sighed and pushed the door open, walking inside the Casino.

As soon as he crossed the threshold, a plethora of sounds and smells assailed his heightened senses—the continuous ringing of slot machines, the buzzing of voices and laughter, the odors of air fresheners, different beverages and food. He could also detect the presence of demonic essence, the energy signatures of vampires, werewolves, shifters and other less-common supernatural beings.

The spacious room had no windows and the dim lights on the walls and ceiling created a semi-dark, almost intimate atmosphere. He looked down, smirking at the brightly colored carpet with a large gaudy design, and was ready to move forward when two massive men dressed in black business suits and ties approached him, blocking his way.

Even though Yaroslav was over six-feet tall, these two towered over him, and a powerful wave of their demonic essence washed over him like muddy waters.

"Sir," said one of the security guards calmly, his voice unexpectedly high for a man of his proportions, "carrying a concealed weapon in our establishment is not permitted. If you wish to proceed, we have secure safes where you can leave your sword for the duration of your stay."

Yaroslav didn't feel comfortable with the idea of leaving his katana behind, but rules were rules, and since he needed to get inside, he nodded at the guard. The demon's lips stretched into a smile which was supposed to be welcoming, but his eyes, cold and calculating, burned with silent warning—toe the line or suffer the consequences.

"Please, follow me, sir," said the security demon, gesturing to the left.

Yaroslav followed him through a side hallway paved with the same taste-deprived carpet until the security guard stopped in front of a large door. He opened it with a light bow, allowing him through into a brightly lit room, each wall of which was lined with cabinets and safes. A tall counter was positioned in front of the door and a middle-aged looking woman—undoubtedly a vampire—sat behind it, a bright smile plastered on her face.

"Your weapons, please, my lord," she said, her pleasant voice bordering on seduction.

Slightly surprised by her salutation—*my lord* as opposed to modern day *sir*—Yaroslav reached under his leather coat and unsheathed his katana, placing it on the counter in front of the woman. She stared down at the blade in awe as her fingers brushed the slick surface of steel.

"That's a gorgeous ancient sword, my lord," she said, gently picking it up. For a moment, her attentive eyes studied Yaroslav, gliding down his long golden hair, and a shadow of recognition crossed her face. "Your Highness, I will take good care of it."

She locked the blade into a safe and gave Yaroslav a round token that looked like a casino chip, but unlike a chip it had the number of the safe imprinted on one side and the casino's logo on the other.

As he exited the room, he noticed that the guard was staring at him with curiosity mixed in with a bit of shock. Yaroslav frowned, putting the token in his pocket. He didn't need any special treatment and had hoped to keep his true identity hidden, but that was no longer an option. Mumbling a quick thanks to the security guard, he headed toward the bar where he sat down with his elbow resting atop a counter, turning halfway toward the gaming floor.

"Can I offer you anything to drink?" asked the bartender, leaning slightly forward.

"B negative, please," replied Yaroslav, his eyes observing the casino floor.

A few minutes later, the bartender placed a red napkin on the bar and a martini glass with B negative blood in it.

"Your drink, sir," he said with a sugary smile that exposed his half-expanded fangs.

Yaroslav threw a few bills on the counter and took a cocktail pick with a couple of maraschino cherries on it out of the glass. Slowly sipping his drink, he kept searching the floor until his eyes stopped on an empty blackjack table. A dealer, a tall dark-haired vampire, stood behind it, an expression of boredom permanently glued to her pretty face.

He put the empty glass on the bar and headed toward the blackjack area, maneuvering between rows of slot machines. Almost every seat was occupied, and he wondered how anyone could spend hours upon hours pressing buttons while staring at a chain of rotating images on the screens. Even though he knew that many enjoyed it, for him it was beyond boring.

As Yaroslav approached the blackjack table, the dealer finally noticed him, and her small coral lips opened. Her hand went up, halting over her heart as her eyes widened, and this sincere expression of disbelief made her look even more attractive, in that strange, almost eerie way of vampiric beauty.

"Hello, Sylvana," he said, lowering himself down on the chair, folding his hands on the table.

For a moment, she kept drilling him with her glowing red eyes, and then the corners of her lips quirked up in a smirk.

"Yaroslav Potemkin," she whispered, shaking her head. "I'll be damned. Are you crazy? What are you doing here, Slavik?"

"Gambling," he replied, a boyish grin splitting his face.

"Gambling my ass," she grumbled, looking around to make sure no one was listening at their conversation. "Santiago is not going to be pleased to see you here. As far as I recall, the last time when you two met, you were at each other's throats. I wouldn't be surprised if he throws you out of here."

Yaroslav chuckled. Since they were surrounded by supernatural beings whose senses were a lot sharper than that of humans, no matter how quietly they spoke, they could still have been overheard.

"Well then, let's not give him the opportunity or the desire to do so," he suggested with a wink.

Reaching into his coat pocket, he produced five stacks of hundred-dollar bills and placed them on the table. Lowering his hand on top of the money, he stared at her with a lopsided grin. As his smile grew wider, he reached into his pocket again, pulling out five more stacks of hundred-dollar bills.

"Hundred thousand," he said, his fingers tracing the shape of the stack closest to him. "I want to bet a hundred thousand dollars."

"What are you doing, Slavik?" she hissed, her eyes darting to the eye in the sky security camera and back to Yaroslav. "Why are you even here? If you wanted to see me, just get a room in the hotel and I'll see you once my shift is over."

"Of course, darling, I'm looking forward to seeing you tonight in my room, which I haven't gotten yet, come to think of it," he purred, his eyes lighting up with a soft scarlet glow at the memory of the smoldering-hot but short-lived romance they had a century ago. "But I think after I'm done, Santiago would be only too happy to take care of my accommodations, our past grievances forgotten."

"Slavik...," Sylvana whispered, her pale complexion getting a shade paler. "I hope you know what you're doing."

"I need your help. We need to talk," he said quickly, barely moving his lips, so only her vampiric hearing could catch his words.

She was about to say something but instead, smiled a casino dealer's dutiful smile and waved her hand at someone behind Yaroslav's back. He turned around in his chair, and watched a cocktail waitress, dressed in a Renaissance style dress that barely covered her private areas, approach them with a tray and a martini glass on it.

The waitress placed the glass on the table in front of him. Yaroslav raised his eyebrows at her, surprised, but she waved her hand in the direction of the bar and flashed a bright smile at him.

"Compliments of the beautiful lady at the bar. B negative

with a touch of cinnamon, sir," she announced and sauntered away.

Yaroslav turned around and saw a woman at the bar. As she met his eyes, she smiled seductively and slowly crossed her long legs, generously exposed by the short black dress. Touching her glossy lips with her fingers, she blew him a kiss. He raised the martini glass, smirking at her over the rim, and brought it to his lips but didn't drink it.

Turning back, Yaroslav placed the drink on the table and met Sylvana's sarcastic gaze.

"Some things never change with you, Potemkin," she said, rolling her eyes. "Women are always draping themselves all over you. Are you going to drink it?"

"Not a chance." Yaroslav chuckled. "My mom told me not to take candy from strangers. Especially in Santiago's casino." Then he took a deep breath and placed his hand over the cash, pushing everything to the betting area outlined by a circle. "Let's get this party started," he murmured under his breath and added louder, "Hundred thousand dollars. Money plays."

"Slavik...," she mumbled mortified, but then turned to the casino pit boss and gestured for him to come over.

As a tall vampire in a black business suit approached her, she pointed at the pile of cash on the table, looking at the pit boss quizzically. "Would you allow a hundred thousand dollars bet? Money plays."

He explored Yaroslav with his icy eyes and stilled, a thoughtful expression settling on his impassive face as he listened to something intently. Seconds later, he smiled carnivorously and nodded to the dealer. "Go ahead."

"Money plays!" Sylvana turned back to Yaroslav and took a fresh deck of cards. With fast, habitual movements, she shuffled it, cards flying under her long fingers. Grabbing a red plastic card, she offered it to Yaroslav. A relaxed smile crossed his face as he took the rectangle and cut the deck with it.

She took the stack of cards, including the red one, from the top, moving it to the bottom of the deck and then burned the first card, placing it to the side. As she did it, her eyes stopped on Yaroslav and she swallowed hard, but he just smiled at her lazily, leaning back on his seat as though he didn't just place a hundred thousand dollars bet on a single hand of blackjack.

Slowly, she took a card from the deck and placed it face down in front of Yaroslav. The next card she placed in front of herself and then reached for the deck again. Her hand shook as she drew the card, positioning it in front of him. He gave her a barely visible nod, encouraging her to proceed. The next card off the deck was the eight of hearts. She put it down on top of hers so Yaroslav could see it and stared at him, waiting for his decision.

He took his cards and flipped them over, eliciting a strangled gasp from the crowd of onlookers that had quietly gathered behind him. The cards were showing seventeen—Jack of spades and seven of diamonds—the infamous *"mother-in-law hand"* every blackjack player dreaded to see in their hands while the dealer showed eight and above.

Yaroslav glanced over his shoulder and noticed the same woman in the short black dress standing right behind him among the others. He winked at her and turned his attention back to the game. Staring directly into Sylvana's dark eyes, he scratched the tabletop with his index finger, telling her to give him the next card.

She arched her brow at him warningly, her hand halting above the deck. As Sylvana drew a card, the tension in the air was so thick, it could have been cut with an axe. She put it on the table face up for everyone to see, and the crowd exploded in excitement, cheering and clapping. A new, shiny four of hearts was decorating his stack of cards.

"Twenty-one," whispered Sylvana, perspiration glistening on her forehead. She flipped her card over, showing a King.

She turned to the pit boss, and he nodded at her, calling to a chip girl. A few minutes later, a young woman in a casino's uniform approached them. She placed one stack of five-thousand-dollar chips in front of Yaroslav and left with a charming smile.

"The house doesn't always win," said Yaroslav with a lighthearted smile on his face and got up. He put his cash back into the pockets of his coat and took the stack of chips, giving one to Silvana as a tip. "It's been a long night and I need to get a room." He lifted his eyebrow at her, and she nodded ever so slightly.

Yaroslav headed toward the cashier's cage, but once he exchanged his chips, putting the cash into his pockets, the same pit boss approached him. He bowed to him with a fake smile plastered all over his face.

"Your Highness, Prince Potemkin," he said. "We're honored to have you in our modest establishment and would like to offer you our Royal Suite for as long as you'd like to stay. Complimentary of course."

Santiago... how predictable. Yaroslav smiled and nodded at the pit boss. "That would be wonderful."

CHAPTER 14

~ YAROSLAV ~

The pit boss stopped in front of a tall double door that looked more like the gates into a medieval tower than the door of a modern hotel. However, a quite up-to-date magnetic lock was attached to the wall next to it. He swiped the card to unlock the door and opened it for Yaroslav with a low bow.

"All the hotel's amenities are at your disposal and I assure you, your stay will be quite pleasant, Your Highness," he said, a predatory smile stretching his lips, exposing the tips of his fangs.

Yaroslav walked inside a spacious room and tipped the pit boss, still wondering why a pit boss would escort him to his room himself instead of sending an employee of the hotel. He waited until the vampire had left and closed the door. The suite looked like a royal chamber any king would love to stay in, complete with a giant four-poster bed surrounded by a rich, dark-purple canopy and a leather armchair that looked like a throne. Despite the medieval theme, the suite was equipped with a big screen TV, mini refrigerator, and a bathroom larger than a room of any regular hotel.

He took a few steps forward and stilled. A barely noticeable, yet familiar scent of perfume lingered in the air. He surveyed the room, all his senses on high alert, but then relaxed and a tiny smile touched the corners of his lips. Next to a small table by the window, concealed by heavy dark-purple panels, Sylvana sat, relaxing in a chair with a tall back. In the dim yellowish light of electric torches attached to the opposite wall, she looked surreal and mysterious. A dreamy smile played on her lips and her eyes glowed with a soft red light.

She got up and approached him, her hips swaying seductively. Her casino uniform was gone, replaced by a sheer black robe which effectively outlined her every curve while leaving enough for the imagination to trigger a desire to see more. The deep cut of her robe partly exposed her breasts, her pale skin emitting a soft glow. Her long, dark hair fell over her shoulders and back in soft, rich waves, and her lips were parted, showing the tips of her fangs.

"Yaroslav...," she whispered his name, her voice fading. She placed her hand on his cheek, gazing up into his eyes.

He exhaled, closing his eyes for a moment, but then seized her wrist, pulling her arm down. His grip was too weak, and she freed herself easily, returning her hand to his cheek.

"We need to talk," he said, but his voice lacked the usual firmness.

She laughed, gently caressing his cheek with her finger.

"And we will, Slavik," she promised, rising on her tiptoes. Her lips touched his for a brief moment, as light as the wings of a butterfly, and even though it could hardly be called a kiss, the desire sprang to life within him. "But the information is not free..."

He grunted, pulling away. "But of course not... what do you want?"

She chuckled. Placing her hands under the lapels of his leather coat, she slowly moved it off his shoulders and let it slide to the floor with a rustling noise.

"Not much, my Prince," she purred, her fingers traveling up his exposed arms, sliding under the sleeves of his black t-shirt, raising goose bumps all over his skin in their wake. "Actually..." She brought his hand up, kissing his knuckles one at the time, speaking between kisses. "I don't want you to do anything... I just want to see these beautiful blue eyes of yours foggy with desire... I want to hear moans of pleasure escaping these tight lips... I want to see this ugly crease between your eyebrows disappear and this hard face relaxed."

"Syl... please," he breathed out. "I have no time for this. Will you help me or not?"

"I will, in more ways than one." She smiled as her hand moved down, gently squeezing his groin over his tight leather pants. "Mphhh, and I can see just how much you want it, love... so, let me have my way with you like we used to..." Her fingers found the button on his waistband, opening it. "We have enough time for everything, Slavik... let me pleasure you... let me help you forget everything that troubles you... even if just for a few minutes."

He heard the sound of the zipper and his body throbbed with need. She pushed his pants down just a little and slipped her hand inside, gently stroking him, sending waves of heat through him with her every move.

"Sit down, love, and enjoy the ride," she murmured, pushing him back gently. A dreamy smile played on her face, her fangs fully expanded, driven by her lust, and he couldn't resist. "It's been years since I had you in my bed."

She helped him lower into the armchair and gazed down at him, her fingers playing with his long hair. Then she leaned forward, seized his shirt, and pulled it off, throwing it on the floor. As her fingers brushed the skin of his stomach and chest, his muscles tightened under her touch. Closing his eyes, he moaned and rested his head against the back of the chair. It'd been a while, and he wanted it. A tiny voice whispered in the back of his mind, telling him it was neither the right time nor the place to do it, but his every cell demanded a few minutes of peace and relaxation, fighting his better judgement.

A soft thud told him that she kneeled before him and a moment later, her lips explored his stomach, slowly moving south. Her hand cupped his groin, her finger tugging at his underwear, and then her cold lips caressed his flesh, her fangs gently grazing his skin, sending electricity up his spine. The world around him melted as the heat waves spread through him, his body responding to her every touch, her every move.

She stopped moving, lifting her hands off of him, and he moaned without opening his eyes, every inch of his body longing for more.

"Don't stop, Syl...," he whispered.

"Yeah, Syl, don't stop," said a deep male voice, sarcasm lacing his every word. "I don't tolerate cock-teasers in my establishment."

Yaroslav recognized the voice and opened his eyes. His hand jerked to his side of its own accord, searching for his katana, but as cold steel nestled below his chin, he raised his hands up in a peaceful gesture.

"Hello, Santiago," he said frostily, his gaze moving from the Spaniard's face to the faces of five vampires, surrounding him with their swords pointing at him.

Santiago del Castillo approached him, picking up a long strand of his hair, and chuckled.

"Prince Yaroslav Potemkin," he said, letting the hair slip from his fingers. "I think I much rather call you Alucard." He stepped behind Sylvana, pushing her head down. "Don't stop what you are doing, sweetheart. I want to see him thoroughly enjoying his stay in my hotel."

As Sylvana resumed her administrations, Yaroslav grunted, trying to push her away. But the security guard who held his sword under his chin pressed it harder, drawing a few drops of blood, and he stopped resisting, leaning back in his armchair.

"I made some serious money betting on your fights, Alucard," continued Santiago. Pulling a chair closer, he sat across from Yaroslav, his well-manicured fingers stroking his short, black beard and mustache. "I knew you were skilled with that katana of yours, but I had no idea how brutal you could be with your bare hands, my friend. Why did you leave the underground fighting?"

"Slavery doesn't become me," replied Yaroslav, shifting a little in a fruitless attempt to stop Sylvana.

"Sit still, Prince." Santiago folded his arms over his wide chest and cocked his head, an uneven smirk twitching his lips. "Let the girl give you some pleasure. Something tells me you need it."

"Santiago, all I wanted was to have a few words with her," said Yaroslav, clenching and unclenching his fingers. "And hopefully with you too... ahhhh... if you tell your boys to lower their swords, that is." He gritted his teeth, a low growl rumbling in his chest, and closed his eyes for a moment as the next wave of physical pleasure engulfed him.

Santiago laughed, throwing his head back, his teeth snow-white against his bronze skin, but then waved at his security guards.

"Lower your swords, boys," he said, still chuckling. "You can leave now."

"But my lord," said one of the guards, staring at his boss with doubt in his glowing red eyes. "We can't leave you alone with him. I saw him fighting. He's deadly."

"Don't worry, the person you saw on TV was Alucard—a fierce fighter," he said, wagging his thick black eyebrows at Yaroslav. "This royal jackass has nothing in common with him except his haircut. I'm absolutely safe." He waved his hand dismissively, but as the guards headed for the door, he twisted in his chair and added, "And give me his katana. I'm sure he feels"—he turned to Yaroslav and winked—"a bit exposed without it."

As a guard came back and gave the katana to Santiago, Yaroslav leaned forward and gently pushed Sylvana away.

"Stop, please," he groaned as she resisted him. "I can't do it with the man, who is your maker, in the room."

For a moment, she lifted her head and glanced at Santiago over her shoulder. He nodded, flashing his bright smile at Yaroslav. "What? *Ménage à trois* is not an option for you, my friend?"

Yaroslav got up, fixed his pants, and picked up his shirt and coat. "Give me a moment to clean up," he said and headed toward the bathroom, ignoring the Spaniard's question. "We need to talk."

He returned a few minutes later and sat down, facing Santiago and Sylvana, who perched herself on the edge of the bed.

"So, what brought you here?" asked Santiago, the mirth gone from his eyes. "Even without you telling me, I know it's something serious, otherwise you wouldn't be here."

"It is," replied Yaroslav. "Something is going on. Something strange and so far, unexplainable."

"You feel it too, don't you?" asked the Spaniard, stroking his beard. "The balance is tipping toward darkness. Something is coming…"

"Yes." Yaroslav nodded, biting his lip. "But besides that, there is something else out of the norm."

"Like what?"

"Like the Sisterhood's slayers going after my mother and her company," replied Yaroslav. "You know how Akira is. She would never do anything to jeopardize the human-vampire relationships in her area. Yet, the Sisterhood sent people to watch us and tried to kill our vampires and me."

He told Santiago everything Peyton told him, including the part where the young witch was killed by one of her own. The King of Nevada listened silently, shaking his head, and sighed heavily once Yaroslav finished.

"You know that the Sisterhood of the Sun is regulated by the Destiny Council," said Sylvana, shifting slightly on the edge of the bed. "If they are persistently going after your mother's company, they have their orders."

"I figured as much." Yaroslav's frown deepened, unease spreading through him. "This is why I came here. Syl, you used to be one of the Sisterhood's slayers until this Spanish jackass"—he waved at Santiago—"turned you. And you, Santiago... You spent years fighting with the Sisterhood until you decided to mainstream. Help me find them."

Sylvana got up, her dark eyes igniting with a fearful scarlet glow. She glanced at Santiago, placing her hand on his shoulder and shook her head.

"Slavik, you're not serious, are you?" she asked and turned toward Santiago. "Father, you need to put some brains into his head, because I am seriously thinking he's having a blond moment."

"He was in love with that girl... Peyton," muttered Santiago, his eyebrows gathering over his striking black eyes. "It's vengeance talking."

"I don't think so...," Yaroslav objected quietly. "Watching her dying in my arms pained me more than I could imagine. She fought alongside me and my friends, and I learned to trust her."

He paused for a brief moment as Peyton's face, surrounded by her sunshiny curls surfaced in his memory. He pressed his hand over his eyes, pushing those memories out of his mind and took a deep breath before continuing.

"I was never in love with her. In the given circumstances, it wasn't possible... At first, she was driving me insane with her duplicity. One moment she hated me, ready to drive a stake through my heart. The next moment, she was kissing me like there was no tomorrow. But when the truth finally came out and she stopped her hot-and-cold behavior, I learned to enjoy spending time with her. She loved me, and I liked her. Liking her was easy and maybe if we had more time, I would have fallen in love with her... But all that was too short-lived..." He dropped his hand onto his lap and met Santiago's gaze. "My mind is not clouded by vengeance and I think clearly when I say I need to find the Sisterhood to understand what's going on."

"They will kill you, Slavik," said Sylvana, leaning forward slightly to touch his hand. "They will put a wooden bullet through your heart as soon as they sense your vampiric energy signature. There will be no conversation. They won't talk to you."

"Yaroslav, my friend." Santiago sighed, a troubled expression crossing his features. "We had plenty of differences in the past, but I actually like you and have nothing but deep respect for your maker, Akira Ida. I'm begging you to leave this idea and stay away from the Sisterhood. If they follow the Destiny Council's orders, they won't stop. The smartest thing you can do is go back to Florida and get ready to fight."

"Thank you. Maybe you are right..." Yaroslav nodded and got up, doubt spreading through him. "But I would still like to find out what's going on. The balance is shifting toward darkness. Akira's vampires, who not only peacefully co-exist with humans but help them fight for their safety, are under the scrutiny of the Destiny Council. Do you think it's a coincidence? Something is seriously wrong, and if we don't get to the bottom of it, we will all suffer the consequences."

He put his coat on and took his katana, sheathing it under his coat. Santiago moved to answer when with an earsplitting bang, all the windows broke at the same time, showering them with splinters of glass. Ten people, dressed in black tactical uniforms and helmets, burst inside, releasing thick black ropes they were attached to.

They stood in a half-circle formation, their strange weapons trained at Yaroslav, Santiago and Sylvana. One of the attackers took their helmet off and their long dark hair fell over their shoulders. Yaroslav held his breath, recognizing the woman in the short black dress who sent him a drink while he was playing.

She smiled icily, pinning him with her cold eyes.

"Yaroslav Potemkin, finally," she said, approaching him without as much as a touch of fear on her face. "I'm tired of running after you all over the human realm. Come with us willingly and we'll spare the lives of these two. Try fighting and we'll kill you all."

Yaroslav looked back and saw horror imprinted on Santiago's and Sylvana's faces. He didn't need to guess who these people were.

"Ask and you shall receive." He smiled bitterly. There was no fear, just sadness coiled in his heart. He turned toward the woman. "Leave them alone. I am coming with you willingly."

For a split-second, the hard, arrogant expression on her face changed to surprise. She grabbed his arm and before he knew what was happening, plunged a hypodermic needle into his neck.

Yaroslav gasped, his hand rising to his neck involuntarily, and his knees buckled. He didn't remember hitting the floor as a mushy, feverish oblivion took hold of him.

CHAPTER 15

~ ZANE BURNS, A.K.A. GUNZ ~

Gunz lay on a hard, tiled floor in a puddle of his own blood, staring at a white ceiling without blinking. Since he didn't feel physical pain and wasn't drained magically, his mind couldn't wrap around the amount of blood on the floor, but the nauseating reek and the warm, sticky feeling under his touch was driving him insane. He raised his hand and watched a thick scarlet liquid coat his trembling fingers, sliding down his wrist to his arm in large, heavy drops. He moaned and dropped his hand. It fell into the puddle with a sickening splash and the sound of it filled his soul with freezing fear.

His body was numb and heavy, and he couldn't make a move even if his life depended on it, which it probably did, since Liam's glacial eyes were glowering at him from above. The young man wasn't wearing the guard's uniform and helmet. He was dressed in blue jeans and a t-shirt, but that didn't change the fact that his hardened features—too hard for his age— breathed with deep loathing and hatred.

"Liam...," Gunz whispered, staring up at him, unable to do anything to protect himself from what he knew was coming. "I didn't kill Hazel. I did what I had to do... It was never my fault.

Alzir killed them both—your mother and Hazel—and you know it. So why—"

Liam's lip drew into a snarl and his fist connected with Gunz's jaw. There was no pain. His head jerked to the side and the metallic taste of blood filled his mouth, but that was it, and as Liam kept kicking and punching him, he felt nothing except the endless torment in his soul that twisted his entire existence into one never-ending nightmare.

The World of Magic had turned this young man into a monster, incapable of rational thinking, driven by pain and revenge, and partially, it was his fault too.

Gunz wasn't fighting back, his muscles laden with terror of what else Liam would do to him. His soul bled, locked in his own useless body as he watched Liam pull the belt out, slowly folding it in two. Unable to do anything else, Gunz screamed and felt an abrupt pain in his side.

HE WOKE up with a start and found himself lying on the floor by the bed, his shirt soaked with sweat clinging to his body. He scrambled into a sitting position, resting his back against the bed, and raised his hands up. There was no blood, but his fingers were trembling uncontrollably and so was his entire body.

Night terrors... It wasn't the first time for him. After his first tour of duty, for a while he could barely sleep without waking up screaming. With time, it got better. But it was the first time he had this kind of nightmare.

He pulled his legs up, wrapped his arms around his knees and rested his forehead atop his hands, struggling to stop his teeth from chattering and his body from shaking. Gunz didn't know how long he sat like that. His exhausted mind was drifting on and off, and reality was warped by nightmarish visions.

When he felt a light touch to his shoulder, he flinched, jerking to the side. His eyes flew wide-open and his body tensed. Karma stood next to him, wearing nothing more than a short bathrobe.

"Shh, Zane," she whispered, lowering herself down to the floor next to him. "It's just me. I heard you screaming. Are you okay? Why are you on the floor?"

He got up and sat on the bed, pulling his feet up. "I'm fine," he said, his voice hoarse. "Just a nightmare."

"That was one hell of a nightmare, I must say." Karma got up, disbelief clearly imprinted on her face. "Do you want to talk?"

"No." He lay down, folding his arms under his head, and closed his eyes. "It's five in the morning, Karma. I want to try to get some shuteye before I have to jump into the next pile of shit the Destiny Council wants us to clean up. I appreciate you checking in on me, but everything is fine. Get back to sleep."

She nodded, wrapping her bathrobe tighter around herself and headed toward the exit, her bare feet stepping softly on the floor. Halting by the door, she turned around.

"Listen, Zane, I don't want to be a bitch—" She cut herself off and chuckled, shaking her head. "It's too late for that, I guess. I am what I am, so I am going to tell the way I see it. When we found you in the Destiny Council compound, we all had seen... um... what we'd seen. I'm sure Lucan, who came a few seconds before us, witnessed even more. So, here is the deal, firetwat. Sooner or later, you will have to talk to someone about everything you went through or it will eat you from the inside."

Everything inside him froze, and the flames surfaced on his chest and arms, responding to his emotional state.

"Not today, Karma," he growled. "I was tortured. Nothing new there. That's all the World of Magic is good for—pain and suffering. And I do not want to talk about it in detail."

He turned toward the wall and closed his eyes.

* * *

After Karma left, Gunz barely got any sleep and when Aidan knocked on his door, he was fully dressed and ready. They walked into the kitchen where Hawk and Theron had set the table for breakfast. He didn't remember what he was eating or the conversation they had, his mind focused on the unknown mission ahead, and when Raoul walked into the room, he felt almost relieved. All he wanted was to get through with it, find Angel and Uri and be on his way to Kendral.

Theron cleaned up the table, and Raoul placed a large map of the United States on it, throwing a few colorful pins on top.

"Well," started the Warden, straightening a corner of the map, "the good news is all three Horsemen are in the territory of the United States. At least for now."

"What's the bad news?" asked Mrak Delar as calm and collected as usual.

"The bad news is that they are all over the map," explained Raoul. He picked up the pins and stuck three of them in. "Well, maybe it's not such bad news. The farther apart they are the better. After all, bringing them back together and summoning their steeds will restart the countdown to the Apocalypse, *mon ami*. Making the Four ride again will speed up the process considerably, breaking the last three seals in no time."

He raised his eyes, staring at Mrak Delar, but the Ancient Master just shrugged and flicked his wrist, signaling the Warden to continue.

"Well, the worst news is that we don't have much time. We'll need to send three separate teams to find each Horseman and bring all three of them here," continued Raoul. "The horsemen are not the kind of beings you can trust blindly. Just like Death, they're not good or evil. They just are. But just like any ancient being of power, they are flaky and vengeful. So, I suggest, no one goes alone."

"Three out of four Horsemen of the Apocalypse together on a tiny Arizona farm," muttered Hawk, jamming his hands into the pockets of his wide cargo-pants. "What could go wrong with this scenario?"

"Look at it this way, Hawk," said Kal, the corners of his lips quirking up in a sarcastic smirk. "If we don't free Death sometime soon, the world will come to an end anyway. You know, with the veil collapsing and the realm of the dead colliding with the realm of the living. Compared to that, we're not risking that much."

"Way to stay positive, Great Salamander," mumbled Raoul, wiping perspiration off his forehead. "But as grim as it sounds, Kal has a point. The sooner we find them the better."

Mrak Delar approached the map and observed it with interest, leaning over the table slightly. "Which of these pins is Conquest... um... Pestilence? Whatever he calls himself nowadays." He touched one pin at the time with his finger. "I'm going after him."

"Pestilence... Here." Raoul pointed at the blue pin on the map. "Boston, Massachusetts. You'll find him somewhere in the downtown business district. Who is coming with you, Master?"

"No one," replied Mrak Delar, his voice flat, his face void of emotions. He straightened, throwing his hair off his face, and calmly met Raoul's gaze.

Gunz got up, ready to argue with the Master of Power, but Mrak Delar glanced warningly at him, and a deep wrinkle materialized between his black eyebrows. Gunz dropped back into his chair, recognizing that arguing with him would be pointless, but it didn't mean he had to like the idea.

"Gunz, you can't go with me," said the Ancient Master, and his eyes traveled from one face in the room to the next. "None of you can. I'm the only one here who is fully immune to Pestilence's power. I can't get sick."

"If I get sick, all I have to do is to revert to heal myself." Gunz gave it another try as dread spread over him at the thought of letting Mrak Delar face Pestilence unsupported.

"Yes, that's true. But you *can* get sick. And how are you planning to revert in the middle of Boston, surrounded by humans? You have no idea what Pestilence can throw at you. Smallpox, Typhoid, Bubonic Plague? How about brain cancer? You name it—he can gift you with it and make it progress within a few hours. I'm not taking any chances," objected Mrak Delar, a barely visible smirk touching his lips.

"How about Aidan?" asked Theron, throwing Aidan a guilty look. "He is a god."

"When it comes to meeting with Pestilence, Aidan is an even worse choice than a Fire Salamander. Yes, he is a god, but in this realm, he has a human body. He can get sick and unlike Gunz, he can actually die," explained Mrak Delar with a sigh. "While Gwyn ap Nudd can restore him back to life with all his powers intact, it will take Aidan out of the game for a while."

"Mrak, you're forgetting that—," started Raoul, raising his hand, but Mrak Delar interrupted him.

"I'm not that old, Raoul. Still remember things… Most of the time." He chuckled darkly. "Yes, I have healing power and I can heal those who fall ill, but the healing magic takes time and a lot of my strength. I can't afford to get weaker while dealing with such a dangerous and devious being as Pestilence. As a Master of Power, I can't get infected. He is powerless against me. This is why I should go alone. Besides, him and I go way back. Wouldn't be our first meeting." He shuddered visibly, his fingers grasping at the edge of the table.

"Even if I couldn't get sick, I won't be able to accompany Mrak or any of you for that matter," said Aidan, and complete silence followed his words as everyone turned, staring at him. "There is something else I must do."

His eyes darted to Gunz, and an expression of guilt crossed his face.

"Listen, Gunz, last night, I had a communication from Yaroslav. First one since he disappeared. I should have told you as soon as it happened, but you were sleeping, and I didn't want to bother you." He glanced down at his clenched hands and sighed. "I don't know what happened to Yaroslav, but something is wrong. I have to find him and bring him here."

"He contacted you?" asked Gunz incredulously.

After they shared quite an unpleasant time being enslaved by the dark soul of Rasputin, Yaroslav had always had Gunz's number on both a supernatural and mundane speed dial, and their blood bond had been reinforced just recently.

What if Yaroslav was trying to get hold of me before and couldn't? Chills ran down his back, and he shifted uncomfortably in his chair.

"He tried you first, Zane, but something is blocking your blood bond." Aidan confirmed his thoughts, sounding troubled. "I can't communicate with you via our psychic bond either."

"Dammit," muttered Gunz and bit his lip, realizing that the powerful shield the Codex had erected in his mind was blocking not only Zmey but also his friends. "Where is he? What did he say?"

"The communication was short, and he practically didn't say anything, except that he can't get hold of you and he needs help. After that something happened, and all I got was his location and..." Aidan's voice faded into silence and he looked away. "And a squall of emotions... Mostly anger, but also some fear. I am going after him, Zane."

"Location?" asked Gunz, his voice a low growl.

"Las Vegas, Nevada," replied Aidan.

Gunz picked up an unused pin from the table and stuck it

into the map with a little more force than he intended, making a hole in place of the little circle that indicated the location of Las Vegas.

"Now we're going into four different directions," he muttered. "I hate this plan more and more. Especially with the assholes from the Destiny Council after us. If they send the Destiny Enforces after us, divided we stand no chance."

"You're right, son," said Kal, leaning back in his chair, making it groan under his weight. "But I don't see any other way it can be done. Besides, if they send a group of Destiny Enforcers, even together we stand no chance against them. So, don't worry about things that are out of your control and tell me where you'll be going."

"War," said Gunz with a wry smirk. "Been there, done that. I don't think he can throw anything my way I haven't seen yet."

"You'll be surprised," interjected Mrak Delar quietly. "Someone is going with you. You're not going alone. Period."

Gunz dropped his head. He didn't want any companions. If he was alone, no one could hold his friends' lives over his head. No one could blackmail him. Alone, he was free. Besides, no one would ask him any questions. Feeling all the eyes in the room staring at him, he knew he had to say something but couldn't bring himself to speak.

"Burns, I'll go with you," offered Lucan from across the room, folding his massive arms over his bare chest. "I hope by now I proved my loyalty to you... and war is what I do best."

Gunz looked up at the elf, searching his emotionless face. "It's not your loyalty I'm worried about, Lucan, it's your life. People around me seem to get hurt and die... a lot."

"I'm an elf." A dark light ignited behind Lucan's angled green eyes. "Not an easy target to kill."

Raoul glanced at Gunz with an expression of doubt on his face but pointed at the map. "You'll find War in Silicon Valley, California. San Jose, to be precise."

"What the hell is War doing in California?" muttered Karma, staring at Raoul in disbelief. "I would expect him to be in the Middle East."

"I have no idea," replied Raoul, sounding slightly unnerved. "Maybe he switched to business wars now. It's for Zane and Lucan to find out and bring him here."

"Doesn't matter, does it?" asked Tessa, jumping off the counter. She walked up to the map, throwing an apologetic glance at Aidan. "I guess I'm taking on Famine. Missi, Karma, are you with me?"

"Tessa...," mumbled Aidan, his face getting a shade paler. "You understand that I must help Yaroslav. Otherwise—"

"Of course, I understand, oldie." Tessa smiled at him, her eyes never leaving his. "I know we are supposed to do things together, and I know you're worried. This is why I'm asking Missi and Karma. My friends, you know? I'll be fine."

"Of course, we're with you." Missi winked at Tessa and turned to Aidan, patting his arm. "We'll take care of her."

"Sounds like a fun road trip," chimed in Karma, jumping off the counter. "Hey, Warden, where are we going?"

"Back to Florida," replied Raoul. "Immokalee."

"Are you kidding me?" Tessa stared at the map, tracing the shape of Florida with her finger. "What is Famine doing in the agricultural center of Florida?"

"Like you said, it doesn't matter." Mrak Delar got up, stopping Raoul with a sharp wave of his hand. "We don't have time, so let's stop asking questions the Warden can't answer and let's get moving."

The Master of Power was always straightforward, but he was never abrupt, and right now he was showing signs of nervousness which was quite unlike him. He cleared his throat and averted his eyes, his fingers twisting a narrow silver band on his left hand—his wedding band.

"Agreed," said Aidan. He walked up to him and gave him a

quick once-over. "But before you can go anywhere, you need to change into appropriate clothing. As much as I like all this medieval knight vibe you have, Master, you can't walk around downtown Boston dressed like this."

Mrak looked down at his outfit, running his hands over his black-silk shirt with ruffled sleeves, tucked into his tight black pants, stopping at his wide leather belt. Then he laughed open-heartedly, shaking his head. "I guess you're right. I am a few centuries behind the latest fashion trends."

Aidan switched his attention to the elf and just shook his head, chuckling.

"I don't even know where to start with you, Lucan. Between your cat eyes, your pointy ears and your long white hair with a blue tint, I am not sure how we can hide all that. Besides, you need something to cover all this"— Aidan smirked, making a wide arch with his hand over Lucan's bare torso—"*Men's Health* magazine, *Gym-Free Abs* edition."

"I'm sorry." The elf shuffled from foot to foot, spreading his arms with a guilty shrug. "When I left the Destiny Council facility, that was all I had on me... And Hawk didn't have anything my size... I can cast an illusion spell and change my appearance."

Gunz raised his hand, a lopsided grin appearing on his face. "Okay, everyone, relax. Lucan and I are going to Silicon Valley. No one is going to look at him twice. They're all going to think he's getting ready for LARPing, or into a cosplay." He shrugged, arching his eyebrow at Aidan. "You know... overly zealous fantasy fan?"

"Yeah... no," replied Aidan, but mischievous twinkles danced in his eyes.

Missi and Karma exchanged a quick look and giggled. "Too bad he's not going to Las Vegas. I bet you anything, any topless show would love to have him."

Lucan gasped—a sound so unfit for the giant elf that Gunz

clasped his hand to his mouth to stop himself from laughing. The elf wrapped his arms around himself. Having a hard time dealing with all the attention, he looked as uncomfortable and shy as he could get.

"Give me one hour," said Aidan. "Get ready for your trips in the meantime." He snapped his fingers and vanished.

CHAPTER 16

~ ZANE BURNS, A.K.A. GUNZ ~

"Shouldn't you get ready?" asked Mrak Delar, leaning back in his chair.

Gunz glanced at him and his eyes darted to Kal who stood silently, staring out the window. Besides the three of them, there was no one in the kitchen, and now the room felt too large and too empty.

"I'm as ready as I can be," replied Gunz with half a shrug, "but something tells me you're not, Mrak. What's with all the anxiety?"

"No, I'm fine." The Master of Power got up and poured himself a cup of coffee out of the coffeemaker. Adding some sugar, he mixed it with a spoon absentmindedly. "Meeting with Pestilence is never fun. I'm just not looking forward to it."

"To be fair, Mrak, the last time you met with him has been years ago and you weren't what you are now," Kal pointed out without turning around. "At the time, you just forfeited your power as a Master, and you were still uncomfortable in your skin as a wizard. So, yeah, you can't compare…"

"I know," replied Mrak Delar lightly, taking a sip of his drink. He grimaced at the taste of the semi-cold coffee and wrapped his hands around the cup, channeling fire energy through it to warm it up. As his regular calm disposition settled over his features, he smiled. "I'm not worried about facing Pestilence. I'm worried about bringing the three out of four Horsemen together."

Turning around, Kal rubbed his chin, and the flames sprung up to life in his eyes. He walked back to the table and planted his massive fists on top of the map, leaning down slightly.

"I have the same concerns as you have, Master," muttered the Great Salamander, touching one pin at a time, frowning. "This is why as soon as all of you are gone, I'm going back to Kendral. I have an idea, but I'm not sure if my memory serves me right, so I want to visit the Riders' library to confirm. I know what I'm looking for, so I should be back before any one of you."

Kal got up and approached Gunz. He made a move to put his hand on his shoulder the way he normally would have done, but then changed his mind and lowered his hand. Gunz noticed his move and guilt washed over him.

"It's okay, Father," he said with a sad smile. "I'll be fine. There is no need to treat me like I'm made of glass."

"No one treats you like you're made of glass, Fire Gecko." Aidan's voice sounded behind Gunz, making him flinch and spin around. "Lately, we have to treat you as if you're made of C4—one wrong word and you explode."

"Aidan! You scared the shit out of me!" Gunz threw his hands in the air. "Can't you knock before teleporting into a room unannounced? Or something."

"Or something." Aidan snickered and put a bunch of shopping bags from different stores on the table. He peeked inside each bag and offered a few of them to Mrak Delar and a few to Gunz.

"Business attire for Mrak, and geek attire for Gunz and Lucan." Aidan winked at Gunz and grabbed the rest of the bags.

"The rest is for the girls and for me. Go change and I'll see you all here in ten minutes."

* * *

A FEW MINUTES LATER, everyone gathered back around the table. All things considered, Aidan managed to find a way to disguise Lucan's elven nature. More or less. The elf was dressed in jeans and a t-shirt which had *"Free the House Elves"* written on it in large silver letters. His cat-like green eyes were concealed beneath sport polarized sunglasses, and his long hair was pulled into a low ponytail on the back of his head, carefully covering his pointy ears.

Gunz tapped Aidan on the shoulder and pointed at his own chest, where white letters printed on the black t-shirt showed, *"I'm not short, I'm a Halfling"*.

"Really, Aidan?" he asked, reproachfully. Tessa and Missi stared at him for a split second and burst out laughing.

Aidan shrugged, a mischievous grin on his face. "I thought it was appropriate."

Gunz was about to give Aidan a piece of his mind when Tessa's and Missi's eyes widened and they stopped giggling, staring at something over his shoulder in awe. He turned around and saw Mrak Delar standing in the doorway. He was dressed in a dark Armani business suit and a white shirt unbuttoned on his chest, holding a tie in his hands, an expression of pure desperation on his face.

"Holy mother of—" Karma didn't finish and cleared her throat. "Master, you make me wish I was still playing for the other side."

Mrak Delar glanced at her, speechless, and the expression of misery got replaced by utter confusion for a split second.

"Aidan," he mumbled, gazing at him pleadingly, "do I have to wear this noose? My wife loves when I wear a suit and this"—he lifted his hand with the tie—"torture instrument, but every time she puts it on me, I feel like I'm wearing a slave's collar again."

Karma approached him and took the tie from his hands.

"You were a slave? Collar and chains and all?" she purred as she buttoned up his shirt and lifted the collar, placing the tie around his neck.

Her nimble fingers quickly made a knot and pulled it up, but not all the way, leaving his neck free and the top button of his shirt opened.

"How does this feel?" she asked, taking a step back, and observing him as though he was a piece of art.

"Thank you, my lady." Mrak Delar bowed lightly to her, his natural elegance shining in his every move. "It's not as bad as I remember it from before."

"Too bad Pestilence is a man," murmured Karma under her breath, arching her eyebrow at him. She approached Tessa and Missi and grabbed the duffel bag which accompanied her no matter where she was going. Pulling a small bottle filled with a shimmering blue liquid out of her pocket, she shook it a little, ready to open a portal. "Are we ready to go?"

"Hold on, Karma," said Tessa, touching Karma's shoulder lightly as she walked by. "We don't need portals. Just give me a minute."

She approached Aidan and, for a moment, stood in front of him, gazing up into his eyes. Rising on her toes, she threw her arms around his neck and kissed him, pressing her whole body to him.

"Be careful, my ancient god," she whispered, "and come back to me."

Aidan didn't reply. He squeezed her tightly in his embrace as though he was afraid to let go, burying his face in her hair. "I'll see you soon, my love."

She let go of him and turned to Gunz. As her fingers brushed his cheek gently, she smiled. "Zane, bring our elf back, would yah?" she asked with a sly grin. "Santa needs his little helper for Christmas." Then she switched her attention to Lucan who looked beyond confused, her eyes sliding up and down his massive frame. "Hey, big boy, you better be guarding my Fire Salamander."

"With my life, my lady," replied Lucan, pressing his fist to his chest as he bowed to her.

"Lady, right..." Tessa rolled her eyes at him and returned to Missi and Karma. "Hold on to me, girls." As soon as both witches grabbed her shoulders, Tessa snapped her fingers, and they vanished from the room.

Once they were gone, Aidan let out a ragged breath, his hands locking and unlocking at his sides. Gunz glanced at him with sympathy, realizing what kind of sacrifice his friend had made to help Yaroslav, and how hard it was for him to let Tessa go on this mission without him.

Kal got up and approached Mrak Delar, giving him a quick once-over.

"I'm wondering where you hide your sword in this weird set of garments," he murmured, pursing his lips.

"I enchanted it. The same way I have done for Gunz's sword years ago," replied the Ancient Master with a smile that left his eyes foggy with sadness. "I'm not worried about my quest, Great Salamander... I just hope you'll find in the Riders' library what we need. The success of this mission depends on you."

Kal nodded and offered his hand to Mrak Delar. The Master of Power glanced down at Kal's hand—the Great Salamander wasn't big on handshakes—and locked his arm in a firm forearm grip. Then he turned to Gunz.

"Young Salamander," he started, but then shook his head and sighed. "Gunz, Gwyn refused to tell me what happened at the Destiny Council trial, and because of that, I know I owe you more than I can ever repay. I'm indebted to you, my friend, for as long as I live." He swallowed hard, his eyebrows lowering over his dark eyes. "War feeds on pain and fear, and right now you're overflowing with both. Clear your mind before you go anywhere close to him. Please... be careful and stay safe." He looked up at the elf. "Both of you. And I'll see you back here soon."

Without giving Gunz a chance to say anything, he snapped his fingers and was gone with a light pop.

"Gwyn didn't tell Mrak, but he told me," said Kal, his voice uncharacteristically hoarse.

"What did he tell you?" Gunz glanced at his mentor, and his shoulders slumped as if he could carry the heavy load no more.

"More than I cared to know, my boy," replied Kal. "You did exactly what I expected you would do, and you paid for it dearly. I'm sure your recent stay at the Destiny Council facility is just the beginning. Unfortunately, right now, we have no time to think about that, but sooner or later, you and I—we'll have to find a way to sort it out."

Gunz nodded, his heart wrenching at the thought of getting Kal involved into his situation with the Destiny Council. Kal observed him, his lips quirking up at the corners a little.

"I remember the day I brought you to Kendral for the first time," he said, his eyes getting distant as his mind travelled back into the past. "You're no longer that scared, lost boy. And between you and my Phoenix, you boys from the human realm are making me run all over the worlds." He tapped Gunz on his shoulder and laughed. "But I wouldn't have it any other way. Take care, my child. See you soon."

He waved his arm and unfolded the fire curtain of his portal. Throwing one more glance at Gunz, the Great Salamander walked through the flames and disappeared on the other side.

With only Aidan and Lucan left in the room, Gunz looked out the window, wondering where Hawk and Theron were. As if hearing his thought, Aidan approached him and glanced outside.

"Hawk and Theron left," he said, sounding distant. "They want to bring a few stronger members of the pack here. Just in case they have to defend the ranch while we all are gone."

"The wards will hold," murmured Lucan.

"Possibly," replied Aidan, turning back to them, "but it's not a bad idea anyway. When you're dealing with the World of Magic, you must expect the unexpected."

For a moment, Aidan stood with his arms dangling powerlessly, his eyes unfocused, and Gunz wondered where his friend's mind had traveled. He looked distant and tired and it seemed like pain had found a permanent residence in his blue eyes.

"Aidan," Gunz called him, touching his hand. "What is your next step?"

Aidan gave a start, but then smirked, rubbing his forehead. "First, I'm going to take you and Lucan to a hotel in San Jose," he said. "I know the area well, so teleporting is not going to be a problem. I made a call and booked a room for you already. It's not far from the business center, so you can rent a car and drive around. See if either of you can sense War's presence."

Gunz nodded. "Aidan—," he started, but fell silent, not sure what to say.

He wanted to tell Aidan to be careful and watch his back, but this advice had never done any good to anyone before. Of course, he was going to be careful. All of them were experienced enough in dealing with the supernatural, but when it came to fighting the followers of Chaos or any other powerful beings of magic, being careful wasn't always the right choice.

Aidan smiled, placing his hands on Lucan's and Gunz's shoulders. "I know, my friend. I'll be careful." Aidan's voice was calm and reassuring as always, but Gunz knew him well enough to see that the god of the Otherworld was a ball of nerves at the moment. "And Zane... you need to open your mind. I don't know which spell you're using to keep Zmey out of your head, but you have to lighten it up a little. At least while you're awake. Just in case."

"I will," promised Gunz, not sure if he was skilled enough with the Codex's magic to deliver on his promise.

Aidan snapped his fingers, and they vanished, leaving the small Arizona ranch behind.

CHAPTER 17

~ MASTER MRAK DELAR ~

Mrak Delar stopped in front of a high-rise located in the heart of the business district of Downtown Boston. Blue skies with a few white clouds reflected in the mirror-like surface of the façade, and the morning sun touched it, bouncing bright flares of light off of it. Above the door, there was a large sign with the name of the company that owned this giant building.

"Conquest Pharmaceuticals," read Mrak Delar, shaking his head. "Hiding in plain sight."

If before he had some doubts, now he knew for sure. *Figures... Pestilence got himself into the pharmaceutical business.*

The Master of Power didn't care to know more about the man with whom he'd had a brief but unpleasant acquaintance a few years ago, or how he had acquired a multi-billion dollar, publicly traded company. All he wanted was to get in, speak with Pestilence and bring him to the Arizona ranch. His goal was to spend as little time as possible next to the infamous Horseman. But now, observing the empire he had built for himself, Mrak started to doubt that it would be easy to talk

Pestilence into leaving it all behind and getting back into the saddle.

He took a deep breath like before a dive and pushed a heavy glass door open. On the inside, the building was just as modern and high-tech as it was on the outside. Mrak stopped, observing the enormous lobby, feeling a little lost. He opened his other sight and checked the area again—there was no doubt he was in the right place. He could see and sense Pestilence's energy signature here, within his reach. Everyone else seemed to be human, no magic of any kind.

At the far end of the lobby, under a large display with the company name, a young woman sat with her eyes permanently attached to a computer monitor. A soft smile lingered on her face as she spoke with someone on the phone. Mrak Delar approached the front desk and halted, waiting for her to notice him.

Without looking at him, she raised her index finger, silently asking him to wait. A second later, she hung up the phone and finally looked up. Her eyes widened and her lips rounded as she froze in place, staring at him.

"Excuse me, my—um—ma'am," said Mrak Delar, his voice a deep and insinuating purr as he weaved some of his magic into it. "I would like to see the owner of Conquest Pharmaceuticals, please."

She blinked at him a few times, her long eyelashes covered in a generous layer of mascara working like an industrial fan. Then she smiled and shifted in her chair, moving forward a little. Her phone rang, and she flinched, tearing her eyes off of him.

"Please hold," she breathed into the receiver without breaking her eye contact with Mrak Delar.

He smiled wider and leaned down slightly, allowing his long hair to fall in soft obsidian waves around his chiseled face, now his eyes just inches away from hers.

"Do you have an appointment with Mr. Vittorio?" she managed to ask.

"No, I don't," replied Mrak Delar, straightening up, "but I'm sure he would love to see me."

"May I have your name, sir?" she asked, her trembling fingers hovering over the intercom button.

"Absolutely." He flashed her a bright smile. "Please tell Mr. Vittorio, Mrak Delar is here to see him."

"Mrak Delar?" she repeated breathlessly. "What an unusual and exotic name... So fitting for someone like you. Are you a model or a—"

She didn't get a chance to finish her question when a soft chuckle sounding behind Mrak interrupted her. He turned around, knowing who it was without looking. A tall man in a dark silver business suit stood just a few feet away from him, his brown eyes twinkling with sarcasm.

"Master Mrak Delar," he said, greeting him with a pearl-white smirk. "Long time no see. To what do I owe the pleasure of your visit? It has to be something serious for you to show up here, looking"—he waved his hand up and down at Mrak—"the way you do and turning on your undeniable charm on my poor, unsuspecting secretary."

"Mr. Vittorio, is it?" asked the Master of Power, mirroring his sarcastic smirk. "Yes, I have a business proposition for you. Can we talk somewhere more private?"

"Enzo Vittorio, at your service." Pestilence inclined his head in a light bow. "I'm holding my breath, Master. Can't wait to hear your proposition." Then he turned to his secretary, regarding her with a reproachful gaze. "Monique, when you're able to think clearly again, please cancel all my appointments for today and make sure no one bothers me. I want to have quality time with my old... yeah... friend."

* * *

ENZO VITTORIO OPENED the door into his personal office, letting Mrak walk inside first. The office was as large as the downstairs lobby and had an amazing view of downtown Boston. He gestured at a wide leather armchair in front of a modern glass-and-metal desk, offering the Master of Power to take a seat, and lowered himself into an identical chair across from him.

As Mrak Delar sat down, Enzo smiled coldly. "Can I offer you anything, Master? Coffee perhaps?"

"No, thank you," he replied, crossing his legs at the knee.

"I promise, it's just coffee, Master. No bubonic plague in it." Pestilence laughed coldly, folding his hands behind his head as he leaned back in his chair and stretched his legs. "I believe that is what I gifted you with the last time we met."

"I'm not worried about that," objected Mrak Delar calmly. "I just don't want our meeting to be longer than is absolutely necessary. If you think I'm enjoying this so-called reunion, think again."

"Aw, my dear friend, why so cold and surly?" whined Pestilence, pouting. "I see you are a Master of Power again, and despite your attempts at hiding your energy signature, I believe you're more powerful than you were while you enjoyed destroying Kendral. You have no reason to be afraid of me. You're immune to my charms."

"Good point," huffed Mrak Delar, narrowing his eyes at him. "But with whom am I speaking? Pestilence or Conquest?"

Enzo Vittorio frowned, the layer of fake cheerfulness and sarcasm gone. "Pestilence, and you know it. So, let's get to business. I believe I know why you're here. So, spit it out."

"We need to find Death," said the Master of Power flatly, staring Pestilence directly into his eyes.

"Summon reapers. I have enough on my plate without all that."

"They can't sense him, and *you* know it," hissed Mrak Delar, tapping his fingers on the arm of his chair. "Otherwise I wouldn't be here."

"Why should I care?" asked Pestilence with an indifferent shrug. "I'm above it all. All Horsemen are. When it comes to the affairs of human realms, we take a neutral position. I'll wait for the Destiny Board to unravel its path."

"Maybe the rest of the Horsemen are, but you are one evil SOB!" growled Mrak Delar. He fell back in his chair and closed his eyes. This man was getting under his skin and he knew he shouldn't let him do it.

"It takes one to know one, Master. Despite what you think, I'm neither good nor evil. I just am." Pestilence leaned forward, his hands grasping at the arms of the chair.

"And what you did with the City of Silver a few years ago, that wasn't pure evil?" asked Mrak Delar through gritted teeth.

"That was a mistake! I was under the influence of—" He got up and walked toward the window where he halted, crossing his arms behind his back. He stood silent for a second and then added without looking back. "Out of all people, I thought you would understand."

"Oh, I understand. I'm an understanding kinda fellow," muttered the Master of Power, everything inside him shaken with the unwanted memories Pestilence brought forth. "So, prove to me that you're indeed not evil, Enzo. Come with me now and let's find Angel."

Enzo turned around and slowly paced to his desk. Leaning on the back of his armchair, he drilled Mrak Delar with a heavy gaze, the energy of his magic rising around him.

"I believe you and the young Salamander have been around Angel for years," he growled. "How could you let it happen?"

"I'm sorry I couldn't guard Death while I was imprisoned by the Destiny Council, wearing Destiny cuffs!" barked Mrak Delar, throwing his hands up.

"So, it's true then?" Enzo observed him with curiosity, disbelief reflected on his face.

"What is true?" Mrak froze in his chair, chills running down his spine.

"You sound like you don't know," muttered Pestilence, frowning. He glanced to the side, looking like a person who was forced into a situation where he had to deliver unpleasant news.

"Enzo, what don't I know?"

"Rumor has it, the young Salamander got into a fight with the Destiny Council over you, ripping them a new one," said Enzo quietly. He sighed and sat down into his chair. "He didn't tell you, did he?"

Mrak Delar shook his head, his heart beating in his throat.

"They said he dissolved the cage, broke the Destiny cuffs and just walked out with you in his arms, Mrak," continued Pestilence. "Who knew that the Fire Salamanders were so powerful? Unfortunately, by doing that he set his destiny in motion. The Destiny Council doesn't take things like that lightly. He'll pay for your freedom."

"Dammit, Gunz... Now I'm starting to understand," exhaled Mrak Delar, icy perspiration beading his forehead. He had known Gunz for years. He knew how loyal and selfless he was when it came to his friends. *Dammit, dammit, dammit... I should have known...* He glanced at Enzo and sighed. "I think he has already paid and it's just the beginning. But how do you know about it? How true are these rumors? From what I know there was no one there, except the Destiny Council, the young Salamander and Gwyn ap Nudd."

"I have no idea how true these gossips are," replied Enzo. "But your young friend is becoming a legend in the supernatural circles. Not everyone has the guts to stand up to the Destiny Council."

"Guts, blind loyalty... stupidity even," murmured Mrak Delar under his breath. "Anyway, Enzo, the young Salamander is with War right now, trying to get him to help us. So, I'm going to ask you the same question again. Will you help us find Death?"

"He is with War?" asked Enzo, his dark eyebrows rising. "Well, things are becoming truly interesting." He narrowed his eyes, and an uneven smirk appeared on his lips. "That's fine, Master. I'll come with you, but not because you asked me. I don't want to miss a chance to meet this young man. One day my curiosity will be my undoing."

He got up and walked to the opposite wall of the room. Moving a painting aside, he exposed the door of a small safe. He pressed the code and opened it. For a quick moment, he stared inside, searching for something. Then he pulled out a small box, took a ring out of it and closed the safe.

"Who's driving?" He put the ring on the middle finger of his right hand, turning toward the Master of Power.

Mrak Delar approached him and placed his hand on his shoulder. "I am," he said dryly. "And Enzo. Just a friendly warning. I'm taking you to a safe-house, and every person there is my friend and under my personal protection. Including the young Salamander. So, don't get cute."

"Cute?" repeated Pestilence, an over-exaggerated expression of horror on his face. "I wouldn't dare, oh mighty Ancient Master of Power. Not with you in charge."

"What could possibly go wrong...," muttered Mrak Delar and snapped his fingers, teleporting them to Hawk's ranch.

* * *

THEY MATERIALIZED on the porch of the house right in front of Hawk. The Alpha hopped aside and the air around him shimmered as he partially transformed. Mrak Delar raised his arms in a peaceful gesture.

"Hawk, this is Enzo Vittorio, also known as Pestilence," he

said absently. "Can you please..." He fell silent for a moment, rubbing his forehead, not sure what he was going to say. "Can you please help him get settled until the other Horsemen arrive?"

Hawk gave Pestilence a careful once-over and nodded. "Master, are you okay? You don't look yourself."

"I'm fine," replied Mrak Delar, his eyes wandering around the ranch. "I just need a few minutes of privacy. I'll be at your smithy. Can you please let me know when Gunz comes back?"

Without waiting for Hawk's reply, he pivoted on his heel and headed toward the small hut at the edge of the property. He walked inside, his eyes gliding over the tiny dark room. The forge was no longer burning, but the traces of fire energy were palpable in the air. He closed his eyes and inhaled, moving his hand from left to right, following Gunz's energy signature.

Then he opened his eyes and drew a rune in the air, infusing it with his power. "Gwyn ap Nudd," he whispered, his voice painfully hoarse, "I summon thee."

An oval communication window materialized, replacing the rune, and he sat down, leaning his back against the anvil. At first, the window remained dark, but then a flash of bright white light announced the arrival of the King of the Otherworld.

"Master?" Gwyn ap Nudd drummed on the surface of the window with his knuckle. "You summoned me?"

"Gwyn," said Mrak Delar without raising his eyes, twisting a hammer in his hand, "you must tell me what happened during the Destiny Council trial. I have to know—"

"I already told you everything you needed to know," Gwyn ap Nudd cut him off.

Mrak Delar dropped his head with a light shake. "Gwyn, please. I must know the truth. Why are you making me beg? Both you and Kal are not telling me everything. Why?"

"Because Gunz made us promise that you would never find out the truth, Master."

Mrak Delar raised his head and saw the Great Salamander standing a few feet away from him.

"Gunz made you promise?" he repeated as he dropped the hammer to the floor, rising, his hands clenching into fists. "And since when do you listen to Gunz? First, he is young and inexperienced as a man, and even younger as a Fire Salamander. Second, he has no instinct of self-preservation. He would put his life on the line to protect those he loves. Including me, or you two!"

He looked from Gwyn ap Nudd to Kal, and since they kept silent, he threw his hands in the air, frustration bottling up in him.

"It's about time all of us started protecting him!" he yelled, his eyes flooding with the darkness of his power. "Fire and Ice, Kalidus! He is just a boy! Your boy! He's not only calling you *Father...* he actually considers you one." He turned to the King of the Otherworld and the ground trembled, responding to his anger. "And you, Gwyn. You knew better than anyone else here how vengeful the Destiny Council could be. How could you keep it a secret from me?"

"And what would you do differently if you knew, Ancient Master?" yelled Gwyn ap Nudd, slamming his fist into the communication window.

Mrak Delar squeezed his head with his hands, his fingers digging into the mane of his hair and screamed. A short howl of anger and despair.

"I would have known where to look for him," he replied, breathing hard. "After my short stay at the Destiny Council prison before the trial, I knew about the existence of their facilities in the human realm."

He fell silent for a moment, anger slowly subsiding, giving

place to sadness, and then continued, his voice strangled and raspy.

"When Aidan had summoned me for the very first time and told me about Gunz's disappearance, I had no idea where to look for him. And since I couldn't sense his energy signature anywhere, I thought he pulled a disappearance act again, like he had done last year."

Mrak grunted, struggling to keep his power under control. "If I had known the truth, the first place I would have looked was the Destiny Council facilities and compounds. I would have leveled them all to the ground. Heaven and Earth, Gwyn! I could have found him in a matter of a few days..." He punched the air and the walls of the smithy trembled. "Destiny Council be damned! Cruel bastards! The abuse and torture they put him through... I would've spared him all that pain."

He fell silent, twisting the ring on his finger, pain gripping at his chest.

"Mrak, I'm sorry." Kal broke the heavy pause, putting his hand on Mrak Delar's shoulder. "You're probably right. It was a mistake to keep the truth from you. Knowing your relationship with Gunz, we were trying to keep you safe. We didn't want you to blame yourself for what happened to him, just like he didn't want it either."

"I'm not a child! Stop protecting me!" hissed Mrak Delar.

"Compared to us, you are," stated Gwyn ap Nudd calmly. "But you're right. Not telling you the truth was a mistake."

"Fine." Feeling drained, Mrak Delar lowered himself to the floor next to the anvil. "Start talking. I'm all ears."

Gwyn ap Nudd went through the events of the trial without sparing any details. It took him just a few minutes, but to Mrak it felt like hours as every word got engraved into his mind. Once Gwyn finished, the Master of Power nodded, chewing his lip.

"Fire Almighty... I wish I had known all that before," he

whispered. "You're forgetting, I'm a Master of Power. Maybe I'm not as powerful as the two of you, but there are things I can do that you cannot. I'll figure out how to deal with the Destiny Council and how to protect Gunz from further prosecution."

"Without sacrificing yourself?" asked Kal warningly.

"Of course. I've been to the Destiny Council prison already, thank you very much. Never again." Mrak Delar shuddered and got up heavily. "Gunz fought for my life. Now it's my time to fight for his. Let's find Death and then I'll deal with those assholes."

"Something is not right, though, Master," muttered Gwyn ap Nudd. "Even when I was there with Gunz the last time, I had a feeling…" His voice trailed away, and his blazing white eyes dimmed down. "I can't take a chance by getting involved again. I had done it for Aidan, Alliandr and for you, Mrak. I should stand down, but if you need my help, count on me."

"Thank you, Gwyn. I'll figure it out," said Mrak Delar, but doubt made his heart speed up with dread.

Someone has to…

CHAPTER 18

~ ZANE BURNS, A.K.A. GUNZ ~

Finding War was easier than Gunz had expected. As he slowly drove the rental car toward the business district, he could easily detect the energy of the Horseman. It was dark and powerful, yet his intuition didn't react to it as it would to any evil presence. Just like Raoul had explained, the Horsemen were neither good nor evil, and Gunz wasn't surprised to notice that War's energy signature reminded him of Angel's, leaving no doubt that he was on the right path.

At first, he thought that War didn't care to conceal his energy signature, but after a while he realized that it wasn't the reason. Lucan, who was sensitive to fluctuations of the magical energy field, could barely detect War's presence. The only explanation he could come up with was that his Salamander senses had taken over for his lost sight when he was blind and had never dimmed down after he broke the curse.

Soon, he parked the car in front of a large three-story building at the edge of the business park. Gunz tilted his head up, staring at the sign with the company name at the top of the building and his jaw dropped.

"*Equitum4 Software Inc.*," he read, his eyebrows rising, and then turned to Lucan. "He's not even hiding."

"Equitum?" repeated Lucan. "It reminds me of Dragon tongue. Sounds almost like—" He cut himself off and shook his head. "No, it can't be. Even he wouldn't be so…"

"Obviously, he would," replied Gunz, chuckling. "I believe it's Latin. One of the dead languages of the human realm and the word *Equitum* means 'horseman'. The only reason I know it is because my friend works at an equestrian center with a similar name." He shook his head with a sigh. "Un-frigging-believable."

Gunz walked into a spacious lobby and halted, observing it in awe. A massive glass-and-metal front desk was situated in the center of the room and a large LED Video Wall took the entire space behind the desk. A marketing trailer of some war game was playing in a continuous loop on the display. A chain of dark-gray leather sofas was positioned on the left side of the room and at least ten people sat there, displaying various stages of impatience and excitement. All of them were in their late teens, dressed in jeans and t-shirts, holding their phones and tablets in their hands.

Carefully, Gunz scanned every person in the lobby with his Salamander senses just to confirm that every one of them was a pureblood human—no magical energy of any kind. He sat down at the end of the sofa and Lucan sat next to him. Pulling out the phone Aidan had given him before they left, Gunz typed in the name of the company into the browser window and hit the search button.

According to the search engine, *Equitum4 Software Inc.* had been around for the last eighteen years. Founded and owned by Viggo Warrington, it had a few hundred employees and a considerable operating income. They specialized in developing first-person shooter and action roll-playing video games, which made them very popular. Recently, they announced that they were working on a virtual reality game which supposedly was unlike anything else available on the market today.

A young man in a t-shirt with a picture of a man with a square jaw and a massive gun in his hands—most likely a character from an *Equitum's* video game—turned to Gunz, giving him a quick once-over, an expression of curiosity and disbelief on his round, freckled face.

"Are you a beta?" he asked.

"No, I am the alpha and the omega," muttered Gunz, his eyes still on the screen of his phone.

"No, dude, I'm serious," huffed the teenager. "Are you here for beta testing of the new virtual reality game? Aren't you too old for that?"

Gunz lowered his phone, but before he could reply, a young woman behind the front desk got up and smiled cheerfully at the assembled crowd, her smile sending the next wave of excitement through the teens. She picked up a tablet and tapped something a few times.

"When I call your name," she said, her voice just as sweet as her disposition, "please approach the desk so I can direct you to your gaming rooms."

After a few minutes, the lobby cleared out and only Gunz and Lucan remained standing by the sofa. The secretary observed them with interest, tilting her head back slightly as her eyes made slow progress up to Lucan's face.

"Excuse me," she said, waving at them to approach. "Your names weren't on my list, I assume. And I think you're a little over the age requirements for this particular game testing…"

"This is the second time today I've been called 'old,'" said Gunz, smirking. "I'll take it as a compliment. Anyway, we're here to see Mr. Warrington."

She threw a lock of her dark hair off her face and peered down at her tablet again. "Hmm," she hummed, her fingers sliding up and down the screen, "I don't see any appointments scheduled for Mr. Warrington—"

Her speech was interrupted by a soft phone ring. The secretary answered the call and a dutiful smile spread over her face almost immediately.

"Yes, Mr. Warrington," she said, throwing a quick glance at Gunz. "I have two adult men here." She fell silent, listening to her boss. "Oh... I'm sorry, sir. No one notified me that they were coming—" She threw a gaze filled with newly found curiosity at Gunz and Lucan. "Yes, sir. I'll direct them to Drew."

She hung up the phone and smiled at them.

"Please follow me." The secretary motioned them toward the door with a sign 'Employees Only'. She swiped her card over the digital lock and let them through first. "Follow this hallway all the way to the end. Drew is expecting you in room number four."

Gunz thanked her and headed toward the end of the hallway. He knocked on the door with a large number four on it, and it swung open right away. A tall, young man stood in the doorway, a wide grin on his face.

"Mr. Warrington said you were the war experts he has been expecting for some time," he announced. "He said that after you go through three of our virtual reality settings, he wants to talk to you in person."

"Virtual reality?" asked Gunz, carefully probing the area with his senses.

While Drew was pureblood human, like every employee of War's company, he detected a soft flow of magic somewhere nearby. Turning his back to Drew, he channeled some of his fire, directing it toward his eyes, and opened his other sight. The entire wall in front of him was shimmering with a magical energy he couldn't recognize. He released his fire and turned back to face the young man.

"Yes, virtual reality," continued Drew, beaming with pride.

"We're in the process of developing a new kind of virtual reality game that wouldn't require the use of glasses. Well, you'll see when you get there."

"Can we talk to Mr. Warrington before we enter your game?" asked Gunz. He knew the answer before he received it. War wasn't going to make it easy on him.

"Sorry, but the boss was adamant about that," objected Drew as he headed toward a computer desk on his left. "First, you play, then he meets with you."

He picked up a small box and walked back to Gunz.

"I'm going to attach a few sensors to both of you. They will help us monitor your vitals and actions while you're inside," he mumbled, attaching small round patches to Gunz's temples. Then he asked him to lift his shirt and attached two more to his chest and one to his stomach.

Once done, he turned to Lucan, observing his massive frame in awe. "Sir, can you please remove your sunglasses?" he asked. "The light isn't bright here, and the games are usually set in the late evening environment. You won't need them."

Lucan threw a quick glance at Gunz and took his glasses off. As Drew met the elf's emerald eyes, he took in a sharp breath.

"Whoa...," he mumbled, stretching up on his tiptoes to attach sensors to Lucan's temples. "I've never seen such... um... unusual eyes. Are those color contact lenses?"

"Of course these are color contacts. Don't you see? He's an Albino," huffed Gunz with a smirk. "They're also prescription, so, he needs to keep them."

"No problem, sir, no problem," muttered Drew, looking like he was all too happy to get as far away from the elf as possible.

Lucan probably noticed it too, because a dangerous grin split his face as he folded his massive arms over his chest, flexing his biceps.

"Okay, you're all set." Drew took a step back, his widened eyes never leaving the elf. "Now that I connected you to the game, it will respond to your mental commands, just like a regular game would respond to a controller in the hands of a gamer."

The young man headed toward the opposite wall, making a large circle to keep at least some distance between himself and Lucan. As Gunz expected, that was the wall infused with magic. Drew placed a small brass key into the lock and turned it twice.

"Your journey will begin here," he announced, gesturing at the open door, and it was obvious that it wasn't the first time the young man gave this speech. "Before entering the game, you will be presented with a choice of weapons. You need to select one to proceed."

"Do I have to?" asked Gunz.

Drew's jaw dropped, but he cleared his throat and regained his composure quickly. "Yes, sir. If you want to pass to the next level, you need your weapon. On every level of the game, there is a *key* which allows you to proceed to the next level. To find the key, you must destroy your opponent's stronghold."

"Sounds like any other video game to me," muttered Gunz with a light shrug. "Do I get points for every killed enemy?"

"It's not like you've seen many other games, but I assure you our game is nothing like all the other video games," objected Drew dryly, giving Gunz an arrogant once-over. "Anyway, the answer to your question is yes, the more enemies you destroy, the more coins you collect. Once you find the key and unlock your next level, you can select better weapons or more than one, using your coins."

"Before we go, just one more question." Gunz seized his arm, stopping him. "Can we die inside the game?"

"Yes, of course," replied Drew indignantly, shaking Gunz's hand off his arm. "What kind of game would that be if there was no risk factor?"

"So, how many lives do we have and what would happen if we die?" asked Gunz, chills rolling down his spine. *What if death within this game was real? After all, it was built by War.* He frowned—there were so many humans in this building. He didn't even want to think what would happen if he died a human death within these walls.

"Well, this is something we're still working on," explained Drew, an expression of discomfort replacing his prior self-assurance. "For now, each of you has only one life. So, if you die, the game will throw you back to the first level's weapons room. Basically, you'll have to start from the beginning."

"I guess we better don't die then," said Lucan, chuckling. "We can't afford to be stuck in some stupid game forever."

"I hate to break it you, buddy, but so far no one has passed the first level. And people who attempted to enter this game were a lot more experienced than the two of you," Drew pointed out, putting his hands on his hips, his discomfort gone. "Don't worry. If you get tired of losing, just knock and I'll let you out."

Gunz glanced at Lucan, but the elf just smirked, shrugging his shoulders. "Losing is not in my nature. Let's go."

"Here goes nothing," murmured Gunz and walked through the door Drew unlocked for them.

CHAPTER 19

~ ZANE BURNS, A.K.A. GUNZ ~

Drew closed the door behind them, and a soft click announced that he had locked it. Gunz looked around, taking in his surroundings. They stood in a small, poorly illuminated room. The air was cool and carried a barely noticeable sweet scent of vanilla. The front wall was semi-transparent, and a dim, bluish light was coming from behind the matted glass with the logo of *Equitum4 Software Inc* on it. A few glass boxes were attached to the wall beneath the logo, and weapons—swords, daggers, throwing knives—levitated inside, slowly and silently rotating like in suspended animation.

Gunz reached for his fire power and magic and noticed that as strange as it was, both were available to him. He opened his other sight and checked the room. Everything inside was breathing with magic, which was expected, but what struck him as weird was that he couldn't see through the glass wall. It seemed like whatever magic had been used to build this barrier blocked his other sight. The weapons in the boxes also shimmered with a soft bluish glow, betraying their magical origin.

"There is nothing virtual about this reality, is there?"

murmured Gunz, narrowing his eyes as he stretched his hand toward one of the boxes.

"Agreed," replied Lucan, grabbing Gunz's wrist to stop him. "Are you sure you want to go any farther? We don't know what lies behind this wall. Even my magic doesn't let me see through it."

Jumping into unknown danger wasn't anything new to Gunz, but he would do everything he could to avoid doing it again. He thought a moment, biting his lip, and then placed his hand over his tattoo, sending a smidge of his fire energy through it.

"Mishka?" he called softly. "Are you with me, my friend?"

Before he finished his statement, the wyvern materialized in the room, levitating between him and Lucan. The elf gasped and hopped aside.

"Why are you carrying a dragon with you?" His cat-eyes widened as he stared at the wyvern.

"Who are you calling a dragon, elf? I'm a mighty wyvern, not some low life dragon," huffed Mishka, spitting a furious fireball in Lucan's direction. Then he turned to Gunz. "Is this elf yours?"

Gunz nodded, stifling laughter. "This is Lucan, Mishka. He's my friend, so be nice for a change."

"A friend?" Mishka cocked his head, his flaming eyes measuring Lucan from head to toe. "How do you manage to find friends who are more ignorant than you are, if it's possible? Has to be a special skill of yours."

"Seems like I have many special skills." Gunz chuckled, noticing an expression of bewilderment on Lucan's face. "Anyway, Mishka, I have a question."

"A question? Ask me! Ask me!" begged the wyvern, hopping up and down in the air in excitement, his mouth stretching into a wide dragon-like grin. "Have you seen me playing Jeopardy? I'm the best at answering questions."

"Yeah, I've seen you playing Jeopardy. You were using your

magic, cheater. Anyway, can you see through this wall?" Gunz asked, pointing at the barrier. "Or better yet, can you manifest on the other side of it and then check the area? In a calm and majestic manner, of course, the way all mighty wyverns do."

"Easy peasy lemon squeezy," sang Mishka and vanished with a light pop, just to reappear almost immediately, confusion showing in the uneven beat of his golden wings. "Hmm... if at first you don't succeed—"

He vanished again.

"He can't go through either." Lucan shook his head, unease reflected in his narrowed eyes.

"Seems that way," said Gunz as Mishka showed up again, angry flames dancing atop his back.

"It's not fair! What kind of dumb magic is this?" he yelled, spinning in the air with a wisp of dark smoke following him.

"It's War's magic," replied Gunz. He approached the wall and moved his hand over its surface without touching it. "His energy signature cannot be mistaken for anything else."

"War?" Mishka landed on Lucan's head, and stared down at Gunz from his height. "As in THE WAR? One of the four Horsemen?"

"Yeah, I know—stupid and reckless," muttered Gunz.

"Then why?" squeaked Mishka. "Do you even know what this thingamajig feels like?"

"What?" asked Gunz and Lucan at the same time.

"You two ignoramuses!" shouted Mishka, dancing on top of Lucan's head, eliciting an annoyed grunt from the elf. "This..." The wyvern's voice trailed as he flew closer to the barrier, pointing at it with its wing. "This barrier has the same magical energy signature as the veil." He twirled in the air, accompanied by a puff of white smoke.

"Excuse me?" Gunz frowned, taking a step closer to the semi-transparent wall. He sharpened his senses, exploring it with his other sight.

"You heard me," said Mishka, landing back on Lucan's head. "This barrier is a mini-veil of sort. I wouldn't be surprised if behind it you'll find some sort of mini reality. A pocket universe, you know?"

Gunz rubbed his forehead and gently tapped the barrier. "You could be right, Mishka. Or it could be just an illusion created by War. He's toying with us." He sighed.

"If you know all that, then why are you still going through with it?" Mishka threw his wings up, staring at him with his rounded, flaming eyes.

"Because, this is our quest," replied Lucan impatiently, waving his hand carefully to get the wyvern off his head, but to no avail. "We must."

"Why would you agree to such a stupid and dangerous quest?" continued the wyvern, slapping the back of the elf's head with his wing.

"Someone has to," replied Gunz.

"Why you?"

"Why not me?" Gunz shrugged.

"It's always you." Mishka pouted. "And every time you're in trouble, I'm the one who has to drop everything and come to clean up your mess and save your fireless ass! That's it! I'm done with it. I'm going back to Kal."

Gunz laughed. "Good idea, my friend. Go to Kal and talk to him about it, since he is the one who sent us on this quest." As bitterness settled somewhere in his chest, he sighed. "Anyway, after this mission, I am done too. I already told Kal that after we find Angel, I'm going back to Kendral. Then you and I can relax and do whatever you want, my friend, volcano diving included."

"Yay!" Mishka danced a happy dance in midair above Lucan's head, showering him with sparks.

Gunz extended his arm and once the wyvern landed on it, he petted his back gently. "Now go, my friend. I don't think you want any part of this not-so-virtual reality we're about to jump into."

"Not a chance." Mishka pressed his mouth into a straight line, but somehow the tips of his fangs were still showing. "I'm not losing you again! I was worried sick all this time when you were missing. Why didn't you call me?"

"I tried," replied Gunz. For a moment, his mind flashing back to his time in the Destiny Council facility. "You couldn't hear me. No one could…" His voice faltered, and he swallowed hard, pushing all the bad memories away.

"I'm not losing you again, firetwat," said Mishka and vanished.

Gunz hissed, pressing his hand to his tattoo as the wyvern merged into it. Without saying anything, Lucan silently pointed up. A red sign appeared above their heads, seemingly hanging in midair, but as Gunz strained his vision, he noticed a dark computer display.

"Please choose your weapons to proceed," he read the sign out loud. "I guess weapons it is."

He approached one of the boxes and touched it. The box dissolved into nothing and a long sword that was locked within it disappeared, materializing in Gunz's hand. Squeezing his fingers around the grip, he moved the sword around and arched his brow at Lucan as the weapon whistled through the air.

Lucan picked a box with two long daggers inside. As soon as he held the weapons in his hands, all light vanished from the room and an impenetrable darkness surrounded them. Something moved and with a loud bang, the floor trembled and disappeared. Gunz cried out as he started to fall into an endless abyss of nothingness. For a moment, everything inside him froze as he felt blind and helpless again. Consumed by fear, he screamed, and suddenly the darkness was gone…

* * *

The steady ground was under his feet.

He could see.

The only problem was, he didn't like the view.

He also didn't appreciate the fact that he couldn't move. Looking from left to right, he found himself tied up to a wooden frame, standing on a tall platform. He could see Lucan's long hair falling over his shoulder, feeling the elf's back pressing against his, so he assumed that he was tied up to the same frame, and they stood back to back.

"Remind me not to buy this game when it comes out," growled Gunz, surveying his surroundings. "The transition between levels sucks."

"Do you know where we are?" Lucan shifted, and the muscles on his back bulged against Gunz's as he strained to break the ropes binding them. "Does it mean anything to you?"

"Yes, unfortunately," hissed Gunz. "We're in the Land of Dreams, in front of the City of Gold. I assume it's not the real nexus, but an illusion created by War's magic. A pocket universe, all right." His eyes fell on the tall white walls and he cringed as the terrible memories of King Alexander and his demonic army flashed before his eyes. "Dammit! I think this asshole is building his illusions based on our memories."

"I hope not," said Lucan, his voice hoarse with strain. "My memories are no fun."

"Neither are mine as you can see." Gunz shuddered, thinking that this whole thing felt a lot more real than any illusion. *Maybe Mishka was right? It is a mini reality...*

The platform they stood on was positioned in front of the main gates into the City of Gold and the entire perimeter of the City was surrounded by a massive army of demons in their pure form. The land was covered in snow and even though it wasn't colder here than in the weapons room, Gunz shivered, reminded of the effect the cold weather had had on him. Everything in this so-called game was realistic, too realistic for his liking, and his stomach twisted as the stench of demonic essence invaded his senses.

The golden domes of the palace rose toward the gray, foggy sky and everything looked just the way he remembered it. He didn't want to remember all this. He wanted to forget everything that had happened from the moment he walked into the City of Gold to the moment when Lucan carried him out of the Destiny Council prison. He didn't need this painful reminder.

"I assume the key to the next level is inside this palace," said Gunz quietly, focusing on the task at hand. "So, we need to fight all these demons and get through the king's guards to get inside."

Lucan chuckled. "Wouldn't be a problem, if we weren't tied up to this goddamn frame."

"Not for long," murmured Gunz, channeling his fire. "How do you feel about fire? Can you protect yourself?"

"Give me a moment…," Lucan whispered something and Gunz felt a touch of elf's magical energy to his senses. "Ready."

Carefully, he probed Lucan's shield and grunted. "It won't be enough," he hissed through clenched teeth. "I'm about to go supernova and your shield is good to withstand a candle."

"Are you going to revert?"

"No." Gunz assessed the distance between the platform and the first line of the demonic army, wondering if his power blast could reach their adversaries. "I can't. I still believe it is just an illusion. And if I'm right, then even though it looks like the Land of Dreams, we're still in the human realm, inside a business district, surrounded by thousands of humans. Maybe it's a pocket universe, but I can't take this chance. I'm not going to revert, but there's going to be a lot of fire and it'll be extremely hot. Brace yourself."

Thinking a second, Gunz muttered a protection spell, wrapping an additional shield around his friend and then let go of his control as much as he could without reverting into the natural state of the Fire Salamander. As the elemental power surged through him, he pushed his head backward against Lucan's back and unlocked his fists. A wild howl tore from his lips as the fire took him over, setting his body ablaze.

He heard Lucan's agonizing scream, but he couldn't do anything to help him. The ropes holding them attached to the wooden frame and the frame itself went up in flames and a second later, crumbled to the ground in a pile of hot ashes. A cloud of dark smoke surrounded them, melting into the foggy, gray sky. Lucan fell to his knees, clutching his throat as he gasped for air. Gunz waved his hand, extinguishing the fire, and then removed the protection spell off of him.

"Are you okay?" he asked, kneeling next to the elf, carefully checking him for injuries.

"Dammit, Burns," exhaled Lucan, sitting back on his heels, "you almost suffocated me with your shield, but I must admit, you know how to bring up the heat."

"Yeah, well..." Gunz eyes darted toward the City walls and he frowned. "Let's see if I also know how to release the Kraken."

A soft whisper rolled over the dark mass of the demonic army and they all stepped forward at the same time, their heavy steps making the ground quake.

"We don't have much time," said Gunz in a quick whisper. "Here is what I think. This level was built especially for me, so my guess, the next one will be yours. Let me take care of these demons. After I'm done, I could be a little bit... um... drained, so I will need your help to fight the guards. Try not to use too much of your magic. Keep your strength for the next level."

"You got it," replied Lucan, but a troubled expression shadowed his face for a split second.

Gunz placed his hand over his tattoo and called Mishka. As usual, the wyvern materialized in front of him right away, but then gasped and twirled around, emitting fountains of sparks.

"Fire Almighty! Déjà vu much?"

"Not déjà vu, Mishka. War, our kind host, wants to play games with me." Gunz let the fire take him over, keeping the elemental energy locked within his body. He roared, rising to Kal's height, flames wrapping around him like slithering serpents. His hair got longer, flowing like a fiery river down his shoulders. "Fine! I am game!" Turning to Mishka, he smiled—a cold and deadly smirk. "Mishka, my friend, can you give me wings?"

"Do I look like a friggin' energy drink to you?" huffed Mishka, but then waved his wings at him. "Fine. Brace yourself!"

As the wyvern merged with him, Gunz threw his head back and spread his arms wide, a low growl rumbling in his chest. Two mighty golden-red wings expanded behind his back and he rose in the air, levitating above the demons. The monsters stopped their slow movement and upturned their heads, watching his every move with malice in their yellow eyes.

Gunz looked down at Lucan. "We are ready." Two voices—his and Mishka's—sounded as one. "Stay back... do not get burned."

Lucan nodded and turned his hands, palms up. A bluish glow of his magic shimmered around him as he erected a powerful shield around himself. Gunz probed his shield and smirked. Lucan had learned his lesson. His new shield was a lot more powerful.

Gunz switched his attention to the demons, and as the first strikes of black lightning bolts and dark energy filled the air around him, he laughed, anger and excitement alike rising in him like a tidal wave.

"*Ignius Amplio!*" he shouted, and his strange double voice bounced off the City walls, reverberating between the hills, disappearing into the distant forest.

In a split second, the entire area between the white walls and the place where the platform used to be was swallowed by a raging fire. The clouds of dark smoke swirled up, lifted by a light breeze and stretched across the gloomy sky over the palace. The stench of burnt demonic flesh made the air thick and the screams of demons devoured by fire rose high above the ground.

For a few minutes, Gunz just levitated above the fiery inferno he unleashed on the demonic army, basking in the power of his own element, adrenalin surging through his system. But as the anger slowly simmered down in him, leaving him hollow and tired, the feeling of joy disappeared.

When the screams had died down and the last demon had turned to ash, he waved his hand, commanding the fire to cease and slowly lowered down next to Lucan. The elf was on his knees with his forehead touching the ground, his arms wrapped around his head. Gunz touched his shoulder, and Lucan lowered his arms, raising his eyes, staring at him in awe.

"We are done…," Gunz breathed out with a soft moan as the wyvern separated from him and then camouflaged himself into his tattoo. Slowly, he assumed his human form and smiled tiredly. "Almost done. Let's go."

"Heaven and Earth…" Lucan wiped perspiration off his forehead with the back of his hand. "I knew you were a Fire Salamander, but I had no idea how powerful you truly were. Now I'm starting to understand why the Destiny Council was doing everything to keep your power and magic blocked. I think they're afraid of you, Burns."

"As well they should be, because I'm coming for them next," replied Gunz softly. With surprise, he realized that there was no anger in his voice. He simply stated the fact. He glanced at the elf and clenched his teeth, a muscle twitching in his jaw.

They approached the gates of the City and stopped, surveying the area. Now that the demonic army was gone, the entrance seemed to be unprotected. There were no guards outside or atop the wall, and as far as Gunz could sense, no one was on the other side waiting for them. He pushed the gates, but they didn't budge.

"Should we knock?" he asked with a crooked smirk on his lips and added without waiting for Lucan's response. "Yeah, I think we should knock. Kal would want me to be polite and behave like a Child of Fire should."

He closed his eyes, reaching for the Codex, and the book presented him with a multitude of spells. With satisfaction, he noticed that the more he used the Dark Codex, the easier it became for him to wield its powerful magic. While he still experienced an excruciating headache every time he connected with the book, the periods of pain were getting shorter with every use, or perhaps he was just getting used to it.

Gunz opened his eyes and placed his hands on the gates, whispering the spell in Dragon tongue. As he continued, a bright white light enveloped him, and the wall started to vibrate. The vibration became stronger, filling their ears with a loud buzz, but Gunz didn't stop. With a thunderous bang, the gates burst inward, disintegrating into a cloud of dust and slivers of wood.

Rising slightly in the air, he plummeted down, landing on one knee, and punched the ground with his fist in the place where the gates used to be just a moment ago. The ground shook and with a deafening bang, the front part of the wall collapsed, falling in a cloud of white powder and debris. As though demolished by an expert demolition team, one section of the wall fell after the next, and soon there was nothing left of it except a pile of mutilated bricks, white rocks and debris. With the wall gone, the entire City stood exposed to the outside world.

Once the dust settled, Gunz glanced at Lucan, and a lopsided grin lifted one side on his mouth. "Knock-knock... Do you think King Alexander and his guards heard me knocking?"

"Those who say elven magic is powerful haven't seen an

angry Great Fire Salamander in action," whispered the elf, respect shining in his spring-green eyes. "Remind me to never get on your bad side."

Gunz pulled his sword out, drawing a figure eight in the air. "When it comes to my friends, I don't think I have a bad side. At least you'll have to work really hard to discover it." He pointed at the palace with his sword. "Now, let's get that goddamn key and move on to the next level."

They followed the main city street all the way to the palace. To his shock, the main entrance wasn't protected either. He shuddered, recalling his escape from the City of Gold. The last time his path had also seemed unobstructed until he was drenched with icy water and thrown half-naked into the snow, that is.

"No way in hell I'm doing that again," he muttered, stopping in front of the tall entrance door. Connecting with the Codex, he redirected the flow of his magic to his hands. An undiluted ray of pure magical energy erupted from his palms and blasted the door. It flew off its hinges, sliding over the tiled floor. Gunz raised his sword and crossed the threshold.

The main lobby was dark, but he could see the dark shapes of the king's guards surrounding them, a few of them lying motionless on the floor. He exchanged a quick glance with Lucan and saw excitement reflected in his cat-eyes. Without saying a word to each other, they sprang into action, cutting through their opponents like they were nothing.

Just like in real life, the king's guards weren't as skilled with their swords as he was, and their courage was questionable, nonexistent even. Neither Gunz nor Lucan had to use their magic, and a few minutes later, they were done. Standing over a pile of dead bodies, Gunz stared at the dark staircase leading to the second floor, and his chest shuddered with ragged breaths as he fought to keep his memories of this place from taking over.

This is just a goddamn game. None of it is real...

"Where to now?" He heard Lucan's voice and snapped around. The elf stood right behind him, clutching the bloodied daggers in his hands, thick, dark drops slipping from the blades.

Gunz extended his arm with the sword, pointing up toward the stairs. "If this game is built based on my memories, I know exactly where to go."

He ran up the stairs, hopping two steps at the time and didn't stop until he reached the spacious lobby. He stood, glowering at the room where he had been tormented by the evil king, where Mrak Delar had suffered for days, and violent rage swept through him, making his body tremble. Scorching flames broke through his skin, rushing up and down his arms, and his fingers squeezed the grip of his sword, setting its blade ablaze.

"Burns..."

Gunz turned to Lucan, a low growl rumbling in his chest, and the elf shied away from him.

"It's just a game, Burns. Try to remember." Lucan approached him carefully, holding his hand up and in front of himself, as if he were trying to placate a wild beast. "War is trying to get under your skin, and he seems to be successful. Clear your mind and pull yourself together."

Gunz took a deep breath but didn't bother suppressing his runaway fire. Blazing with scorching flames, he approached the door and kicked it with his foot, sending it flying off its hinges. For a moment, he lingered in the doorway as his eyes halted on the back of the man whom he hated so deeply it made his teeth ache. Then he crossed into the room and stopped a foot away from him.

"King Alexander!" Gunz growled and there was nothing human in his deep voice.

The man turned around and gawked at Gunz, arrogance and loathing reflected on his narrow features.

"Salamander," hissed the king, clenching the bony fists of his skinny arms.

"Finally, I can give you what you deserve," exhaled Gunz, and before the king could say or do anything, he thrust his sword upward into his jaw.

The blade exited through the top of the king's skull with a nauseating crunch and thick streams of blood ran down the shiny metal to his arm, permeating the air with a coppery scent. Gunz shuddered with rage, observing the bulging eyes and the expression of horror imprinted on the king's face, and then yanked the sword out.

The dead body collapsed to the floor and dissipated in a fountain of golden sparks, leaving a small golden key lingering in the air in front of Gunz. He reached for it and carefully wrapped his fingers around it. As soon as he took the key, a door shining with a bright bluish light materialized in front of him.

Gunz looked up at Lucan and smiled, exhaustion settling in his shoulders. "What did they say about not going for the light?"

He touched the door with the key and the eye-watering glow enveloped both of them.

CHAPTER 20

~ ZANE BURNS, A.K.A. GUNZ ~

The light dwindled down, and when the red and black spots stopped dancing in his vision, Gunz found himself standing in a semi-dark room. It looked exactly the same as the first room they had entered when they started the game. His eyes halted on a few glass boxes with new sets of weapons rotating inside them. Each box had a price in coins marked at the top. A red sign lingered above.

"Please choose your weapons to proceed to the second level. You have 10,560 coins," Lucan read and visibly cringed. "You were right, Burns. This level is built for me."

"How do you know?" asked Gunz, observing the set of weapons with curiosity.

Lucan pointed at the boxes. Just like in the first level, most of the weapons were swords, throwing knives and daggers, but the blades of the swords and daggers were curved, and the pommels had strange symbols engraved on them. Besides all that, there were bows and arrows which hadn't been available in the first level.

"These weapons look like the ones my clan used during the —," he started to say, but cut himself off and shrank back, his pale skin almost blue in the dim light of the room. "If that is what I think it is, I can't..." He bowed his head, his long hair falling over his face. "I'm sorry, Salamander, but I can't live through all that again."

Gunz approached him, thinking with remorse that he was about to talk a man into going through his personal hell once again and how much he wished he didn't have to do it. He didn't know what kind of memory War had fished out of Lucan's mind to create this next level, but there was something there the elf was terrified to think about.

"Lucan," he started softly, putting his hand on the elf's arm. "Look at me, my friend."

The elf raised his eyes, meeting Gunz's steady gaze. "I know, it's not real, Zane, but I don't think I can survive it again... even if it's just an illusion..." His voice trailed off, and undiluted fear reflected in his widened eyes.

Just the fact that he called him Zane instead of Burns told Gunz how deeply terrified and shaken Lucan was.

"Lucan, it's okay to be scared. If you know how to control it, fear doesn't have to be your enemy," said Gunz with a deep sigh. "We don't know what lies behind this wall, and I'm sure you are right. War used one of your most painful memories, just like he used mine, to construct the illusion. But I also know for a fact that the Horseman was expecting us to arrive here. Probably has for a while."

Lucan frowned and stepped away from him until he reached the wall and there was no more space to back out. "Why would you think so?"

Gunz chuckled. "You realize that we are still in California, inside a modern business center, surrounded by humans and human technology, right?"

Lucan nodded.

"I just used my magic to conjure an enormous amount of real, physical fire, obliterating War's illusion into ashes, yet did you hear any fire alarms or smoke detectors going off?" asked Gunz with a soft chuckle. "The sensors they attached to me are also fireproof since they survived me wielding my element.

"So, it's either Mishka was right and every level of this game is located in a separate pocket universe, or all these so-called game rooms are fire-proofed, and the fire proofing spell is quite potent. I'm not a hundred percent sure, so I'm not going to take a chance to test my theory, but I'm almost positive that no matter what these rooms are, they're built to withstand the Fire Salamander's natural state. And that tells me that War has been expecting my visit for a while."

"So what?" asked Lucan, rubbing his knuckles with his thumb. "Even if it's true, it doesn't change anything."

"It does, Lucan. Let me explain," objected Gunz. "What you have just witnessed was one of my most recent memories. But it wasn't how it ended in real life." He fell silent, searching Lucan's expressionless face. "In real life, I didn't get a chance to kill the evil king. He got the best of me, tortured me until the Ancient Master arrived and saved me. Mrak Delar was the one who killed the king, not me."

He rubbed his forehead tiredly, and for a split second closed his eyes, biting his lip.

"I hate to even think like that," he continued, his voice barely audible, "but by killing this evil asshole in the game, I felt like... As strange as it sounds... it helped a little. It was the closure I needed."

Lucan huffed with a half-shrug. "You're not suggesting that one of the Horsemen—War—is trying to help us. You can't be serious."

"God, no. War couldn't care less about any of us." Gunz laughed bitterly. "But I knew one of the Horsemen, the scariest one of all. Death. He was honest and fair..." He pinched the bridge of his nose and his forehead creased as pain gripped at his heart. "He was a friend... Angel would do the right thing no matter what. So, what I'm trying to say is that War is playing some kind of messy cat-and-mouse game with us, but whatever he is doing, he has a reason for it and unless we push through it, we'll never find out."

"Zane..." Lucan turned his head to the side and leaned his back against the wall, his arms dangling powerlessly.

"Lucan, through everything we've been together, I've never seen you so... terrified," said Gunz. "Whatever it is that pains you so much... we'll go through it together. I'll stand by your side, my friend. I promise, I'll never leave you behind, no matter what happens there."

The elf swallowed and nodded, but his pale face was still contorted with pain and the haunted expression never left his darkened eyes. Pushing himself away from the wall, he approached the glass boxes and touched one with the bow and arrows, selecting his weapon. Gunz stopped in front of the box with a sword and a dagger inside and slipped Lucan a calm glance.

"Ready?" he asked, and once Lucan nodded, he touched the box.

As soon as he did, a belt with a sword and a dagger sheathed in simple leather scabbards materialized around his waist. Something clicked, and the room submerged under the cover of gray nothingness. The wind howled and the air spun around them in a continuous nauseating motion. Gunz felt weightless as if he was lifted by a tornado, his body sprawled in the air, oblivious to the commands of his mind.

A moment later, the wind ceased, and he hit the ground hard, losing his breath.

* * *

GUNZ FELT the steady ground under his back and pushed himself up into a sitting position, gasping for air. Looking to the side, he saw Lucan on one knee with his fists planted into the ground and his head bowed so low his white hair brushed the dirt.

Quickly surveying his surroundings, Gunz got up to his feet, unsheathing his curved sword. They were in a deep, dark forest. Giant trees the likes of which he had never seen before stretched high, their massive branches weighed down by hefty crowns obscuring the sky. The air was fresh and cool, infused with the scents of wet dirt, fresh grass and wildflowers. Liana vines stretched from tree to tree, covered in small leaves and patches of moss, and a thick rag of foliage was soft and damp under his feet.

Despite the calm, Gunz could sense the heavy presence of his element in the area and a barely noticeable smell of smoke hung in the air, mixed in with the other scents of the forest. Sharpening all his senses, the screams of fear and pain reached his ears, and he tapped on Lucan's shoulder. The elf got up, his chest rising and falling with ragged breaths as if he just ran a half-marathon.

"Lucan, is this what you expected?" Gunz threw a sideways glance at him.

"Yes...," the elf breathed out, staring intently ahead, where the bright red flares of fire broke through the darkness of the forest.

"I sense my element," whispered Gunz. "It's overwhelming. Are you ready to face your fears, my friend?"

Lucan didn't answer, but a deep shudder rushed through him as he got up, taking his bow off his shoulder and pulling an arrow out of the quiver. They ran through the forest and with each step they took, the screams of horror and pain got louder. The clatter of metal on metal and the wild crackling of fire fused into a continuous pandemonium, and a general atmosphere of chaos and fear was palpable.

At the edge of the forest, Lucan came to a screeching halt

and squatted, hiding behind thick shrubbery. Once Gunz lowered down next to him, he separated the shrubbery and peeked through the opening. The view which unfolded in front of him made Gunz hold his breath, clenching his teeth in anger.

A wide field was surrounded by a sizable army comprised of different supernatural beings. Sharpening his already stretched senses, Gunz detected vampires, werewolves, and demons. There were also other beings of magic, but he didn't recognize their energy signatures. Clad in heavy armor and armed to the teeth, they encircled the entire field and what looked like a small village situated at the other end of it.

Every house was set ablaze and the entire space of the field was covered in dead bodies of elves intermingled with corpses of their enemies, blood soaking the ground, coloring the grass scarlet. The way the dead bodies were sprawled around suggested that every single elf, including women and children, put up a mighty fight before perishing under the overwhelming forces of their opponents.

In the center of the field, five giant pyres were erected, surrounded by the opposing army. A raging fire was set into the piles of dry wood and scorching flames rose, wrapping around their helpless victims, slowly devouring their contorted bodies one lick at a time.

The reek of burnt flesh, blood and sweat was so heavy, Gunz had to hold his breath to suppress the rising nausea. He glanced at Lucan, terrified to even think how the elf must be feeling reliving all these horrors again. Lucan looked like an unmoving statue, his shoulders tensed, his emerald eyes veiled with grief.

"Lucan," whispered Gunz, carefully touching his shoulder. The elf gave a start and snapped his head toward him, but Gunz wasn't sure he actually could see him. "What do you want me to do?"

Lucan shuddered and closed his eyes, a deep wrinkle materializing between his eyebrows as he frowned.

"Extinguish the pyres, if you can," he said, his voice so deep and low, it sounded like a feral growl. "And then we'll kill... Every... Single... One of them." He pronounced his last words clear, one word at the time, and then added something in the elven language Gunz couldn't understand, but by the look on his face it wasn't anything good.

"Cover me," Gunz whispered and pushed his way through the bushes into the open field.

No one paid attention to him and before anyone noticed his approach, Gunz connected with his element and stretched his arm toward the pyres.

"Cease," he yelled, his voice deep with anger commanding the fire to obey.

Not only the pyres but all fire died out at once, as if someone had just sucked out all the oxygen from the area, creating a perfect vacuum. The houses stood half-destroyed by the flames, dark clouds of smoke rising above the malformed ruins. With glassless windows, blackened support beams protruding from the walls and the caved in roofs, they looked like skeletons, just as dead as the elves who used to occupy them.

Five elves, who were condemned to be burned at the stake, hung limply in their restraints, their heads bowed low, and Gunz couldn't say whether they were dead or alive. Their formerly long hair was burned to the roots and most of their skin was either incinerated by scorching flames or covered in blisters, melting with whatever was left of their clothing.

The invaders snapped around, glowering at him, and he couldn't stop the lopsided smirk from appearing on his face as he observed their infuriated faces. He raised his sword to his shoulder, flicking his eyebrow at a vampire nearest to him and hissed, "Come get me, asshole."

As the vampire charged him, moving so fast he was nothing more than a blur, Gunz connected with his magic, set his curved sword ablaze, and opened his other sight. With speed that could rival any vamp, he sidestepped his opponent and swung his sword, decapitating him in one fluid motion. A few more assailants turned around and rushed him, but before they could come close enough to engage him, they fell, arrows glowing with elven magic protruding from their chests.

The vampires disintegrated into ash as soon as the wooden arrows sent by Lucan's steady hand penetrated their non-beating hearts. The demons weren't in their pure form and their hosts' dead bodies were as easy a target to the elf's arrows as to Gunz's flaming sword. It was harder to kill werewolves, but the fire was an equal opportunity destroyer, devouring any creature of magic with ease.

"Ignius!" Gunz roared, and the next group of attackers went up in flames, their wild howls of pain rising over the bodies of their victims.

"Burn them all..."

Gunz turned to see Lucan standing by his side with a new arrow nocked to his bow, an expression of outrage distorting his hardened features. His hand squeezed his weapon till his knuckles turned white, trembling with unadulterated fury, and his chest shuddered with uneven breaths.

Sensing how deeply his friend suffered reliving the worst moment of his life, Gunz nodded and increased the flow of his element. *"Ignius Amplio!"*

A few minutes later, the fight was over. Except Gunz and Lucan, no one was standing, nothing was moving, and a deafening silence enveloped the field that looked like a scene from a horror movie.

"Lucan...," Gunz called once he caught his breath.

The elf turned to him, regarding him with his lifeless gaze, and there was no recognition in his eyes. There was nothing there except endless torment.

"Lucan, I'm sorry, but this level was yours..." Gunz cringed inwardly at the thought that he had to bother him with a stupid question at such a grievous moment. "Do you know where to look for the key?"

"I don't know. Give me a moment, please," whispered the elf, his lips barely moving.

He touched Gunz's shoulder while staring straight ahead at the pyres where the disfigured shapes of elves were still attached to the stakes. Without saying anything else, he moved forward, stepping over the dead bodies of his people and their killers.

Gunz followed him, nausea rising to his throat with every step he took. While he remembered that all of this wasn't real, just an illusion created by War to play this stupid and cruel game with them, he couldn't help feeling sick. As he approached the pyres, he carefully started checking the victims' vitals to see if any of them were still alive. They were dead. Their bodies, malformed by fire and blackened by smoke, were still attached to the stakes, their faces distorted by pain no one in the right mind could survive.

Suddenly, a soft, barely audible moan sounded from the left. Before Gunz could react, Lucan dropped his bow and in one jump, reached the person on the left-most pyre. His hands ripped the enfeebled restraints apart. It was hard to say, but Gunz thought it was a woman. Lucan took her into his arms and carried her off the pyre. Going down to his knees, he pulled her to his chest, slowly rocking back and forth as if she were a child he was trying to put to sleep.

She opened her eyes, and her turquoise gaze as deep as an ocean on a sunny day met Lucan's. Her cracked, dry lips quirked up at the corners just a little.

"Lucárion...," she whispered, and it was clear that every word she said was taking all the strength she had in her dying body. "You're here... you came for me..."

"Elora...," Lucan moaned. Silent tears escaped his eyes,

running down his cheeks, dropping on her face. "I am... so sorry... I wasn't here to protect you..."

Her angled eyes closed for a moment and she swallowed with effort. Then she forced herself to open her eyes again and her hand that rested on her chest twitched as if she was trying to lift it. He seized it gently and brought it to his lips, kissing her blistered, raw skin, then he pressed her palm lightly to his cheek.

"I love you, Luca...," she whispered. "Now the blue-sky eternity is ours"—she sucked in some air, something wheezing in her chest—"and no one... can take you away from me..."

"Elora..." His body trembled with grief and agonizing sobs as he pressed his lips to her hand. "I love you too... I'm sorry I've never had a chance to tell you that... You are... were my heart and my soul. I will always love you..."

She smiled and a soft breath escaped her lips, her heart stopping forever as her gaze never left his.

"I love you...," he moaned, gently pressing her to his chest.

At his words, her body dissipated into a fountain of golden sparks and a small golden key lingered in the air above Lucan's hands. For a split-second, the elf stared at it bewildered as if he couldn't remember where he was or why he was here. Then he grabbed the key and got up to his feet.

A large door shining with a bright blue light materialized before them. Without looking back, Lucan touched the door with the key and the blinding light swallowed them both.

CHAPTER 21

~ ZANE BURNS, A.K.A. GUNZ ~

As soon as the door closed behind them, Lucan slid to the floor with his back pressed against the door. Gunz glanced up at the usual red sign urging them to choose their weapons and move on to the next level. The amount of coins they had was enormous. He ignored the sign and lowered himself down to the floor next to the elf. They didn't talk. There was nothing to say. Lucan was deeply shaken, and he was trying to deal with it the best he could, and Gunz wasn't going to rush him.

Minutes had passed when Lucan finally lifted his head and threw his hair off his face, glancing sideways at Gunz.

"You were right, Zane," he said, his voice raspy.

"About what?"

"The closure... I told her, you know... that I loved her and that I was sorry I couldn't save her...," he whispered, squeezing his hands together, his nails digging into his own skin. "What you had witnessed wasn't an exact replica of what had happened then."

Gunz nodded, not daring to ask any questions in fear of disturbing his friend's old wounds.

"I couldn't save her," said Lucan, dropping his head to his chest. "I couldn't save any of them. In real life, I was on my knees, restrained and held by three vamps as they forced me to watch her dying in the fire..."

"Who were those people and why did they attack you?"

"Mercenaries. I have no idea who they worked for, but it had to be someone of extreme power since they were able to block elven magic." Lucan shrugged, resting his arms on top of his bent knees. "My clan was one of the warrior clans, protectors of the realm." He rubbed his forehead, a painful smirk curving his lips. "And I was a common soldier in love with the daughter of the clan chieftain. An impossible relationship, you know?"

Gunz nodded, and Lucan sighed, dropping his arm by his side with a heavy thud.

"Anyway, it was many years ago... in a land far away from here," he said. "Elven wars... A terrible time, indeed. You can ask your friend, Mrak Delar. Although it happened before his time."

"Where is your realm, Lucan?"

"Kendral," replied the elf. "The northern forests, far away from the main city."

"I spent over a year in Kendral," said Gunz. "I had no idea there were elves there."

Lucan chuckled humorously. "Kendral is a lot bigger and more complicated than you realize, little Salamander. There are lands that stretch for miles outside the Elemental realms." His emerald eyes got veiled with distant memories and a shadow of deep sorrow crossed his hard features once more. "I can never go back there..." His voice trailed into a whisper.

"Why?" asked Gunz. "I'm sure the Master of Kendral would welcome you with an open heart. Alliandr is—"

"Alliandr?" asked the elf, interrupting him. "You're on a first name basis with the young Master of Kendral?"

"Alliandr is my friend." Gunz chuckled. "I met him when he just took over the Power and the throne. We go way back."

Lucan nodded. "Trust me... Master Alliandr is not going to let me back in. I can never go back there. Besides, my clan has been destroyed. Whoever survived the massacre, including myself, has been sold into slavery into different realms. There is nothing there for me."

Lucan got up, his every movement slow and heavy, and offered his hand to Gunz.

"Let's go, Burns," he said as Gunz took his hand and got up to his feet. "Let's finish this evil game once and for all."

Gunz regarded the glass boxes and cringed. Judging by the set of weapons inside, the next level was his. Even though he expected it, he was terrified to think about what the next illusion could be. Glancing at the amount of coins they had, he turned to Lucan.

"I think we should select a couple of weapons each," he suggested.

He approached the box with a sniper rifle inside and touched it. The box vanished and he ended up with a duffle bag in his hand. He placed it on the floor and checked its contents. Inside, he found a VKS sniper rifle and a few boxes with ammunition. Walking along the wall, Gunz stopped in front a smaller box with a Swiss army knife inside, identical to his own. He shook his head in disbelief and touched the box. As usual, the box disappeared, and the knife materialized in his hand.

"These look like the modern-day weapons of the human realm," said Lucan, sending a look full of sympathy in Gunz's direction. "Next level must be yours?" He found a box with a bow and arrows and another one with a sword.

"Let's get it over with," muttered Gunz as the floor dissipated beneath his feet and he fell into the sickening nowhere.

* * *

As the darkness melted away, the last rays of the setting sun illuminated the area, making Gunz's blood run cold. He stood on a hill, staring down at a sandy mountain. Surrounded by green forests, it looked dead, cold and sinister in its nakedness. Dark silhouettes of people were prominent at the foot of the mountain, and their magical signatures were screaming Masters of Dark Arts.

"No," he growled, his chest rising and falling with heavy breaths. "NO! Not this!" He punched the air as a suffocating fury enveloped him, taking his breath away. "Motherfucker! Out of all the shit stored in my head, he had to fish this out??? When I'm done with this goddamn game, I'm going to rip him apart with my bare hands!"

As anger surged through him, the fire broke through his skin, tiny flames dancing on his arms and shoulders. He took a few deep breaths and closed his eyes, getting in control of his element.

"What is this place?" whispered Lucan, his hand clutching his throat as if he couldn't breathe. "It's... evil. We shouldn't be here."

"No shit! This is Mount Karasova," replied Gunz through gritted teeth, dropping his duffle bag onto the grassy surface of the hill. "The un-resting place of the Lord of Chaos, cursed by the Slavic god of the Three Realms, mighty Veles himself." He pointed at the mountain. "I know exactly where we're going to find that last key."

"What do you want me to do, Burns?" asked Lucan and stepped back as Gunz turned to him, a wave of heat expanding around him.

"Stop calling me Burns!" he yelled, his hands squeezing into tight fists.

"Zane, I'm sorry," said Lucan quietly. "Please, tell me what I can do to help."

Gunz pressed the heel of his hands to his eyes and stilled,

breathing hard. A moment later, he lowered his arms and met Lucan's gaze.

"I'm sorry, Lucan. That was uncalled for." He inhaled a ragged breath, making an effort to restrain his raging emotions. "On the serious side though. Stop calling me Burns. Every time you say that I feel like I need to take you to the nearest hospital or a burns center." He sighed. "My friends call me Zane or Gunz."

Lucan just nodded, saying nothing.

Gunz glanced down and smirked. This illusion was almost identical to his real memory of the fight for Mount Karasova, but it wasn't quite the same. He wasn't the same person he had been then. He squatted next to the bag and pulled his rifle out, loading it. His military training took over, calming down his battered nerves. Straightening out, he pointed toward the dark wizards by the mountain.

"Lucan, do you think your arrows can reach that far?" he asked.

"With some help, yes," replied the elf and pulled an arrow out, readying his bow.

"Okay," said Gunz, "I'm going to silence the area and we'll take out as many of them as we can. After that, conjure the most powerful shield around yourself you can and let me do all the talking."

Lucan gave him a curt nod and stretched his bow, the bow string touching his tightly pressed lips.

"*Silenties*," whispered Gunz, lowering himself down to the ground.

As an impenetrable silence enveloped the area, he held the stock of his rifle to his shoulder, aiming at the dark figure in front of the mountain. He exhaled and softly pressed the trigger, feeling the familiar jerk of the kickback. He watched one of the men falling and right away another one fell, an arrow infused with elven magic in his chest.

The scent of gunpowder mixed in with the metallic odor of ammunition touched his senses, bringing back more memories, most of them unpleasant. He reloaded his rifle and aimed again. Lucan kept sending his arrows flying, every shot taking one of the dark wizards down.

Gunz wasn't sure what triggered the change, but all the remaining wizards turned around and ran toward the hill. The air buzzed with the strikes of magical energy and electrical discharges. Throwing his rifle to the ground, Gunz got up, staring at Mount Karasova and the approaching wizards with disdain.

"*Incanto Comlium,*" he muttered, removing the silencing spell, and turned to Lucan. "I don't know about you, but I'm done playing by War's rules. Do me a favor, stay back and take care of your safety."

Without looking back at the elf, Gunz walked down the hill. He didn't channel his elemental power as he normally would have done. Instead, he reached for his magic and the magical energy around him spiked to a new high.

"*Ventius,*" he roared, pointing at the mountain. "*Ventius Amplio.*"

The winds picked up, seemingly blowing from every direction. Gunz muttered another spell, collecting the winds between his wide-spread arms and spinning them into a gargantuan twister. As the twister moved toward Mount Karasova, dark stormy clouds veiled the sky. Gunz followed the storm, adding more magic into its already turbulent nature.

"*Ignius Amplio,*" he hissed, weaving the fire into the winds and soon, a raging inferno unfolded over the mountain.

As pandemonium broke loose, Gunz closed his eyes, throwing his head back, and screamed, releasing his bottled-up rage. He let the elements rampage wild for a few long minutes, then he took a deep breath and waved his hand, extinguishing the fire and dropping all the magical energy.

The dust and debris settled down, slowly unveiling a new view. Mount Karasova was gone. In place where it once stood, there was nothing but a large stone table, a reflection of silvery moonlight throwing sinister flairs at the deep grooves of the designs on its surface.

Heading toward the table, Gunz switched to a run. He reached for the Swiss army knife he had taken from the glass box, wondering if it would work. But as he called his sword's name, to his surprise, the knife vanished from his hand, replaced by an exact replica of his sword.

He raised it, infusing the blade with his magic and elemental power, ready to crash it onto the table, when a deep fracture split its surface and a moment later, the table exploded with a thunderous bang. Reacting to the explosion, he dropped to the ground, covering his head with his arm, holding his sword in the other and quickly muttered a spell, erecting a protection shield over himself.

As the distant echo of the blast disappeared into the night sky, he lowered his arm and scrambled to his knees. Raising his head, he saw a woman standing over him, her foot tapping impatiently. Gunz tried to get up, but she raised her arm, whispering something under her breath, and he froze in place, an icy wave spreading through his body. Unable to make a move, he calmly met her dark gaze.

"Angelique…," he croaked, but then cleared his throat and smirked. "I mean, Zmey. You're not her."

She leaned forward, gently brushing her fingers through his hair, slowly moving her hand to cup his cheek.

"This is where you're wrong, lover," she said, and her voice—the voice of the woman he loved so much—cut through his heart like a deadly dagger. "I'm more her than you could ever imagine. I have her memories, her emotions, her feelings. Her soul is merged with mine. Your Angie and I are like this, Salamander." She crossed her fingers, showing them to him. "Best pals for eternity."

Gunz grunted, fighting against the restraints of Zmey's magic, in his mind hoping that Lucan listened to him and stayed back in the safety of the forest.

"She loves you more than you know," continued Zmey. "Right now, her soul is bleeding for you. I can feel it."

"You don't have a soul, Zmey," growled Gunz.

The monster smiled and his malignant smirk distorted Angelique's tender features into a terrible, evil mask. He bent down, cupping Gunz's face with his hands that looked and felt so much like hers and upturned his head, staring directly into his eyes.

"Now you're mine, lover," Zmey grumbled, the hiss of a serpent escaping Angelique's lips. "There is nothing you can do to fight me. The Great Fire Salamander. The guardian of all good and pure. The protector of human realms." He laughed, his laughter musical and clear just like Angie's, yet laced with venom and darkness. "Protector my ass. You're nothing but a scared, little boy who tried to play with fire and got burned."

Gunz jerked and pushed against Zmey's magic but couldn't break free. Abruptly, he heard a soft whistle and an arrow flew past him, grazing his skin with its tip. He gasped, reacting to a sudden zing of pain, but as the energy of elven magic spread through him, he felt the restraints of Zmey's dark magic lighten up.

Thank you, Lucan, he thought, connecting with the Dark Codex. Fueled by his boiling rage, the Codex provided him with a number of spells. He hissed in pain and clenched his teeth, his mind processing the new information. A brilliant white light surrounded him, dissipating the remaining dark magic, and he rose to his feet, his fingers squeezing the grip of his sword.

"Angie," he said more to himself than to the illusion in front of him. "I love you and I will never give up on you. You're my perfect world."

He swung his sword, and in one powerful strike, decapitated Zmey who was still in Angelique's form. As he watched her head hit the ground with a repugnant thud, an expression of disbelief still reflected on her beautiful features, he exhaled and swayed a little.

"You're not her, Zmey," he repeated, his voice shaking with anger. "You will never be her."

Waves spread through Angelique's headless body and it started to morph, slowly changing into that of Zmey. Gunz stepped over it, positioning his feet on either side and raised his sword once more. Once the transformation was completed, he plummeted his sword down, piercing Zmey's chest with *Ardenium* steel.

A terrible chaos, violent and deafening, enveloped the area, and the ground trembled. Ignoring the racket, Gunz remained standing, holding his sword down, pinning Zmey's body to the rocky surface.

Suddenly, the mayhem was over and Zmey exploded into a fountain of golden sparks. In front of Gunz's face, a small golden key was lingering in midair. He grabbed it, wrapping his fingers around it, and his tightly pressed teeth squeaked. As a door materialized in front of him, he hurtled the key at it with all the strength he had.

A blinding whiteness surrounded him, and he raised his arms, protecting his eyes.

CHAPTER 22

~ ZANE BURNS, A.K.A. GUNZ ~

Gunz rubbed his eyes and blinked a few times, adjusting his vision. Once he could see again, he stared at the computer screen with a large red sign: "Congratulations! Game over!"

"Damn right, game over," growled Gunz, taking a few deep breaths to get in control of his ragged nerves. His hands were still shaking, and anger was still spiking the adrenalin and fire in his system, but he managed to rip the game sensors off his skin, throwing them to the floor. "Lucan? Are you okay?"

"I think so," replied Lucan. "Zane—"

Before the elf could finish, the door opened and Drew rushed in, his eyes sparkling with excitement.

"Whoa! Dudes!" he yelled. "You are the first two peeps who passed through all three levels! I'm stoked!"

Gunz turned around to face him, his rage subsiding little by little, getting replaced by something a lot scarier than that—deadly determination. Heavily, he walked toward the young man and halted a step away from him. With the speed and precision of a snake, his arm snapped forward, seizing his neck in a vice-like grip. He pinned Drew against the wall, eliciting a yelp of fear out of him.

"If you know what's best for you," he said, his voice steady and calm, "you will escort us to your boss right now. No. More. Games."

He let go, and Drew stepped to the side, trying to put some distance between them as he clutched his throat with his hand.

"Whoa, man," he said fearfully, "didn't they teach you in kindergarten to keep your hands to yourself?"

Gunz cocked his head, raising his eyebrows. "Now would be a good time."

"And no need to threaten me," said Drew indignantly, his eyes flashing from Gunz to Lucan. "I was going to take you to Mr. Warrington's office anyway. He's expecting you." He opened the door, gesturing for them to follow and walked out.

Drew walked into a large waiting area and headed toward the front desk where a young man sat, typing something on his computer, hitting the keys as though they were his personal enemies. When Drew approached the desk, he lifted his head and stared at him with a silent question in his eyes.

"Hey, Justin, Mr. Warrington is expecting these two." He waved over his shoulder at Gunz and Lucan. "Can you please let him know that his war experts are here?"

"Please, sit down," said Justin flatly, readjusting his headset. "Can I get you anything while you're waiting?"

"I don't think so," growled Gunz.

Followed by Lucan, he walked past Drew toward a tall door and kicked it in with his foot. The door flew open, hitting the wall with a loud bang. Both Drew and Justin screamed something behind his back, but he couldn't care less.

Gunz halted in the doorway of a large, brightly lit office. Even though there was enough space, the room was furnished with the laconism of a warrior—no unnecessary luxury or pointless decorations. A large mahogany desk was situated at the far end, but besides dual monitors, a standard office phone unit and a digital tablet, there was nothing else on top of it. Except for three leather armchairs—one behind the desk and two in front, there was nothing else in the room. The walls painted in a light gray color were bare, absent family photos or any kind of artwork.

With his hands balled into fists, Gunz stared at the man behind the desk. The man got up, a light smirk tugging at his lips as he observed first Gunz and then Lucan. Justin squeezed past them, mumbling his apologies, but Mr. Warrington just waved his hand, telling him to leave and close the door.

The infamous Horseman wasn't what Gunz had expected. He wasn't tall, no more than five-foot-nine, but he had an athletic build and even his stylish business suit couldn't conceal his well-defined muscles. He looked like a man in his late forties, but Gunz knew that this powerful supernatural being was as old as creation itself.

His pale gray eyes were as hard as steel. They measured Gunz and Lucan with an attentiveness beyond regular curiosity, and Gunz felt as if War was scanning him, searching for something only he knew about.

"I hope you don't mind, I let myself in," said Gunz, his voice as cold as Mr. Warrington's eyes, but a layer of sarcasm was undeniable in his every word.

War smirked, a lopsided smile lifting one corner of his mouth, and pointed at the two large armchairs in front of his desk.

"Not at all," he replied lightly, lowering into his own chair. "Please sit down, son."

"Son?" huffed Gunz, throwing his hands in the air. "Why is it every supernatural asshole loves to call me that? I'm not your son."

Mr. Warrington's smile grew wider, and his eyes sparkled with humor. "But you are my sons. Both of you," he purred, gesturing at the chairs again. "War is what makes your hearts beat. Maybe some people live for love, but you two are alive only when you fight."

Gunz and Lucan exchanged a look and walked toward the desk where they kept standing, staring down at War. He leaned back in his armchair, making a steeple out of his fingers, meeting their eyes calmly. Then he ran his hand over the dark stubble on his cleft chin and smirked his lopsided smirk again.

"Please sit down." He pointed at the chairs once more. "We need to talk."

Gunz and Lucan exchanged a quick look, and as much as Gunz wanted to wipe the grin off of War's face, he pulled the armchair back and sat down, folding his arms over his chest.

"You two are more alike than you think," continued Mr. Warrington, his glacial eyes flashing from Gunz to Lucan and back to Gunz. "You both went through a lot, learning what war was all about from a young age. You both witnessed the death of the woman you loved more than yourselves. And you both found solace in war later."

"How so?" asked Lucan, leaning forward slightly, his hands grasping at the arms of his chair.

"You, Lucan, were forced to watch the only woman you'd ever loved perish in flames," said Mr. Warrington. "It destroyed you, and despite the fact that it wasn't your fault, you blamed yourself. You were grieving—you still are—and the only way you could deal with your grief without going insane was by spilling blood. Even though it wasn't the blood of those who wronged you, it helped. Didn't it? You gave in to your slavers and obeyed their command in exchange for a sword. War was your painkiller, am I right, elf?"

Lucan dropped his head, falling back in his chair, and closed his eyes, swallowing hard. Mr. Warrington smirked and switched his attention to Gunz.

"No," growled Gunz, his forced calmness slowly abandoning him. "Don't you dare say it. Don't you dare say her name."

"Fine. I'll say yours instead. Vladislav Kirilenko. Zane Burns. Gunz," continued War, bending the fingers on his hand as he counted. "You, Child of Fire... You are changing your name faster than I'm changing my gloves. You hide behind your names, or behind your friends, or behind your silent anger. But in the end, you are a Child of War as much as you are a Child of Fire.

"You were just eighteen when you experienced *real* war for the first time—your first tour of duty. Being a part of Captain Svetlov's special unit, with your trusted friends by your side, even in the midst of hostile territory, you felt more comfortable than back at home. In a war zone, you knew who your friends and who your enemies were. It was easy. Simple..."

Mr. Warrington's voice faded away, and he took a short pause, observing Gunz with the same undying interest in his eyes. "You never stopped fighting since then. For all the right reasons, of course... But still... Tell me, how did you feel when you pressed the trigger of your sniper rifle for the very first time, aiming at a living, breathing human being? How did it feel watching your enemy fall, lifeless, through the scope of your rifle?"

"Shut up," hissed Gunz, his face a stone mask, his anger slowly rising to a boiling point, threatening to spill. Everything inside him was shaking, partially because he couldn't help but admit to himself that in some strange, perverted way War was right.

Warrington smirked, his narrowed eyes drilling into Gunz. "Just like your elven friend, you witnessed the death of the woman you loved. Even though you talk yourself into believing that her death wasn't final, it threw you over the edge. At first, you attempted to drown your sorrow in alcohol, but soon you realized that it wasn't enough. And this was when you found out that the only time you were alive and not in pain was—"

"I said, shut the hell up!" yelled Gunz, jumping to his feet, sending the chair rolling across the spacious office.

Mr. Warrington tilted his head, observing his reaction with a light smile. "War and Fire. An explosive mix."

He waved his hand, and the chair rolled back, hitting Gunz under his knees. He snapped his fingers, and an invisible force field pressed on Gunz's shoulders, forcing him to sit down.

"I know what you're going to say, Mr. Burns. You jumped into the underground fighting pits because your boss, Agent Andrews, sent you there… or because you wanted to find your undead friend, Yaroslav Potemkin… or because you suspected that the Head of the California House was the dark soul of Grigory Rasputin. All these facts are true." He waved his hand dismissively. "But your main reason—the one you fail to admit even to yourself—was that the only time you could breathe and forget about your pain was while you were fighting."

For seconds, Gunz just stared at him while working on getting in control of his emotions and his raging power. Then he sighed and relaxed in his chair, dropping his tense shoulders.

"You're wrong, War," he said softly, sounding almost wistful. "I did admit that. I'm surprised you didn't know. In my conversation with Mr. Kogan, ex-Head of the Florida House, I told him exactly that."

War inclined his head slowly. "I'm glad to hear you can be honest and objective with yourself, son. Not too many people can do it."

Gunz signed. "Don't call me son. Kal is my only Father, and he is not going to appreciate it," he said quietly, but then just bit his lip, averting his gaze. "Why, War?"

"Why what?"

"Why did you put us through hell?" asked Gunz, shuddering. "Why did you make Lucan and me relive the worst moments of our lives? What's in it for you?"

Viggo Warrington got up and leaned forward, bracing himself against the desk. He tucked a strand of his shoulder-length dark hair behind his ear, and a cold, calculating smile stretched his lips.

"That's simple. It was a test," he replied, his voice a low growl. "Now I know where your buttons are and how far I can push them before you break. I've seen your magic and power in action, and I have learned what you're capable of, magically speaking. I know that you two are loyal to each other and I also know that the both of you would do what must be done when the time comes."

Gunz got up. "Does it mean—"

"Yes, Mr. Burns, I will go with you," said War calmly, straightening up. "Since the disappearance of Death, I expected someone would come looking for me, seeking to bring the Four back together. I was hoping it would be you, and you didn't disappoint me."

"Why would you think I would get involved?" Gunz shrugged.

War walked around his desk and halted in front of him. Placing his hand on Gunz's shoulder, he peered into his eyes.

"Because you're the Great Fire Salamander. The protector of the human realm." He lifted his shoulders in a slight shrug, raising his eyebrows. "It's in your nature."

"Oh, really?" Gunz pursed his lips, hooking his thumbs into the waistband belt loops of his jeans.

"Of course not." Viggo Warrington chuckled, rolling his eyes as he shoved his hands into the pockets of his pants. "Not really. Mostly because you and your band of supernatural misfits are the only beings of magic who are crazy and powerful enough to risk bringing the Four back together."

He laughed louder and grabbed Aviators sunglasses from his desk. With a light flick of his wrist, he opened a portal. There was nothing usual about his portal. Just like any portal, it swirled in a continuous counterclockwise motion, but its color was bright red, the color of arterial blood, and scorching flames danced around its perimeter.

Gunz stilled and held his breath as the undiluted energy of War encapsulated him. Out of the corner of his eye, he could see that Lucan's reaction was similar to his.

"Where does this portal lead?" he asked, getting over the initial shock.

"A little Arizona farm in the middle of the Sonoran Desert, of course." Viggo turned around with a dark smile on his face, his gray eyes crinkling at the corners.

"I never told you—"

War laughed, shaking his head, and Gunz fell silent.

"You're forgetting something, Salamander. I've been in your head." He shuddered exaggeratedly, rubbing his arms with his hands as if he was freezing. "I must tell you—your head is one dark, twisted and terrifying place. Even for me. Nevertheless, I managed to gather some useful information too."

He arched his eyebrow at them and waved at the portal.

"What are you waiting for, soldiers? A special invitation? Go!"

CHAPTER 23

~ TESSA ~

Tessa's car sped along Alligator Alley toward Immokalee. Since Raoul couldn't give them the exact coordinates, they decided to drive all the way to the final destination and see if they could detect Famine's presence. As they passed endless everglades and swamps of natural preserves, the scenery stayed unchanged, and little by little, Tessa's mind drifted back to Aidan.

Her chest tightened with worry as she thought of all possible and impossible dangers he could be facing. Yaroslav was a capable fighter and if he had sent a distress signal, asking for help, his situation had to be desperate. Even though she knew that Aidan was a god and killing him wasn't an easy task, the feeling of dread hadn't left her since she teleported from Hawk's house.

Always and together... She sighed, thinking that with their lifestyles, it was impossible. At least in the World of Magic.

My knight in shining armor. She smiled at her thought. *Incorrigible. When is he going to put it through his blond head?* Aidan was always so worried about her safety, her powers and her ability to use them, and her situation with the Guardians Order, that no matter how many times she had proven to him she could hold her own, he still tried to shelter and protect her. She didn't need his protection. She didn't need him to take care of her. She just needed him. Why couldn't he understand that?

For the first time ever, she felt that she needed someone in her life. Someone to wake up next to every morning, someone she could laugh and cry with, someone who could understand both her lives—human and supernatural—without asking any questions. Not someone—she needed Aidan. The truth was, she wanted to protect him and make sure he was safe just as much as he wanted that for her.

I love you, my ancient god.

A light fluctuation in the magical energy field touched her senses, bringing her back to reality. She squeezed the steering wheel tighter and pressed the brake pedal softly, slowing down. Looking around, she didn't notice anything out of the ordinary —the same chain of trees, dry and deformed in places, endless swamps and puddles of lakes shining in the morning sunlight as far as she could see. Yet something was definitely off.

The entire area carried traces of magical energy, and while Tessa had never sensed anything like this before, somehow it felt familiar.

Angel...

It reminded her of Angel. It wasn't the energy of Death. Not exactly. She could never mistake it. Death or any magical being related to Death had such a specific energy signature that it couldn't be mistaken for anything else. Yet, what she was sensing right now had a strange similarity to it, and no matter how hard she tried, she couldn't pinpoint what it was.

"Tessa, what's up?" asked Missi sleepily from the back seat.

Tessa glanced into the rearview mirror. Both Missi and Karma were up, staring at her quizzically.

"I detected some kind of presence," she said, pointing to the right and slightly ahead. "All that area. Do you feel it too?"

Missi and Karma exchanged a bewildered look and shook their heads.

"The farther we go, the stronger it becomes," said Tessa airily, more to herself than to her friends.

"But we're literally in the middle of nowhere. There is nothing here except swamps and alligators." Missi waved her hand at the swamp, looking out the window. "And it's still going to be a while before we reach Immokalee."

"I know…," murmured Tessa, keeping her attention on the flow of magical energy.

She drove another few miles, then pulled over to the side of the highway and parked the vehicle. Leaning back in her seat, she opened her other sight and inhaled deeply. An earthy, swampy smell of everglades, intertwined with the scent of pines heated in the morning sun, invaded her senses.

As much as she enjoyed it, she forced everything normal out of her mind, focusing on the supernatural only. She could still feel the strange energy easily, but now she could also see it. It was flowing all around them, shimmering with a dark purple, almost obsidian glow. Deeper into the marshlands, it became brighter and thicker, as if pointing in which direction she needed to go.

Feeling a soft touch to her shoulder, she turned around and saw Missi standing next to her with an expression of wonderment on her face.

"I feel it too," she said, her eyes wandering over the swamps.

"Hard to miss," murmured Karma as she pulled her duffel bag out of the car and threw it over her shoulder. "I assume that's where we're going."

Tessa nodded, heading toward the fence. She moved her hand over the wires and glanced back at her friends.

"It's electric." A wide grin split her face. "Just what the doctor ordered."

She channeled her power and lightning bolts flashed in the

depths of her eyes. Putting her hands on the electric wires, she spread them wider apart and redirected the flow of power. High voltage electricity surged through her, doing her no harm, leaving the path open.

"What are you waiting for?" she asked, jerking her chin toward the fence. "Go through already. I'm not gonna hold it forever, you know."

Without waiting for a second invitation, Missi and Karma slipped between the wires and Tessa went after them. Following the flow of the magical energy, she walked down the hill toward the water covered in algae and overgrown greenery. She chose her every step carefully, but as the unsteady ground wobbled under her feet, she stopped and took a deep breath, trying to calm her nerves.

"It just a swamp," she said to herself, the sound of her own voice providing her with some reassurance.

Missi whispered a few words and a tall oak staff materialized in her hand. "Let me go first," she suggested quietly. "Something is not right here. I feel it in my skin." She shivered even though it was a hot morning and the air was thick with humidity.

Moving past Tessa, she progressed forward, carefully probing the land before moving her foot. Tessa started after her, but a metallic click of a cocked weapon made her stop and look over her shoulder.

"I don't think a shotgun would help us with whatever"—she waved her hand around—"is ruling this area."

"We'll see," muttered Karma, but it was visible that her mind was focused on something else.

Tessa shrugged and moved forward, cautiously stepping on the unsteady green path. While she knew that her friends trusted Karma, she couldn't say she understood her, and even though she had never showed it, the presence of the supernatural assassin always made her feel a little uncomfortable. Nevertheless, the current situation called for every capable warrior, magical or otherwise, and Karma was a gifted witch and skilled fighter.

The farther they progressed, the more lifeless the surrounding forest became. The trees stood naked, their bare branches stretching toward the sky like the skinny, dried-out arms of a beggar. With their crooked trunks, even the pines looked dark and abnormal as they leaned in every direction, crisscrossing and entwining with each other.

As dirty gray fog swirled over the swamp, silence—eerie and unnatural—enveloped the area. It pressed on Tessa's nerves, raising the small hairs on the back of her neck, making her every move sharp. Like a prey expecting a predator to hide behind every rock, she kept surveying the everglades, ready to spring into action at the first sight of trouble.

A bubble surfaced next to her feet, blowing up with a light pop, and she flinched, at the last moment stopping herself from jumping aside. She squinted her eyes, straining to see through the layer of murkiness. Something moved. A dark shadow glided silently below the surface, and a bird screeched somewhere in the distance.

She took a deep breath, feeling cold perspiration covering her forehead, and moved after Missi. The dead forest got denser. With malformed tree trunks standing so close to each other, Tessa had a hard time squeezing between them. She ignored the dried branches scratching her skin to blood and pushed forward, fighting the desire to turn around and run without looking back.

Soon, even the birds stopped screaming, and the silence thickened, swallowing the tiniest sound into its asphyxiating nothingness. The air became considerably colder despite the sun blasting from above, and goose bumps covered the exposed skin of her arms. She shivered and pressed her teeth tighter together to stop them from chattering.

Suddenly, Missi came to a sharp halt and raised her hand, signaling them to stop. Tessa and Karma caught up with her and halted in front of a clearing covered in tall sawgrass and billowy pink and purple clamps of Mushy grass flowers. There was no wind, but the grass was moving in continuous, shallow waves as if ruffled by a breeze. Tessa touched Missi's shoulder, staring at her quizzically.

"I don't know," murmured the young mage. "Something is off."

Her voice was no more than a whisper, but somehow her last words spread around, bouncing from tree to tree like an echo. However, unlike the typical echo, the sound didn't dim down. On the contrary, with each reverberation, the words sounded louder and louder, until Missi's voice was shouting through the everglades, forcing all three of them to press their hands to their ears, bending down.

The reverse echo disappeared as suddenly as it began, and they straightened up, lowering their arms. Tessa was about to say something, but Karma raised her finger to her lips and shook her head no. Missi moved her hand from left to right, and a streak of dark-purple light followed her motion. She raised her hand and started writing in the air with her index finger.

A moment later, the words "power shield" hung in the air, glowing with the bright white light of Missi's magic. The mage struck the shield, trying to break through it, but to no avail. She made a gesture as if she was punching through it and turned to Tessa and Karma. They both nodded at her, but Karma raised her index finger, asking to wait. The magical energy spiked around her as the witch channeled her magic.

"*Silenties*," she whispered and pressed her hands to her ears.

There was no reverse echo. Magically induced silence that enveloped the area was thicker and heavier than before.

"Together?" asked Tessa, but no sound came out from her mouth.

All three of them connected with their magic at the same time. Karma held out her hand with three fingers extended and counted, bending down one finger at the time. They blasted the power shield at the same time, and it lit up with a blinding purple light, making them step back, shielding their eyes with their hands.

"One more time," mouthed Karma, pointing at the shield.

Tessa touched her shoulder and raised her hand, gesturing for them to wait. Then she channeled her power, rising high above the ground and nodded at her friends. Karma held out her hand with three fingers extended and started a countdown. On three, Tessa reached up, and lightning struck through the cloudless sky, impacting the power shield.

The air vibrated with electrical discharges and the shield gave in under the pressure of the triple attack. The ground trembled and a silent wind rushed through the dead forest, raising clouds of dust and particles in the air. The shield collapsed, leaving the path forward unobstructed. But as Tessa made a move forward, Karma stopped her, shaking her head. She breathed out and pointed at a soft white cloud forming near her lips. Then she wrapped her arms around herself, shivering, and just now Tessa noticed how cold it had become.

Tessa surveyed the area but didn't notice anything new. The magical energy she had been following was getting thicker toward the other end of the clearing.

"Must go there," she mouthed, pointing forward to where the dark-purple mist of magic was swirling and moving in soft waves. To support her words, she took a step forward, placing her foot onto the rich grass of the clearing.

"No!" Missi and Karma yelled soundlessly at the same time, reaching to stop her, but they were too late.

As soon as her foot touched the ground, night fell over the everglades. The temperature dropped by a few more degrees, and dirty flakes of something resembling ashes or dirty snow started to fall. Tessa glanced up and gasped, grabbing Missi's arm. She pointed into the void of the dark sky, biting back a scream.

"Hell no!" mouthed Karma, stamping her foot on the ground angrily.

A dark cloud, swirling like a tornado funnel, was slowly descending toward them. It was hard to say what this cloud was comprised of, but clearly it was something supernatural and the energy it emitted was so dark and sinister that Tessa could barely breathe. She touched her lips and then jerked her finger across her throat, asking Karma to kill her silencing spell.

Karma threw a troubled look at Missi, but her lips moved as she whispered, *"Incanto Comlium"*, removing her spell. Although the spell was gone, the silence remained unchanged, and it seemed like the rotating darkness was swallowing all the sounds as it progressed down toward them.

"What is it?" whispered Tessa and covered her ears, expecting the reverse echo which didn't follow.

Karma exhaled a rugged breath. "This rotating cloud looks like the phantoms from the Dark Nav, but I know it's not possible. Chernobog would never let this number of phantoms run around the realm of the living. It's something else."

"It's not phantoms," said Missi, looking up. "I think it is—"

She didn't finish her phrase as something dark and semi-transparent flew through her chest. Missi cried out and leaned forward, pressing her hand over her heart. Another translucent creature flew through Karma, causing her to yelp, and soon the air around them was infused with hundreds if not thousands of them. They flew around with considerable speed, zooming in wide circles with a light hiss like some nightmarish merry-go-round.

"Let's see what they think about salt," murmured Karma.

She raised her shotgun and shot the nearest creature. To Tessa's shock, the creature moaned and dissipated, leaving behind a puff of dark smoke. Missi tried to raise a protective shield around them, but the creatures were merging through it as if the shield didn't exist at all.

With a light whistle, one of the monsters zoomed forward toward Tessa. Before Karma could reload her shotgun, it attempted to fly through Tessa's chest. However, as soon as it touched her, it spun in place and howled, going in and out of focus. Its dirty-gray translucent shape lost its darkness, becoming almost clear and then disappeared. The rest of the monsters screeched all at once and the silence got replaced with a terrible ruckus complimented by gunshots, curses, and occasional cries of pain.

"I know what they are," yelped Missi as another creature sailed through her shield. "These are ghosts or specters. Malevolent spirits that didn't cross the veil and were stuck in the realm of humans."

"Are you saying, all these monsters are dead people?" asked Tessa.

"Pretty sure they are," answered Missi.

"I think I know what I have to do," said Tessa, grabbing Missi's arm to yank her out of the way as the next specter flew through the shield.

She closed her eyes, allowing the reaper in her to take center stage. Even though she had helped spirits of dead people cross the veil before, it had always been one spirit at a time. Besides, those other spirits had wanted her help, whereas these malevolent manifestations didn't look like they were ready to move on.

As the magical energy of Death took over her entire being, she opened her eyes and glanced down. She was levitating a few yards above the ground and above the rotating mass of ghostly creatures. Her whole body, from her shoulders down to her feet, was covered by a black hooded cloak not unlike those she had seen on reapers before. In her right hand, she was holding a large scythe shining with a soft light in the surrounding darkness. She squeezed the weapon, wondering where it came from but had no time to think about it.

As her power surged through her, bringing to life every cell in her body, she laughed, and the rotating mass of ghosts came to a sharp halt. All of them turned their distorted faces up to stare at her, their soft whispers rising all around her. Her laughter rushed through the dead forest, spread around by a normal echo, and the energy of Death surrounded her like a dense shield.

She swung her scythe, and the ghosts wailed, trying to get away from its touch, but they could no longer move. Her weapon cut through the dirty, translucent swarm, leaving only shimmering wisps where the ghosts had once been. Rotating faster and faster in the air, she soon looked like a little tornado. A few minutes later, it was all over.

Tessa glanced around to make sure that all the spirits were gone and released the magic of Death, slowly lowering down to the ground. The scythe and the robe disappeared as she returned to her human form, and she sighed tiredly, a light smile touching her lips.

"Well, that was something new," she said with a half-shrug.

"No shit," murmured Karma, staring at her incredulously. "Now I can see what the Otherworld's very own Cerberus found in you, girl. You've got some serious moves there."

Tessa just nodded. Karma's words brought forth all the thoughts and worries about Aidan, but she took a cleansing breath and forced them to the back of her mind. There would be plenty of time to think about that when she was done with her mission.

Now, she needed to focus on what lay ahead.

CHAPTER 24

~ TESSA ~

The night disappeared together with the ghosts, and now, the bright Florida sun was blasting from the clear blue sky. Tessa observed the area and held her breath, gesturing at Missi and Karma to look forward. At the other end of the clearing, there was a small house they hadn't noticed before. There was nothing special about its appearance—just another modern house with large windows and tiled roof. But in the given surroundings, it looked unnatural and ominous.

"I guess this is where we're going," said Karma, squatting next to her duffel bag. She reloaded her shotgun, slung her bag over her shoulder and headed toward the house.

Tessa followed her, but the feeling of dread just intensified, sending chills down her spine. She could feel and see the strange energy washing over the building in soft, continuous waves and the closer they got, the faster it moved. As they approached the house, the door opened up with a high pitched squeak. It stood ajar like a faceless black hole, silent and sinister.

"Let's go," whispered Missi, staring intently into the darkness behind the threshold, but didn't make a move.

Tessa felt an icy touch to her mind and a soft voice, almost a whisper, sounded in her head. At first, she thought it was in her head only, but by the way Missi tensed and Karma raised her shotgun, she quickly realized they could hear it too.

"Therasia...," whispered the voice, a soft and insinuating sound invading her mind. "Come in... Theras-s-ia..."

"I'm going." Tessa took a deep breath ready to walk inside, but Missi grabbed her hand.

"Not alone, you're not," she hissed, her fingers digging into Tessa's skin. "I promised your divine lover that I'd keep you safe."

"How about I'll go first," said Karma. She cocked her shotgun and crossed the threshold without waiting for their response.

Tessa and Missi exchanged a quick look and followed Karma inside the house. As soon as Tessa stepped across the doorway, the door shut tightly behind her with a loud bang, leaving her in complete darkness. She gasped and snapped around, searching for her friends or for a way out.

"Missi? Karma?"

Her voice sounded muffled and hushed like a whisper of a scared little girl who lost her mommy. Even though she could see nothing, she was positive she was alone here. Tessa had no idea how she knew it. It was as if she could sense it with her very skin—there were only two alive entities in this place, her and this house. For a moment, fear consumed her, scrambling her thoughts.

She took a deep breath to get in control of her stretched nerves. *I'm not a child. I can do it. Famine wants me to be here alone? So be it.*

She wondered where her friends were. The mere idea that something could have happened to them tightened her chest with worry, and fear reared its ugly head again. She couldn't allow herself to be scared. She had to believe that they were fine —safe outside this hellhole.

A deep moan filled with anguish and despair sounded somewhere in the depth of the house. Its sound chilled her to the bone, making her hair stand on end, and for a split-second, she could hear nothing but her pounding heart and the rush of blood in her ears. Tessa swallowed and sharpened her hearing, blinking to adjust her vision, but the darkness was all-consuming, and she still couldn't see anything.

"Tessa... help..." A man moaned, notes of pain ringing in his deep voice, and Tessa shuddered inwardly. He sounded just like Aidan.

She took a few steps in the direction of the sound and stopped. *It's not Aidan. It can't be. He's somewhere in Las Vegas with Yaroslav. Famine is toying with me...*

"Famine!" she shouted, squeezing her hands into fists at her sides. "I know it's you. Enough with your stupid games! Show yourself." She extended her hand and an energy ball crackling with electrical discharges materialized in her palm, partially illuminating the area.

A loud feminine laughter was the only response to her words. It bounced against the walls and ceiling and died out somewhere in the darkness. Tessa gasped and twirled around, sending more of her magic toward the energy ball in her hand. As far as she could see, she was absolutely alone in the empty room.

"Famine! Goddammit—," she yelled, but got interrupted by a melodious giggle that bounced from one side to the other, jingling like silver bells.

"You don't like to play, Therasia?" purred the voice. "Pity. Just one little game, darling. You play and if you win, you'll get rewarded." The voice laughed again.

"No!" Tessa yelled, spinning around. "I have no time for your games!"

"My house, my rules." Famine chuckled. "It's my way or the highway, darling. If you want to meet me, you must play first."

"Crap," whispered Tessa, admitting to herself that Famine

was right at least about one thing—she had no choice but to play by her rules. She made the energy orb dissipate and sighed. "Fine! One game. What do you want me to do?"

A loud click sounded somewhere on her right, and a blinding white light filled the room. Staggering back, Tessa grunted and shut her eyes, involuntarily raising her arm to shield her face. When her vision adapted to the brightness, and she was able to see again, she froze in place, pressing her hand over her heart as her chest tightened with anxiety.

She stood in an empty, spacious hall. It was too large to be natural. Recalling the way the house looked from the outside, she didn't think this hall could fit into it. However, it wasn't the size of the room that made her heart pound desperately against her ribcage. A massive balance scale stood at the opposite wall. An enormous black void spread under the pans on both sides of it, seemingly leading into nowhere.

On the right side of the scale, in front of the pan, Aidan kneeled with his arms tied behind his back. His blue eyes were wide with fear, his face contorted with pain. He was so close to the void that one wrong move could send him plummeting down.

"Tessa," he moaned, his voice hoarse, "help me."

"Aidan," she whispered, stretching her hand toward him, "oh, no..."

"Tessa, help me..." She heard another familiar voice and snapped her head to the left.

In front of the left pan, just outside the void, she saw Zane. He was on his knees with his arms tied behind his back just like Aidan, but a wide circle of black flames danced around him.

"Zane," she cried out. "Don't move! I'm coming."

She rushed toward him, but as soon as she deviated off center of the scale, Aidan screamed, raw agony in his voice making her stop and turn to him. His body shuddered, his muscles twisting with such force she was afraid his bones would snap. White feathers were slowly breaking through his skin as his arms, no longer bound, started to turn into wings. She froze, her eyes darting from left to right, and then softly stepped back. Once she reached the midline again, both Aidan and Zane stopped screaming and relaxed to a degree.

"Famine!" she yelled, tears burning behind her eyes. "What the hell is this? What kind of twisted game are you playing?"

Soft giggles bounced from one corner of the hall to the next.

"Twisted? I think not," replied Famine, arrogance and mockery lacing her voice. "The rules are simple—pick one. Two men enter, one man leaves. Who is it going to be, Therasia? Your lover or your friend? Pick one and do it quickly or both will die."

Tessa froze, biting back a scream of terror. *This is just an illusion. A twisted, perverted illusion. Zane is in California. Aidan is in Nevada. They can't be here. Just an illusion.* She pressed her hand to her chest and took a ragged breath, trying to get her fluttering heart to slow down.

"But it is real, Therasia," said Famine, a soft chuckle following her words. "Choose, or doom them both to a slow, painful demise."

"I refuse!" hissed Tessa. "I refuse to choose between the man who's the love of my life and the man who's my friend, who saved my life more than once. It's an impossible choice."

As soon as the words escaped her lips, both Aidan and Zane screamed. The circle of Black Fire got smaller, encroaching closer to the Fire Salamander and even though the flames hadn't touched him, his skin got covered in terrible blisters. Aidan's situation was just as bad as an unknown spell was slowly and torturously transforming him into a swan.

"Please, stop!" yelled Tessa, squeezing her head with her hands, her fingers digging into her hair.

"Choose!" shouted Famine. "Or lose both!"

"NO!"

Tessa looked from Aidan to Zane, shaking her head, tears running down her face, but she didn't get a chance to say anything else. With an earsplitting bang, the wall behind her exploded, showering her with pieces of wood, dirt and debris. The air got infused with the stench of gunpowder and dust, making her cough. Sunlight flooded the room and for a moment everything became blurry and disappeared soon after.

* * *

When the spots stopped dancing in her vision, Tessa found herself standing inside a small empty room. There was no scale and both Aidan and Zane were gone. She felt a touch to her shoulder and flinched, twirling around.

"Missi... Karma...," she exhaled with relief. "You're okay."

"We're fine," replied Karma, kicking a pile of rubble out of her way with the tip of her boot. "Sorry, we were thrown out of this house and across the clearing. Took us a while to break through." She smirked, raising a grenade launcher to her shoulder. "So, what's going on here? You look like you've seen a ghost." She glanced around, cocking her head a little.

"I wish I'd seen a ghost. At least I would know how to deal with it," muttered Tessa, just now noticing that her shirt was soaked with cold sweat. "Unfortunately, it was Famine."

"Where is he?" asked Karma dryly.

"She, thank you very much." An already familiar voice boomed through the room.

Tessa turned around and stomped her foot, placing her hands on her hips. "I've had enough of your friggin' games," she yelled, her hands gathering into fists of their own accord. "Show yourself, before I make you."

"Was that a threat, Therasia?" the voice asked snidely and snickered, but it was no longer hollow and distant.

Tessa snapped to the left and saw a tall woman moving

toward them, swaying her hips as if she were walking the catwalk. She wore a simple light shirt and wide beige cargo pants. With her long hair more silver than black, she looked like she could be in her late forties. However, Tessa knew that in the World of Magic appearances could be deceiving and Famine was thousands of years old.

Karma raised her grenade launcher, training it on the woman, and Missi channeled her magic, ready to fight. Famine's thin lips lifted in a smirk, and she glanced at them with reproach.

"A grenade launcher enhanced by magic. How very progressive of you, Karma," she said, rolling her eyes. "I hate to disappoint you, but no mundane weapon, even reinforced by magic, can harm me." Since Karma didn't move, she sighed and added with a layer of sarcasm in her every word. "Usually people pay you to raise your weapon, but I don't mind paying you for lowering them. What do you say, Sword for Hire?"

Karma grimaced but lowered her weapon.

"And you, Guardian mage," continued Famine mockingly with a dismissive wave of her hand. "Your magic is too weak to deal with someone like me. Don't waste your breath."

She approached Tessa and stared down at her, the heavy gaze of her pale-yellow eyes moving up and down her body as if measuring her. Then she shrugged and tilted her head slightly.

"I wonder what he sees in you?" she murmured, hooking her thumbs into the belt loops of her cargo pants. Tessa didn't reply, and she continued. "Anyway, I know why you're here."

"Good," muttered Tessa. Annoyed by Famine's arrogance, she had a hard time keeping her temper under control. But a small voice in the back of her mind kept reminding her that getting in a fight with one of the four Horsemen probably wasn't the hottest idea. "So, you're coming with us then."

It wasn't a question. Tessa didn't want to give Famine an

open invitation to say no, and she probably realized it too, because she laughed.

"Yes, I am." Famine smirked, but her smirk quickly faded away, and she frowned. "But not because of you, Therasia. You failed my test. I'm coming because of Death and his strange attachment to your boyfriend, Aodh mac Lir."

"Excuse me?" hissed Tessa, taking a step closer to the Horseman. Missi grabbed her arm, but she shook it off. "How did I fail your test? I didn't make the choice! I didn't submit to your stupid demands. I stood my ground."

"And you killed them both! You lost everything!" roared Famine, and the walls trembled, responding to her powerful magic. "The goal of my test was to see if you were capable of making a tough decision." She took a breath and her eyebrows knitted together in a deep frown. "The darkness is rising the likes of which you have never seen before, and we all have to be ready to make some sacrifices. None of us will walk away from this fight unscarred. You're not ready, Therasia. Perhaps you're just too young to understand... I'm sorry, but you failed my test."

"Do you think if anyone else was in my place, they would be capable of making a decision like that?" shouted Tessa. "No one in their right mind could make that choice, killing people as a result. Especially people they love!"

Famine huffed, "Ask your friend, the young Fire Salamander." She lifted her shoulders in an indifferent shrug. "He had to make this kind of decisions since he was younger than you're right now."

She fell silent for a brief moment, and Tessa lowered her eyes under her drilling gaze, stubbornly staring at Famine's yellow construction boots.

"You can also ask your boyfriend," Famine continued, her voice even and unemotional as if she was reading from a phonebook. "He's been making choices like this and tougher ones for centuries. I don't judge you. You're new to the World of Magic and still have a lot to learn, child. Usually, the hardest and most painful path is the right one and you are the one who has to make the choice—do what's right and follow it at your own peril or choose the path of less resistance and fail."

Tessa cringed inwardly and bit her lip, feeling heat creeping up to her cheeks. She didn't agree with Famine, but her words sent a painful jolt through her, making her eyes water with unwanted angry tears.

"Anyway," continued Famine, more to Missi and Karma than to Tessa, "it's time to go. I believe two of my brothers are already waiting for us. I can sense their closeness. So, let's not make them wait any longer."

She waved her hand and a black portal opened up. Unlike any regular portals, it wasn't shimmering or rotating. It looked almost like an opening into the void. Dark and motionless, it stood like a faceless hole punched in the fabric of reality, leading nowhere good.

Famine approached the portal, gesturing at them to proceed.

"After you?" She bowed slightly and a derisive smirk curved her thin lips.

CHAPTER 25

~ AIDAN ~

Aidan stared at the two demons blocking his entrance into the *Crimson Creek Casino* and sighed, pursing his lips. *Are they really as dumb as they look?* His aggravation rose to a new high as the demonic security guards dressed in black suits and ties kept explaining to him the casino rules which didn't allow for any form of concealed weapons. *Blah blah blah...*

"If you follow us, sir—," continued the guard, but Aidan waved his hand impatiently, interrupting him.

"I'm not here to gamble. I'm here to see Santiago del Castillo, the owner of this casino," he said dryly, "and there is no power in this world that could separate me from my sword."

The demons exchanged a ferocious look and stepped closer to Aidan.

"Then we must ask you to leave, sir," growled one of them, the dark mist of his demonic essence rising around him. The second guard seized Aidan's arm above the elbow, ready to force him out the door.

Aidan grimaced as the stench of sulphur invaded his senses and slowly lowered his eyes, glowering at the demon's hand pointedly.

"Remove your hand," he said icily. "If you want to keep it."

The demons glanced at each other, and the second one grabbed Aidan's other arm ready to throw him out.

Why does it always have to be so violent? Why can't we all just get along? I don't have time to deal with these dumbasses...

More annoyed than angry, Aidan looked heavenward and transformed into his godly form. A black mask concealed his face, and his eyes ignited with a brilliant white light, shining through the slits of the mask. He folded his arms over his chest, shaking off the massive demonic guards effortlessly, and the floor, covered in a gaudy carpet, trembled beneath his feet.

"Santiago del Castillo!" he shouted, and his magically magnified voice rushed through the casino, consuming all other sounds.

Every guest stopped whatever they were doing and turned toward him, some staring at him flabbergasted, some horrified. The magical energy field spiked up inside the room, assailing Aidan's senses with a wild mix of different supernatural energy signatures. The electric lights flickered on and off, and the illumination in the casino got even dimmer than it had been before. The shrill noise of slot machines seemed to become louder as the rest of the sounds died out.

Aidan observed mortified visitors and grunted, returning to his human form. He didn't need it. All he wanted was to ask Santiago a few questions about Yaroslav and be on his merry way to search for him.

He glanced up at the eye in the sky security cameras and took a step forward, but as a soft rush of air touched his face, he stilled. A tall dark-haired man, seemingly in his forties, stood in front of him, his dark-brown eyes observing him with curiosity. His thick black eyebrows rose as understanding dawned on him, and he bowed deeply and ceremoniously, like a medieval courtier.

"Aodh mac Lir... My lord," he said, keeping his humble position. "Please forgive my guards' disrespectful behavior. My casino is an official sanctuary and we have a strict no-weapons-allowed rule. They had no idea who you were."

"Please rise," said Aidan impatiently. "I assume you're Santiago del Castillo?"

"Yes, my lord."

The Spaniard gave a short nod to his security guards. Both demons bowed to Aidan, mumbled some kind of apologies, and walked away swiftly.

"We need to talk." Aidan looked around the casino, not sure he wanted to discuss the matter at hand in an open space with so many sharp supernatural ears around. "Is there a place where we could have a quick conversation without being overheard?"

"Please follow me." Santiago bowed lightly, gesturing toward a sparkling, blinking and ringing ocean of slots.

Following the owner of the casino, Aidan maneuvered between the rows of machines and gaming tables. Now that the initial shock of his power-display was over, the supernatural visitors returned to what they loved most—gambling, and no one paid attention to him. At least not openly.

Santiago led him toward an elevator which opened immediately, allowing them in. He pressed a button with the number two on it and once they arrived, followed a long brightly lit corridor all the way to the end, stopping in front of a door with his name written on it.

"After you, my lord," he said, opening the door for Aidan.

Aidan walked inside and observed the room, his eyebrows rising. Santiago's office had a modern black-and-gray desk with a widescreen computer monitor on it, a few black leather chairs and a low leather sofa by the wall. Just like everywhere in the casino, there were no windows, and the only source of light was a beautiful wall lamp behind the desk.

But what shocked him the most was that every available inch of wall space was covered with bookshelves. Books, varying from modern fantasy novels to old religious manuscripts—undoubtedly first editions, were carefully placed on the shelves. The older, more expensive volumes were encased in glass boxes to protect them from the destructive forces of time and air.

Aidan heard the soft click of the closed door and turned around.

"Stop bowing, Santiago, and stop calling me 'my lord'. In this realm, my name is Aidan McGrath." He pulled a chair to sit down, but halted for a moment, waiting for the Spaniard to approach.

"But, my lord," purred the vampire, stopping in front of Aidan, his deep eyes twinkling with something other than respect. "I'm humbled by your presence. It's not every day a god of the Otherworld pays a visit to my modest establishment."

"Humbled. Modest." Aidan pursed his lips, narrowing his eyes at him. "You don't know the meaning of these words, vampire. Sit your ass down. Sorry, but I don't have time for the exchange of pleasantries, so let's get down to business."

"As you wish, Aidan," replied Santiago, lowering himself onto the leather sofa by the wall. He leaned back and folded his arms. "What can a vampire do for a god?"

"You can tell me where my friend Yaroslav Potemkin is," replied Aidan dryly, sitting down. "I received his distress signal from your casino."

"I should have known," whispered the Spaniard, stroking his black beard.

"What are you talking about?" growled Aidan, and the walls of the office trembled a little, responding to the feeling of dread that swirled through him. "What have you done to him?"

"Whoa, Aidan, relax." Santiago raised both his arms up in a peaceful gesture. "I'm just trying to say that Yaroslav is the only vampire I know of who's capable of creating a blood bond with a god, getting his loyalty. I swear, I haven't done anything to him. We go way back. Trust me, while we've had our fair share of disagreements in the past, I've always liked the kid, my lord."

"I don't have a blood bond with Yaroslav," muttered Aidan. "A while ago, I created a psychic link with him and one more person." He paused for a split second, recalling the day when he created that link with Yaroslav and Gunz. Then he shook his head and frowned. "Anyway, do you know where he is?"

Santiago leaned forward, resting his arms on his lap, and a dip wrinkle crossed his forehead. "The Sisterhood of the Sun has him. Sorry, Aidan, but most likely, he's dead. The slayers don't schmooze with our kind. They kill anything without a heartbeat."

Aidan closed his eyes, reaching through his link to Yaroslav. There was nothing there except a terrifying empty void, but since the link was still open, Slavik was alive.

"He's alive. I can sense him," said Aidan breathlessly. He opened his eyes, peering down at the ancient vampire. "How did it happen?"

Santiago sighed and brushed a lock of his dark hair off his face, straightening up. "My guess, they followed him here. Yaroslav told me that the Sisterhood's slayers targeted his mother's vampires, actively destroying her organization, and he was trying to find out why. He had come to me for the information on how to find them."

Aidan got up, feeling stiffness in his muscles. "How can I find them?"

"But my lord, they're ruthless killers..." Santiago's voice wavered as he got up, a muscle twitching in his chiseled jaw.

"I'm a god of the Otherworld, Santiago. They don't kill gods," objected Aidan quietly. "And if they try..." A dark chuckle escaped his lips. "Nothing will help them then."

Santiago nodded and headed toward his desk. Pressing an intercom button on his phone, he said, "Sylvana, I need you in my office immediately."

A few minutes later, a beautiful woman with long, dark hair walked into the office. She wore a casino dealer uniform, which only accentuated all the seductive curves of her slender figure. For a moment her eyes lingered on Aidan and then her lips parted in shock. She bowed low to him, pressing her hand to her chest.

"My lord...," she whispered, her voice soft and tender like the touch of a summer breeze.

Before Aidan could say anything, Santiago stepped forward. "My lord, allow me to introduce my progeny, Sylvana Erickson. She used to be one of the Sisterhood's best slayers until..." He cleared his throat and a crooked smile appeared on his face as he flicked his eyebrow at the woman. "Well, until I turned her. Centuries ago."

Aidan's jaw dropped as for the first time he saw the shrewd Spaniard in a new light. To turn a Sisterhood slayer into a vampire was unheard of. Taught to kill vampires without thought, without mercy or remorse, these women were skilled fighters and powerful witches who could wield not only their weapons but also anti-vampire magic with unparalleled ease and precision. For a vampire to get close to one of the Sisterhood slayers was practically impossible, let alone turn one.

Santiago stroked his mustache, hiding his delighted smile, and turned to Sylvana.

"Darling," he purred, not without some sarcasm in his deep voice, "please say hello to our honored guest, Aodh mac Lir, a god of the Otherworld. He needs our help to locate the Sisterhood and save your blond—um—friend with benefits."

"My lady," said Aidan, slightly inclining his head. He took her icy-cold hand, bringing it to his lips without actually kissing it. "Nice to make your acquaintance. Aidan McGrath."

"Finally, someone with balls," muttered Sylvana, throwing a scorching gaze at her maker. "So, when are we going?"

"We?" asked Aidan flabbergasted.

"You didn't think we'd let you go alone?" She gave him an arched stare, putting her hands on her waist. "If you're planning to kick a hornets' nest, at least have someone with you who'll stop you from getting stung."

"Fine," agreed Aidan. "Where are we going?"

"Phoenix, Arizona," replied Sylvana.

It was a day full of surprises. All this time Yaroslav had been a few miles away from him… A cold wave of shivers ran down his back, and he held his breath for a split second, clenching his teeth.

What the hell? How come I couldn't sense his presence?

CHAPTER 26

~ AIDAN ~

The merciless Arizona sun was in its zenith, blasting from the cloudless blue sky when Aidan parked a rental car across the street from the gates of a giant mansion. A wide asphalt road led to the house, and a state-of-the-art security monitor was positioned next to the entrance.

The building itself looked like a modern-day masterpiece with soaring windows, a tall roof, and steel, wood, and stucco detailing on the outside. All in all, it was a peaceful luxury paradise any suburban middle-class dweller could only dream about owning.

"Is that it?" asked Aidan, staring at the house incredulously.

"Yes," replied Santiago from the back seat, sounding slightly unnerved.

Even though vampires could walk in daylight without bursting into flames, they were extremely sensitive to sunlight and preferred to stay inside their homes during the day. If they had to go outside, they wore dark sunglasses and dressed to cover as much skin as possible.

The harsh Arizona sun wasn't something Santiago appreciated, and Aidan silently wondered why the old vampire had chosen Las Vegas as a location for his establishment.

"I didn't expect it to look so... hmm... modern and peaceful, I guess." Aidan's eyes traveled over the well-groomed front yard with a few Saguaro cacti and other spiky representatives of local flora planted around the entrance. A perfectly aligned desert-adapted lawn with colorful pebbles and decorative rocks just didn't fit his vision of the Sisterhood HQ.

"But it is not," said Sylvana, leaning forward to touch Aidan's shoulder. "Don't look with your eyes, young god."

"I'm not that young," murmured Aidan absentmindedly.

"I'm sorry. Well-preserved god," Sylvana corrected herself with a soft chuckle. "Open your magical sight or cast a spell that can reveal the unseen."

Aidan glanced back at her and she gave him a nod, jerking her thumb toward the house. He turned around and opened his other sight, observing the Sisterhood HQ. The modern dwelling was gone, replaced by a building resembling a tenth century French Château. Fortified like a medieval fortress, it looked like it could withstand a year-long siege by an army of vampires.

The entire perimeter of the property was surrounded by protective spells and wards, and anti-vampire runes gleamed dimly on the walls of the Château. Aidan bit his lip, wondering if Yaroslav was inside this building. If he was, he had to be experiencing constant pain being so close to these runes.

"He must be tormented every moment he spends there..."

Aidan heard Sylvana's voice, hollow and sad, and turned to face them.

"Neither you nor Santiago can go with me," he said, thinking that after seeing Peyton's apartment, he should have expected all these anti-vamp tricks and more in the Sisterhood HQ. "Thank you for getting me this far."

The Spaniard shook his head. "I think, we'll hang around a bit longer. Just in case you need a getaway vehicle," he stated, and by the tone of his voice, Aidan knew that arguing with him would be pointless.

"Thank you," he said gratefully, truly meaning it.

Opening the door, he got out of the car and quickly shut it to make sure Santiago and Sylvana wouldn't get exposed to the scorching rays of the afternoon sun. He headed across the road and halted in front of the security screen. He skimmed through the instructions and pressed an intercom button.

"How can I help you?" asked a pleasant female voice.

"I'm here to see the Grand Master of the Sisterhood," replied Aidan, feeling strange butterflies fluttering in his stomach. Suppressing the unusual nervousness, he glanced to the right at a security camera to make sure they knew who he was.

Something clicked on the other side, and with a soft thud the heavy iron gates split in the middle and slowly moved aside, allowing him to pass. Now that he knew how the building truly looked, the illusion no longer worked on him and he could clearly see the distance to the fortress. Instead of walking all the way, he snapped his fingers and teleported, manifesting in front of the steps leading toward the main entrance.

As soon as he placed his foot on the first step, the tall, heavy door opened and a young woman dressed in regular jeans and a shirt walked outside, a cold smile playing on her lips. Her hand causally slipped to the pommel of a dagger sheathed at her belt, which looked out of place with her modern attire.

"My lord," she addressed him with a title that was supposed to demonstrate her respect, but neither the tone of her voice nor her behavior supported it. "Grand Master Elony is expecting you in the Main Hall. Please follow me."

Without waiting for his reply, she turned on her heel and walked away. Aidan frowned, unimpressed by such a strange greeting. *They can't know why I am here, can they?* Whether they knew or not, he couldn't care less. He was going to get Yaroslav out of here no matter what.

He headed up the stairs and followed the young woman. Inside, the fortress looked like a museum. A soft, burgundy carpet covered a long hallway illuminated by the flickering yellow light of electric torches designed to maintain the medieval vibe of the house.

The walls were lined with pictures in heavy frames decorated with silver ornaments, undoubtedly old and expensive. The portraits themselves seemed to be authentic oil paintings, and they were just as old as their frames. Most of them depicted women who, judging by their fashion and hairstyles, represented different centuries and epochs.

Anti-vampiric runes gleamed softly on the ceiling, walls and floor, shining through the carpet, and thin strips of silver were embedded everywhere he looked.

Still paying no attention to him, the woman turned a few corners and finally stopped in a spacious lobby in front of a tall red-oak double door with silver inlays and ornaments. Armed with modern firearms, two young women in black tactical uniforms guarded the entrance. One of them conversed with Aidan's guide in hushed tones and then opened the door, gesturing for him to proceed.

Aidan crossed the threshold of the Main Hall and halted, his heart giving a painful jolt. The large room was long and narrow like a pencil box. The light of electric torches wasn't enough to illuminate every corner and the tall arched ceiling seemed to be melting into the darkness. A heavy scent of lavender lingered in the air. It seemed to be artificial, like an air freshener, but it triggered something in Aidan's memory—something he couldn't quite place.

A large table was positioned at the far end of the room. Just like any modern conference room table, it was surrounded by twelve leather office chairs. A woman in her late fifties sat at the far end, her curly black hair cropped close to her head in a military style haircut.

She got up, her pale, gray eyes sliding up and down Aidan's body as if sizing him up. On her ebony skin, those eyes, cold and unyielding, seemed to live a separate life. She was tall and too masculine for a woman—flat-chested with well-defined muscles of her arms bulging under her simple black t-shirt.

Twelve more women stood behind her, all armed with swords and firearms, looking as cold and ferocious as their leader. Aidan took a deep breath and slowly headed toward the table.

"Aodh mac Lir," said the Grand Master frostily. "Since we're mostly dealing with the undead, we're not in the habit of receiving"—she gave him one more once-over and shrugged—"gods of deathly realms here. What is the reason for your visit?"

Aidan regarded her with a gaze that could freeze Hell and smirked. "I'm here because you hold my friend in your fortress against his will. I'm taking him home."

"And who might that be?" she asked, arching her black eyebrows.

"Yaroslav Potemkin," replied Aidan, keeping a calm facade. But while he looked relaxed and reassured on the outside, on the inside he was slowly channeling his magic, assessing his position and getting ready to fight if needed.

"Are you saying that this disgusting vamp is your friend?" asked Grand Master Elony, disdain distorting her full lips. "You keep pretty low company for a god."

Aidan grunted as anger flared in him, for a moment blinding him with the desire to smite everyone in this room, disassembling this fortress brick by brick. Instead, he took a cleansing breath and smiled.

"Since Yaroslav is such low company in your opinion, perhaps you wouldn't feel bad parting with him, would you?" His smile grew wider, leaving his eyes cold and deadly.

She huffed and glanced back at her sisters who were lined up behind her. They responded with soft chuckles. "What makes you think he's still alive? After all, since the dawn of humanity, we are in the business of killing undead monsters. That's what we do." She laughed icily and added, "My lord."

"And since when is the Sisterhood of the Sun going after the vampires who co-exist with humans in peace?" asked Aidan, his arms slowly sliding down to his hip, ready to manifest his sword. "Like the Scarlet Queen's company?"

For a moment, Grand Master Elony lost her arrogance, and a shadow crossed her face. She frowned and rubbed her forehead like a person who was trying to recall something that was slipping away.

"We have orders," she replied at length, but there was no self-assurance in her voice.

Something is off...

Aidan nodded. "Fine. I know Yaroslav is alive and he's here. I can sense his presence. Please let him leave with me. That's all I need. No arguments, no fights. I'll leave, and you'll never see me again."

Grand Master Elony looked over her shoulder at her team and nodded to one of the young women. She walked away through a small back door he hadn't noticed before. A few minutes later, she came back with Yaroslav following her. They stopped next to the Grand Master, but the woman kept holding Yaroslav's arm above his elbow.

To Aidan's surprise, the vampire wasn't restrained and didn't look like he was hurt. He even had his katana sheathed under his leather coat. But as their eyes met, Aidan shuddered. Even though Yaroslav's pale face remained calm and emotionless, his haunted gaze told him more than any words could. He made a move to get closer to the vampire, but two of the women blocked his way, stopping him.

"Yaroslav, are you okay?" he asked, his voice a low growl.

"Aidan—," started Yaroslav.

"Silence, vampire," Grand Master Elony hissed, interrupting him.

Yaroslav flinched, a pained expression crossing his features. His mouth snapped shut, and his hands clenching into fists at his sides. He groaned, helpless fury reflecting in his blue eyes.

"What did you do to him?" Aidan snapped around, taking a step closer to Grand Master Elony.

She laughed arrogantly, folding her arms over her chest. "I did my job. But I think I'll let him give you an explanation." She turned to Yaroslav. "Yaroslav Potemkin, please explain to your friend what was done to you. You can show him."

Yaroslav winced as if she had slapped him across the face, but then slowly shrugged his coat off, dropping it to the floor, and lifted his shirt, exposing his chest. A large rune was glowing, deeply embedded into his skin.

"Aidan," he croaked, his voice painfully hoarse, "this is necromancy." He pressed his hand over the rune and looked away for a moment. "They have complete control over me. Please leave, my friend. There is nothing you can do. If they order me to run you through with a sword, I'll do it. I'm not in control."

"But I am," growled Aidan, "and you're forgetting *who* I am, Yaroslav." He turned to Grand Master Elony, death staring from his blazing eyes. "Remove this rune at once and release him."

She met his eyes without blinking and smirked. "No. What are you going to do about it, huh? We receive our orders from a power mightier than yours!"

Destiny Council? What the hell is going on? Aidan took a deep breath and the sweet odor of lavender flooded his senses. *Lavender? Oh, no... I remember... I know...* His thoughts scattered around, and for a moment, he couldn't organize them into anything coherent. He grunted, forcing the wild stampede of thoughts out of his mind, and allowed the god of the Otherworld to take over.

Turning to Grand Master Elony, he laughed. "And how are you going to stop me, little witch?"

He waved his hand and the witches of the Sisterhood flew all the way across the long hall, propelled by the mighty force of his godly power. They hit the wall and crashed to the cold tiles in a senseless heap of bodies.

"Last chance, witch," he roared, the walls reverberating with the sound of his deep voice. "Remove the rune and live to see another day. Disobey me, and I'll torment your spirit in the Otherworld for eternity!"

"No!"

"Fine." Aidan waved his hand and a dense shield glowing with the white light of his magic enveloped the entire hall, blocking all ways in and out. "If my father, Gwyn ap Nudd, taught me anything at all, it was how to do a thorough spring cleaning."

The witch turned to Yaroslav and yelled, "Kill him! He has a human body. Destroy it! Use your sword, disgusting vamp!"

Yaroslav howled, squeezing his head with his hands, blood dripping from the corners of his eyes. Unable to fight the necromancy rune, he bent down, grabbed his katana and turned to Aidan.

Aidan just laughed and vanished. He reappeared behind the vampire. Moving with a velocity that would rival any vamp, his arms snaked under Yaroslav's armpits and he clasped his hands on top of the vampire's head in a firm s-lock, securing him in a full nelson hold. He pushed his knuckles into the back of his head, forcing his arms up, and the vampire cried out, dropping his sword.

Before Grand Master Elony realized what was happening and could gather her magic, he released Yaroslav, turning him around, and placed his hand over the rune. The brilliant light of his magic encapsulated both of them, and the vampire screamed, his entire body convulsing violently in Aidan's firm hold. When Aidan let go of him a few seconds later, the rune was gone, a terrible bleeding lesion marring his skin in its place. Yaroslav moaned and collapsed to the floor, clasping his hand to his chest.

"You'll heal... You're a vampire after all," muttered Aidan more to himself than to his friend, remorse twisting his insides. Then he turned to Grand Master Elony and his power spiked with new strength within him. "Time to do the highly advertised spring cleaning."

"No, no..." The witch extended her arms toward him, fear contorting her face, but he ignored her.

Aidan spread his arms wide, and the shield he erected responded to his move, expanding farther, now encapsulating the entire building. He lowered his arms and started to sing. The word of a forgotten language older than Dragon tongue flowed through the air, entwining with his magic. As his light became brighter and his voice carried through the fortress, Grand Master Elony fell to her knees, covering her head with her arms and moaned.

A few minutes later, he let go and swayed on his feet, overwhelmed by sudden fatigue. Even though Gwyn ap Nudd had taught him how to break mind-controlling spells and incantations, he had never had to perform the so-called *cleaning* magic himself. Nevertheless, he knew that the spell had been broken.

"I had no idea that housekeeping could be so exhausting," he mumbled, turning to Grand Master Elony. "I'm taking Yaroslav Potemkin and we're leaving. I want you to know that Akira Ida and her company are under my personal protection. You try to touch her or any of her employees again, and I won't be as merciful next time."

"Yaroslav Potemkin?" she asked, rubbing her forehead, a confused expression suffusing her features. As her gaze fell upon Yaroslav, she gasped. "What is he doing here? We're not at war with the Scarlet Queen!" Slowly she got up and looked around in shock. "What's going on? Why are my sisters unconscious?"

"They're unconscious because you decided to fight with a god, my lady," replied Aidan snidely with a light bow.

"Christ All Mighty," mumbled the witch, rising. "I'm sorry, my lord. I have no idea what came over me."

"I have no idea either," replied Aidan calmly, "but I'll get to the bottom of this bullshit even if it's the last thing I do."

He bent down, picked up Yaroslav's coat and sword from the floor, and helped the vampire to his feet. The wound on his chest was gone, but he still was weak and unsteady, slowly getting over the effects of the rune. Aidan turned toward the witch one more time.

"The darkness is rising from beneath and terrible times lie ahead, Grand Master Elony," he said softly. "Keep your sisters safe and stay vigilant."

He inclined his head at her as she bowed low to him and walked out of the Main Hall with Yaroslav.

* * *

As soon as they approached the car, Sylvana walked outside and halted in front of Yaroslav. She moved his disheveled hair off his face and threw her arms around his neck, pulling him closer. Still weak, he swayed a little, embracing her awkwardly.

"I'm fine, Syl," he said into her hair, stepping away.

"You look like shit," she mumbled, "and what's with the crying, man?" She pulled out a small package with Kleenex and took one out, rubbing the dark-brown streams of dried blood off his cheeks.

He chuckled, sarcastic twinkles dancing in his eyes. "I missed you so much, I just couldn't hold it together."

Santiago approached them and tapped Yaroslav's shoulder.

"Nice to see you're still alive, man. Tell your mother that if she needs help, I'll stand by her side."

"Thanks, Santiago, I'll tell her." A wide, boyish grin split Yaroslav's face. "As long as standing is the only thing you are going to be doing with my mother," he added and quickly ducked down as Santiago's fist sailed in the place where his face had been just a moment ago.

Still smirking, the Spaniard turned to Aidan and offered his hand. Aidan squeezed it in a tight handshake, feeling the coldness of the vampire's skin.

"Santiago, thank you for your help," he said. "I hate to leave you and Sylvana like this, but Yaroslav and I must go. Our friends are waiting for us."

"I know... The darkness is rising." Santiago's dark eyebrows gathered over his eyes as he stared somewhere over Aidan's shoulder.

Aidan nodded, seized Yaroslav's elbow and snapped his fingers, teleporting back to Hawk's ranch.

The darkness is rising... and someone better be there to stop it...

As soon as Aidan and Yaroslav walked into the kitchen, everyone turned, facing them. With relief, he realized that all his friends were back and seemingly unharmed. Gunz got up, his steel eyes darting from Yaroslav to him, and a soft lopsided smile tugged at his lips. Warmth expanded in Aidan's chest—it was nice to see this uneven grin on his friend's face again. It'd been a while since he'd seen him smile.

Besides all the familiar faces, he noticed three new ones—two men and a woman. They sat around the table with steaming cups of coffee in their hands. He didn't need an introduction. Their magical energy signature spoke loud and clear. These were the three Horsemen out of four.

He greeted them, slightly inclining his head, but before he could say anything, Tessa approached him and grabbed his hand, squeezing it in her unusually cold fingers. Then she turned back toward the assembly and a guilty expression crossed her face.

"Before we start, could you please excuse me and Aidan for a moment?" she asked, squeezing Aidan's hand tighter. "We'll be quick. No more than five minutes."

Aidan sent her a veiled gaze full of surprise but walked out the door after her. He followed her outside as she nearly ran all the way to the fence. Stopping there, she turned to face him and pressed her back against the rails, breathing hard. Silently, he pulled her into his chest, wrapping his arms around her, and inhaled the familiar scent of her hair.

"I'm so glad to see you," he said, planting a soft kiss on top of her head.

She pushed against his stomach lightly and looked up, tears gathering in her velvety brown eyes. Tessa wasn't the type to fall apart crying at the first sign of trouble. She was a fighter and seeing her in this kind of distress sent Aidan's thoughts into a wild frenzy.

He wiped her tears with his fingers and sighed. More than anything he wanted to see her happy, to protect her from anything that would make her bottomless eyes swim with tears. He didn't think she was weak and needed his protection. Yet, he had this deep, all-consuming desire to always be there for her and protect her, because the mere thought of losing her was scarier than anything he had ever faced in his long life.

"What's wrong?" he asked gently.

"I'm okay," she whispered, averting her eyes, but then looked up again. The tears were gone, and an expression of determination changed her face. "Aidan, I wanted to tell you that I failed the quest. I wanted you to hear it from me before anyone else would say anything."

"What do you mean?" He frowned, shaking his head. "I don't understand. I saw all three Horsemen drinking coffee in Hawk's kitchen. One of them has to be Famine."

"Famine came with me willingly. From what I understand, all three Horsemen were expecting us and were willing to cooperate. But I still failed, Aidan... Famine gave me a test, and I screwed it up." Tessa shrugged. "Lucan told me that War put him and Zane through a test also and they both passed. I didn't..."

She told Aidan all that had happened since she went on the mission with Missi and Karma. As he listened to her detailed description of the test and everything Famine had told her after, he knew full well what Famine expected Tessa to do, and his jaw tightened as he stifled a sigh. When she finished her story, he placed his hand against her cheek, gently caressing her skin with his thumb.

"Don't kill the messenger, my love," he said softly, "but I think Famine is right."

"How so?" She glanced up at him. There was no anger in her eyes, just disappointment. "Would you have done something differently? If you had been in my place, would you have killed the person you love?"

His shoulders tensed, but he didn't break their eye contact. "I can't answer this question. Unless I am in the exact same situation, I don't know what I would or wouldn't do. But hypothetically speaking, taking into account everything that's been going on lately, I would choose to save Zane's life, not mine. And I wouldn't take a stand, refusing to make a choice the way you did either, because by doing it, I would lose both lives."

"But why? I don't understand," Tessa yelled, throwing her hands in the air. "Why Zane? He's just a little Fire Gecko. You're a god. If we have to face the followers of Chaos, wouldn't you be better suited to fight them and win? And why should I choose between two men who mean so much to me?"

"Aw, sweetheart," whispered Aidan, running his fingers through her hair. He tried to pull her closer, but she pushed him away, refusing his embrace. "From what I understand, that was the point of the test—to see if you were capable of making a strategic decision, disregarding your personal feelings."

"So why would you choose Zane?" she asked, the frustration in her voice getting an underlying tone of sarcasm. "Please enlighten me."

"Zane is not a little Fire Gecko as we all call him. He is a Great Fire Salamander. A protector of the human realm. The truth is, none of us knows the full extent of his power. Not even Kal," started Aidan. "Gathering from the latest events, his destiny was set in motion. It means he is destined to face Skiper-Zmey, eventually. Not me, not you, not Yaroslav. Sooner or later, he will face Zmey in mortal combat. The rest of us can only help and support him."

"I had no idea his destiny was set in motion. I don't even know what that means. So, Famine couldn't have expected me to make my choice based on something I didn't know." She lifted her shoulders in a shrug. "There has to be more to it. What is it?"

"Basic common sense," replied Aidan. "From what I recall, you said Famine showed you an illusion of me turning into a swan. It means that technically, if something like this would happen, Gwyn ap Nudd could restore me back to my human or godly form. The spell wouldn't kill me, but the Black Fire would kill the Fire Salamander at first touch." He gazed at her with a soft smile, thinking how young and inexperienced she still was. "So, even if I didn't know about Zane's destiny, I would choose to save him and then summon Gwyn ap Nudd so he could help me. By choosing Zane, you would have saved both of us, my love."

A slow, almost lazy clapping sounded behind him and he

turned around, finding himself face to face with a tall woman. She gave him a quick once-over and put her hands on her hips.

"Aodh mac Lir?" she asked, slightly narrowing her eyes. "I thought you would look older."

"Sorry to disappoint you," replied Aidan dryly, stepping between her and Tessa. "Famine, I presume?"

She nodded and her smile grew wider but not warmer. "I thought you'd like to know... You just passed my test, god of the Otherworld."

CHAPTER 27

~ ZANE BURNS, A.K.A. GUNZ ~

The conversation in the kitchen died out. Aidan and Tessa were still out, and Famine followed them soon after. Raoul sat on the kitchen counter, softly conversing with Missi and Karma. Kal stood in front of the window, both his hands placed on the glass. With his forehead rested against it and with his flaming hair in disarray, the Great Salamander exuded a vibe of unease. Yaroslav left accompanied by Hawk to clean up, and Gunz noticed that the absence of the vampire in the room put Lucan at ease.

I need to talk to both Yaroslav and Lucan... They must learn to work together, thought Gunz. Having a clear idea of why the elf was so anxious around vampires, he was more worried about Lucan than about Yaroslav. The vampire was old enough to be able to control his impulses no matter how attractive the elf's blood smelled to him.

Gunz leaned his back against the doorframe and closed his eyes, folding his arms over his chest. He felt drained after the test Viggo Warrington, a.k.a. War, put him and Lucan through, but he knew that any kind of rest wasn't anywhere in their foreseeable future.

The shrill ring of a cellphone broke his train of thought and he opened his eyes. Enzo Vittorio, better known as Pestilence, answered his phone and walked away from the table, halting by the window next to Kal. The Fire Elemental threw one glance at him and walked away, taking a seat next to Mrak Delar.

"Enzo Vittorio," he said dryly and fell silent, listening to someone on the other end of the line. After a moment, he waved his hand. "What types of flu virus are expected this year?"

He fell silent again, drawing something on the glass with his long finger as he listened to the report.

"Quadrivalent? Which strains?" He laughed, shaking his head. "Yes, we will also produce quadrivalent... Yes, just like the last year. Besides that, I want you to put into production something extra. Get everything ready for A(H5N1)—"

He probably got interrupted, because he grunted and pursed his lips, tapping his finger on the phone.

"Don't you think I know that? Yes, they updated A(H1N1) and A(H3N2). We did that too. But I need our company to be ready for the outbreak of H5N1," he repeated through his gritted teeth. "I know it's rare and not expected! Goddammit, Jeremy, there will be no overproduction! Have I ever been wrong? Trust me. Get the vaccine ready and be prepared to satisfy the demand."

He hung up the phone and rolled his eyes, muttering something under his breath that sounded like, "Humans! What do they know about infectious diseases?"

"So, you use your power to improve your bottom line, eh?" asked Mrak Delar, his lips curved in distaste. "Is that how you got your publicly traded Evil Incorporated to be—ah... whatchamacallit—a Fortune 500 company?"

Pestilence snickered, staring at him with derision. "I told you, Master. I'm not evil or good for that matter. I just—"

"Yeah, so I've heard. You're not good or evil, you just are," retorted Mrak Delar sardonically. "So, what would you call creating an epidemic in the human realm where thousands could suffer just so you could be the only pharmaceutical company who could provide the vaccine on short notice? You wouldn't call it pure evil, would you?"

"Of course, I wouldn't." Enzo laughed openly, throwing his head back. "I would call it a *creative entrepreneurial mind*. Thinking outside the box, you know?" He rolled his eyes and sighed. "Trust me, Master. Your precious humans do things a lot worse than that to improve their bottom lines."

The entrance door opened with a soft squeak, interrupting the heated conversation, and a moment later, Aidan and Tessa walked into the kitchen, followed by Yaroslav, Hawk and Famine. To Gunz's amusement, Yaroslav was wearing jeans and a plaid shirt, which was absolutely out of the vampire's taste and style. His long, golden hair was clean and shone with the reflected light of the late afternoon sun, and he looked refreshed and rested which made Gunz wonder how it was possible.

Yaroslav greeted everyone with a light bow, but as soon as his eyes fell on Lucan, they lit up with a hungry scarlet glow, and his fangs started to expand. He grunted, pressing his hand over his mouth, and closed his eyes, getting his thirst under control. Once he opened them again, they were a normal blue color. He threw an apologetic glance at the elf and stopped next to Gunz.

Kal got up, bearing down heavily on Mrak Delar's shoulders to keep him seated as the Master of Power kept eyeing Pestilence angrily.

"I need you all to put your differences aside," Kal growled, giving a pointed stare to Pestilence. Then he glanced at Lucan and Yaroslav. "What I'm about to tell you may come as a shock to some, and it will require complete understanding and cooperation between all parties in this room. Am I clear?"

Mrak Delar jerked, but Kal seized his hair, pulling his head backward. "Ancient Master, do you think I expressed myself clearly? Or shall I remind to these three"—he pointed at each Horsemen—"that even though they consider themselves the mightiest power here, there is always a bigger fish?"

Kal let go of Mrak's hair and started to transform, allowing the cold fire to consume his giant frame. Gunz had just a moment to shield Yaroslav from the effects of the purifying Fire before Kal spread his arms, and the air inside the room got infused with undiluted elemental energy. It didn't burn anything but made it hard to breath for those who couldn't command it. Everyone fell silent, staring at the massive blacksmith. He laughed, his deep voice filling every corner, making windows vibrate.

"Well, now that I have everyone's attention, we can begin," said Kal, brushing his flaming hair off his face. He commanded the fire to cease and leaned forward, planting his fists on the table. "As I promised, I went back to Kendral and did some digging in the Riders' Archives and Library. The good news is that I found everything I needed almost immediately. The bad news... Just as I suspected, we can't let the Horsemen ride again. That would break the remaining seals, bringing forth the Apocalypse."

"Isn't that what I warned you about?" said Raoul with a shrug. "I told you that once the Horsemen ride again, we'll have very little time to find Angel before all hell breaks loose."

"Yes, you did," agreed Kal, his lips stretching into a frosty smile. "What you forgot to mention—or didn't know perhaps—is that once the Horsemen start riding, there is no way of stopping the Apocalypse. Even if we separate them again."

"I knew that. I'm sure Pestilence and Famine knew that too," chimed in War calmly. "So, what do you want us to do?"

"You will do nothing," said Kal, sounding cold and unyielding. "All we need are your horses. They can sense Death's location as well as you do, and if other powerful beings of magic ride in your stead, we will prevent the Apocalypse. Am I correct, War?"

War frowned, tapping his fingers on the table. "It's true," he admitted finally, and the other two Horsemen nodded. "And I'm sure none of us would mind lending our horses to you. On one condition though."

"What's your condition?" Kal folded his arms and flames went up to life, dancing on his shoulders.

"We get to choose who ride our horses," said War, his hard, steel eyes lighting up with a deep reddish glow.

"Fine," agreed Kal. "Each of you can choose anyone in this room."

Famine stretched in her chair and a lazy smirk ghosted her lips as she folded her hands behind her head. "Not gonna work, ladies and gents."

"Why is that?" asked Kal.

"You all forgot how to count. Back to first grade perhaps?" She got up, held out her fist and opened one finger. "Famine and her mighty steed." She opened her second finger. "War and his little red pony." She opened her third finger. "Pestilence with his cute white horsey." She demonstrated three fingers, spinning around. "One, two, three. You need four horses—four riders. Where are you going to get another horse who can ride as fast as our three?"

Kal turned to Mrak Delar. "How about your Amicus?"

The Ancient Master shook his head. "Amicus is a great stallion, but he is not magical. He won't be able to keep up with their horses. Besides, he has no magical energy."

Gunz sighed, pressing his hand over his eyes. "I can't believe I'm saying this. I know a horse that can keep up with your three. I need a few hours to bring him here."

Yaroslav pushed him on his shoulder, a youthful grin appearing on his face. "No, you're not serious. Please tell me you are not going after that four-legged swindler?" He laughed.

"What is he talking about?" asked Kal and War at the same time. They exchanged a troubled look and then stared at Gunz.

"He's talking about Sivka-Burka," replied Yaroslav, still chuckling. "You know, that magical horse from Russian fairy tales."

"Do you know any other horse that can stay up with theirs? If you do, I'm all ears," muttered Gunz. Since Yaroslav just shrugged, he turned to Kal. "Father, I need to make a quick trip to the Land of Dreams. I'll find Siv and bring him back here."

"That's fine," said Kal, "but you're not going alone. Remember, we had an agreement. No one goes alone anywhere."

"I'll be faster alone—," started Gunz.

"Not faster than with me," Mrak Delar interrupted him. Before Gunz could object, the Master of Power grabbed his shoulder and snapped his fingers.

CHAPTER 28

~ ZANE BURNS, A.K.A. GUNZ ~

Gunz sighed, taking in his surroundings. As he expected, the Master of Power had teleported them into the catacombs under his city, and they stood next to the portal-door into the Land of Dreams. He frowned and turned to Mrak Delar, staring at him reproachfully.

"If you tell me that I'm slowing you down, boy..." The Ancient Master chuckled darkly, slightly tilting his head.

"I wasn't going to," replied Gunz. "I just wanted some—"

"As usual, I know what you wanted," Mrak interrupted him. "And as usual, I don't care. Instead of what you want, we are going to do what's right. Even though the nexus has been purified, it's still not safe for any of us to travel alone. Especially not for you, when the Destiny Enforcers can show up at any moment."

Gunz grunted and averted his eyes, kicking a gold coin with the tip of his shoe. It slid across the ground, hitting a pile of coins with a soft cling.

"Gunz, if you have something to say, now would be a good time," said Mrak Delar softly. "Before we enter the nexus."

Gunz lifted his head and smirked tiredly. "No, Mrak," he

objected, his voice barely above a whisper. "As always, you're right. Let's go?"

Mrak Delar stepped through the portal, and Gunz followed him. He felt a heavy load settle in his soul, and he couldn't understand why. Mrak hadn't said or done anything out of character, but a feeling of dread spread through him, setting his nerves on edge.

* * *

ONCE GUNZ STEPPED out of the portal, magical energy enveloped him, and he bent forward, struggling for breath, feeling unsteady and intoxicated. When he was able to straighten up, he found himself in a wide-open field in front of the Gatekeeper's house. She stood just a foot away from him with her arms folded over her chest. Mrak was next to her, a drunk smile lingering on his full lips. With his eyes flooded with the darkness of his power and his face relaxed, he looked about the same age as Gunz.

"I can never get used to the effect the nexus has on me. The amount of magical and elemental energy here is jarring," Gunz mumbled, but then noticed that the Gatekeeper was tapping her foot impatiently and bowed to her. "I'm sorry, my lady. Please forgive my lack of manners."

"Don't waste your time bowing to me. You modern men never learned how to do it properly anyway." She readjusted her kerchief, tucking the loose strands of her silvery-gray hair under it. "You're not here to just have a small talk with me, Fire Salamander. You're looking for that pesky stallion."

Gunz's eyebrows climbed up, but then he chuckled, shaking his head. "You're a seer, Baba Maria. I keep forgetting."

"My lady, do you know where we can find Siv?" asked Mrak Delar.

"Only mighty Stribog, the god of the Wind, Air and Sky,

knows where this four-legged monster is today," muttered Baba Maria, turning heavily in Gunz's direction. Her blind eyes were shut, but Gunz knew she could see him perfectly well. "Why don't you call him, Gunz? You're an Eastern Slav, I believe. You should know how."

"You can't be serious," mumbled Gunz, scratching the back of his head.

Baba Maria just shrugged, and a web of small wrinkles materialized around her eyes as she grinned at him.

"You *are* serious," murmured Gunz. "Why do I always have to look like an idiot, reciting some children's bedtime stories?"

He put two fingers into his mouth and whistled. As he weaved some of his magic into the whistle, the wind rushed through the field, bending the tall grass down, rustling the threes.

"Sivka-Burka, come!" yelled Gunz, his magically enhanced voice echoing through the forest.

Nothing.

"Just as I thought—didn't work," announced Gunz.

"Of course, it didn't work!" Baba Maria huffed, throwing her hands in the air. "What the hell was that? A web translation of the summoning spell? Say it in Russian, boy, the way you should."

Gunz threw a tortured gaze at Mrak Delar, but the Master of Power just bit his lip to suppress his laughter and twirled his hand, gesturing for him to go on.

"Fine!" grumbled Gunz. "Here goes nothing…" He whistled again and yelled at the top of his lungs, infusing his words with fire. "*Sivka-Burka, veschaya kaurka! Stan' peredo mnoj kak list pered travoj!*"

Nothing.

Gunz gave Baba Maria an arched stare, placing his hands on his hips, but before he could say anything, a loud phone ring interrupted him. Baba Maria flinched and pulled the device out of her pocket, muttering something under her breath. On the outside it looked like a normal iPhone, but the apple on the back of it shone with a bright green light.

"Darling Lily?" asked Gunz, a wide grin splitting his face at the thought of the little guiding spirit inhabiting the magical phone.

Baba Maria nodded and put the device on speaker, showing him the screen with a photo of a beautiful stallion with a rich golden mane.

Darling Lily cleared her throat and announced with the best voice of a newscaster, "We're sorry; the number you have dialed —S-I-V-K-A-B-U-R-K-A—has been disconnected or is no longer in service. If you have an emergency, please hang up and dial your local stables."

Mrak Delar burst out laughing, and even Baba Maria smiled, shaking her head.

"I'm going to kill this magical grifter, I swear," growled Gunz, sending Mrak into the next fit of wild laugher.

"I think I already like this horse," murmured the Master of Power once he stopped laughing.

"As long as you don't have anything sparkling on you," said Baba Maria with a sarcastic smirk, "you can like him all you want."

"I have nothing except my sparkling personality," replied Mrak Delar, chuckling.

"Sparkling, alright," grumbled Gunz as he took over the magical device. "Darling Lily, can you please show us where Sivka-Burka is?"

The screen of the phone flashed with orange-red flames, looking like a digital fireplace. A moment later, the fire got replaced with a bouncing scarlet heart.

"Yum, who do we have here?" purred the guiding spirit, making the heart bounce faster from one side of the screen to the other. "The young Fire Salamander and the Ancient Master of Power. What a wonderful picture you two present. You make my SIM card sing. So, you're looking for Siv... one moment, please..."

The device flashed, maps and photos moving so fast it was impossible to recognize anything. Suddenly the flashing stopped, and Lily said in a robotic voice, "We're sorry... The number you have dialed—" She cut herself off and displayed a picture of a laughing monkey, jumping up and down. "Just kidding. You should've seen your faces."

"Ha-ha," said Gunz, rolling his eyes. "Everyone is a comedian. Did you find him?"

"Who do you think I am?" asked Lily indignantly, displaying a set of blazing angry eyes on the screen. "Of course, I did. He's in the forest, right on the border between the Kingdom of Copper and Kingdom of Silver." She displayed a standard GPS map with a giant red cross in the middle.

Mrak Delar peered at the screen over Gunz's shoulder. "I know where he is," said the Master of Power. He bowed to the Gatekeeper respectfully. "Thank you for your assistance, my lady. I'll take it from here."

Baba Maria approached him and took his hand into hers. Then she opened her milky-white eyes and locked her gaze with his. The Master of Power stilled, his shoulders stiff, his chest shuddering with laborious breaths. After a moment she let go, and he closed his eyes, relaxing his rigid body with a soft moan.

"Ancient Master," she said so softly Gunz could barely make out her words, "you're in the right place, as always. When you get back to Arizona, please say hello to Aodh mac Lir and tell him that I sense a lot more lavender in his destiny."

"Lavender... In his destiny? Did you mean, in his future?" asked Mrak Delar, troubled. "I don't understand."

"No, in his destiny. Tell him exactly the way I told you. Word for word." The old lady chuckled, patted his hand and added, not without a thin layer of sarcasm. "Don't worry your pretty head over it, Master. Just give my message to the young god." She stopped talking and sighed, getting back into a serious mood. "Take care of your fiery friend. He doesn't know it, but he needs you now more than ever... And that little story Pestilence told you?" Mrak Delar nodded. "Keep it to yourself."

She squeezed his hand before turning around to face Gunz. "Child of Fire," she said gently, "you're doing the right thing—"

"...Said no one ever," murmured Mrak Delar under his breath, but Baba Maria threw a warning stare at him, and he raised his hands up, a wide grin on his face.

"Two court jesters," said the Gatekeeper with a deep sigh, but her blind eyes crinkled at the corners. "Maybe your sarcasm and humor are what's needed to survive this magical turmoil."

She patted Gunz on his shoulder and pulled him closer into a motherly embrace. He stilled in her arms, then exhaled, lowering his head to her shoulder. For the first time in days, he felt relaxed and safe. He wasn't sure why or where this feeling came from, but it soothed his stretched nerves, giving him the few moments of peace he needed so desperately. But the feeling was gone too fast as the Gatekeeper let go, her wrinkled hand caressing his cheek.

"Be careful, child," she whispered, deep sadness shadowing her words, "for riding a steed of the Apocalypse is not a joking matter."

As Mrak Delar put his hand on Gunz's shoulder and snapped his fingers, the world around Gunz swirled and then dissolved into a continuous roller-coaster of colors and sounds.

* * *

"Down," hissed Mrak Delar and dropped to the ground, pulling Gunz with him. "Something is not right here."

Gunz didn't expect that and fell awkwardly, hitting his forehead on the trunk of a fallen tree. He grunted, clasping his hand to his head, feeling the wetness of blood under his fingers. Mrak Delar pressed his finger to his lips, asking him to be silent, but it was too late. Somewhere close by, wings flapped, and the dry sound of broken branches echoed through the forest. An annoyed neighing of a horse followed the commotion.

Gunz slowly scrambled into a sitting position and peeked from behind the tree. Two birds as large as any ostrich were steadily gaining height, supported by their powerful wings. Despite the late hour, their plumage shone with red and orange colors as though they were set on fire. Their long beautiful tails and wings emanated smoldering heat and the distinct energy of elemental fire, and that fact alone made them attractive to him.

"Firebirds. Quite rare, even for the nexus. Their feathers are priceless," whispered Mrak Delar. He channeled his power, and the ground shook slightly as he probed the area. "Gunz, I think we have a bit of a problem on—"

He didn't get to finish his statement as the irritable neighing of a horse interrupted him. "Three thousand white mares, Salamander!" Siv muttered, kicking the tree with his hind leg. "You can stop hiding now."

Gunz got up and looked around. Mrak had teleported them into the heart of an ancient forest. Tall trees with enormous limbs, weighed down by a canopy of heavy green leaves, stretched high into the sky. Their thick trunks were wrapped in patches of brown moss, and long vines hung from their branches like strange emerald garlands.

They stood on the border with a large meadow, covered in tall grass dotted by specks of white and yellow flowers. Smack in the middle of it, there was a sizable mountain of pure silver. The metal sparkled dimly in the reflected light of the last rays of the setting sun. Two large washtubs were positioned next to the silver mountain. One of them was filled with grain and wine, its bittersweet aroma wafting through the air, overpowering the scent of wet greenery, wildflowers and foliage. The second one was empty, lying upside down.

Siv danced in front of them, his round purple eyes darting left and right nervously. Gunz frowned, observing the horse's behavior warily, and sharpened his Salamander senses. The Master of Power was correct—something felt off about this entire area. Even though the forest and the meadow looked absolutely normal, his senses were throwing one red flag after another.

He opened his other sight and gasped. A large territory, at least a mile around the meadow, was surrounded by a shining wall of magic. It wasn't a God's snare—both Gunz and Mrak Delar would have sensed it immediately, yet this magic was just as potent and had a dangerous vibe to it.

"Siv, stop hopping around," said Gunz, grabbing the stallion's mane and yanking it down, "and explain to me what you got us into this time."

"Oh yeah? That's interesting," neighed Siv, shaking his head to loosen Gunz's grip on his mane. He stopped dancing and narrowed his purple eyes, glaring at him. "I got you into something? I didn't summon you here. You showed up unannounced, made all this ruckus and scared my Firebirds. Now what am I supposed to do?"

"I don't care what you do," hissed Gunz as the energy field of the unknown magic somehow doubled, assaulting his senses. "What the hell is this place, and why do I feel like we just walked into a trap?"

"Gunz, forget about the horse. I think we have a bigger problem on our hands," whispered Mrak Delar, touching his shoulder. Gunz glanced at him, noticing that the Ancient Master had his black sword in his hands, and his eyes were flooded with the darkness of his power. "We're no longer alone."

Gunz spun around, pulling his Swiss army knife out of his pocket in one fluid motion and turning it into a sword.

Blocking all their ways out, a large group of armed men surrounded them, standing with their swords at the ready. They were dressed in dark tunics and pants, but the soft clinks of metal on metal betrayed the presence of chainmail beneath their clothes. All in all, they didn't look like a friendly bunch.

Three tall women in long, dark cloaks stood outside the circle of armed men. Their arms were stretched wide and their lips kept moving as they chanted something soundlessly. Gunz touched them with his senses and threw a quick glance at the Master of Power—all three women were powerful witches. He had no doubt they were the ones who placed and supported the magical barrier around the meadow.

Another dark shadow separated from a nearby tree, and a tall man in his late forties approached them. He had the hard face of a warrior with a thin white scar crossing his face from his right temple to his chin, cutting across his lips. He regarded Gunz and Mrak Delar calmly and sheathed his sword.

"Who are you and what are you doing here?" he asked, his voice just as emotionless as his face.

Mrak Delar lowered his sword and stepped forward, gesturing for Gunz to lower his weapon.

"I'm Mrak Delar, the Ancient Master of Power," he introduced himself, slightly inclining his head, and then pointed at Gunz with his hand. "This is Zane Burns, the young Fire Salamander. May I ask who you are and on whose authority you're holding us within the circle of your magic?"

For a split-second, the man's eyes widened as his gaze slipped from Mrak Delar to Gunz, but the tiny moment of shock was gone so quickly that Gunz wasn't sure it happened at all. The man pressed his hand to his chest and bowed low, nearly touching the ground.

"Master of Power… my lord, please forgive us. It wasn't our intention to hold you imprisoned here," he said softly. "I'm Svetozar, the personal bodyguard of the Moonlight Princess, the only daughter of the Moon. We're here only to make sure that the stallion keeps his word."

"Siv, what did you do this time?" asked Gunz, glowering at the horse with murderous intent in his eyes.

"Well...," Siv whined, rotating his overly wide eyes, a guilty grin exposing his large teeth. "You're not going to believe me if I told you."

"Try me," growled Gunz, turning his sword into the knife before placing it back into his pocket.

"I didn't do anything... I swear. I just wanted—," started Siv but fell silent as Svetozar frowned and shook his head, his lips pressed in a straight line.

"This stallion stole the feather of a Firebird from Her Highness' collection," the warrior explained, distaste and aggravation shadowing his features. "Our witches managed to trace him, and we captured the thief. But he already sold the priceless artifact. In her infinite kindness, the Moonlight Princess offered him one last chance to redeem himself. He must deliver a new Firebird feather to her. If he fails, we have orders to execute him by sunrise."

"Dammit," muttered Gunz, throwing his hands up. "Why is it every time I lay my eyes on this pesky horse, I find myself neck-deep in trouble?"

Mrak Delar smiled calmly, giving Gunz a little nudge on his shoulder. "Svetozar, unfortunately we need Siv alive and with all four legs attached. I can see you're a good man who's just doing his job, and neither I nor my young friend here"—he waved at Gunz—"want to fight you and your men. What can we do to convince you to let us go and release this stallion into our care?"

"My lord... with all due respect..." Svetozar inclined his head slightly, but his face remained as hard and unrelenting as ever. "I can allow you and the young Salamander to leave, but Siv must deliver on his promise or die."

"They scared my Firebirds away! It's their fault I couldn't get the feather!" whined Siv, rearing away from Svetozar.

"Shut up when I'm trying to save your useless, lying hide!" Gunz hissed, anger spiking the fire within him.

He threw a scorching stare at Siv, small flames bursting through his skin, dancing on his arms and shoulders.

"Svetozar," he addressed the bodyguard, ignoring Siv's indignant snort. "What if I offer you a feather of the Phoenix instead? I believe the feathers of the Phoenix are just as valuable and rare as the feathers of Firebirds. Would that make the Moonlight Princess happy?"

Svetozar glanced back at his witches and all three of them nodded energetically, their faces alight with excitement.

"If you can deliver a feather of the Phoenix, I accept it with much gratitude and allow you and the Ancient Master to leave with the stallion," replied Svetozar. "But may I ask you, where are you planning to find a Phoenix. Extremely rare creatures of Fire they are. I haven't seen a Phoenix in the Land of Dreams for ages."

"I'm well connected," muttered Gunz, pressing his hand over his tattoo as he sent a burst of his Fire through it. "Mishka, are you with me?"

The wyvern materialized above his head and twirled around, taking in his surroundings.

"Wow," he said, landing on Gunz's shoulder. "You know what I like the most about our relationship, boss?"

"No, but I am sure you're going to tell me," muttered Gunz, glancing at Svetozar apologetically.

"It's the element of surprise," continued Mishka, migrating to the top of Mrak Delar's head, away from Gunz as his fire energy spiked again. "I never know what kind of shithole I'm going to find myself in when you summon me."

Mrak Delar chuckled and extended his arm, allowing

Mishka to move there. "You and me both, little brother," he whispered loudly, winking at the wyvern.

"Mishka, how long would it take for you to travel to Kendral and back?" asked Gunz, ignoring the fact that the wyvern was whispering something into Mrak's ear, his fiery eyes staring at Gunz with a humorous twinkle.

"Five minutes." Mishka lifted his head, staring at Gunz suspiciously. "Why?"

"I need you to go to Kendral and find the Phoenix," replied Gunz, bracing himself for an onslaught of questions.

"Why?"

"As you know, the Phoenix is our brother in element and my friend. I need one of his feathers and I hope he's not going to say no to me in time of need." Gunz sighed. *If he is going to ask me why—*

"Why?"

"I need to give it to Svetozar." He stared at the wyvern tiredly. *Why me...*

"Why? This Svetozar and his men don't look like nice people," muttered Mishka, spreading his wings. "I don't like angry people with sharp pointy things in their hands."

Gunz sighed again and said as patiently as he could muster. "The feather is a payment for Siv's life, Mishka. We need Siv's help."

Mishka's eyes settled on the horse and he hissed angrily, emitting a fountain of bright sparks followed by a small cloud of light smoke. "Why do you need this conhorse?" He flew, hovering in the air between Gunz and Siv, spitting angry fireballs at the stallion. "What kind of scam did you get my ignoramus-boss into, Siv?"

"Scam? Me?" Siv neighed innocently and moved to the side, endeavoring to peek around the wyvern at Gunz. "Hey, Salamander, can you control your teacup dragon?"

"Teacup dragon???" yelled Mishka, his entire body bursting

into furious flames. "Who are you calling a teacup or a dragon for that matter, you ignorant mule!"

"Enough!" yelled Gunz, and a wall of fire expanded between Siv and Mishka. "I don't have time for this bullshit!" He lifted his arm, ordering Mishka to land and once the wyvern settled down, he asked, "How long would it take for you to find the Phoenix and bring his feather back?"

"Five minutes, if he is at home," grumbled Mishka, pouting. "Twenty minutes if he's anywhere in Kendral. Forever, if he is roaming the worlds of magic and different realms."

"Go!" barked Gunz, barely able to contain his anger and spiking elemental energy.

Mishka huffed indignantly but vanished. Mrak Delar approached Gunz and squeezed his arm. "Control your power, my friend, or I will have to do it for you."

"Sorry... I know..." Gunz pressed his hand over his eyes and exhaled heavily, moving his fingers over his face.

Neither Svetozar nor his team said anything, and he was grateful for the short reprieve. When the wyvern materialized in front of him with a flaming feather in his paw, Gunz experienced an instant relief, feeling as though he had been holding his breath all this time. He held out his hand, and Mishka placed the flaming feather in his palm.

He was about to offer it to Svetozar when Mrak Delar stopped him. The Master of Power whispered something and a small silver box, bedazzled with gemstones that looked like rubies, materialized in his hand. Channeling the power of Fire, he took the feather of the Phoenix and placed it inside the box.

"Svetozar, I believe we honored our word," he said, offering it to the warrior. "Now, you must hold your side of the deal."

The man took the box with a respectful bow, then turned around and nodded to his witches. They stopped chanting and the magical barrier dissipated a moment later.

"You and your friend are free to go, Master," he said, handing the box to one of the women. "The stallion is yours, at your own peril." He smirked. "It was a pleasure doing business with you."

He waved at his people and they softly stepped into the shadows of the forest, quickly disappearing from view.

As soon as they were gone, Siv made a circle around the meadow and stopped in front of Gunz.

"Well, it was fun chatting with you," he said, his shameless purple eyes showing no gratitude, "but on that note, I must go."

"No, you don't." Gunz seized his golden mane, wringing it around his arm. "You're coming with us—"

"Or else," added Mrak Delar, sending a touch of his magic toward his eyes, making them completely black.

Siv froze, his entire body stiff with fear. Then he turned his head to Gunz and whispered, "Hey, little Salamander, where is your defective vamp? I think I like him better than this terrifying Master of Power…"

"Defective vamp?" Mrak Delar almost choked. "Is he talking about Yaroslav?" Gunz nodded, giving him a warning stare. "I don't even want to ask." The Master of Power raised his hands, taking a step back, but a wild grin spread across his face. "I got to remember this one…"

"First of all," growled Gunz, yanking the horse's mane before letting it go, "I already told you—you don't get to call me little Salamander. Second, Yaroslav is not defective, and I don't ever want to hear you saying it again." He sent some fire toward his eyes and smirked as Siv took a step to the side, trying to get away from him. "Now that we got all that straight, you're going to take us to the door out of the Land of Dreams and we'll take it from there."

"Fine!" snapped Siv, inching his way around Gunz, his eyes carefully following Mishka's every move. "But at least tell me what kind of emergency brought the almighty Fire Salamander to seek out lowly old me."

"I can do that," replied Gunz dryly. "We're looking for a

horse who can run as fast as the four horses of the Apocalypse. If you're as fast as you say you are, you should have no problem, right?"

"You have to ask?" huffed Siv, pride reflected in his shameless eyes. "I'll leave them in the dust. Big friggin' deal—four horsemen of the whatever. Four immatures, that's what they are."

"I guess we'll see?" murmured Mrak Delar.

Approaching the stallion, he ran his fingers through his long mane, patting his neck and the dark fur of his back. Siv stilled, visibly enjoying Mrak's touch.

"There is nothing to see," announced Siv. "Hop on. Both of you."

Mrak Delar flew on top of the horse in one easy motion and offered his hand to Gunz. He took his friend's hand and mounted Siv, wishing he could be as good at horseback riding as the Ancient Master.

"Now, hold on to your hats, boys!" the stallion neighed happily and pushed off the ground, rising high above the tallest trees in the forest.

CHAPTER 29

~ ZANE BURNS, A.K.A. GUNZ ~

"Oh, my God! He's so cute!" Tessa squealed, running toward the stallion. "I've never seen such a beautiful horse!"

Gunz exchanged an all-knowing glance with Mrak Delar and both snickered, expecting the stallion's reaction. Siv didn't disappoint. As soon as Tessa put her hand on his golden mane, threading her fingers through it, he shook his head, taking a few steps to the side, away from her.

"Whoa, whoa... No touchy...," he neighed indignantly, raising one hoof up. "Who do you think I am, girl? A fluffy kitty-cat?"

"Oh, my God! He is a *talking* horse to boot!" Ignoring Siv's displeasure, Tessa caught up with him and wrapped her arm around his neck, caressing his back gently.

"Ahhh...," Siv exhaled, closing his round eyes, an expression of pure bliss reflected on his face. "I can get used to that..."

Mishka hissed, spitting fireballs in Siv's direction, and then landed on Tessa's shoulder, pressing his hot head to her cheek.

"I thought you liked me?"

Tessa laughed, letting go of the stallion. "I love you, Mishka."

She waited until the wyvern moved onto her arm and kissed the top of his head gently. "But you know, I've never seen a horse, and this one is so beautiful. Don't be jealous."

"Jealous?" Mishka huffed, throwing his wings in the air. "Why would I be jealous? That would mean that I think he's better than me. Thank you very much." Mishka pouted at first, but then sighed and migrated to Gunz's shoulder.

Gunz just chuckled, caressing the wyvern's back absentmindedly. He sat down on the porch, watching Tessa, Missi and Karma talking to Siv, exchanging jokes with the sharp-tongued stallion. They looked so peaceful and so normal that for a moment he forgot that none of these young women could be called normal, or human for that matter—a demigod, a mage and a witch-slash-supernatural assassin.

He felt a burning in his tattoo and brushed his fingers over it, in the back of his mind realizing that it was Mishka hiding there. With a soft groan, he leaned against the railing and closed his eyes. His thoughts were scattered and foggy, and he couldn't focus on anything at all. His body was heavy, and he didn't think he could move even if his life depended on it. The voices of his friends, the neighing of Siv, the soft whispering of the wind—everything blended into a continuous white noise, and he wasn't sure whether he was still awake or dreaming some strange, surreal dream.

Feeling a soft nudge on his shoulder, he lifted his head and saw Aidan and Yaroslav sitting on his right. He smiled tiredly at his friends, looking at them through his half-closed eyelids.

"How was your trip to the Land of Dreams?" asked Aidan. Glancing sideways, he leaned forward to rest his elbows on his lap.

"Uneventful." Gunz turned slightly to face his friends. "Compared to my previous trips to the nexus, that is."

"Uneventful when it comes to a meeting with Siv?" Yaroslav laughed, shaking his head. "Impossible."

Before Gunz could say anything, Mrak Delar approached them and halted with his hands shoved into the pockets of his pants.

"Aidan, Lady Gatekeeper gave me a message for you," he said. Even though he was as calm as usual, a tiny modulation in his deep voice betrayed the concern he felt. His dark eyebrows knitted above his eyes as he regarded the god of the Otherworld. "Her message was a little strange, so I hope you know what it means."

"What is it?" asked Aidan, stiffening, his relaxed look gone.

"She asked me to tell you that she senses a lot more lavender in your destiny." Mrak Delar lifted his shoulders in a light shrug. "Does it mean anything to you?"

"She said *destiny*, not future?" Aidan's voice was so quiet and strained that Gunz raised his eyes, staring at his friend with surprise.

"That was my exact question," said Mrak Delar, his frown getting deeper. He sighed and rubbed his forehead. "She said destiny and made sure that I would repeat her words exactly as she said them."

"Dammit...," Aidan exhaled, covering his drained face with his hands. "I was so hoping it wasn't the case."

"Aidan, I'm tired of riddles and the truth being concealed from me by people I'm supposed to trust." Mrak Delar grabbed his arm, and his grip wasn't light. "We need to talk. I must understand what's going on."

Aidan glanced at the Ancient Master and a sad smirk touched his lips. "You're right. We should talk. But I also need Kal and Gwyn in on this conversation." He thought for a moment and then added, "Actually, Zane and Yaroslav should come too."

Gunz got up, his every move slow and weary. Opening the entrance door, he gestured toward it. "So, let's have a talk."

* * *

They settled in the small room Gunz used as his bedroom, and Aidan summoned Gwyn ap Nudd. As briefly as possible, he described everything that had happened in the Sisterhood of the Sun and what had been done to Yaroslav to keep him under control. After he finished, a heavy silence spread over the room.

"Lavender...," Gunz whispered, cringing inwardly at the thought of what he was about to say. "When Gwyn and I were at Mrak's trial in the main hall of the Destiny Council headquarters, I detected a very light scent of lavender there... It was so light, and it felt so artificial... I thought it was just an air freshener."

He glanced at Gwyn ap Nudd, but the King of the Otherworld just shook his head. "I wish you had told me," he said, bracing his arms at either side of the communication windows. "I don't understand how you could sense it while I sensed nothing. I'm a lot more powerful than you are, so I should be more sensitive to things like that..." He dropped his head and his long black hair fell over his face. "I'll be damned..."

"I think the only reason I could sense it was because of my blindness," suggested Gunz. "At the time, my Salamander senses had taken over for the lost vision, and I felt like a dog, sensing every tiny smell around me. To be honest, it was making me sick." He chuckled humorously, but the same concern surfaced in his mind—anything related to magical energy, Gwyn should have sensed before he did. "What does it mean, anyway?"

Noticing that Gwyn was staring at someone over his head, he turned around. Aidan got up and his expression hardened as his darkened gaze halted on Gunz.

"But you know it, Zane," he said softly, and a cold shiver ran down Gunz's back as understanding dawned on him. "Magical energy is not odorless. Some magic, like demonic essence, for example, has a strong, putrid smell which can be easily detected even by humans. Some magic has a barely noticeable scent that even gods have a hard time catching."

He stopped talking, observing everyone in the room. Kal nodded and waved his hand, asking Aidan to proceed.

"Anyway," he continued, throwing a quick glance at Yaroslav, "the scent of lavender is associated with a particularly powerful spell which sole purpose is to control someone's mind. Imagine my shock when I entered the Sisterhood of the Sun building and noticed the smell of lavender. It wasn't strong, and just like Gunz said, it felt artificial. But it was enough for me to suspect that something wasn't right."

He covered his eyes with his hand and took a deep breath as if the mere thought of what he was about to say was hurting him.

"The Gatekeeper said that she sensed a lot of lavender in my destiny, not future…" Aidan's voice faded away, and he cleared his throat before continuing. "I know what her message means. It means that the same person who invaded the Sisterhood and placed a spell on them, is possibly controlling the Destiny Council and all other supernatural organizations which report to them, including Guardians and Wardens. Zane's statement just confirmed my theory."

"Fire Almighty," whispered Mrak Delar, shaking his head. "Again? For an organization who can't hold their own, they wield way too much power."

Gwyn ap Nudd smirked bitterly. "Fresh after the trial, I can imagine how you feel, Ancient Master," he said, his unnerving white eyes bored into Mrak. "As you're well aware, I don't have warm and fuzzy feelings toward them either." He glanced around the room and added, "None of us do. But let me ask you, Mrak… You said they can't hold their own… So, how many times do you recall through your long life that the Destiny Council itself was compromised?"

Mrak Delar frowned, his gaze becoming unfocused for a

split-moment as he traveled back in his memory. "Two," he said finally. "First time when the Master of Kendral was falsely accused and had to stand on trial and now."

"Two," repeated Gwyn ap Nudd with a short nod. "My life is thousands of years longer than yours, Master. Even Kalidus is younger than I am. But two times—that's all I can recall as well. Through thousands of years, the Destiny Council was compromised only twice."

The King of the Otherworld exhaled and bit his lip, falling silent. No one said anything, and Gunz averted his eyes, staring down at his tightly clenched hands. A dull ache spread through his back, reminding him about his recent stay at the Destiny Council compound. It was just too fresh, and he wasn't sure he could ever forgive everything he went through. Let alone forget.

"As much as I hate to admit it, we need them," continued Gwyn ap Nudd at length, his soft voice making Gunz flinch. "And even though in most cases, we don't understand how they work and why they do certain things, I still believe that whatever they do is for the greater good."

"Gwyn is right." Kal leaned forward slightly, propping his elbows on his lap, and the bed moaned under the weight of his body. His wrists dangled powerlessly as he dropped his head, his flaming hair obscuring his face. "We don't understand them. We hate them. And we still need them."

"When Master Alliandr was falsely accused, the Destiny Council had been truly compromised," continued Gwyn ap Nudd. "They had a traitor in their midst. This time it's different." He took a pause, observing everyone in the room. "It's a lot worse. Someone managed to break through the defense system of the Destiny Council realm. The defense system which is supposed to be unbreakable! Whoever did that, has to be an extremely powerful Master of the Dark Arts. The spell they used to control them is one of the forbidden ones." He stopped talking and his blazing eyes halted on Gunz.

Gunz cringed and raised his hand up, as if he was trying to protect himself from what was coming.

"I understand everything you explained, Gwyn," he said, a bitter uneven smirk appearing on his face. "But please don't ask me to help them..." His voice disappeared into a heavy silence, and he lowered his head, rubbing his forehead. "I can't... I'm sorry."

"I wish I could ask you, but that won't be wise, young Salamander." Gwyn ap Nudd shrugged his unclothed shoulders. "Until we break the spell, you should keep away from any organization controlled by the Destiny Council. Ideally, Aidan as an oath-breaker"—he threw a stern stare in his son's direction—"should stay away from them too. But unfortunately, besides me, Kalidus and Zane Burns, Aidan is the only one who has what it takes to break this malevolent magic. So, he'll have to take a chance."

"Father, but what about Angel? I must—," Aidan started but got interrupted by a loud knock on the door.

"Kal," said Gwyn ap Nudd with urgency in his voice, "summon me as soon as you sort out the Horsemen business and send them on their way." He nodded at the Fire Elemental and closed the communication window.

The door opened with a soft squeak and Viggo Warrington walked inside. His mere presence added to the already heavy tension in the room. His hard, gray eyes slipped from one person to the next, halting on Gunz. The corners of his mouth lifted ever so slightly, but the semblance of a smile was gone a heartbeat later as he waved his hand at the door.

"It's time," he said and walked out.

CHAPTER 30

~ ZANE BURNS, A.K.A. GUNZ ~

The sun was gone, and the unblemished sky was colored in the electric ultramarine shades of late evening, preceding nightfall. The air—cool and crisp—was filled with the dusty, earthy scent of the desert, and crickets accompanied by cicadas started their shrilling concert.

Except for Hawk and Theron, everyone had gathered outside already, taking all available chairs on the porch. Famine and Pestilence stood by the house, conversing quietly in a strange language Gunz couldn't recognize. Since his magic couldn't help him with the translation, he assumed that this language was at least as old as the Dragon Tongue if not older.

Lucan, who stood by the door, leaning his back against the wall, turned around and gave Gunz a short nod. His bright eyes halted on Yaroslav, but he didn't cringe or shy away from the vampire. *I guess they had a talk,* thought Gunz with relief as he sat down on the steps next to Mrak Delar.

Pestilence stepped forward, observing everyone who had gathered in front of the house and his dark eyes lit up with the glow of his magic.

"We shouldn't wait anymore," he said, his normally velvety

voice filled with urgency. "The three of us can't spend much longer together without grave consequences to this world. Besides, the longer Death is missing, the feebler the veil becomes, which is fraught with terrible danger."

He stopped talking and War stepped forward. "In a minute, we'll summon our mounts, and even though we're not going to ride, the world will become unstable. So, the sooner you complete your mission and come back here, the better it is for your realm. Do you understand me?"

"Oh, we understand you just fine," muttered Kal, folding his massive arms over his chest. "Most of us weren't born yesterday. So, let's get to the point. Who is riding your steeds?"

Famine walked up to him, looking up into his flaming eyes, and a slow smile stretched her thin lips.

"Hmmm...," she purred. "It's true what they say—fire and patience are mutually exclusive."

He grunted and moved away, eliciting a soft giggle from her.

"We'll let you know in a moment. Those who are chosen, must be ready to leave immediately." She winked at Kal and turned to Pestilence. "The stage is yours, brother."

Pestilence took a ring off his finger. Squeezing it in his left fist, he started to chant. Using the same ancient language the Horsemen used to communicate with each other, he weaved a complex spell, sustaining it with his words and the fluid motions of his right hand.

As he kept chanting, stormy clouds gathered over their heads, and a blinding lightning bolt arched through the sky, forking into hundreds of directions. The thunder rumbled, making the windows jingle drearily, and a bright, white portal opened before him.

"Come...," he whispered, and even though his voice was soft and quiet, there was so much power in it that every other sound seemed to dim down. A powerful wave of magical energy spread around him, rushing in all directions, and whatever sounds still remained died out immediately, leaving them under the pressure of silence—deadly and unnatural.

The portal swirled faster and a beautiful white stallion walked through it, halting next to Pestilence. With a quick wave of his hand, the Horseman closed the portal. He approached the horse and wrapped his arm around its neck, softly whispering something into its ear.

A moment later, Pestilence pulled away so slowly as if letting go of his horse was causing him physical pain. He walked toward Mrak Delar and halted, staring down at him. The Master of Power raised his eyes, and his lips parted, an expression of horror on his face.

"No," he said, rising, taking a step up the stairs. "Not me. Choose someone else, Pestilence. After everything you put me through, I don't want to have—"

Pestilence laughed, a cold and dry sound that made the Master of Power visibly cringe and stop talking mid-sentence. The Horseman seized Mrak's arm and yanked him down the steps.

"I don't care what you want, Ancient Master. You're the *only* person here who's more or less suitable to ride my steed. No one else will be able to control him."

"Ancient Master," Kal growled warningly. "Try to remember..."

Mrak Delar grunted, closing his eyes for a few long seconds as a painful crease settled between his eyebrows. "Fine," he said finally. "What do you need me to do?"

"Your hand, Master." Pestilence seized his wrist, pulling him closer, and put his ring on the middle finger of Mrak's right hand. "Do not take this ring off until you're back here."

As soon as the metal touched his skin, Mrak's appearance began to change. His usual black shirt and pants got replaced by a completely white attire of an ancient warrior. A large bow and a quiver with arrows materialized behind his back, and his black sword was replaced by a long dagger. At the last moment, a gold crown appeared on his head, and a thin golden collar encircled his neck.

Feeling the cold touch of metal to his skin, Mrak Delar cried out like he was in pain and grasped at the collar, struggling to rip it off. Pestilence seized his hands, stopping him.

"Patience, Master!" he yelled, forcing his arms down. "Both the collar and the crown will be gone in a moment. They're just a symbol of what you've become once you took over my ring... and my mantle."

Breathing hard, the Master of Power stopped struggling, raising his eyes at the infamous Horseman. "Why me?" he croaked.

"Because..." Pestilence let go of his arms as the crown and the collar dissipated. "You are the only one who has it all in you. You're the darkness and the light. You're the King and the Slave. You're the savior and the destroyer. You are Conquest and Pestilence." He gave him a quick once-over and smirked. "And judging by your appearance, the ring has chosen you as Conquest."

Enzo Vittorio gathered the reins of his horse and walked it to Mrak Delar.

"Take care of my best friend, Ancient Master." As Mrak Delar easily flew into the saddle, Pestilence brushed his horse's white mane and stepped away, raising his eyebrows at War. "Your turn, brother."

Viggo Warrington took a few steps forward and his steel eyes glanced over everyone present, halting on Raoul de Beaumont.

"Warden," said the Horseman frostily. "The events you're witnessing as we speak are of historical significance. I hope you're recording everything you see for your Warden's Archives."

Raoul met his heavy gaze without blinking. Silently inclining his head, he said, "Yes, my lord. I do record everything that's going on here right now as I believe you to be right. However, it'll be awhile before I can face my brothers after what I have done."

War smirked. "It may happen earlier than you think."

He turned away from Raoul, his eyes halting on Gunz and then darting to Kal. He took his ring off and just like Pestilence before him, he started his chant, pronouncing the words of the ancient tongue clearly.

A portal shimmering with a bright, scarlet light expanded in front of him. Scorching flames danced around the perimeter of the portal, permeating the air with smoldering heat. Moving his hand in a wide arc, he glanced back at Kal, a sly twinkle dancing in his glowing red eyes.

Then he returned his attention back to the portal and whispered, "Come..."

The ground trembled as the sound of his voice rolled through the desert, and the second blast wave of magical energy rushed away from the epicenter. The portal ignited brighter and a flaming-red beast erupted through it, carrying the smoldering heat in its wake. Its long mane and tail swayed around, rising like a weightless cloud of flames. The red stallion halted next to Viggo and playfully pushed him on his side. War greeted his horse by gently stroking its neck and back.

As the Horseman headed back toward the porch, the beast followed him. For a split-second, the stallion stalled, his flaming eyes checking every person. Then he neighed softly and approached Gunz, lightly nibbling on his shoulder. A wave of heat enveloped him, and Gunz held his breath. While the fire emanated by War and his horse somehow felt familiar, it wasn't quite the same as the elemental energy.

Gunz got up and stretched his hand, carefully running his fingers over the horse's fiery mane. The stallion took one more step forward and bent his head, placing it on Gunz's shoulder.

"Gunz, my boy," whispered Kal, stepping by his side, "this fire is not elemental by nature. I don't know if you and I can control it."

"I know," Gunz murmured breathlessly, transfixed by the fire flowing over the entire horse's body. "But somehow..." His voice trailed away as he brushed his fingers over one of the flames, allowing it to move onto his palm. The fire licked his skin, doing absolutely no damage, and its touch didn't feel dangerous or threatening.

Kal gasped, but Viggo Warrington just smiled. He touched the flame on Gunz's palm, extinguishing it, and took the horse's reins, walking him a few steps back.

"I guess my stallion made the choice for me," War announced with a nonchalant shrug. "I can live with it. Your hand, young Salamander."

Gunz glanced at his mentor and extended his hand to Viggo. As soon as War slipped the ring on his finger, the flames of the same foreign fire surrounded him, burning so bright his eyes started to water. When the fire disappeared, he looked down and his annoyance flared.

"You can't be serious!" he yelled, throwing his arms up.

He was dressed in the short tunic of a Roman legionary uniform, covered by a breastplate and shoulder plates made of metal strips. In his hand, he held a massive sword, and his feet were wrapped in leather strips of sandals studded with metal. He sheathed the blade and folded his arms over his chest. The elemental fire as well as the war flames responded to his frustration, breaking through the skin of his bare arms.

"Hell no!" he grumbled. "I'm going nowhere dressed like this. How am I supposed to fight in this skirt and sandals?"

"I think you look just fine," said Aidan, biting on his fist to suppress his laughter quite unsuccessfully.

"Like father like son?" asked War, giving Kal a quick tap on his shoulder.

Kal, as serious as ever, just nodded and didn't say anything. Mrak Delar also remained calm, but his face got paler by a shade.

Gunz turned to War and snarled, "Give me back my jeans and sneakers."

A lopsided smirk graced Viggo's face. "No can do, Child of Fire. You're War now and you should look the part." He thought for a moment. "How about this?"

He snapped his fingers, and the flames wrapped around Gunz once more. When the fire dwindled down, he stood dressed in a modern camouflage tactical uniform, combat boots included, but the leather scabbard with the sword was still attached to his belt.

"Better," replied Gunz. "I wonder why this sword is so massive and heavy. Judging by the first outfit you gave me, I would expect a short one, like a gladius."

Since Viggo didn't reply, he approached the red stallion, grabbed the pommel of the saddle and placed his left foot into the stirrup, just now realizing how high it was. With a strenuous grunt, he pulled himself up onto the horse's back and gathered the reins, looking down from the height of the flaming beast.

Gunz had never enjoyed horseback riding and had never mastered it to the same level as his friends. Mounting a horse was always a slow process that he had to muscle through. But sitting on this giant stallion, he admitted with surprise that it felt right, as if he and this massive steed were one.

War observed Gunz approvingly and turned to Famine. "I'm done. You can proceed."

Famine sauntered up front and started to chant. There was no preamble with long speeches, no storms and no raging elements. Her portal opened up silently, stagnant darkness spreading menacing cold around. Gunz shivered and his shoulders tensed as he stared down at a gaping black hole that reminded him of the portal into the Dark Nav. He glanced at

Karma and saw the reflection of his thoughts on her ashen face.

"Come..." Famine's musical voice whispered through the desert, and a soft and deadly energy blast spread around her.

A mare as black as night emerged from the portal and halted next to her. It was slightly smaller than the other two horses, but somehow, it looked more powerful and a lot more menacing. The horse neighed, digging the ground with its huge hoof.

"Whoa...," whispered Siv, his round eyes as large as two purple plates. "What a beauty! I wonder if I can get her number?"

Famine approached the porch and put her foot on the step, bending forward slightly to prop her elbow on her lap. Her pale-yellow eyes bored into Tessa, and she flicked her eyebrow.

"Therasia, I really wish you were ready to ride in my stead, but you are not. You're powerful, girl." Famine straightened up, carefully sizing up every person before her. "Believe it or not, you're more powerful than a few of the good folks here."

"Then give me a chance to prove that I'm ready." Tessa got up, stepping around Aidan to be closer to the Horseman. She wasn't begging or pleading. She was demanding. "I've been in situations where I wasn't ready, yet I handled them. I'm sure a few people would vouch for me."

"No," objected Famine coldly. "We're not in a position where I can take chances." She walked up the steps and approach Aidan, staring into his eyes over Tessa's head. "Aodh mac Lir, earlier you had passed my test. Unfortunately, I believe your hands are full with something as equally important as recovering Death. So, both you and the great Salamander are out."

Tessa twirled around, peering at Aidan with shock. "What is she talking about, Aidan?"

Aidan put his hands on her shoulder, squeezing it slightly. "I'll tell you later. This is neither the time nor the place for this discussion."

In the meantime, Famine sauntered her way to Lucan. She halted a step away from the giant elf, looking up at him with the admiration of a cat staring at a fat, juicy mouse. She brought her hand up, running her fingers up the massive muscles of his chest, then to his shoulder and down his bicep. The elf shuddered at her touch and grunted, his entire demeanor displaying just how much he wanted to throw her hands off of him.

"Lucárion—"

"The name is Lucan, my lady," the elf interrupted her, gently taking her hand off his arm.

She smiled snidely. "Lucárion, my brother has tested you, and he believes you to be the man for the job," she continued, ignoring him. "I trust my brother, so your hand, please."

The elf turned around, and Gunz met his troubled eyes. He sighed and gave an encouraging nod. Famine stretched up a little and seized Lucan's chin, forcing him to look at her.

"Don't look at the young Salamander, elf. He's not your master." She snickered and grabbed his hand.

Before Lucan could object, she slipped her ring on his finger. As the dark, shimmering mist embraced him, the elf struggled fruitlessly against its hold. Black, wispy tendrils slithered around him, encapsulating him into a tight cocoon. He groaned and then cried out, throwing his head back.

When the darkness finally dissipated, the elf stood, clad in black linen pants and a shirt with a picture of silver weighing scales imprinted on his chest. Two long daggers in plain leather scabbards were sheathed at his belt. His wide-open arms were trembling with strain as if he were still fighting against the mist. Famine led her black mare to him and gave him the reins.

"She's yours for now, elf. Take good care of her," she purred. "And don't disappoint me. I promise, I'll know."

Lucan cringed but took the reins and easily flew up into the saddle.

"Our job is done," said Pestilence, rubbing his hands together.

"So, what do we do now?" asked Mrak Delar, patting the snow-white stallion's neck.

"Since all of you can communicate with your steeds telepathically, order them to find Death, of course." Pestilence shrugged nonchalantly as if it was common knowledge. "Because there are only three steeds of the Apocalypse, it may take them a little longer to find him. But as long as there are four magical horses riding together, they should generate enough magical mojo to tap into the collective power of Four. They'll find him." He waved his hand dismissively, and then murmured under his breath, "Sooner or later."

"Understood." The Master of Power gathered the reins, getting ready to get going, but Pestilence tapped his knee, stopping him.

"Before you can be on your way, you must tell me who's riding this"—he twirled his wrist in Siv's direction—"um... little pony."

Siv hopped up in the air, indignation pouring from his every pore. "Who are you calling a little pony, you great and powerful Syphilis?" he yelled, pushing Pestilence on his chest with his hoof.

Gunz gasped and bit his lip to stop himself from laughing out loud.

"My bad. I apologize, oh mighty stallion." Enzo raised his hands up in a placating manner, a wide grin on his face. "So, who would you chose as your rider?"

"You better," neighed Siv, turning around, and hit the ground, raising a small fountain of dirt in the air. "Hey, defective vamp. I choose you."

"Uh-oh...," muttered Gunz as Yaroslav just vanished—one second the vampire was standing next to Aidan and the next, he was gone.

A split second later, he reappeared, holding his katana to Siv's throat.

"Call me defective one more time," he hissed, applying some extra pressure on his blade.

"Jeez, man!" neighed Siv, rotating his fearful eyes. "Lighten up! It was a compliment. Don't you know? The beauty is in imperfections." As Yaroslav lowered his sword and then sheathed it beneath his coat, he sighed with relief and winked. "Hop on, old friend. Someone needs to lead these three losers of the Apocalypse."

"Siv, the time for jokes is over," said Gunz, directing his horse closer to the magical stallion. "Tune in and try to keep up with me."

The ground trembled as the four magical steeds took off at the same time, raising a cloud of sand and dirt in the air. For a short while, the sensation of complete weightlessness descended upon Gunz and he gripped the pommel of his saddle with his left hand, praying to all the gods he knew that his horseback riding skills were enough to survive this trip.

He felt the powerful muscles of the red stallion moving beneath his legs and then a wave of heat spread through him. He held his breath, realizing that it was the way the War horse was communicating with him. He didn't hear him talking. As the magical energy surged through his body, his mind just accepted the meaning of his words.

"Hold on to something, young master," projected the stallion. "The Arizona farm is no more..."

Gunz gripped the saddle with both hands and as a powerful wind impacted his chest, he grunted and leaned forward, hiding his face into the horse's mane.

CHAPTER 31

~ ZANE BURNS, A.K.A. GUNZ ~

Gunz couldn't say how many hours he had spent in the saddle. The horses moved softly and soundlessly without touching the ground with their hooves, as if the wind itself carried them on its wings. All sounds dissolved into a soft and even hiss of the air, and the only thing he could hear was the pumping of blood in his ears.

The beasts moved too fast, turning the surroundings into a continuous blur of colors. He couldn't see the other horses or their riders, but he could feel the presence of his friends nearby and it made him feel more at ease. A few times, he heard Yaroslav speak to him through their blood bond, joking about Siv and his one-sided competition with the other three horses.

The vampire sounded as lighthearted and relaxed as always, and Gunz thought with regret that he should have clocked more hours in the saddle when he was back in Kendral. Kal had insisted on his training in horseback riding, swordsmanship and other useful medieval style activities he had never thought he would need.

Kal was right, he thought, squeezing the pommel of his saddle, holding on for dear life. Then he chuckled, thinking about his stern mentor with affection, and corrected himself. *The old man is always right.*

When the horses finally touched the ground and came to a smooth stop, he exhaled with relief and then inhaled deeply, refilling his lungs with oxygen as if he had been holding his breath all this time. Feeling sore all over, he dismounted awkwardly, stepping on the soft surface covered with a carpet of pine needles. His every muscle was agonizingly stiff, and he wasn't sure he could ever straighten his knees again. Still grasping the saddle like it was his lifesaver, he closed his eyes, resting his forehead against the horse's warm side. Everything was swaying and shifting, and he grunted, suppressing the nausea.

He felt a tap on his shoulder and slowly turned around. Mrak Delar, Lucan, and Yaroslav stood behind him, identical grins on their faces.

"I see a horse is not your favorite type of transportation, Burns... um... I mean, Gunz?" asked the elf, his cat-eyes sparkling with humor.

"When we get back, I'll make sure you spend a few hours riding Siv every day," promised Mrak Delar, wagging his eyebrows at him.

"How about, when we get back, I'll make sure you take some driving lessons, Master," Gunz snapped back, but a tiny smile lifted the corners of his mouth.

"Cars..." Mrak Delar shuddered exaggeratedly. "No, thank you very much. Nobody puts a Master of Power in a metal box. Besides, no one uses cars in Kendral anyway."

"No one rides horses here either," Gunz retorted snidely.

"I do," chimed in Yaroslav with a shrug. He stood, light and relaxed as usual, as if he didn't just spend an unknown number of hours in the saddle. "All the time."

"Well, you three are medieval freaks." Gunz chuckled, observing his friends. "I don't even know how old you are,

Lucan. But something tells me you're older than both of these jokers." He waved at Mrak Delar and Yaroslav.

"You're probably right." The elf laughed openheartedly, and Gunz thought that through all the time he had spent in the Destiny Council compound, he had never seen Lucan smile. Despite the gravity of the situation they were in, it was a welcome change.

A soft gust of wind rushed through the tiny clearing they were standing on, ruffling Gunz's hair, and he looked around, taking in his surroundings. They were in the midst of a forest and since it wasn't dense, the rocky slopes of a mountain were clearly visible between the trees up ahead. A barely noticeable scent of rotting vegetation and algae suggested the presence of a swamp or some kind of body of water nearby. A narrow path led toward the mountain, and as far as he could see, it didn't seem to be too steep or hard to climb.

He sharpened his Salamander senses, probing the area. Even without opening his other sight, he knew that this place was infused with magical energy. Around the clearing, it was almost tangible, but it got a lot thicker and more potent closer to the mountain.

"If you want to find Death, this is where you need to go, young master. We'll be awaiting your return here."

Gunz felt the red stallion's voice invading his mind and flinched, turning to face him. The horse lifted his leg, pointing toward the mountain.

If you want to find Death, Gunz repeated the stallion's words in his mind. *That just didn't come out right... I hope not...*

"Aren't you going with us?" he asked out loud, surprised and unnerved by the idea that such powerful magical beings as the horses of the Apocalypse looked uneasy and troubled.

"We cannot...," replied the white stallion, shaking his head, his long white mane flowing in the wind.

"Why can't you?" asked Mrak Delar, and just now Gunz realized that it wasn't only him who could hear the horses' communications.

"The same magic that keeps Death imprisoned in this place, blocks us from entering..." explained the red stallion.

"After all," added the black mare, her voice unexpectedly melodious, "we and our riders... we all have the same magical energy signature..."

"We'll be waiting for you here...," repeated the War horse, gently pushing Gunz on his shoulder. "Godspeed, young master..."

"How about you, Siv?" asked Yaroslav, turning toward the magical stallion.

"Me?" neighed Siv, taking a step away from the vampire. "What about me?" His eyes grew round, and he pressed his ears down while baring his large teeth in the semblance of a smile.

Yaroslav smirked, giving an arched stare. "Are you coming with us, Siv?"

"Me?" Siv's grin was getting wider and faker by the moment. "Thank you for the invitation, but I have to respectfully decline. I think I'll stay here with them." He waved his hoof at the other three horses. "If the mighty steeds of the Apocalypse don't want to go there, who am I to argue. I'll stay with my kind."

"Oh, now they are mighty steeds and your kind?" Yaroslav huffed, rolling his eyes. "Four-legged coward."

"Defective vamp!" grumbled Siv, lowering his head, staring directly at Yaroslav.

Before the vampire could make a move, Gunz seized his elbow, pulling him back. "Slavik, don't start it. And don't you dare tell me that he started it!"

Yaroslav opened his mouth but snapped it shut, raising his hands up. Siv snorted, giving the vampire a sarcastic look, and as the other the three horses vanished from the clearing, he stuck his tongue out at Yaroslav and neighed, "Adios, amigos", before disappearing himself.

***

AFTER THE HORSES HAD LEFT, they took the trail, hiking toward the top of the mountain. They walked in silence, following Mrak Delar. The Master of Power was uncharacteristically tense, and even though he had never been the chatty type, now he looked plainly grim. He was moving fast without as much as a quick glance back to check if the rest of them followed him, and his unusual behavior set Gunz's nerves on edge.

"Mrak," called Gunz, catching up to him, "do you know what this place is? Where are we?"

"I do," the Ancient Master answered sharply, without looking at him, his jaw set. "This is Vottovaara mountain. Haven't you heard of it, Salamander? This place has a long history and…" His voice faltered, and he swallowed with an effort, like a person who had a sore throat. "And magical significance."

"Salamander," muttered Gunz, shaking his head, wondering what kind of memories about this place his friend had that made him so jittery. "Yes, I've heard of this place. It's in Karelia. Some ancient pagan beliefs are associated with it." He frowned, trying to recall whatever he knew about it. "And of course, all the non-magical events that have happened here during World War Two. Is there anything you want to tell me, Master?"

For the first time since they took the trail, Mrak Delar slowed down slightly and glanced at Gunz. But then he just shook his head and his black eyes warmed up just a little.

"No, Gunz," he said softly. "Nothing you need to worry about."

"Something bothers you, Mrak," objected Gunz. "I can see it."

"The usual stuff, you know? This place is sacred and as such, it holds powerful magic within it. Ancient one. Possibly as old as creation itself. Out of all the magical places and nexuses in this realm, whoever captured Death, chose this one. There has to be another reason for that. It can't be only the magical significance of this place," muttered Mrak Delar, nibbling on his lip. "I feel like I'm missing something, but I have no idea what. Just give me a few minutes, my friend. Don't worry, I'm okay."

Without waiting for Gunz's response, the Master of Power sped up again. Gunz sighed and slowed down to let Lucan and Yaroslav catch up.

"What's going on, Gunz?" asked Yaroslav, falling into step with him. "The Ancient Master is not quite himself, is he?"

"I am not sure," replied Gunz.

He glanced at Yaroslav and Lucan, thousands of thoughts flashing through his mind at once. Then he gestured for them to stop, not sure what he was going to tell his friends. The elf and the vampire halted, exchanging a quick look filled with surprise. For a moment, Gunz stilled and closed his eyes, rubbing the bridge of his nose with his fingers. Then he sighed and opened his eyes, lowering his hand.

"Guys," he started softly, shifting uncomfortably from foot to foot. "I don't know how to explain, but I have this strange feeling..." He shook his head, biting his lip. "Not even a feeling, it is more on the intuition level..." He took a pause and added with a sigh. "I wanted to ask you to keep an eye on Mrak. Something tells me, he'll need our protection."

"Fire Salamander's intuition? I would take something like that seriously. But what *really* troubles you?" Lucan accentuated the word 'really', folding his arms as he stared down at Gunz with narrowed eyes. "Out of the four of us, the Ancient Master is the most powerful. He's nearly a god, and you're asking us to protect him? Why? What do you think we'll find there?" He waved his hand toward the mountain and folded his arms again.

"I am not sure. Like I said—it's something on the intuition level," repeated Gunz with a light shrug. "You're right, Lucan. Mrak is nearly a god, and not only in his power but also in his knowledge of magic and history. If anyone can solve this puzzle and find Angel, it's him. But while he is more powerful than the three of us put together, he is also more vulnerable than any of us."

He looked up at Lucan and then his gaze halted on Yaroslav's eyes that were glowing with a dangerous scarlet light.

"Slavik," he said, and as a warm boyish grin split the vampire's face, he couldn't help but smile back at him. "You're an old vampire—fast and strong. While your immortality is conditional, it's not easy to kill you."

Yaroslav's smile grew wider, showing the pointy tips of his half-expanded fangs. "They can try killing me"—he twirled his wrist nonchalantly—"whoever they are… I promise, I'm not going to make it easy on them."

Gunz nodded and switched his attention to the giant elf. "Lucan, you're an elf. Your body is built to heal fast, no matter how damaging your injuries are. Unless you know how, it's practically impossible to kill an elf. Am I right?"

Lucan gave him a curt nod, throwing his long bluish hair off his face.

"I'm a Great Fire Salamander," continued Gunz. "Immortal. Unless I choose to do so, I can't die. I can't be killed by any weapon except the Black Fire. This leaves Mrak. As godly as he is, he is the only one among us who has a fragile human body. And as such, he can easily be killed by any weapon, human or magical. I'm sure whoever holds Angel already knows that we're coming, and they'll try to take Mrak out first. Believe me, it's not his power that they're afraid of. It's his knowledge."

"Understood and agreed," said Lucan, slightly inclining his head. He glanced ahead, over Gunz's head and flicked his eyebrow at him. "Well, if you want us to keep an eye on the Ancient Master, then I suggest we stop gossiping behind his back and catch up to him."

The elf walked around Gunz and picked up speed, heading up the trail after Mrak Delar.

"I wasn't gossiping," murmured Gunz, following Lucan. Yaroslav just chuckled, giving him a quick tap on his shoulder.

* * *

As the path kept climbing up, the surrounding air became noticeably colder, white puffs forming at Gunz's lips every time he exhaled. While it was early fall, the weather seemed to be a little colder than he expected, but since he had never been in this region of Russia before, he couldn't say if it was normal for this time of the year.

Closer to the top of the mountain, the trail started to level, making their progress easier and faster. The surroundings began to change too and not in a good way. The ground became rockier and small stone formations were popping up here and there along the way. The forest—if one could call it a forest—also changed. The trees stood far apart from each other, distorted and twisted to such a degree that Gunz couldn't believe they grew like this naturally, without a helpful hand of some dark magic. The entire area looked anomalous and freakish, stretching his already overly extended nerves.

The light presence of the magical energy he had sensed before got a lot heavier and denser here, overwhelming his Salamander senses and making it hard to breathe. He was positive that his friends felt it too. Mrak Delar slowed down. His white shirt, soaked with sweat, plastered to his back, and his shoulders were tensed as if he were carrying a heavy load. Lucan looked like he ran a marathon, his mouth opened slightly, his chest shuddering with ragged breaths. Only Yaroslav was seemingly unaffected. But taking into account his vampiric nature—he didn't need to breathe, and demonic essence had no effect on him—it was understandable.

As a large rock formation blocked their path, Mrak Delar came to a sharp halt. He placed his hand on the boulder and closed his eyes, his magical energy spiking around him. Gunz observed the formation with interest. An enormous boulder was balanced on three small stones beneath it, and it was hard to believe that such a strange contraption could be of natural origin. A wave of dark energy emitted by the stones touched his senses, and he took a step back involuntarily.

"Seid...," muttered Mrak Delar, rubbing his forehead, unease present in his every move. "There will be more of them..."

"What are these?" asked Lucan, tilting his head slightly as he observed the rock with curiosity. He touched it with his fingers, and it lit up slightly, responding to the invasion of elven magic. "I can sense its magic, but it's unlike anything I've ever sensed before. It's dark..." He shivered.

"Old magic, my friend," explained Mrak Delar louder, lowering his arms. "Ancient Saami sorcerers erected these stones over five thousand years ago, infusing them with their old magic, mostly forgotten nowadays. From what I know, the Seids are... hmmm... hard to explain. They are like stone guardians of this sacred place. Imagine wards and protection spells we cast today, but a lot more powerful and, I would say, a lot darker."

For a moment, he stared at the boulder, craning his neck, but then bit his lip and sighed.

"But I detect more than just the normal energy signature of Saami magic in these rocks. It feels almost like it was modified, mutated—" The Master of Power cut himself off and frowned. "I guess we'll have to wait and see."

He motioned forward and went around the Seid, following the trail. Gunz followed him silently, but his general agitation just increased. His Salamander senses were screaming, and he could feel some strange, malignant presence with his very skin.

Mrak Delar was right. The closer they moved toward the top of the mountain, the more Seids surrounded their path, each weird contraption accompanied by an even stranger tree.

Twisted and malformed, every tree was blackened as if a blast of fire had devastated the area a while ago, burning everything in its wake. Gunz sharpened his senses and to his shock detected a light presence of fire energy in the area, but just like everything else here, even his own element seemed to be slightly off—mutated.

By the time they reached the plateau at the top, the ground became more rock than dirt. Assorted stone blocks, shaped perfectly as if they were cut by a modern-day machine, were spread around among Seids. Heavy silence blanketed the area, swallowing everything, even the sounds of their steps. The dark presence became almost palpable, and Gunz felt cold perspiration soaking his uniform, his hand reaching for War's sword at his hip.

"In the center of this plateau, there is a crater with a small round swamp in the middle," said Mrak Delar, pointing forward. "I think this is where we need to be. The accumulation of magical energy seems to be the heaviest in that—"

The Master of Power suddenly stopped talking, choking on the last word. His face lost any color he had, becoming pale-gray, and he swallowed hard, sweat glistening on his forehead. He twirled in place, searching the rocky ground intently. Then he channeled his power and magic. His eyes swirled with all the colors of the four elements, and his jet-black hair surrounded his face like a dark cloud.

"I can't believe I missed it," he exhaled, turning to Gunz. "How could I miss it when it was right in front of my eyes…"

"Missed what?" asked Gunz, grabbing his friend's arm, the sound of Mrak's voice making his hairs stand on end. Yaroslav was already next to him with katana in his hand, and Lucan's magical energy field spiked around him, giving his eyes a bright green glow.

The Ancient Master ignored his question, as if he didn't hear it. "All this time. Goddamnit!" He cursed, squeezing his fists, and the ground trembled slightly beneath their feet, responding to his emotions. "All these rocks, the cold, the silence—"

"Mrak, what are you talking about!" yelled Gunz, but as the dark magic rose around them to the next level, almost suffocating them, he pressed his hand to his throat, struggling to breathe. Mrak slowly turned toward the center of the plateau and extended his arm forward.

"This...," he breathed out, reaching for his black sword that wasn't at his belt. His fingers found the hilt of Pestilence's dagger, and he unsheathed it, a thin metallic sound swallowed immediately by the silence.

Gunz looked into the direction Mrak was pointing at and shuddered, icy fear making his blood run cold. Wrapping his fingers tightly around the grip of War's long sword, he unsheathed it. Then in one move, he connected with the Dark Codex and gathered all the magic and elemental power he could safely control in his body.

"Why me?" he muttered, setting the blade ablaze.

CHAPTER 32

~ AIDAN ~

"Gwyn ap Nudd, I summon thee," whispered Kal, infusing the fiery rune with his fire energy.

As soon as the communication window materialized on the wall of the small smithy located at the far end of Hawk's property, the King of the Otherworld stepped into view, separating from the absolute darkness behind him.

The expression of concern made his angled features harder than usual, and his white cat-eyes glowed with the light of his magic. He slowly explored the three people standing in front of the communication window and frowned.

"Kalidus," he called the Fire Elemental, "where are the Horsemen?"

"Back in the house with the Warden," replied Kal, leaning against the anvil while twirling a large hammer in his fingers as though it were a kid's toy. "Hawk and Theron returned with five more werewolves. Big boys, all seven of them, you know."

"That's good," murmured Gwyn, and Aidan wasn't sure what his father referred to—the fact that the Horsemen weren't here or that Hawk and Theron were back with five strong wolves. "I assume Mrak Delar was chosen for the mission? Pestilence picked him?"

"Yes, Pestilence always had a soft spot for the Ancient Master. Since the day Mrak kicked his ass in the City of Silver. Good days... good days..." Kal chuckled humorlessly. "Anyway, Mrak, Gunz, Yaroslav and that elf... um... Lucan are gone."

Gwyn ap Nudd nodded, his unnerving eyes drilling into Tessa. She gasped, squeezing her hands tightly, but held the King's heavy gaze.

"Father," said Aidan reproachfully, stepping in front of her. "Stop. You don't need to read her."

The corners of Gwyn's mouth quirked up a little under the thin line of his well-groomed mustache. "Therasia," he said softly, "I thought Famine would choose you or one of the other two witches for the mission. Usually, she prefers to deal with women. And the more powerful they are, the more she's attracted to them. You're the most powerful out of the three of you."

"She had," replied Tessa with a sigh, moving forward from behind Aidan's back, "but I failed her test, my lord. I guess I'm not good enough." She shrugged, but as much as she tried to hide her disappointment, it was apparent in her every word and move. "Aidan was the one who passed her test."

"Not good enough? That's not true, child," objected Gwyn ap Nudd, warmth suffusing his features. "My son can tell you. I have a very rare gift which I bestowed upon him as well. I can read human souls. And yours is beautiful. You're young and just like anyone of your age, you bring things to the extreme. For you everything is black and white, and there are no gray areas in between."

"But the world *is* black and white, my lord," objected Tessa. "Good and evil. Heaven and Hell. Life and Death. It's simple. How can there be anything gray between that? And Famine? I could never let her kill Aidan. Not even for a stupid fake test. I love him too much, and his life..." She trailed off, averting her gaze for a moment, but then met Gwyn's smiling eyes again and continued, "Anyway, I don't believe there are any shades in between. Even though I understood everything Aidan explained to me, I still would never sacrifice him. His life means more to me than my own, than this entire world... or any other world... I would protect him with my dying breath."

At Tessa's words, something swelled inside Aidan's chest, filling his entire being with warmth and pride and more love than he could ever imagine his soul could hold. He glanced at his father over Tessa's head, his hands gripping her shoulders. All he wanted to do was embrace her and never let go.

"Aidan," called Gwyn ap Nudd, ripping Aidan out of his daydreams, "when all this mess is over, come back to the Otherworld with Therasia. I would love to continue our philosophical discussion about the colors of life at a better time." He winked at Tessa, but then quickly sobered up, and turned to Kal. "Kalidus, we need to take care of the little lavender issue and we need to do it fast."

"What's your plan, Gwyn?" asked Kal, pushing off the anvil. He dropped the hammer, and it fell with a loud thud, the vibration of the impact spreading through the ground.

"The plan is simple." Gwyn ap Nudd came closer to the window, placing his hands on either side of it. "Aidan will go to the Guardians HQ and deal with the infection there. If he was able to clear it at the Sisterhood, I believe he can do the same again."

"I can do it," agreed Aidan.

"Kalidus, you will open your portal to the Wardens HQ in Paris," continued Gwyn ap Nudd. "I hate to do it to you, my old friend, but you'll have to suppress your fire energy the way Gunz does. I know you haven't been doing that for centuries and you hate the idea, but Paris is a city of humans and we don't want to have millions of dead bodies just because you decided to enjoy the view of the Eiffel Tower."

"Fine," grumbled Kal, pursing his thin lips, flames rising on the bottom of his deeply set eyes. "This one time for the greater good... That greater good will owe me big for that."

Gwyn laughed. "I'm sure the greater good will pay you back... as soon as never." He stopped laughing and sighed. "Once both of you are done with your tasks, I need you to come back to the Otherworld. Something tells me it'll take all three of us to deal with the enchantment that was placed on the Destiny Council."

Kal and Aidan exchanged a quick look and nodded. The plan was simple, but the execution wasn't. Aidan thought back to his fight at the Sisterhood. That had taken a lot of his power, and the slayers of the Sisterhood were nothing compared to the mages of the Guardians Order.

"My lord..."

He heard Tessa's voice and looked at her. She stood in front of the communication window, barely reaching up to Gwyn's chest, but somehow, she managed not to look tiny and insignificant next to him.

"My lord," she repeated, demanding the King's attention. "What would you like me to do? Can I do anything to help?"

Gwyn ap Nudd peered down at her and gave her a short nod.

"I need you to stay here, Therasia. You and the other two witches must work with the werewolves to protect their property," he said softly. "Until Aidan deals with the enchantment placed on the Guardians, this ranch is in danger of another attack. Your task is not easy, child. You must protect the Horsemen. Under no circumstances can they get involved in a fight and use their powers against the Guardians. Especially War. The more they use their powers while they are together, the more unstable the foundation of the realm will become, moving it closer to doomsday. Do you understand me?"

"Yes, my lord," replied Tessa calmly. "I'll make sure the Horsemen don't leave the house. Missi, Karma, and I can handle a few Guardians. Besides, we have Hawk and his wolves." She smiled with a lighthearted shrug.

"All you have to do is keep the Guardians away from the Horseman until I return," added Aidan, and even though the doubt was tearing him up from the inside, he made sure not to show it. "As soon as I break the spell, the Guardians will stop attacking the ranch."

Gwyn nodded in agreement, but before he could say anything, the ground trembled and a deafening, screeching pandemonium broke loose outside the hut. A powerful wave of magic invaded Aidan's senses, and he held his breath, pressing his hand to his chest. Tessa's eyes widened, and she covered her ears with her hands. Gwyn ap Nudd was shouting something, but Aidan couldn't hear him over the mayhem. Breaking out of his stupor, he ran toward the communication window but still couldn't make out anything Gwyn was saying.

The King of the Otherworld rolled his eyes and waved his hand. Words, glowing with the brilliant light of his magic, materialized in midair above his head.

"Aidan and Kal, leave now! Tessa, take care of the Horsemen!"

Gwyn ap Nudd snapped his fingers and closed the communication window. Tessa ran toward Aidan and threw her arms around his neck, pulling him down slightly. He felt her hot lips pressed to his for a split second.

"I love you, my ancient god," she said. "Be safe."

He couldn't hear her words but rather read her lips. Before he could say anything to her, she turned on her heels and bolted out of the smithy. For a moment, he just stood there, breathing heavily with his arms dangling by his sides, as all sorts of worst-case scenarios of what could happen to Tessa flashed through his mind.

A heavy tap on his shoulder made him flinch and snap around. Kal had already unfolded the flaming curtain of his portal, ready to walk through it.

"I'll meet you back here when you're done!" he shouted and waved at Aidan, gesturing for him to leave before disappearing behind the fire.

Aidan threw a desperate glance at the exit door, wishing with all his heart that he could be next to Tessa now. As the buzzing of the wards increased and the next wave of the Guardians' magic rushed through the area, Aidan snapped his fingers and vanished.

CHAPTER 33

~ AIDAN ~

Aidan materialized outside the fence surrounding the Guardians HQ. It was close to midnight, and the area was submerged under a heavy cloak of darkness. The display of a security monitor radiated a dim blue glow, and a streetlight projected a thin beam of light down to the ground, creating a fuzzy-edged yellow circle in front of the gates. A nasty mist of autumn drizzle hung in the air, its shiny streaks and droplets visible in the ray of light.

Within moments, Aidan's shirt and hair became wet, and the next gust of the infamous Chicago wind made him shiver, running his hands over his exposed arms that were covered in small droplets. Ignoring the unpleasant weather conditions, he closed his eyes and took a deep breath, opening his other sight.

Now that he knew what to look for, he registered a dome of magic encapsulating a large area behind the gates. From where he stood, he couldn't see the actual building, but he was positive that the magical dome covered it completely. It was the powerful spell the Guardians mages had cast to capture him and strip him of his power. Since Missi had described it in detail, he knew exactly what to do with it.

However, this wasn't the spell he was looking for. Even though from this distance, he still couldn't sense the mind-controlling enchantment placed by a Master of the Dark Arts, he had no doubt it was there. He thought about Jamie Coldwell, the guard who had helped him more than once, and a heavy knot settled in the pit of his stomach. All he could do was hope that the young man wouldn't cross his path at the wrong moment. But right now, the future of this realm was at stake and he had to do whatever was needed to break the dark spell.

I will trigger the broken oath alarm as soon as I touch this monitor... Who cares? I won't receive a warm welcome anyway...

He channeled his power, allowing the god of the Otherworld to take him over entirely. As his appearance changed into that of an ancient hunter, and the black mask covered his face, he collected the power in his hands and blasted the entrance into the Guardians HQ with it. The heavy wrought-iron gates were ripped off its hinges and propelled a few yards inward, warped by the enormous force. The wards and protection spells howled furiously, and the screeching noise of the broken oath alarm shattered the silence of the night.

Aidan smirked and stepped through the entrance. Even though he felt the resistance of the wards, they weren't powerful enough to keep a god in his natural form from entering. If the Guardians were expecting him and didn't want him to enter, they surely underestimated his power.

Perhaps they wanted me to enter... Well, I'm glad to oblige...

Moving at the fastest pace he could muster, he ran toward the building. He knew he couldn't teleport on the territory of the Guardians' property, but even if he could, he wouldn't have done it, anyway. Since he couldn't point out the exact location of the trap the mages created for him, he didn't want to give them a chance of capturing him.

He didn't care to conceal his presence—the blazing light of his magical energy and the ground trembling with every step he took gave away his location regardless. So, when he approached the circular driveway in front of the building, he wasn't shocked to find a large group of witches and armed guards waiting for him just inside the dome of magic.

Aidan halted a few feet away from the magical trap, folding his arms over his chest. Quickly, he checked every single person who stood silently, waiting to see what he would do. With relief, he noticed that Jamie wasn't there. Trying to negotiate with these people was useless—they were under a spell, and frankly, he had no time for that. Tessa was in danger, protecting the Arizona ranch from the attack of the Guardians. So, the sooner he broke the spell, the sooner she and everyone else there would be safe.

Without long speeches or any preface, Aidan opened his arms wide and blasted the magical shield with an undiluted flow of his power. The brilliant light of pure magic of the Otherworld impacted the dome, quickly devouring it as Aidan slowly progressed closer to it. Muttering a quick spell, he entwined it with his power, and the dome collapsed with a deafening bang. For a split second, he couldn't hear anything, but when his hearing readjusted, he realized that the wards crumbled, and now, a heavy silence lingered over the terrified crowd.

The witches and guards gasped, frozen in place, their faces masks of terror. Aidan unsheathed his icy sword, and the weapon exploded in his hands with the eye-watering light of his power.

"Let me pass and I will let you live," he said softly, but his voice, infused with his power, boomed through the area, making the walls of the Guardians HQ shake like from an earthquake.

The Guardians looked at each other, nothing but fear reflected in their wide eyes and pale faces. Nevertheless, the guards raised their weapons—anything from ancient swords to modern firearms—and the witches channeled their magic.

"As you wish." Aidan rolled his eyes and sighed. *Why does nobody ever choose the easy way?* He conjured a light protection shield around himself, just enough to protect his human body from bullets and blades, but not enough to slow him down or restrain his movement. Even in his godly form, his body was vulnerable and even though it wasn't easy to kill him, getting injured wasn't part of his plan.

As soon as he made his first move, the air buzzed with magical strikes and flying bullets. He waved his hand, easily deflecting all the attacks while throwing the Guardians out of his way as though they were some raggedy dolls. They screamed —some in pain, some in fury—and charged him from every direction.

Aidan rose in the air, for a moment hovering a foot above the ground as he collected all the power he could in his hands and plummeted down, striking the asphalt with his fist. The ground trembled, deep waves spreading around the epicenter of the impact like circles on the water. The blast of his power rushed through the property, knocking all those who were still standing off their feet, propelling them a few yards away.

Breathing heavily, Aidan straightened up and surveyed the area. The circular driveway was covered in sprawled bodies— some unconscious, some squirming and moaning in pain.

"What did you think you were doing?" he grumbled, shaking his head. "I'm a god of the Otherworld. The emphasis is on the *god*!" The last words he shouted, punching the air with his glowing fist. "You didn't think your feeble spell would hold me down for longer than a second, did you? Puny humans…"

Remaining in his godly form, Aidan ran toward the driveway, carefully maneuvering between fallen Guardians. As soon as he reached the steps leading to the main entrance, the familiar scent of lavender invaded his nostrils. It was barely noticeable and perhaps the only reason he detected it was because he was searching for it. Slowing down, he walked up the steps and pushed the door into the Guardians HQ open.

The door swung inward with a soft squeak, giving him a view of a pitch-black lobby. Opening his second sight, Aidan knew that at least a few magically endowed people were hiding in the shadows, expecting him. A few of them stood right next to the doorway, ready to strike him with their spells as soon as he crossed the threshold.

"Seriously?" he mumbled, gazing heavenwards. Instead of entering, he pointed at the entrance and whispered, *"Exitius..."*

The walls in front of him exploded, sending bricks and debris flying through the air. With his magical sight, he saw that all the Guardians who stood by the door were knocked out by the explosion. Without a moment of hesitation, he walked inside, ready to smite anyone who dared get in his way.

The light of his magic spooked the darkness inside, and it slithered away, hiding in the far corners of the room. At least six wizards and witches lay sprawled on the floor, in awkward poses, unconscious. Aidan halted by the doorway, dropping his arms down.

Archmage Allerton stood in the middle of the lobby, holding Jamie Coldwell as a shield. The young guard was restrained, his hands tied up behind his back, and the Archmage held a long dagger under his chin.

Aidan took a step forward, but Quinn Allerton pressed on the dagger, drawing a few drops of blood, and Aidan stopped.

"Aodh mac Lir," said the Archmage, his voice horse and shaky. "You broke your oath and I have an order to bring you in front of the Destiny Council. Assume your human form at once and give yourself up."

"Uh-huh," muttered Aidan, a crooked smirk curving his lips. "Anything else you'd like me to do while I'm at it?"

He took another step forward, not without shock realizing that the closer he got to Arlington, the heavier the odor of lavender had become. Now he could actually see the presence of the dark magical energy surrounding the Archmage, its slithering tendrils weaving in and out of his body.

He sharpened his senses, carefully probing Allerton with his power. Now he had no doubt. The spell that was cast on the Guardians Order was different from the one he had encountered in the Sisterhood of the Sun. If in the Sisterhood the enchantment had been placed upon the building, here the epicenter of the spell was a living person—Archmage Arlington, and his infected aura was affecting everyone within the Order, exposing them to the mind control of the dark spell.

"Do it!" squealed the Archmage. "Obey, or I will kill him!" He pressed the dagger deeper and a few rivulets of blood ran down Jamie's skin.

"Aidan, don't listen to him... My life means nothing... Leave, save yourself..." whispered the young guard and then stilled as the Archmage jerked him back. His lips opened, and his pupils dilated into two black abysses of pain and fear.

Aidan smiled, sadness settling in his heart. Being one step away from crossing the veil, Jamie Coldwell was still trying to protect him. *How did I earn his loyalty? And why is he not affected by the spell?* A thought flashed through his mind and quickly disappeared.

"Jamie, don't move," he said calmly and waved his hand.

A dense bubble of his power wrapped around the Archmage, Jamie and him, leaving the rest of the Guardians outside its walls. From the corner of his eye, he noticed that the other Guardians were slowly coming back, shifting and moaning, and he didn't want any interruptions while he was working on the cleansing spell.

A soft yelp reached Aidan's ears as Archmage Allerton backed away from him, hitting the wall of Aidan's spell with his back. Just to be sure, he opened his other sight and probed the Archmage again, this time more forcefully.

"Dammit... Gwyn, what do I do with that?" whispered Aidan, biting his lip. It looked like the center of the spell was rooted deeply into the heart of the Archmage. *How can I cleanse him without killing him in the process?* He knew that Gwyn couldn't hear him, and he wasn't expecting any help.

Taking a step forward, he met Jamie's terrified eyes, and sighed. "Jamie, there is something I need to do," he said. Noticing that his voice sounded almost apologetic, he cringed inwardly and took a short pause, thinking if there were any other ways. But since nothing better came to mind, he continued, "You're not going to like it. But it must be done."

Quinn Allerton growled as he pulled Jamie closer, shrinking behind him. Even though the man was hidden from his vision, with his magical sight, Aidan could see the slithering tentacles of the dark spell squeezing his heart tighter into its deadly embrace. While the virulent miasma of the malicious magic filled the bubble he created, it seemed to stay clear of Jamie, weaving around him without touching his skin. The young man was scared, his body trembling in his captor's hands, yet the spell had no effect on him whatsoever.

Aidan smirked. "You can play your games, but you can't run," he muttered, realizing that he was talking to the dark spell and not to the man it was feeding on.

He opened his arms and threw his head back, allowing the power of the Otherworld to flow freely through him. The brilliant white light filled the bubble as he started to sing, clearly pronouncing the words of the ancient tongue that Gwyn ap Nudd made him memorize hundreds of years ago. The dark spell responded with a high-pitched hiss, and the Archmage cried out in pain.

Out of the corner of his eyes, Aidan saw the Guardians on the other side of his bubble rise to their feet and attack his protective shield, but he didn't care. They weren't powerful enough to defy the Otherworld's purest magic. His song filled the space, getting stronger and growing more powerful as he continued.

Quinn Allerton screamed, unlocking his arms, and Jamie collapsed to the floor, his hands pressed to his chest as he was taking short, strenuous breaths. The spell retaliated to his invasion violently, raising the man it was feeding on a foot above the ground. In one stride, Aidan closed the distance between them and seized the Archmage, pulling him down.

He pressed his hand to his chest, pinning his back to the wall of the bubble, and directed the flow of his power to his heart. Quinn Allerton thrashed, and an agonizing howl escaped his lips. Aidan didn't stop, increasing his powerful assault on the blob of malignant magic hidden within Allerton's heart. To his shock, he noticed that the dark shades of the spell met the ray of his light, entwining with it, forcing it back.

Fighting the resistance of the dark magic, Aidan growled and pressed his hand tighter to the Archmage's chest while bending his knees slightly to look directly into his eyes. He channeled more of his powers, and the sound of his deep voice became deafening. Like through a wall, he caught Jamie's constrained moan, but he didn't stop, increasing the assault of his power.

The dark spell fought him, pulsating faster and faster, and with horror, Aidan felt it touching his mind, trying to invade it with its poisonous presence. A burst of anger flashed through him, and a low growl rumbled in his chest, interrupting his singing for a brief moment. The thought that Allerton was not going to survive this fight crossed Aidan's mind, but he resumed his song, sending more and more of his power through the man's heart, channeling his rage into it.

The dark spell twisted and screeched. Quinn Allerton cried out as if someone was tearing his heart out and then passed out. The light of Aidan's magic became so bright that even his magical sight got flooded with it. Aidan shouted the last words of his cleansing spell and a deafening boom rattled the building.

A malevolent wave rushed from the epicenter of dark magic and everything went dark.

* * *

"Mr. McGrath... Aidan... please don't be dead..."

Aidan cracked his eyelids open and blinked a few times, readjusting his vision to the surrounding darkness. Jamie Coldwell kneeled next to him, gently shaking his shoulder. Once he noticed that Aidan opened his eyes, an expression of concern on his face lightened up, replaced by a warm smile.

"I'm a god, Jamie...," he mumbled, scrambling into a sitting position. "I can't die."

"You *are* a god, my lord," replied the young guard with a happy grin. "A powerful one. No one doubts that anymore."

Aidan muttered a quick spell and threw a few light orbs in the air, noticing that this simple spell took more effort than it should have. In the shimmering blue light of the orbs, he surveyed the lobby that resembled a battlefield with a few motionless bodies sprawled on the floor, covered in dust and debris. Quinn Allerton sat a few feet away from him, surrounded by Guardians and luckily alive.

"Yeah..." Aidan pushed himself off the floor and rose to his feet with a strenuous grunt. "It is generally a bad idea to underestimate a god just because he doesn't like violence and prefers not to use all his power in the human realm."

"Lesson learned, my lord," said Quinn Allerton, getting up with the help of the Guardians. "I don't understand though..." He pressed his hand to his chest and winced in pain. "What happened? Why were we fighting you?" He took in Aidan's appearance, his eyes searching his chest. "You don't have your pendant... You broke your oath, my lord. But why?"

Aidan sighed, a light smirk touching his lips. In so many words, he told the Archmage everything that had happened in the last few weeks, including his visit to the Sisterhood of the Sun.

"Jesus Christ...," muttered Quinn Allerton, rubbing his forehead. "How could it happen? And you think the Destiny Council is infected as well?"

Aidan nodded. "I'll be visiting them next. In the meantime, Mr. Allerton, I would appreciate it if you could call back a group of Guardians you have sent to attack a small ranch in Arizona. If your witches and wizards are still alive, that is." He smirked darkly, observing the expression of shock on the Archmage's face.

As he listened to Quinn Allerton giving orders to the Guardians, Aidan turned to Jamie.

"Thank you, my friend," he said, meeting the young man's eyes. He still wondered why he hadn't been affected by the dark magic, but right now wasn't the right time to get into it. "Is there anything I can do for you to show my gratitude, please let me know."

Jamie smiled—a shy smile that made him look younger than he was.

"If you're planning to teleport back to Arizona, my lord," he started, sounding slightly uncomfortable, "would you mind giving me a lift to Blue Creek? It's a small town right outside Phoenix. I think it's about time I had a talk with my father. He is a powerful wizard, but I've never thought I had any talents for the art..." He shrugged, staring down at his hands. Then he raised his eyes at Aidan, staring at him in puzzlement. "I want to know why this spell didn't affect me. I could actually see it as you were fighting it... I must learn what I am."

Aidan narrowed his eyes, peering deep into the young man's soul, but quickly let go, knowing that the sensation of being scanned by his power wasn't a pleasant one.

"I sense a very small amount of magic in you, Jamie. I always have. Most likely, you're a wizard," he said, placing his hand on the guard's shoulder. "But it's a good idea to dig deeper. Everything in the World of Magic is deceiving. Powers can be concealed or blocked. So, your father may know something you don't."

He nodded at Archmage Allerton and snapped his fingers, teleporting himself and Jamie out of the Guardians HQ.

CHAPTER 34

~ TESSA ~

Tessa ran out of the smithy and rushed toward the house. She found Raoul de Beaumont, Missi and Karma standing a few yards away from the porch. The Warden held his sword in his hands above his head, pointing it at the top of the protective dome clearly outlined by the light of the wards. Staring at him with concern, Tessa couldn't help but wonder how long he could stay in this position before his arms would get numb.

Missi and Karma stood on either side of him with their hands placed on his shoulders, and all three of them were chanting something in Dragon Tongue continuously. She couldn't hear their words over the buzzing and screeching of the wards, but their lips were moving, and their bodies emitted a soft glow of their magic. A bright ray of light ran from the tip of Raoul's blade to the dome above their heads. Channeling any magical energy they could collect, including the energy of their own life force, they were trying to reinforce the failing wards.

Outside the protected area, a long chain of people stood with their arms raised. Even if she didn't possess the other sight, the combined magical energy of the Guardians witches was so powerful, she could probably see its bright glow with her normal vision.

The enchantment they cast now was different from the one they had used in their previous attack. And whatever this new spell was, it appeared to be working. The wards were still buzzing and glowing with a bright white light, fighting the vigorous assault of the Guardians, but the darker spots of negative energy had marred the surface of the protective dome in a few places already.

If we don't make them stop now, the wards will collapse. I don't think we have longer than thirty minutes...

Tessa glanced at Raoul, Missi and Karma and any doubts she had left her mind—all three of them knew it too. Their faces were tense, and Raoul's arms were shaking with strain. Fear coiled in her chest, and a thick lump stuck in her throat. Her friends were overusing their magic and connecting their life forces to the failing wards put them in serious danger.

Not gonna work... at least not for long...

She heard a low guttural growl and snapped her head to the side. Stepping on large, soft paws, Theron in his tiger form moved toward her, his long orange tail swiping from left to right. Six giant wolves followed him, fur standing on their withers. The weretiger approached her and pushed her slightly on her side, showing her that he was ready to fight.

Just ten of them against half of the Guardians Order... She stared at the dark shapes outside the fence and shuddered. She knew most of them. Some of the people behind that white fence weren't even Witches or Wizards yet—just Apprentices. *If they were here because of Zane and Aidan, how could the Order do that? How could they send such inexperienced people to fight with a god of the Otherworld and a Great Fire Salamander?*

"These wards are not going to hold longer than a few minutes," said a soft feminine voice next to her, but somehow, she could hear it through the pandemonium of the failing wards. "If you don't do something now, you'll get a bloody battle on your hands."

"Famine," Tessa growled, pointing at the house. "Go back inside. You shouldn't be here."

With her peripheral vision, she caught a bright flare of red light on her right. Tessa pivoted and froze in place, trying to figure out what the Guardians were up to. They separated into two teams. The bigger group continued sustaining their initial enchantment, working on breaking through the protective magic Aidan had placed around the farm. The other team conjured fire, adding it to the original spell. Despite the coldness of the desert night, the fire the Guardians were wielding burned so hot, she could feel it even from a distance.

"If you don't do something quick, you all are going to be dead in a few minutes," said Famine indifferently. "I wonder if fried tiger tastes like chicken."

She winked at Theron, and he responded by baring his terrifying fangs at her. Famine chuckled at his displeasure and quickly scratched him behind his ear as if he were a cute house kitten. The weretiger growled and snapped at her, but she pulled her hand back faster than he could react.

"If you don't do something quick, we will," said a deep voice behind her, making Tessa flinch and spin around. War and Pestilence stood barely a foot away from her with their arms crossed, identical smirks on their faces.

"No!" yelled Tessa, her voice breaking on the high notes. She swallowed and took a deep breath to calm her nerves. "I said no. You can't get involved. None of you! Go back inside the house. I will take care of the Guardians."

Viggo Warrington laughed mockingly. "Little girl, do you seriously think you can take care of so many witches and wizards, most of whom are a lot more powerful than you are?"

"I can't kill them! Don't you get it? They are innocent in all this… It's that stupid spell!" Tessa yelled, throwing her hands up.

"I just need to hold them until Aidan cleanses the Guardians Order! I can't... I can't kill them..."

She repeated her last words quietly, her anger dying down as she realized with horror that the Horsemen were right. As soon as the wards collapsed—and they would collapse soon—she would have to face the Guardians in a kill or be killed combat situation. She glanced back at Missi and saw tears glistening on her strained face. She knew it too.

"Say one word, little girl," purred War, putting his hand on her shoulder, "and I'll make them kill each other. Nice and clean... none of you here will have to fight at all... I just need to use a smidge of my power to get it done."

"Say one word, child," Pestilence whispered into her ear from her other side, "and they will fall ill, unable to fight... never to rise again... Your command and an ounce of my power... that's all it takes."

Tessa stared at them, her mind clouded by the influence of their powerful magic. *"Under no circumstances, can the Horsemen get involved in a fight with the Guardians,"* Gwyn's voice sounded in her head, clearing it instantly. Making an effort, she closed her eyes for a brief moment and took a deep breath.

"No," she said firmly, pointing back at the house. She extended her arm up, summoning the Axe of Perun. As the deadly weapon materialized in her hand, she turned to Viggo Warrington, gazing calmly into his steel eyes. "I'm not a little girl, Mr. Warrington. I am the only daughter of Perun and a powerful demigod, and you'll do well to remember it."

She gathered the electricity from the air and a bright lightning bolt split the night sky, getting absorbed by the axe. Theron and the wolves shifted back, growling at the Horsemen.

War made a move away from the animals, but before he could reply, the wards collapsed. The sound of a loud explosion rattled the desert, and a brilliant flare of white light blinded them. The nonstop cacophony that was pounding the area just a moment ago got replaced by a deafening silence, and for a few seconds, everything stilled as though time ceased its movement.

Stunned, people on both side of the fence stood still. Then, like by someone's command, everything came to motion. The fire-wielding witches shouted something, and a wall of smoldering flames moved toward them. Tessa swung the Axe in a wide arc and yelled, *"Praecidio Amnia!"*

The pale-yellow glow of her shield unfolded between them and the fence. The fire hit the shield, flowing around it, doing them no harm. She knew that her basic protection spell wouldn't hold for longer than a minute, but that was enough for her to get rid of the Horsemen.

"Mr. Warrington, please take your...um... siblings and get back into the house," she commanded in a no-nonsense tone. She knew that she was bossing around three ancient beings of magic, but at this moment she couldn't care less. "You must stay there, and you must keep your power under control. As long as you three are together, this world is in danger. Using your power will shift the balance toward the apocalypse. I can't fight these crazy witches and worry about you sending the world into the stone age. Do you understand me?"

"Yes, ma'am," replied War, lifting his hand to his temple in a military style salute, but his gray eyes were crinkling at the corners. He gestured at Pestilence and Famine and all three of them vanished.

As the next fire strike hit her protective shield, she grunted, channeling more power through it and looked back, searching for Raoul, Missi and Karma. In the flickering light of the flames, she saw them lying sprawled on the ground unconscious. Raoul's sword lay next to him, its shiny blade reflecting the orange flares of the fire.

She screamed in frustration as she watched her worst fears come true. Just like her, Raoul, Missi and Karma had hoped that Aidan would break the dark spell before the wards would fail.

Since they were channeling their life energy through the dome, when it collapsed, it knocked them out cold. The overuse of their magic didn't help either.

"Theron, Hawk!" she yelled, breathing hard. "Get ready! I am dropping the shield!"

As soon as the glow of her protective magic vanished, all hell broke loose. The fire strikes and energy orbs flew through the air, spreading electrical discharges and sparks around. The Guardians charged all at once and were met by the infuriated tiger and six giant, ferocious wolves.

Theron seized one of the Guardians witches by her leg while she tried to hit him with an energy orb. She screamed, her face contorted in pain as she struggled to unlock his iron jaws.

"Try not to kill them!" yelled Tessa, deflecting a magical energy strike with the Axe.

Theron growled, unhappy with Tessa's order, but unlocked his jaws, spitting, and hissing like a house cat who smelled a lemon. Then he swung his mighty paw and hit the witch on the side of her head, knocking her out.

Since she didn't want to kill any of the witches and wizards, at first, Tessa tried to be careful, keeping her magical strikes to a minimum, resorting to hand-to-hand combat and use of low voltage energy orbs. However, as more and more witches came from the darkness of the desert, vaulting over the fence, she realized that she wouldn't be able to keep the Horsemen safe for much longer. And if the Guardians attacked them, she had no doubt—they would use their full powers. With the future of the entire world at stake, it wasn't an option.

Tessa lowered the Axe of Perun and looked around, cold sweat trickling down her spine. It seemed like the attackers were coming from all directions at once. As they kept pushing her, Theron, and the wolves closer to the porch, she realized that soon they would have no more space to maneuver. The fire was encroaching on the house and dirty smoke partially obscured her vision, making her eyes itch and burn.

The Warden, Missi and Karma were still unconscious, and she had no other help coming. One of the wolves yelped and fell, a sword protruding from his chest. Hawk spun toward Tessa, his lips curving in a furious snarl.

"No, please...," mumbled Tessa, but Hawk howled, and the remaining four wolves repeated his war cry.

They charged the Guardians closest to them at full force, and Theron followed suit. Their mighty jaw ripped throats, severed ligaments and crunched bones. And even though it was only six of them, the Guardians staggered back a few steps, horrified by the brutality of their attack, leaving their dead and wounded behind.

Tessa swung the Axe, channeling her power, and the sky lit up with the bright zigzags of lightning bolts. The thunder rumbled from the cloudless sky. She raised her arms up, holding her weapon with both hands. With a painful scream escaping her lips, she redirected her strike at the attacking Guardians. A few fell, dead and wounded, their bodies convulsing uncontrollably.

Aidan, where are you?? What's taking you so long?

Everything inside her was crying and bleeding at the thought that she had to kill her own. She had studied with them. She had practiced magic with them. She had lived with them in the same building. They were her classmates, her neighbors. They were supposed to be on the same side, not facing each other in mortal combat. They all gave the same oath—to fight on the side of the light, protecting the realm of humans and keeping the World of Magic safe.

Why???

Through the noise of the battle she caught a strange shuffling sound somewhere behind her. She tried to turn around and take a look, but being under constant attack, she couldn't take her eyes off of her opponents. When she finally got a moment to breathe, it was too late.

Throwing a quick glance over her shoulder, she saw dark shadows moving forward from behind the house, surrounding it. Missi and Raoul were still unconscious, but Karma stirred weakly, struggling to sit up.

Moving slowly like in a nightmare, a few witches surrounded her friends, raising their swords. Tessa yelled something, not fully understanding what she was saying or doing. She turned around and ran toward her friends, swinging her Axe at anyone who tried slowing her down. One of the witches raised her sword, standing over Karma.

Gathering electricity in her hands, Tessa redirected it at the enemy. The blinding zigzag of a lightning bolt struck the witch in her shoulder. She cried out, but before she fell, she plummeted her blade down, putting the weight of her entire body behind it.

Time slowed down.

All sounds melted into the pounding of Tessa's heart.

All thoughts disappeared in her mind consumed by debilitating terror.

She didn't hear Karma's scream. She saw her eyes widen as the blade pierced her left shoulder just above her clavicle, sinking deep into her chest. Her hands wrapped around the cold steel, blood bursting between her fingers, running out of her open mouth. Slowly, she sunk down, falling on her back, her legs bent awkwardly under her.

Tessa was almost there when she saw another witch standing over Missi, a deadly energy orb, crackling with electrical discharges, twirling in the palm of her hand. Tessa knew her. They started as the Guardians Apprentices at the same time. She knew her name—Lucy. They used to study together, had fun together and ate lunch at the same cafeteria in the Guardians HQ.

As Lucy raised her hand ready to propel the energy orb at Missi, Tessa screamed—a roar of anger and pain erupting from her lips—and swung the Axe of Perun, decapitating the Guardian witch in place.

Numb, she watched the head of the witch roll off her shoulders, bright red liquid spurting out of her neck. She couldn't process what happened, her brain refusing to accept the reality. The head fell, rolling to her feet, and Tessa backed away, almost tripping over Karma's body, bile rising to her mouth. She sunk to her knees next to Karma. Dropping the Axe, she grabbed her face into her hands, peering at her black eyes with dead, dilated pupils, and tears, hot and painful, spilled from her eyes.

"Tessa…"

A soft whisper touched her mind, and she slowly turned her head in the direction of the sound. Missi was struggling to get up into a sitting position, but her body, weakened by the overuse of her magic, didn't obey her. Raoul sat next to her, carefully supporting her with his arms.

"Tessa…," she whispered barely audibly. "Karma… is she…"

Tessa didn't answer, but Missi's voice brought her back to the terrible reality she was living in. The sounds came back rushing, and with shock she realized that she heard the sound of the wind, the songs of midnight crickets and the crackling of fire. And even though she still heard moans of the wounded, the noise of the battle was gone.

It was quiet. Too quiet.

Afraid of what she was about to see, she rose to her feet and turned around. Theron, covered in blood, some of which was undoubtedly his, stood in front of her in his human form, his bloodied arms dangling at his sides powerlessly. Hawk and two other werewolves stood behind him, also back to their normal appearance. The Guardians were scattered all over the property, at least fifty of them still on their feet, but they looked shocked and disoriented, like people who couldn't remember why they were here and how they got to this point.

"Tessa," whispered Theron, approaching her.

She raised her hands covered in blood, and then her eyes darted to Lucy's headless corpse. She looked back up at Theron and her lips quivered, tears running down her cheeks, leaving clear paths in dirt and blood covering her skin.

"I killed her... Theron, what did I do? And Karma... I couldn't—" She cried, and he came closer, wrapping his massive arms around her, pulling her tiny trembling body to his chest.

Sobbing against Theron's chest, she didn't notice when Aidan materialized next to her. She felt Theron stiffen as he whispered Aidan's name. She lifted her head and her eyes fell upon the only face she wanted to see right now.

"Aidan...," she mumbled, barely able to produce coherent words. "You were too late... I had too... Aidan... Karma..."

Aidan replaced Theron, and she fell into his embrace, clutching to him as if she were that ten-year-old girl again in need of his protection.

"Tessa, I'm here," he whispered into her matted hair. "I came as soon as I could. I'm sorry, my love."

"Aidan, summon Mrak Delar." She lifted her head off his chest, staring into his eyes pleadingly. "He has healing power. Please, he can still save her." She twisted in Aidan's arms and stared down at Hawk, who was kneeling next to Karma. The werewolf looked at her and shook his head, his face shadowed by grief.

"I can't summon Mrak Delar, my love," whispered Aidan, stroking her shoulders gently. "But even if I could, it's too late. He can't bring back the dead—"

She didn't listen to him. "No, please." She turned back to face him, grabbing his arms. "Then summon this other Master of Power... The one that looks just like Mrak. Master of Kendral. Please, Aidan, please!"

He pulled her back into his chest and wrapped his arms around her, placing his cheek atop her head.

"I'm so sorry, Tessa," he said softly. "It's my fault… It took me too long to break this goddamn spell…"

She stopped crying and pulled away. The Guardians still stood around them. Anger, powerful and all-consuming, surged through her like a tidal wave. The thunder rumbled above, and a bright lightning forked through the sky, hitting the ground next to her feet.

"Leave…," she hissed, pointing at the Guardians with her trembling hand. Then she punched the air with her fist and shouted at the top of her lungs. "Leave! All of you! Out! Out! OUT!"

The Guardians exchanged a shocked look but turned around and walked away into the darkness of the desert, leaving a few bodies behind. Hawk and Theron checked every person lying on the ground. They were all dead, including three out of five werewolves and Karma.

"Tessa…" She heard a whisper and a touch of cold air brushed her skin.

She sighed, knowing exactly what she was going to see. As her vision flashed to negative and back, she found Karma's spirit standing in front of her. Crowding behind her were the spirits of the dead Guardians and fallen werewolves.

"Karma." Tessa reached for her, wanting to hug her, but then pulled her hand away. "I'm sorry. I couldn't save you."

Karma smiled, a sad but warm smile, and shrugged. "I guess it was my time? When you find Death, can you please tell him that he can take his list and sh—" She stopped talking and chuckled. "No, better give my message to Zane. Tell him that he's the best firetwat I've ever met. Tell him not to give up on his love."

She closed her eyes and the soft glow of her human soul ignited brighter.

"I will give both of them your message," whispered Tessa, wiping tears off her face with the back of her dirty hand. "Are you ready?"

Karma nodded. Instead of taking her hand, Tessa approached her and pulled her into a last embrace. Karma sighed with relief and vanished. Feeling dead on her feet and debilitated by grief, Tessa walked slowly among the spirits. With parting words of encouragement, she touched their hands, directing them through the veil. A few minutes later, all the spirits were gone.

Tessa turned around, meeting Aidan's gaze filled with love and sympathy. She took a step toward him, but a blazing curtain of fire unfolded between them, making her jump aside. Kal walked out of his portal and quickly surveyed the area.

"Cease!" he boomed, pointing at the house.

Tessa twirled around and saw that the fire the Guardians used to attack the wards was still burning, slowly creeping toward the building. At the Fire Elemental's command, all fire died out immediately, leaving wispy gray tendrils of smoke hanging in the air.

Kal shook his head and his brows snapped together as he observed all the dead people lying in the space between the gates and the house. His flaming eyes lingered on Karma's body for a few moments and he sighed, sadness clouding his features. It seemed like he understood everything without the need for words. He turned to Tessa and seized her chin with his hot fingers, gently lifting her face.

"You did well, child," he said softly. Letting go of her chin, he tapped her lightly on her shoulder and peered at Aidan over her head. "Aidan, we need to go. As tired as we both are, we must take care of the Destiny Council situation immediately."

Just now Tessa noticed how uncharacteristically weary the Great Salamander looked. His enormous shoulders were hunched, and he was clasping his hand to a deep laceration on his left side, blood mixed with liquid fire still trickling from under his fingers. His face was covered in a thick gray layer of dust and ashes, and his clothes were stained with blood.

"Brother Raoul," called Kal.

The Warden picked up his sword and got up with a strained grunt, leaving Missi sitting on the ground by the porch. He approached the Fire Elemental and bowed.

"Yes, my lord." His voice was weak and shaky, and it looked like he barely had any strength left in him to carry his heavy blade.

Kal stared down at him and a deep sorrow reflected in his eyes.

"Raoul," he said softly. "You must go back to the Church by the Sea. Both you and Father Collins are needed at the Wardens HQ in Paris as soon as possible. The Grand Master is dead. He was used as an anchor for the dark spell that was placed on your Order. I broke the spell and cleansed the minds of those infected. Luckily, not all the Wardens were affected..." He took a short pause and a deep sigh shuddered his chest. "I couldn't save your Grand Master, Raoul. And for that, I'm deeply sorry. He was a great man..."

Raoul swayed on his feet, and his pale face became ashen. He dropped his head, pressing his hand to his eyes, and for a few seconds remained silent. When he raised his face, he looked calm, but his bloodshot eyes betrayed suppressed tears.

"My lord... Aidan," he said quietly, his voice hoarse. "Would you kindly teleport me back to the Church by the Sea? If you no longer need me here, that is."

Aidan nodded. "We'll drop you off there on the way to the Otherworld."

He approached Tessa and pulled her into a tight embrace. Tessa closed her eyes, listening to the steady beat of his heart. She wanted to go with him, but she knew it wasn't possible. The Horsemen were still here and both Missi and she had to keep an eye on the situation. As long as Zane, Mrak, and Lucan were riding the steeds of the Apocalypse, the world wasn't safe.

As if reading her thoughts, Aidan bent down slightly and kissed her, a quick and gentle touch of his lips to hers. "As soon as we're done with the Destiny Council, we'll come back here. You and Missi"—he threw a quick glance at the mage—"still have a job to do. Keep the Horsemen safe and don't let them use their powers no matter what."

Aidan nodded to Theron, Hawk, and the two other werewolves. Then he seized Kal's elbow, put his hand on Raoul's shoulder, and all three of them vanished.

Be safe, my ancient god...

CHAPTER 35

~ ZANE BURNS, A.K.A. GUNZ ~

A giant, winged monster—an enormous serpent with a body as black as night—hovered over the center of the plateau where the small swamp was supposed to be. In the surrounding darkness, it was hard to assess its full grandeur, but it seemed like the blackness of its scales absorbed all the light without reflecting it.

The flat head of the serpent ended in a massive iron beak, and two large trunks hung on either side of it. Dark mist rose beneath it in long slithering tendrils, obscuring the bottom part of its body. The monster spread its wide wings and a piercing hiss, accompanied by a powerful jet of fire, escaped its beak.

Gunz screamed and threw himself in front of the fire to shield his friends, absorbing most of it with his body. Mrak Delar grabbed Lucan and Yaroslav, pulling them behind the nearest Seid and into a small trench in the ground.

Gunz fell to his knees, breathing hard, and glanced up at the serpent. Its wings were opened to full extent now, obscuring the entire valley in the center of the plateau. Unlike its body, its wings sparkled as if they were covered in precious gems—diamonds, rubies, emeralds—emitting all the colors of the spectrum. Its eyes shone with a sinister red light, but Gunz was positive that it wasn't the glow of fire energy.

The monster's dark magical essence permeated the air, suffocating him. Gunz fell on all fours and coughed, clutching his throat. For a heartbeat, he couldn't move, his body heavy and stiff. Even though the monster was using his element, absorbing its fire gave Gunz neither strength nor the usual burst of energy. On the contrary, he felt ill and weak as if he was poisoned.

Since he discovered the fire, he met quite a few monsters and evil beings, including the Lord of Chaos, Skiper-Zmey, but never had he sensed an energy signature as dark and ominous as this one.

"Gunz..." He heard Mrak Delar's voice and glanced back over his shoulder. "Be careful. Don't let the serpent look into your eyes. I need you to get here, behind the Seid. Do it fast, before he attacks again."

Did Mrak just call this snake 'he'? A thought materialized in Gunz's mind, but he ignored it, focusing on the monster's giant wings to avoid his blazing eyes. He grabbed his sword and carefully sheathed it, trying to produce as little noise as possible. Slowly, he moved backward toward the Seid and then rolled on his shoulder, falling into the trench behind it.

Lying on his back, he stared up at his friends, still gasping for air. "What the hell... is that?"

"Our worst nightmare," Mrak Delar whispered, helping him to sit up. "Aspid."

"Never heard of it," mumbled Gunz. "How do we kill it?"

"That's the problem," murmured Yaroslav, exchanging a look with the Master of Power. "Last time it took three gods to destroy this monster—Semargl, Stribog and Dazhbog."

"Needless to say, they barely survived the encounter," added Mrak Delar, shaking his head. He leaned his back against the rocky wall of the trench, pulling his bent legs to his chest and bit his lip. "I can't believe I missed all the signs. The rocks, the cold, the silence."

"I'm sorry, Mrak, but I really don't know anything about this monster," mumbled Gunz, searching his memory for anything useful he could find and coming up with nothing.

"Aspid can never land on the ground," explained the Master of Power, speaking in a quick whisper. "Mother Earth doesn't accept his venomous presence. So, he lives in mountains, moving around by landing on rocks. This place"—he waved his hand around—"is infested with stone blocks, Seids, and the ground barely has any dirt over it. He loves solitude and cold temperatures. I should have known we were dealing with Aspid. It was right in front of my eyes all along."

"How do we get rid of it?" asked Lucan, carefully peeking over the side of the Seid.

Yaroslav yanked him down, giving him a warning stare. "Lucan, you lock your eyes with Aspid, and he'll have another stone to land on."

All of a sudden, the ground trembled and a loud hiss that could be easily called a roar shattered the silence. A heavy slithering noise followed the war cry of Aspid as the monster moved closer. The energy of fire tripled in a heartbeat and the reek of Aspid's malicious presence assailed them.

"*Praecidio Amnia,*" yelled Mrak Delar, infusing his protection spell with all four elemental powers.

As soon as the shield unfolded over them, a blast of darkened flames swallowed everything around them. Even though Mrak's protective magic saved them from the direct impact, the smoldering heat of the monster's fire strike was unbearable. Yaroslav screamed, wrapping his arms over his head, and fell to the bottom of the trench.

"*Praecidio Amnia Circula Archni,*" Gunz yelled, manifesting a second, more powerful shield around Yaroslav.

The vampire lowered his arms, raising his bloodshot eyes at

Gunz, and nodded. Aspid hissed again and another fire strike followed. This time, the dark flames kept flowing without stop. The heat intensified, and the swirls of gray smoke spread over them. The reek of burnt wood invaded their senses, and soon, the lack of oxygen became noticeable.

"What do we do?" asked Lucan, coughing. "Neither you, Master, nor the Fire Salamander can keep the protection spells forever. Sooner or later, the use of magic will drain you both. Besides, if we do nothing, we'll suffocate."

"If we have any chance of killing this monster at all, we must work together. All four of us." Mrak Delar closed his eyes for a moment and swallowed hard, wiping sweat off his forehead. "When we're ready, I'll distract Aspid. I have to bring his full attention to myself, so all of you can do your part."

"Mrak, no," objected Gunz, fear squeezing his already tight throat. He coughed and sucked in a gulp of air poisoned by smoke. "Why you? I'll do it. Aspid uses fire, and even though his flames are darker than normal, it's not the Black Fire. There is nothing he can do to me. The rest of you are vulnerable."

"No. It must be me," Mrak Delar cut him off dryly, and the way he said it stopped Gunz from any further objections. Quickly, the Master of Power explained what each of them would have to do.

"Dammit," Gunz cursed, adding a few choice words in Russian. "There are more holes in your plan than in a spaghetti strainer."

"His plan is based on history," objected Yaroslav calmly, throwing his long hair back. "There are no other plans."

"Yeah, but the last time this plan was executed by three gods," muttered Gunz. "As powerful as you are—"

"I know, I'm not a god. None of us are. But it isn't the first time we have to do something everyone considered impossible," growled Mrak Delar, interrupting him. "Besides, it is you who will have to step into Semargl's shoes and play a god for a change. None of us can do that. Use all the resources you've got. *All of them*, am I clear, young Salamander?"

"Yes, sir," replied Gunz, all the blood draining from his face as the feeling of dread intensified.

In his mind, he reached for the Dark Codex again, channeling more of its power and its knowledge. With a constrained groan, he suppressed the instant headache and searched the spells presented by the Codex, trying to find anything that would tell him how to kill Aspid. Except for the legend Mrak had told them already, he couldn't find anything else, and the longer he stayed connected to the book, the brighter his eyes shone with a blinding white light. Yaroslav and Lucan gasped, staring at him in awe, but asked nothing.

"No more discussions," grumbled the Ancient Master, cutting the air with his hand. "We must defeat Aspid and find Death, and right now, we're wasting time this realm doesn't have. Each moment the Horsemen and their horses spend together in this world, the more unstable it becomes."

"On your command, my lord," said Lucan, getting into a crouching position, ready to spring into action.

Yaroslav took one knee, unsheathing his katana. His eyes lit up with a scarlet glow and his fangs expanded as his lips curled into a feral snarl. "I'm ready, Master."

"Gunz will remove his shield off Yaroslav first. Then on the count of three, I will bring the protective magic down," said Mrak Delar, his face strained, his eyes swirling with the color of the four elements. "Take your positions as fast as you can. Each of you must wait for my command. I'll make sure you hear me."

Gunz unsheathed War's sword, wishing it was his own, and whispered, *"Incanto Comlium."*

Yaroslav grunted but remained still despite the heat of Aspid's continuous fire strikes scorching his skin.

"Get ready," hissed Mrak Delar, glowering at the nonstop river of flames flowing over the surface of the protection spell above his head. As the stream of the fire dwindled down slightly, Aspid sucked in some air with a loud hiss. The Master of Power counted to three and quickly removed his magical shield.

Gunz jumped out of the trench, landing on the rocky ground into a crouching stance and then bolted to the nearest stone formation, hiding behind it. He didn't see where Lucan went, but out of the corner of his eye, he caught Yaroslav shifting into a large white bird and disappearing into the night sky.

With his chest shuddering with short breaths, Gunz watched Mrak Delar through his other sight. The Master channeled all four elemental powers, entwining them with his magic. Gunz couldn't hear his words but judging by the spikes of magical energy around him, Mrak was summoning something.

A loud hiss drew his attention back to Aspid, and Gunz peeked over the side of the rock he was hiding behind. The serpent's chest expanded as he sucked in a large gulp of air, the black scales covering his body pulling apart slightly. A moment later, a sweltering jet of fire escaped his beak again. He flapped his wings, raising clouds of dust and ash in the air.

Gunz's knee-jerk reaction was to throw himself in the path of the fire to protect his friend, but remembering Mrak's command, he stayed down, his fingers squeezing the grip of the sword. Fire flowed over the trench, and with relief, he realized that the Master of Power managed to conjure a protective shield over himself again.

A new sound came unexpectedly—a high pitch, vibrating note of a horn. Tender and pure, it was inept for the given situation, seemingly coming from every direction at once. Thin and weak at first, it grew stronger, forcefully invading every nook and cranny of the plateau, and soon it was so loud that it overpowered the hisses and roars of the monster.

The flow of the fire ceased, and Aspid rose higher in the air, searching for the source of the sound. If the terrifying look on the monster's face could've been called an expression, the serpent wore one of annoyance and scorching fury. Gunz twirled around, surveying the area with his second sight, until his eyes stopped on the trench where Mrak was hiding. He couldn't see the Master of Power, but the glow of his magical energy easily identified his position.

Reinforcing his other sight with his magic, Gunz got a clear picture that made chills run down his spine. Holding a small horn in his hands, Mrak Delar lay on the bottom of the trench, blowing into the horn and magically magnifying its sound.

Aspid emitted a mighty roar, shaking his head like a wet dog, and his death-dealing eyes shone brighter. Following the direction of the sound, the serpent flew closer to Mrak Delar and stilled in the air, lingering right above him. The Master of Power didn't stop playing and with every next note, the frustration of the monster took on a whole new level.

Spiraling down, the serpent slammed into Mrak's shield, beating it with his powerful wings and spraying it with fire. The Master of Power screamed, and for a brief moment, the music of the horn vanished.

"Not yet," Gunz whispered to himself, his own voice sounding foreign to his ear. "Stay down... Mrak knows what he is doing..."

The sound of the horn rose again, more powerful and brighter than before, and Gunz let out a strained breath, dropping his tense shoulders. The horn drove Aspid into the next outburst of anger. Ignoring everything around him, the monster attacked the shield with all he had.

Gunz rose slightly, pressing his chest to the rough surface of the stone. His heart thudded against his ribcage, cold sweat trickling down his back.

Come on, Mrak... we're ready... don't wait too long...

Like in response to his thoughts, the magically reinforced

voice of the Ancient Master boomed through the plateau. "Lucan, now!"

The elf rose from behind a stone block that was lying right next to the trench. Gunz had seen Lucan fight before. But what he was witnessing now was unlike anything he had ever encountered in his previous experience. The elf's body emitted a soft blue light, the air around him shimmering with cerulean sparks. His long hair elevated slightly, fanning around his face and shoulders.

He raised his arms toward Aspid, chanting something in his ancient language, and two blue rays of elven magic burst out of his hands. Distracted by the music of the horn, Aspid kept attacking Mrak Delar, and when he noticed Lucan, it was too late.

A shimmering blue noose of elven magic materialized around Aspid's neck, right behind his head. Lucan pulled down on the blue rays of his magic as though they were real ropes. The noose squeezed tighter, and the muscles on Lucan's arms and shoulders rippled as he strained to keep the monster in the vice-like grip of his magic.

Aspid flapped his wings, trying to break the restraints and rise higher, but somehow Lucan managed to keep him down. The elf screamed, dropping to one knee as he leaned his massive torso back. The sound of the horn grew louder. Aspid roared, thrashing from side to side, beating his wings vigorously.

"Yaroslav, now!" shouted Mrak Delar, his magnified voice barely heard over the roars and hisses of the snake.

Aspid pulled back as far as he could. He opened his iron beak and directed a stream of his fire at Lucan. In one swift motion, Mrak Delar removed the shield from the trench and got up to his full height.

"*Praecidio Amnia,*" he yelled, pointing at Lucan, and the wall of his protective magic surrounded the elf with its soft yellow glow.

The serpent's long tail swung around, striking the Master of Power across his chest. Mrak cried out and fell backward into the trench, hitting the edge with his head. Nevertheless, Lucan managed to hold the monster.

A large white bird appeared above Aspid. It twirled in place, and the air around it shimmered like a mirage in a hot day. A heartbeat later, Yaroslav materialized in its place, holding his katana above his head. The serpent was hissing and beating in the restraints of elven magic, making it hard for him to aim the strike properly. Catching the right moment, Yaroslav screamed and plummeted the blade down into the serpent's neck.

A piercing howl of pain and anger made the Vottovaara Mountain shudder, and its echo reverberated far through the forest. Black goo gushed from the deep wound on the serpent's neck, drenching Lucan from head to toe. Ignoring the foul stench of the monster's blood, Lucan pulled tighter on the ropes of his magic. Yaroslav yanked his sword out and lowered it again, this time cutting the head cleanly off Aspid's neck.

As the head of the monster rolled down on the rocky ground, Gunz channeled his power and rose in the air supported by the flow of the elemental fire.

"Slavik, get the hell out of the way!" he shouted, redirecting his power toward his hands.

One second, the vampire was hovering over the serpent's body that was twitching and thrashing between the rocks, and the next moment he was gone.

"*Ignius Amplio!*" yelled Gunz, adding some of the Dark Codex magic into the flow of his elemental fire.

Streams of blinding white flames hit the monster's remains, setting it ablaze. Even though Aspid's entire body was engulfed in smoldering fire, Gunz didn't stop, channeling more and more of his power and magic into it. The headless serpent flailed and twirled on the ground, but to his shock, Aspid was still alive and a tiny head materialized in the place where Yaroslav severed the neck.

"Mishka! I need! More! FIRE!" roared Gunz.

Without waiting for the wyvern to materialize, he switched his position slightly and struck the newly forming head of the serpent with his fire. The white flames turned bloody red, burning hotter than any fire Gunz had ever conjured before, but he had no time to dwell on it.

"Boss!" squeaked Mishka in horror, his golden wings beating faster and faster as he assessed the situation. This time he didn't play the twenty questions game and added his fire to the flow of Gunz's power.

A terrible, strained holler escaped Gunz's tightly pressed lips as he reverted into the natural state of the Great Fire Salamander. For a moment, a golden lizard lingered in the air above Aspid's body and then dissolved into a wall of scorching flames. When he assumed his human form, Aspid was gone and only a pile of dirty ashes remained in his place.

Gunz lowered down to the ground, softly dropping to his knees. The wind picked up, raising a cloud of ashes in the air, spinning it into a funnel. As the wind dissipated, the ashes fell to the ground, forming a massive rock. Mishka landed on Gunz's shoulder and sighed with relief, making a move with his wing as though wiping his brow.

"Boss," said the wyvern with a soft hiss. "Next time you decide to have barbecue snake for dinner, give me some advanced warning, would yah? At least I would bring the right sauce with me."

Gunz didn't hear his words. Slowly, he got up to his feet, feeling as if the ground just disappeared from under his feet. Lucan stood next to the trench. He was bleeding and burnt, his white hair matted with sweat and disgusting black goo. But it wasn't his look that shocked Gunz, turning him into a motionless statue of all-consuming grief. In his arms, the elf held Mrak

Delar. The Ancient Master's head was thrown back lifelessly, a thin rivulet of blood streaming from his temple, his arms dangling limply with every step Lucan took.

"No...," Gunz moaned, shaking his head.

"Gunz...," whispered the elf.

CHAPTER 36

~ ZANE BURNS, A.K.A. GUNZ ~

"No..." Gunz staggered back, his eyes glued to the lifeless body in Lucan's arms. "No."

He took another step back and stilled, squeezing his hands into tight fists. A brush of cold air against his cheek made Gunz flinch. Before he realized what happened, Yaroslav materialized next to Lucan. The vampire closed his eyes, and his lips parted a little, showing the tips of his fangs. He gently touched a deep laceration on Mrak's temple and brought his finger coated in fresh blood to his lips.

"He's still alive," he whispered airily, his scarlet eyes getting darker. "I can hear his heartbeat, his blood rushing through—" The vampire growled and turned away, pressing his hand to his lips—a sure sign of him fighting the thirst.

"Can you heal him, Slavik?" Gunz asked, cringing inwardly from how flat and emotionless his voice was.

"Yes-s-s-s... Ahhh..." Yaroslav closed his eyes, a deep crease materializing between his eyebrows. "I just need a minute to deal with..."

"Don't deal with anything," snapped Gunz. "If you need to

feed before you can touch him, feed on me. Wouldn't be the first time."

"No, Gunz," objected the vampire. "We are still far from done here. If I feed on you, I'll make you weaker. Just give me a moment."

He turned away, locking and unlocking his fingers at the sides of his body. When he opened his eyes again, turning to face him, they were no longer scarlet but normal blue. Lucan placed the Master of Power down on the ground, and Yaroslav knelt next to him. He upturned Mrak's head gently and then bit his own wrist. Two dark-red streams ran down his arm from small puncture wounds, permeating the air with the metallic scent of the vampire's blood. Yaroslav pressed on Mrak's jaw, opening his mouth, and moved his wrist to his lips, letting a few drops spill inside.

Nothing happened. The Adam's apple in his throat didn't move, and the Ancient Master remained as still and lifeless as before. Yaroslav sat back and shoved his hair out of the way, a thoughtful expression on his face. Then he positioned his wrist over the laceration on Mrak's temple and squeezed a few drops directly into the wound.

Gunz had experienced the healing magic of vampire blood himself, but every time he witnessed it in action, he couldn't help but feel awestruck. Slowly, the edges of the wound closed, the bleeding stopped, and Mrak Delar's eyes moved under his tightly shut eyelids. He swallowed and exhaled, his breath coming out in a soft moan.

"Mrak," called Yaroslav, leaning forward slightly.

The Master of Power opened his eyes and his gaze halted on the vampire's face first, but then slowly moved down to his wrist, smeared with blood, where two puncture wounds were gradually closing. He swallowed with an effort and grimaced.

"Vampire's blood... too sweet for my taste..." He smiled

weakly and touched Yaroslav's knee. "Thank you, my friend." He looked up at Lucan and then at Gunz. "Aspid?"

"Dead," replied Gunz.

"Dead as a pile of rocks," squeaked Mishka from Gunz's shoulder.

"We are not done," Mrak Delar muttered, struggling to sit up, bearing heavily on Yaroslav's arm. "I need a moment."

The Ancient Master closed his eyes and leaned back, allowing the vampire to support him. His body tensed as he channeled his power, starting the self-healing process, and the ground trembled slightly, responding to his actions.

"Earth?" asked Lucan, approaching Gunz.

"Healing power," replied Gunz with a short nod.

A few minutes later, Mrak opened his eyes and got up to his feet. But as soon as Yaroslav let go, he swayed, his knees gave in and he would have fallen if the vampire hadn't caught him.

"Mrak, you need some time to recover," said Gunz gently. "Tell us what we need to do next and I swear, we'll follow your every command. But you have to sit this one out. You're going to have to wait for us here."

"Like hell I am. And you're too young to give me orders, Salamander," grumbled Mrak Delar and waved at the wyvern. "Mishka, can you fly down and do a quick check of the crater before we go there?" He pointed toward the center of the plateau.

"Yes, sir!" Mishka raised his wing in a military salute and vanished from Gunz's shoulder.

He came back a minute later, flying at full speed, his eyes like two red saucers. Hovering in front of the Master of Power, he whimpered, "There is nothing there. Just a swamp. Dark, scary, stinky swamp. What were you expecting to find there, Master? A few leeches?"

"I hope that's all we find there," murmured Mrak Delar and

carefully moved down the slope, following a barely visible path toward the crater.

"If there is nothing there, why do you look so scared, huh?" asked Gunz, a lopsided smirk making a quick appearance on his face.

"Didn't I make it clear? The dark and scary part," Mishka whispered, flying next to him. "We mighty wyverns, do not get along with dark and scary... We're the Fire. We like warm and bright."

Yaroslav threw a concerned look at Gunz and followed the Master of Power closely, holding his katana at the ready, prepared to act at the first sign of trouble. Gunz tapped his shoulder, inviting Mishka to land, but the wyvern looked at him with round eyes and shook his head, disappearing into his tattoo.

"Chicken," muttered Gunz, starting on his way down.

"Firetwat!" He heard Mishka's voice in his mind, and a light electric shock surged through his arm, making him wince.

The farther down they moved, the darker it became. Even though Aspid was gone, the residue of his evil energy still lingered in the area. The darkness was so thick that Gunz could barely see Mrak and Yaroslav who were only a few steps ahead of him.

Catching up with him, Lucan muttered a spell and sent a few light orbs in the air. It didn't help as the shimmering light produced by his magic got suffocated by the darkness. The sounds seemed to be muffled too, and Gunz felt like he was submerged under water. Mrak and Yaroslav came to a sharp stop, and he almost ran into them.

"Do you hear it?" whispered the Master of Power, his words falling flat and disappearing into the dense emptiness.

"Hear what?" asked Gunz.

"Exactly," muttered Mrak Delar, giving him a pointed stare.

"There are no sounds. At all. And it's not a silencing spell. I would sense it right away. Besides, we can still hear each other."

He held out his hand and conjured a fireball. Usually, fireballs produced enough noise, rotating, crackling, and sending sparks in the air. But while this fireball was rotating, the sounds were muted, almost nonexistent. Even the bright light of the fire seemed unusually dim and weak.

Something moved soundlessly ahead of them—a shadow darker than the darkness of this endless night. A soft gust of wind rushed through the plateau, ruffling Gunz's hair, but even the wind produced no sound.

"Do you hear that?" asked Yaroslav, pointing in the direction they were supposed to be walking. "Right there. Just listen…"

Gunz shook his head, frowning. He took a deep breath and allowed the Fire Salamander in him to take over. As his hearing became sharper, he detected a distant noise, harsh but familiar. He raised his eyebrows, staring at the vampire.

"Sounds like a… well… a duck." He shrugged with a light smile.

The quacking sound became louder, moving closer to them, and soon it was close enough for everyone to hear. A soft light broke through the darkness, illuminating the black circle of a swamp at the bottom of the crater. Fuzzy green orbs that resembled the light of a candle rose above it, coming in and out of focus. The flames danced, inviting Gunz to come closer and join them, promising warmth and peace. He wanted it with all his soul. He was tired… tired of fighting, of pain and loss… He needed it.

Gunz stared at the swamp, mesmerized by the movement of the light. A soft whisper touched his senses, but he couldn't distinguish the words and for some reason, he didn't care. His vision blurred, and an unfamiliar wave of magical energy rushed through him. It didn't feel dangerous. On the contrary, it felt inviting, clouding his already entranced mind.

The duck quacked again, ripping him out of the trance, and when he could see clearly, he realized that he was only a few feet away from the swamp. Lucan stood right behind him, his green eyes wide open, staring into the space without blinking. Mrak and Yaroslav were even closer to the swamp—another step and they would fall into the muddy darkness of the deadly trap.

"Mrak! Slavik! Stop!" Gunz yelled, but no sound came out from his dry throat.

Fighting the weakness and dizziness, he reached for the fire within him and allowed it to consume him without reverting into the natural state of the Fire Salamander. Yaroslav was too close, and he wasn't sure that in his current condition, he could control the purifying fire. As the elemental energy rushed through him, instantly clearing his mind, he bolted forward, quickly closing the distance between him and his friends, and seized their arms, pulling them back.

"What the hell was that?" Yaroslav muttered, staring around in awe as if he couldn't remember where he was and why he was here.

Mrak Delar grunted, rubbing his eyes like a person who had just awakened from a long, deep slumber. He surveyed the area, an expression of shock imprinted on his face, and whispered, "Heaven and Earth..."

"Will-o'-the-wisp," whispered Lucan, his cat-eyes following the green lights dancing over the swamp. "Some call it swamp lights... some call it ghost candles..."

"I think you're right," agreed the Master of Power. "I can't believe I fell for its trance... The mystery is, who conjured them and why?"

"Well, that's not a mystery at all, boys."

Gunz turned around at the sound of a pleasant female voice. Perched on a large boulder, right at the edge of the crater, a young woman sat, her fingers playing with her long blonde hair.

She smiled at him, flashing a perfectly white set of teeth, readjusting her short dark slip which generously exposed her curvy figure.

"Oh, hello there," she sang, waving her hand at him cheerfully.

Her eyes were bright green and even more unnatural than Lucan's, but her ears weren't elongated, so she couldn't have been an elf. Suspicion flashed through his mind as he kept staring at the young woman, but since he wasn't sure, he decided to wait before saying anything.

Gunz turned to his friends. "Can you all see her?"

Lucan nodded, his hands landing on the daggers sheathed at his belt.

"Unfortunately," Yaroslav hissed, his fingers clenching his katana tighter. "Bad omen… really bad one." He shook his head, throwing his hair off his face.

"What do you want?" Mrak Delar took a step closer to the young woman, his formidable frame towering over her. "What are you?"

"Who would you like me to be, hon?" she asked mockingly, unfazed by his attempt to intimidate her. "You come with me"—she pointed at the swamp—"and I can become whoever you want me to be."

The swamp lights got agitated, zooming closer, circling around the young woman. Her body shimmered with bright green sparkles, and for a brief moment, she disappeared from view. When she manifested again, her appearance had changed. Now, she looked even younger, her youthful frame willowy yet curvy in all the right places. Her short slip was replaced by a long linen dress that was common for women in Kendral, and her golden hair flowed down her shoulders and back in rich waves.

Mrak Delar roared like an angry beast, the energy of his magic spiking around him.

"Dammit," muttered Gunz, but before he could make a move to stop him, the Master of Power had a bow and arrow ready.

"Get the hell out of my wife's body!" he shouted, letting the arrow fly. The ground quaked and a few rocks slipped down the slope. Stormy clouds gathered above their heads and thunder rolled through the plateau, reverberating against every Seid and stone block.

The arrow, infused with the power of Pestilence, flew through the woman's chest, doing her no harm as if she were incorporeal. She frowned, and her emerald eyes ignited with displeasure.

"Tsk, tsk, tsk." She clucked her tongue, staring at the Ancient Master reproachfully. "And here I thought I was dealing with Conquest, but you're nothing but repulsive Pestilence."

Mrak jerked forward, but Gunz seized his arm, holding him in place. "Mrak, we can't fight her. All we can do is talk to her and find out why she's here."

With his chest rising and falling with angry breaths, the Master of Power lowered his bow. The woman got up and approached Yaroslav, her fingers raking through his long hair, brushing dust and dirt off his blond strands. The green dancing lights surrounded her again as she dissolved into nothing. When she manifested, she was taller, athletically built, wearing a black shirt and jeans. Her hair, the color of copper, was braided into a single braid, and a soft smile lingered on her full lips.

Gunz held his breath as he raised his eyes at Yaroslav. The vampire became a statue, just as motionless and cold as any rock on this cursed mountain. A single tear of pure blood escaped his eye, leaving a dark red path in its wake, but he didn't bother wiping it, remaining painfully still.

"You're the only one here who is actually yourself, Your Highness," she said in Peyton's voice, lowering herself down in a light curtsy filled with mockery. Straightening, the woman looked around and pointed at Gunz. "You are War, in more ways than one." She switched her attention to Lucan. "You're Famine... hmmm... an unusual choice for her." Then her unnatural eyes stopped on Mrak Delar, and she chuckled. "How can I expect you to know who I am, when you don't even know who you are—Conquest or Pestilence."

She turned back to Yaroslav, arching her eyebrow at him.

"How about you, Prince?" she asked snidely. "Do you know who I am?"

"Please...," said Yaroslav, his voice dry and hoarse. "I know who you are. Please take your real form... not hers..."

He dropped his head, and even though his hair obscured his face, concealing the reflection of his true feelings, there was so much torment in the vampire's voice that Gunz shuddered, fighting to remain in place.

"Guilt is a terrible burden, Prince." The woman nodded and once again dissolved into a cloud of green sparkles.

When the mist around her dissipated, an old crone stood in her place. Her back was bent by age, and she was leaning heavily on a crooked staff, her skeletal fingers clasping its top. Old rags, covered in dirt and moss, partially concealed her twisted body, and her gray, unkept hair hung in limp, dirty strands along the sides of her head. Her eyes—bright green and young—looked unfit for her face, wrinkled like an old prune.

She tilted her head slightly, staring at Yaroslav sideways. "Who am I, Prince Potemkin? Say my name, boy." She cackled, her dry, elderly laughter jarring in the surrounding silence.

"Kikimora," whispered the vampire, barely audible. "*Kikimora Bolotnaya.*"

"Swamp Kikimora," echoed Gunz, his worst suspicion confirmed.

"You're the evil spirit of this swamp. Some say you're a death omen, Kikimora," continued Yaroslav. "There are four of us here. Whose death are you prophesying now?"

Kikimora lifted her head as far as her unbending neck would

allow her and cackled, pointing with her deformed finger at each of them. "All of yours." She lowered her hand and smirked, displaying yellow, rotted teeth. "If you keep climbing up this mountain, searching for Death, death is what you shall find."

"Is that a threat?" asked Gunz calmly, exhaustion settling in his very bones—another monster, another attempt to intimidate him.

"No, Fire Salamander, it is not," objected Kikimora frostily. "If I were threatening you, you wouldn't have to ask. It is a warning from my master."

"And who might that be?" asked Gunz with a crooked smirk. "Skiper-Zmey?"

The old hag snickered, mockery dripping from every sound coming out of her foul mouth. "I bet you sleep and dream of him, don't yah, boy? In your wet dreams." She wiggled her gray, bushy eyebrows at him, and Gunz shifted back involuntarily, cold sweat covering his forehead. "I hate to disappoint you, but the warning is not from him. While my master is in alliance with the Lord of Chaos, I do not serve Zmey."

"If it's not Skiper-Zmey, then who is your master?" asked Yaroslav.

"Well, that's none of your business, is it, vamp?" Kikimora laughed, throwing her skinny arms into the air, dust, and moss falling off her clothes.

"Then why does your highly secretive and powerful master care to give us the warning at all?" asked Lucan, not without a fair share of sarcasm.

"Oh, he doesn't care, elf." The hag cackled again, a thin rivulet of muddy swamp water dripping from the corner of her mouth. "You can go right ahead. If you want, I can even give you the directions to your imminent demise. All four of you. I'm sure both my master and the Lord of Chaos will appreciate it."

Mrak Delar stepped closer, placing his hand on Lucan's

shoulder. He cocked his head slightly and a dark smirk appeared on his face.

"Thank you, but no thank you," he said with a nonchalant shrug. "But while I'm really not the type to ask for directions, I'm still extremely grateful for your assistance."

Kikimora's green eyes darted to him and narrowed. "What are you talking about, Master?" she hissed, spluttering swamp water all over him.

"I know where your master holds Death," he replied calmly, grimacing in disgust as her foul breath assailed his senses. He produced a small handkerchief and wiped his face. "And thank you so much, dear, for telling us that the Lord of Chaos has a powerful ally. You see, before we met you, I thought it was Skiper-Zmey who ran the show, puppeteering his followers. So, the information you provided was invaluable to us." He bowed ceremoniously. "My deepest gratitude."

Kikimora screeched in anger, and the swamp lights rose around her again, starting their sickening dance. The energy of her toxic magic polluted the air, and Gunz coughed, clutching his throat. The world around him got blurry and shaky, and for a heartbeat, he felt like he was falling into the Dark Nav again. He cried out, reaching for his magic and fire, but couldn't find them. The Dark Codex twitched in his mind, responding to his internal turmoil, and a blinding headache consumed him. The energy of the Codex swirled in his head, wiping out the effects of Kikimora's magic.

"*Emunius Amnia*," he croaked.

He'd never used this spell before and wasn't sure what to expect. The swamp lights disappeared, the fog and mist surrounding the swamp cleared, and the normal sounds of the night rushed back in. Gunz let out a harsh breath and massaged his forehead, waiting for the headache to let go. Kikimora was gone and together with her, gone were the constant pressure on his senses, the feeling of someone watching him, and the suffocating darkness.

Mrak Delar stood, leaning heavily on Yaroslav's shoulder, and he looked so drained that Gunz wasn't sure he'd be able to walk let alone fight if the need arose. Lucan sat on a stone with his elbows rested on his lap. Even the vampire showed some signs of weariness, or maybe it was just the layer of dirt and dust and the brown stains of dried out blood on his face that made him look so tired. This was the first moment of peace they had since they vanquished Aspid, and he felt just as tired as his friends looked.

"Mrak—," started Gunz.

"I'm okay, Gunz," the Master of Power cut him off, straightening. "I can keep going... I must."

"I know that," continued Gunz. "I was going to ask you if you really know where they are holding Angel. You said that to Kikimora."

"Oh, that?" Mrak Delar chuckled humorously. "Actually, I told her the truth. I do know where to look for Death, and she was the one who pointed me in the right direction."

"What did she say?" Lucan turned his head to the side to see the Ancient Master. "I didn't catch anything that remotely sounded like directions."

"That's because none of you know Vottovaara as well as I do." He winked, tucking his long hair behind his ear. "She said that if we keep climbing up, we'll find Death. Now, look around." He waved his hand. "Where are we standing?"

"In the center of the plateau," muttered Yaroslav. "I still don't understand, Master. We're at the topmost point of the mountain. There is nowhere else to climb."

"But there is." Mrak Delar glanced at Yaroslav and then at Gunz and Lucan, his drained face lighting up with a soft smile. "You just don't know where to look." Mrak Delar pointed in four directions, slowly turning in place. "Open your other sight, Salamander. What do you see?"

Gunz did as the Master of Power told him and observed the area. "Fire almighty," he whispered, taking in the view presented by his second sight. "What the hell are these?"

Four stairways rose into the sky at the four opposite sides of the plateau. The energy of strange magic the likes of which he had never encountered before flowed through each stairway, seemingly disappearing into nothing.

"Stairways to heaven," replied Mrak Delar.

"As in *the Heaven*?" asked Gunz, his eyebrows rising.

"Of course not." Mrak chuckled, shaking his head. "It's just a name. But these stairways lead into something else—another small world, very similar to the realm of the Destiny Council. Perhaps it is even a part of their realm. I'm not sure... Anyway, I believe this is where the followers of Chaos, or whoever they are, are holding Angel. And possibly Uri, too. That would explain why no one, including the Reapers, can detect his presence."

Gunz spun around, registering the location of each stairway. "They are quite far apart. Which one are we going to use?"

"All four of them," replied the Master of Power.

He channeled all four elemental powers at once and shut his eyes, whispering something. A crystal-like orb materialized in the palm of his hand. A tiny flame danced inside the orb, glowing with the red light of the elemental fire.

"Fire," he murmured, offering the orb to Gunz.

Gunz took it, staring at it with interest. While he had millions of unanswered questions, he decided to wait until the Master of Power was done. Mrak's fingers moved as he channeled his power and another orb materialized in his hand. Inside, there was a small plant. Its wide, green leaves glistened with morning dew. The soft green color of the elemental energy of Earth filled it, shimmering with bright sparkles.

"Earth," he announced, giving it to Lucan. "I think this element is most appropriate for your kind."

Lucan nodded and carefully took the orb, gently caressing its slick surface with his fingers. As Mrak continued working his magic, the next orb appeared in his hand. Glowing with a light beige color, a soft cloud hung inside it. He offered it to Yaroslav with a tired smile.

"Air... You in your bird form seemed quite comfortable up there." He pointed into the dark sky as Yaroslav took the orb from his hands.

Mrak moved his hands, muttering something under his breath, and one more orb appeared in his hand. The last orb was filled with water, emitting a soft blue light.

"Water—this one is mine." He pointed south and tapped Gunz on his shoulder. "You will take the southmost stairway. The fire energy is the strongest there. Use your portal to get in place." He turned to Yaroslav. "Fly to the east one. Move as fast as you can."

Mrak Delar fell silent, staring at the orb in his hands.

"I'll take Lucan to his stairway, and that should give you two a few minutes to take your positions," he continued. "When I tell you—and you *will* hear my voice, don't worry about that—I need each of you to smash the orb against the topmost step of the stairway. That's all you need to do." He observed the three of them, his eyebrows slightly raised as if he were expecting a question, but since no one said anything, he put his hand on Lucan's shoulder and commanded, "Go!"

He snapped his fingers, and they both vanished from the crater.

"I'll see you on the other side, Fire Gecko." Yaroslav winked at Gunz and twirled around, turning into a giant white bird. With one flap of his wide wings, he rose high in the air and melted into the darkness.

I wonder what we're going to find on that other side... Gunz waved his hand, unfolding the flaming curtain of his portal and walked through it.

* * *

Gunz walked out of the portal and found himself standing on the last step of a stairway. Looking down, he had a perfect view of the plateau with the crater and the dark circle of the swamp in the center. He opened his other sight and surveyed the area, searching for his friends. He couldn't see them, but the magical sight showed him where each of them was, their energy signatures loud and clear in the surrounding darkness.

He glanced down at the fire orb in his hands, wishing Mrak had given them a better explanation on what to expect. Even when they were at their full strength, facing the followers of Chaos had never been easy. Now, all four of them were exhausted physically and drained magically, and after the conversation with Kikimora, he was positive that the situation was going to be a lot worse than they had thought originally. He had no idea who her mysterious master was, but if this unknown monster considered himself equal or even above the Lord of Chaos, the prospects of facing him didn't give Gunz a feeling of comfort.

He kneeled at the edge and took a few deep breaths to calm down his stretched nerves. *Mrak is barely keeping it together and Yaroslav is constantly at his side to catch him if he falls.* He turned his head from left to right, flexing his sore muscles. It took all they had to kill Aspid... *What if the giant serpent was just the flower, and the berries were ahead—*

"Now!" Mrak's voice sounded in his head, tearing him out of his thoughts.

Gunz slammed the orb against the rough steps of the stairway. He expected it to shatter like any crystal orb would, but instead it melted softly, and the bright light of the fire energy shimmered out of it like a soft cloud. For a moment, it hung around him, caressing him with its friendly presence. Then it moved slightly up and forward, and as it progressed toward the center of the plateau, its red light exposed more steps that weren't visible before.

Looking up, he saw three more shimmering stairways reaching forward, seemingly supported by nothing. Once they connected, a portal, swirling with a brilliant blue light, opened in the middle. There was nothing dark or sinister about this portal, but the expectation of something terrible struck Gunz, taking his breath away. As the Fire Salamander in him was screaming bloody murder, he stilled, staring at the shiny doorway into an unknown realm with wide eyes.

"Gunz!" He heard Mrak's voice in his head and flinched, noticing that the Master of Power, Yaroslav and Lucan stood by the portal already. "What are you waiting for? Get over here! Now!"

Shaking off his stupor, he stepped on the airy stairway and swayed. The magical steps were see-through, and he could see the dark land covered in sharp rocks spread beneath him.

"Don't look down, Fire Gecko!"

He heard Yaroslav's voice laughing through their blood link and looked up at him, showing him the middle finger. He ran across the power bridge, making a point to stare straight ahead, and didn't stop until he reached the portal.

"Here goes nothing..." Mrak Delar sighed, still leaning on Yaroslav for support, and they both walked through the swirling threshold.

Lucan tapped Gunz on his shoulder and followed them. Throwing a last look at the dark Vottovaara, Gunz headed after him, stepping through the rotating lake of lights. As soon as he crossed over to the other side, he froze in place, and his jaw dropped, his arms dangling along the sides of his body.

"Fuck...," he exhaled mournfully and reached for his sword.

CHAPTER 37

~ ZANE BURNS, A.K.A. GUNZ ~

It wasn't just dark. It was black.

They stood on a narrow plateau of some mountain. Just a few feet in front of them, there was a sharp cliff, and a wide valley unfolded down below. The tall wall of another cliff, no more than a few yards away, loomed behind them. The surrounding rocks were black, the ground they stood on was black, and the valley in front of them was blacker than black. Low stormy clouds veiled the dark sky, void of light, and Gunz wasn't sure if it was nighttime or if daylight didn't exist in this strange realm.

As soon as they passed the threshold, the portal closed behind them, removing the only way back they had. The elemental powers were practically nonexistent, and Gunz felt as though he was standing on top of Mount Everest, cold and deprived of oxygen. He could barely breathe, and his body, already exhausted from the previous fight, was even weaker now.

Mrak Delar, deprived of all four elemental powers, was in an even worse condition. Drained by the use of his healing power and sore from the injuries he had sustained earlier, he dropped down to all fours, struggling to breathe, his eyes bloodshot.

A large castle was visible at the far end of the valley. Its tall, massive walls made of rough stonework glowed with a dim purple light which made the entire building stand out in the starkness of this monochromatic realm. From this distance, the castle looked like an impenetrable fortress. However, that wasn't the reason Gunz felt so hopeless and desperate. The entire space between the castle and the cliff they stood on was filled with demons.

Not any demons—pureblood abominations of Hell stood shoulder to shoulder, emitting ungodly amounts of demonic essence, polluting the already thin air. Their eyes glowed with the sickening yellow light of Chaos, and they all stared at them with abhorrence, their heads upturned.

Despite the stench of sulphur, Gunz could sense Angel's energy signature clearly, and that told him they were in the right place. However, this knowledge did nothing to make him feel better. Staring down at the motionless army of demons, he couldn't see a way to get anywhere near the castle. Yaroslav approached him silently. Even though the absence of the elemental powers didn't affect him, the vampire shivered, unsheathing his katana.

"This place is not for the creatures of elements," he said softly. "It renders you and Mrak powerless. Without your powers and with everything that you've had to endure before we got here, you're not much of a fighter."

Gunz nodded. "I still have some fire in me." He smirked, scratching the back of his head as he tried to get in touch with his element with nothing to show for it. "Well… maybe not the elemental fire. This place is worse than the Dark Nav."

Lucan approached the Master of Power. Placing his hands on Mrak's shoulders, he channeled some of the elven magic through him. A few seconds later, he let go, and Mrak Delar sat back on his heels, his hand rubbing his thighs mindlessly.

"Thank you," he said, his voice a low growl. Supported by Yaroslav, he got up and walked to the edge of the cliff. Glancing down, he frowned. "Looks like we are up for a hell of a ride."

"And here I thought these were the stairways to Heaven," murmured Gunz, his fingers wrapping tighter around the grip of his sword. "They led us straight to—"

He didn't finish his statement and gasped as an enormous blast of fire energy rose in the air above the castle. It was so powerful that he could easily sense it even from this distance. It lingered over the fortress for a few seconds and then imploded, sucking whatever minuscule elemental energy had been available in this hell-realm before.

A thunderous bang rolled through the valley, and the ground quaked, unbalancing him. He fell to his knees, dropping his sword with a loud clatter, nearly falling over the cliff. Yaroslav's strong hands seized his shoulders, yanking him away from the deadly gorge.

Lucan hissed something in elven and a dense power shield unfolded over them just in time to block the downfall of rocks and debris sliding from the mountain above them. Gunz looked forward and the small hairs on the back of his neck stood on end. A giant black vortex materialized over the castle. It wasn't moving, and there was no light or color to it. It looked like a dead black hole in the fabric of reality itself.

"Void...," exhaled Mrak Delar, his dark eyes growing more intense. "What the hell is Angel doing? What's going on?"

"And that flair of elemental fire. Was that—," Lucan started to say but cut himself off, staring at Gunz in horror.

"Black Fire," confirmed Gunz. "But it's gone now. I can no longer sense it."

Another wave of magical energy swept through the valley, and the void above the fortress vanished. A soft whisper, light as a gust of wind, reached their ears and suddenly turned into a piercing howl filled with so much hatred that Gunz shuddered, feeling its menacing presence with his skin. The sound—he could hardly call it a voice—felt familiar, but for the life of him, he couldn't figure out what it was.

The clatter of metal on metal and a dull thud from beneath drew their attention. The presence of the demonic essence seemed to double as the army of demons slowly moved forward. They drew their weapons—terrifying swords, massive spears and battle axes, and the roar of their battle cry rose above the valley.

"I think they know we're here." Gunz chuckled, picking up his sword.

"Was that a hysterical laughter, Burns?" Lucan stood by his side with his daggers in his hands. "Between the four of us, we have two and half fighters and we're facing an army of hundreds of pureblood demons."

"Who are you calling a half-fighter?" growled Mrak Delar, rising to his feet.

"I didn't call you a half-fighter, Master." Lucan smirked, mischievous twinkles dancing in his eyes. "I wouldn't dare to disrespect a Master of Power by lying to him. If my math is correct, I called both you and Burns quarter-fighters."

Mrak Delar glanced at Lucan and burst out laughing, but the sound of falling rocks cut his amusement short. Gunz stared down over the edge of the cliff and turned back to his friends.

"We have a few minutes at the most until these monsters reach us. Ready or not, we must fight." He pointed down with his sword, and blood-red flames enveloped the blade, making it shine with a deadly scarlet glow.

"The flames of War," muttered Mrak Delar, and his eyes got unfocused for a split-second as though he traveled some distant memory lane. Then he seized Gunz's sword hand, raising it as his expression darkened. "The flames of War! Except for Yaroslav, we're not ourselves."

Yaroslav turned to the Mater of Power. "Are you okay, Ancient Master?" he asked, staring at him with shock. "You make no sense."

"I am fine." Mrak Delar laughed again, a short and nervous sound that chilled Gunz to the bone. "Oh, I am better than fine. We're going to fight these monsters, but not as ourselves. We're going to fight them as ancient beings of enormous power. Destructive power to boot."

"I don't understand—," Gunz started but fell silent.

"Kikimora said that Yaroslav was the only one here who was himself," explained Mrak Delar impatiently. His speech was fast and agitated, and Gunz had to put some effort to keep up with him. "And she was right! Once the three of us assumed the mantles of the Horsemen, we became one with them. While it was enough for us to handle their horses, we've never activated the actual power of Four. We have used some of it here and there but could never tap into it fully."

"So, what changed now?" asked Lucan with a light shrug.

"This." Mrak Delar pointed at the fortress. "I can sense the fourth Horseman. Angel is so close to us that we can activate the power of Four."

"But if we activate it, wouldn't it shift the balance toward the Apocalypse?" asked Yaroslav, doubt clearly written on his face.

"It would, but this is our only chance to survive and complete the mission," replied Mrak Delar, frowning, and for a moment his eyes got unfocused again. Then he looked up at the vampire. "So, whatever we have to do to break through into the castle, we better do it fast."

"I don't think even the power of Four can give us what we need to defeat hundreds of demons." Lucan shifted closer to the edge and then hopped back as a giant rock whistled past his head, his green eyes widening.

"What hundreds?" Gunz huffed. "Thousands probably."

The second battle cry of the demonic army sounded closer and was followed by the sounds of their heavy breaths, the clatter of weapons and armor, and the grinding noise of rocks stumbling down as they slipped from under their feet. A few blackened, warped hands grabbed at the edge of the plateau. Gunz swung his sword, cutting the malformed fingers off, and followed the falling demons on their way down with his eyes. Their bodies hit the shifting mass of others, taking down a few more monsters.

"Beggars can't be choosers," Gunz yelled, turning back to his friends. "Mrak, what do we need to do to activate the power of Four?"

"Come here!" yelled the Master of Power. He raised his hand up, pointing at the ring, and then clenched it into a fist, extending it forward. "Bring the rings together."

Gunz glanced down at the red stone in War's ring on the middle finger of his right hand and a strange surge of heat traveled through him, settling in his chest. He held his breath, wondering what that was all about. Then he extended his hand forward, touching Lucan's and Mrak's.

As soon as their fists connected, the rings lit up with a bright light, and a powerful blast wave spread through the valley, reaching as far as they could see and beyond. For a brief moment, all sounds died out, and it seemed like time itself stopped moving. A tall wall of brilliant light rose around them and when it dwindled down, Gunz felt stronger and more powerful than he had ever felt before.

Slowly, he moved his head from left to right, rolling his shoulders, and then looked down. He was still the same, but besides the sword, he had a long dagger sheathed at his belt. He pulled the dagger out, and it lit up with the blood-colored flames of War.

"Damn," he mumbled, raising his eyes at his friends. "You were right... You aren't yourselves."

Mrak Delar's eyes—normally black or swirling with the colors of elemental powers—were shining bright white with the energy of Conquest, reminding him of Gwyn's and Aidan's eyes in their natural forms. The Master of Power spread his shoulders and flexed his arms, visibly enjoying his restored strength. A cold, deadly smile stretched his full lips as he raised his bow and Gunz shuddered inwardly, reminded of Mrak's dark side.

Maybe his dark side is exactly what we need right now, thought Gunz, cautiously observing his friend.

"A bow and arrows are not my weapon of choice, and they are useless in the close combat we're about to face." He quickly fastened the bow behind his back. "I guess, I'll have to get myself a sword as I go." The Master of Power laughed darkly, stepping closer to the edge.

"I'm ready," said Lucan, and when Gunz met his eyes, his jaw dropped. The elf's eyes were flooded with darkness. His white hair was raven-black, and somehow, he managed to look even more massive and intimidating than before.

Just as Yaroslav joined them with his katana in hands, all hell broke loose. At least twenty monsters reached the top of the plateau at the same time. Gunz brought his sword down, cutting their claws, hands and talons, sending them flying down the hill, but more and more were coming, and soon demons flooded the space, surrounding them.

Mrak Delar reacted fast. Seizing the arm of a demon closest to him, he twisted it, forcing him to drop his massive sword. In one fluid motion, he repositioned himself and threw the monster down to the ground. Quickly picking up the long demonic blade, he ran it through the demon's chest and infused it with the power of Conquest, disintegrating the monster in place.

Without stopping, he swung the demonic blade, decapitating

an enemy next to him. "This feels right," he roared, turning the next demon into a puddle of dirty goo with one blast of his newly gained power.

Even standing among the giant abominations of Hell, Lucan towered over them. With his black hair and black eyes, he looked terrifying. His daggers projected blood-chilling black beams, cutting through the monsters as though they were butter. Moving with his usual fluidity, he carried death in his wake, leaving sticky puddles of slime behind.

As soon as the fight began, Yaroslav disappeared. Even though he didn't have any new powers, he was just as dangerous as any of them. As the vampire moved with blinding speed, liquid and silent among the heavy opponents, screams and shrieks of pain and anger followed his progress.

In his peripheral vision, Gunz caught a few dark shadows moving on his right and snapped around. Three more demons charged at him, each one at least a foot taller than him and a lot heavier. He felt no fear and that fact alone shocked him more than anything else. It wasn't his first fight, but he always felt at least some uneasiness facing a stronger opponent—at least until the moment the fight began. Once the first punch was thrown, any fears or doubts were gone instantly, expelled by the intensity of combat, by the adrenalin pumping through his system, and by the fire charging him from inside.

He moved forward at full speed, and as he came within reach of the first demon, he easily side-stepped him, running his flaming blade through his side. The scarlet fire set the monster ablaze, eliciting terrible howls from him. Gunz didn't care to see what would happen to him. He already knew it.

Keeping his forward momentum, he met the battle axe of the next opponent with his sword. The giant monster pressed down, his ugly, lipless mouth stretching into an ominous smirk, exposing rows of hideous fangs. In one swift motion, Gunz seized his dagger with his left hand and threw his arm forward.

Moving it in an upward motion, he drove the flaming blade into the demon's stomach, spilling his black, putrid guts to the ground. The demon screeched, dropping his weapon, clasping his enormous talons to the terrible, burning wound. Gunz spun around, and his sword cut through the monster's short neck, decapitating him.

As he set on fire the third demon attacking him, Mrak Delar came into his view. The Master of Power—or maybe Conquest—made his way closer by cutting through the mass of monsters with his newly found sword.

"Gunz!" he yelled, his voice sounding strained as he cut the demon's head off his shoulders and push-kicked his body off the hill. "We need to move down! If we keep fighting in the limited space of this plateau, sooner or later they will overwhelm us. Besides, we need to make our way to the castle."

"The sooner the better!" shouted Lucan. "Let me make some space first..." With a mighty roar, the elf spread his arms, and jumped off the cliff, taking a few demons with him. The monsters plummeted down, screaming, but Lucan lingered in the air, supported by the misty energy of Famine, and then slowly lowered himself down to the ground in the midst of the enemy's army.

He spun around, his deadly daggers wreaking chaos and devastation into the demonic lines, and the monsters shied away from him. Soon, the elf straightened, his wide chest shuddering with heavy breaths, and gestured for them to move down. Mrak Delar and Yaroslav jumped off the cliff, landing softly next to Lucan. Holding their weapons at the ready, they straightened, staring up at Gunz.

Still standing on the plateau, Gunz turned around to face the few demons still standing before him. He channeled the fire of War and unleashed the fiery inferno, with relief realizing that the blood-red flames of War did the job just as well as his elemental fire would. The cries and howls of the demons devoured by a smoldering fire rose into the dark sky, and dirty swirls of smoke lingered above his head, carrying the suffocating reek of burnt flesh and demonic essence.

Gunz didn't wait to make sure that they were all dead and jumped off the edge of the hill, softly lowering himself down next to his friends, right in the middle of the fight. Working with the powers of the Horsemen, using their blades and their magic, they slowly started to make their way to the castle. But the farther they moved, the more resistance they received. It seemed like for every demon they killed, three took the place of the fallen.

Even recharged by the power of Four, Gunz soon started to feel tired, his blade seemed to be heavier than before, and his fire strikes weren't as powerful as earlier. Besides, he received numerous injuries, and even though none of them were bad enough to stop him, they added to the overall fatigue.

Glancing at Mrak Delar, he realized that the Master of Power started to slow down too. Covered in black goo and blood, he still was as dangerous as before, yet Gunz could recognize the symptoms of exhaustion in him. Since the demons in their natural form didn't bleed red, Gunz was positive that by now, the Ancient Master was wounded, probably not once.

Gunz didn't see it. He felt Lucan appear by his side and threw a quick glance in his direction. The elf lost one of his daggers and his left arm seemed to be broken, hanging limply alongside his body at an awkward angle. Yet, ignoring the obvious pain, the elf kept fighting.

"If nothing is going to change, we're not going to make it!" he yelled, his spine-chilling black eyes staring over Gunz's head at the fortress no more than a couple of hundred yards away from them.

The castle stood dark and silent, its purple glow gone now. For a split second, Gunz took his eyes off the fight to check the area ahead and that was enough for one of the attackers to seize his arms and pull him back into the demonic mob. Gunz roared, struggling to free himself when he felt a sharp pain. Looking down, he saw a spear protruding from his left side just above his hip. A dark stain materialized on his uniform as blood soaked through. He screamed, throwing his remaining strength into channeling the power of War and his entire body went up in flames. The demons let go of him, cowering away from the fire.

Gunz grunted, falling down to one knee, and immediately felt Yaroslav's hands on his shoulders, pulling him up. The vampire looked terrifying in his anger, his long hair matted with blood and black slime, his lips drawn back into a feral snarl. He yanked the metal part of the spear that was still embedded into Gunz's side and threw it to the ground. Gunz cried out, pressing his hand over the bleeding hole, his eyes watering from pain.

"Hang in there, Gunz," Yaroslav yelled, blocking the next attack. "I'll heal you as soon as we get a moment to breathe."

As if to prove him wrong, the gates in the castle wall opened up, and a black mass of demons and some other monsters he had never seen before, spilled out, running toward them with ear-splitting roars.

We're not going to get a moment... With horror, Gunz realized that even the power of Four was getting depleted, leaving all of them drained, injured and weak. They needed help, and they needed it now.

"Aidan!" He reached to his friend through their psychic link. *"I don't know if you can hear me... I don't even know where we are... but we won't be able to fight for much longer. We need help..."*

CHAPTER 38

~ AIDAN ~

Aidan stood between Kal and Gwyn ap Nudd, a rush of jitters making his heart beat faster in his chest. He wiped his clammy hands on his pants and squeezed them into fists. It wasn't his first visit to the Destiny Council's realm, but he'd never had to worry about fighting them.

Cleansing the Sisterhood of the Sun was bad enough but compared to the enchantment placed on the Guardians Order, it was a walk in the park. According to Kal, the spell cast on the Wardens had been even more complicated, intricately embedded into the heart of the entire Order.

It wasn't uncommon for Masters of the Dark Arts to place a curse on an entire organization or a group of people, using one of them as an anchor. However, the way the enchantment had been placed on the Wardens Order made it impossible to break the spell without destroying the Grand Master, who was used not only as an anchor but also as a life-force that sustained the curse.

"Do you sense anything?"

Kal's rough voice broke Aidan's train of thoughts and he sharpened his senses, exploring the area around them as far as he could reach. Nothing. He couldn't detect anything out of the ordinary. He glanced up at his mentor and saw him shaking his head slowly, his lips pressed together in a straight line.

"Neither can I," said Kal, a muscle working in his tightly clenched jaw.

"I guess there is only one way to find out." Gwyn ap Nudd waved his hand and the shiny rectangle of a door materialized in front of him. But as soon as he tried to walk through it, he was thrown back with such force that he slid a few feet across the ground. He got up, rubbing his lower back, and exchanged a bewildered look with Kal.

The Fire Elemental stepped closer to the door Gwyn ap Nudd had created and moved his arm over its surface. A thin stream of fire followed his motion, but his flames were weak and flickering, switching color to deep purple from time to time.

"Did you see that?" Kal whispered, looking around warily. "There is something here..."

"Something that is powerful enough to block my magic," agreed Gwyn ap Nudd.

Assuming the form of the Lord of the Wild Hunt, he channeled as much of his ancient magic as he could, and his whole body shone with its blinding light. He sang just a few words, touching the air with his fingers as though there was an invisible glass panel in front of him. At his touch, the entire space as far as they could see lit up with dark purple symbols and lines crisscrossing in every direction.

"What the hell?" muttered Aidan, reaching forward, but Gwyn grabbed his wrist, stopping him.

"Dark magic," he whispered. "It seems to have no end... the size of this enchantment is remarkable. I haven't seen anything like this in centuries."

"So, whoever this Master of the Dark Arts is, he should be

extremely—," Aidan started but cut himself off, as both Kal and Gwyn shook their heads.

"Not a Master of the Dark Arts," mumbled Kal, craning his neck as he stared up at the wall of symbols disappearing into the dark sky.

"We're not dealing with a Dark Wizard, son," explained Gwyn ap Nudd. "We're dealing with a dark god. One of the old ones. And this spell… It feels more like a deadly curse if you ask me."

"The only way we can find anything out is by getting inside." Catching Aidan's puzzled expression, Kal chuckled. "I'm the Fire, am I not? Nothing can stop me." He waved his hand, unfolding a fiery curtain of his portal. Arching his brow at Aidan, he bowed slightly and gestured at it, his flaming eyes twinkling with sarcasm. "After you, my lord."

Gwyn seized Aidan's elbow and pulled him through Kal's portal.

* * *

THERE WAS nothing human about the main chamber of the Destiny Council building. It was cold, empty, and void of any hope or compassion. Even during their infamous trials, this round hall was never lit well, but now it was darker than ever. The multiple rows of the theater seating were vacant, and the only stairway leading down was barely visible in the dim gray light of this windowless space.

"Do you sense anything?" asked Kal. His deep voice bounced against the tall ceiling, reverberating through the room.

"No." Gwyn ap Nudd shook his head and a heavy shudder ran through his body. "I hate this place…"

He moved his finger, conjuring light orbs, and ran down all the way to the massive marble desk positioned on a tall platform. He halted there and moved his hand from left to right in a wide arc while singing softly. The air around him shimmered, and soon after, the bright purple runes and symbols lit up the entire perimeter of the chamber.

"Dammit," muttered Aidan, joining his mentor and Kal. "I've never seen anything like this." He frowned, a heavy knot twisting in the pit of his stomach. "Both the Sisterhood and the Guardians HQ were infected with dark magic, but not like this."

"I have an unpleasant feeling that this spell covers the entire realm, including the Dark Side," muttered Kal, lowering himself into a large armchair on the right of the desk. It was made of dark wood, had a tall, straight back, and looked as comfortable as any torture device from the times of the Spanish Inquisition.

"Agreed," said Gwyn ap Nudd, taking in every rune and symbol of the ominous spell.

The Destiny Council realm wasn't big. Nevertheless, some parts of it were never visited either by the members of the Council or by their staff. They called it the *Dark Side* of the realm. Even the Destiny Enforcers, whose main purpose was carrying out the Council's orders, avoided the Dark Side like the plague. Trained to fight different monsters and a variety of supernatural evil from a young age, they weren't afraid of the darkness, but there was never a reason for them to venture to that part of the realm.

"What I don't understand is how Zane could detect the energy of this dark magic when I'm standing right in the middle of it and I sense nothing," said Aidan softly. "I'm a god, and he's just a Fire Salamander. Not even an Elemental like Kal."

Kal and Gwyn exchanged a heavy look, and Kal nodded.

"That's because Zane is the Codex," said Gwyn ap Nudd with a nonchalant shrug. He said it so evenly and simple as though there was nothing to it. "He merged with the Dark Codex a while ago. That was the only way he could keep it out of Chernobog's hands."

"Impossible...," breathed out Aidan, thousands of thoughts

rushing through his mind at once. "One must be a god or a being of equal power to complete the merging process."

"Everything you said is true, Aidan, yet there is no doubt—Gunz is the Dark Codex. Accept it and keep your mouth shut," Kal cut him off, rising. He approached Gwyn ap Nudd and tapped him on his shoulder. "I believe we all know what needs to be done, so let's get things rolling, my friend. Summon them already." He grimaced as if he just ate something sour.

A dark smirk touched Gwyn's lips as he drew a rune in the air, infusing it with his power. Placing his hand over it, he said a short summoning spell and stilled, staring at the area behind the desk.

A brilliant white light flooded the entire chamber, and Aidan raised his arm involuntarily. When the light finally subsided, he lowered it and blinked a few times to clear his vision. Three people appeared on the platform behind the desk. Their eyes shone so brightly that it was impossible to look at their faces, let alone distinguish their features.

Gwyn ap Nudd grunted, holding his hand over his eyes, and then shouted, tones of annoyance unmistakable in his voice, "Shut down your high beam headlights!" He folded his arms over his chest and added quietly, looking to the side. "Assholes."

As their lights dwindled down, Aidan glanced at the people behind the desk and gasped, staggering back. The effects of Gwyn's spell hadn't worn off yet, revealing the energy of the dark magic clearly. In the dim light of the chamber, a giant three-headed serpent was rising slowly behind the members of the Destiny Council, growing bigger and more sinister with each passing second.

Its thick body didn't look corporeal, but rather like a hologram shimmering with bright purple light. Coiling around them tightly, the thick pipe of the serpent's body weaved in and out of their torsos. Its massive heads hovered over each member with malice, moving from side to side slightly. Three sets of eyes with narrow vertical pupils burned with malignant energy, and their semi-transparent tongues forked in and out of their fanged mouths in perfect unison.

"Fire Almighty," exhaled Kal, taking a few steps back as smoldering flames broke through the skin on his shoulders and arms. "It's embedded into their hearts... Gwyn? We can't..." His voice trailed off, and he swallowed with an effort.

Aidan opened his sight, checking the members of the Council. Their bodies shimmered and glowed with white light, and there was nothing human about them. To a degree, they reminded him of Uri and the way his body looked through his other sight. However, the pure brilliance of the Council members' energy was severely polluted by the dark purple inclusions, and a heavy purple mass pulsated in place where their hearts were supposed to be. The shimmering body of the serpent was connected to that mass, pulling through it and exiting through their chests.

Gwyn ap Nudd frowned, his face motionless and void of emotions like a stone mask. "Take your positions. We're still going with our plan. Kal, don't use your full power. Until I give you the signal, use only the purifying fire."

"Gwyn, brother! What's going on?" the man in the middle asked, stretching his hand to the King of the Otherworld.

"Be quiet and trust me, Magnus," hissed Gwyn ap Nudd. "You're experienced enough to know when to fight and when to shut up and pray." He lowered his head and rubbed the bridge of his nose, a long crease cutting through his forehead. "And right now, is the time to pray... I'll explain everything later. If you survive, that is."

As soon as Kal assumed his position in front of the desk, Gwyn and Aidan stepped next to him, halting on either side. Both Aidan and his mentor let go of their control, allowing the powers of the Otherworld to consume them. As they started to weave their magic, the three-headed monster responded with an earsplitting hiss. Despite the magical storm that unfolded around the councilmen, they stood still and motionless, their shoulders tensed, and their hands clenched into fists.

Little by little, the light of the Otherworld's magic invaded every corner of the chamber, overpowering the purple glow of the evil spell. But whatever they were doing wasn't enough. The serpent seemed to be unfazed. It slithered over the terrified members of the Council, its coils squeezing them tighter and tighter.

Throwing a quick glance at Magnus, Aidan saw that his face was distorted with pain, but he didn't stop. On the contrary, he channeled more of his power, his voice rising in perfect harmony with Gwyn's. The dark spell retaliated violently. The walls of the building trembled and the floor quaked, making him check his balance. A deep fracture marred the unblemished white ceiling, and dust and debris fell from the crack.

A noise, loud and vicious, assailed his senses. He didn't just hear it. It seemed like it was coming from everywhere at once. Vibrating within him, it exploded with a blinding pain in his head, but he didn't stop chanting. The winds howled through the large hall, blowing in every direction, and the strong, sweet odor of lavender invaded his nostrils. Focusing on the task at hand, Aidan and Gwyn kept pushing the dark magic back, taking care of one square foot after another, and soon the chamber was cleared of runes and symbols.

Despite everything they had done, the terrible snake was still there, feeding on the magic and energy of the Destiny Council. And that put everyone within the Destiny Council realm in danger.

"Kal!" yelled Gwyn, the muscles on his arms bulging as if he were lifting something heavy. "Now! Burn it out and the rest will follow."

At Gwyn ap Nudd's command, Aidan redirected the flow of his power at the snake, seizing its heads. Kal channeled his fire and hit the monster with an undiluted stream of purifying energy. Out of the corner of his eye, Aidan watched the Fire Elemental wielding his element, and he had to admit that while it felt very similar to the way Zane did it, it wasn't quite the same. He couldn't say what was different—the difference was insignificant—and right now he had no time to think about it.

A ray of purifying fire hit all three members of the Destiny Council at once, burning through their hearts. The phantom-serpent screeched and thrashed violently. Gwyn ap Nudd roared, struggling to hold the manifestation of the dark spell within the grip of his magic. Aidan channeled all the energy he could, helping his mentor.

It seemed impossible, but Kal managed to increase the flow of his element. As he rose above the floor, his massive arms ripped with the thick ropes of his muscles, and his flaming hair framed his strained face. The spell wavered, and the serpent shimmered like a mirage, its massive body coming in and out of focus.

The screams of torment, the hissing of the monster, and the buzzing of the dark spell—everything mixed into one blaring commotion. Kal roared like a wild beast, adding more to his already powerful fire blast, and now the entire body of the serpent started to glow with red shades of purifying fire. The cacophony of sounds overwhelmed the chamber, and its walls trembled again.

With a deafening bang, the serpent exploded, and a glistening purple mist hung in the air, surrounding the Destiny Council. All sounds ceased at once, and a deafening silence consumed the hall. Kal didn't lower down, still keeping his fire at the ready. Slowly the mist started to rotate, rising higher. The dark, malignant energy emitted by this ominous cloud was so overpowering that for a brief moment, Aidan held his breath.

Abruptly, it stopped its sickening rotation, and a heartbeat later, it imploded. For a split second, a dark purple jewel the size of a golf ball lingered in the air above the Destiny Council. Then a few purple rays of light broke through it, and a number of ugly, dark fractures marred its shiny surface. Transfixed, Aidan couldn't take his eyes off the evil spell's last moments. The rays became brighter and longer and soon, a blazing light consumed everything.

It ceased as suddenly as it had started, and once again, the three-headed serpent was lingering in the air over the heads of the Destiny Council. While the monster still looked the same, the color of its eyes had changed. The head in the middle had vicious dark purple eyes. The left head had blue eyes, and the eyes of the right one glowed yellow with the energy of Chaos.

Slowly, the serpent's heads moved from left to right, glowering at everyone in the chamber. Then the left head lowered down, its piercing blue gaze drilling through Aidan, sending shivers down his spine.

"I s-s-s-see you...," the snake's head hissed in a soft, insinuating female voice. "Now, I s-s-s-see you, boy..."

"We s-s-s-see you all," growled the head with the purple eyes, and there was so much aversion and unadulterated ill-wish in its voice, that Aidan froze, unable to take a breath.

"We're coming for you-s-s-s...," hissed the yellow-eyed head in the voice of Skiper-Zmey. "S-s-s-soon..."

All three heads hooted with laughter and the serpent vanished.

Kal slowly lowered down to one knee and leaned forward, bracing himself with his fist against the floor.

"Aidan, I need you to shield them." Gwyn ap Nudd gestured at the mortified Destiny Council. Then he kneeled next to Kal, placing his hand on his shoulder. "I know you're tired, but I need you to finish it, my friend," he said softly. "Revert, Kalidus. Purify this realm as far as you can reach."

Kal shook his head, his red hair no longer in flames, and raised his face, exhaustion changing his strong features.

"I'll try..." He got up with a grunt and sighed. "I don't think my energy will spread all the way to the Dark Side, but at least I can take care of the Light one. Now stay back... or better yet, get under the protection of Aidan's shield."

As soon as the King of the Otherworld stepped under the cover of the protective shield, a dense wall of fire surrounded the Great Salamander. Then the fire vanished, revealing a giant flaming lizard in the place where Kal had stood just a moment ago. A powerful blast of purifying fire energy spread around him and rushed through the walls.

Kal reverted into his human form and stood with his eyes closed, his chest expanding with heavy breaths.

"The Light Side of the realm is clean," he said, opening his eyes. "Aidan, you can let go now."

With a sigh of relief, Aidan released the shield, in his mind admitting that the energy blast produced by the Great Salamander was a lot stronger than that of Zane. He had conjured the most powerful protection shield, yet he could still feel its touch.

"Gwyn... brother..."

Gwyn ap Nudd turned to face the Destiny Council, and a deadly smirk slowly stretched his lips. "Yes, Magnus?"

"What just happened?" Magnus fell back into his chair, pressing his hand to his chest as if he had a shortness of breath. "I don't understand—"

Gwyn's smile grew wider while his gaze became frostier. He remained silent, measuring the man in front of him with his wintry eyes. For the next few minutes, the King of the Otherworld explained to the Destiny Council everything that had happened from the moment they brought Mrak Delar to stand trial to the moment they broke the dark spell. Delivering news, he was neither gentle nor diplomatic, and he didn't spare any details, describing everything that had been done to Zane while he was held in their compound.

When he finished, Magnus got up, his face ashen. He wiped shiny drops of perspiration off his forehead and leaned forward heavily, planting his hands on the top of the desk.

"We did all that?" His voice shook in unmistakable fear, but somewhere deeper under the surface, there were layers of regret and shame.

"That and who knows what else," confirmed Gwyn ap Nudd with a shrug, but his blazing eyes narrowed ever so slightly.

The man frowned, shaking his head. "We'll set it right... I swear... I'll talk to the young Salamander myself... And the Ancient Master..." He dropped his head low and his shoulders sagged. "Oh God, how did it happen? Who was behind the invasion?"

"We don't know," replied Kal, folding his arms across his chest resentfully. "We believe the spell was placed by one of the dark gods. As far as Gunz... Good luck talking to him." He rolled his eyes, and this gesture was so unusual for the Fire Elemental that Aidan couldn't help but smirk.

Magnus threw his arms in the air, a desperate look on his face. He moved to walk around the desk but stumbled and stilled, taking in short breaths. His eyes got unfocused for a moment and then lit up so brightly that now they truly resembled the headlights of a car. The other two members of the Council got up too, channeling their magic.

"A battle...," whispered the woman on Magnus' righthand side. She placed her hand to her throat, gasping for air, and her eyes widened.

"A terrible one...," the younger man on the left echoed her. "Dangerous powers have been awakened, threatening the balance of the human realm... I feel... Death, Conquest, Famine and War... The Four are riding again... and the Doomsday Clock is ticking..."

"Gunz," whispered Aidan, his heart beating in his throat. *It's not possible... They can't be here...*

He closed his eyes, transforming into his godly form, and scanned the Destiny Council realm as far as he could reach. Somewhere in a considerable distance, he detected a weak flair of familiar energy.

Zane... Mrak... What's going on?

He sucked in a sharp breath. Now that the dark spell that was blocking all their senses was broken, he could feel their presence. It could only mean one thing—they were in *this* realm, indeed.

How is that possible?

Aidan approached the desk, glowering up at Magnus, and growled through gritted teeth, "Do you know where this battle is?"

Magnus flinched, and his eyes returned to normal. "Right here. On the Dark Side of our realm. I can see them... on the Destiny Board... They're greatly outmanned..." He spoke in short punchy sentences, as if he had a hard time pronouncing the words.

He held out his hand, and an image of a strange three-dimensional map projected from his palm. Touching the map with his fingers, he rotated it, panning and zooming as if it was a chessboard displayed on the screen of a tablet.

"The three who are not meant to handle such dangerous powers, evoked the power of Four... I can feel the presence of Death. All this time, he was held here... right under our noses... And we were all none the wiser."

"You were all under a powerful enchantment, controlled!" snapped Kal, heat rising around him. "Get over it and tell me where I can find my child, you useless—"

Aidan raised his hand, stopping Kal's furious speech. Feeling a soft touch to his mind through the psychic bond he had created with Yaroslav and Gunz a while ago, he stilled, listening to the voice of his friend.

A moment later, he turned to his mentor and the Great Salamander. "Gunz needs our help, and now I know exactly where he is. Are you with me?"

Both Kal and Gwyn nodded, and Aidan waved his hand, opening the door of a brilliant white light, ready to walk through it, but Magnus stopped him.

"Wait, god of the Otherworld. It's not wise to bring Kalidus with you to the Dark Side," he said, throwing a careful glance at Kal. "The elemental powers don't flow well there—"

"I don't give a damn!" roared the Great Salamander, interrupting him. "My boy is there, deprived of his element. I'm not going to stay behind and wait. I'm going. Period." He slammed his fist against the side of the desk, leaving a deep indentation in its marble surface.

"Fine, fine..." Magnus raised his hands up in a peaceful gesture. "But at least take my team with you. You'll need all the capable fighters you can get."

He waved his hand and a tall wooden door materialized in the left wall of the chamber. Sending a small amount of his magic toward it, he whispered, "Destiny Enforcers, special team... you're summoned."

CHAPTER 39

~ ZANE BURNS, A.K.A. GUNZ ~

The brilliant burst of light was too much for his eyes accustomed to the darkness of this realm. Gunz looked down, blinking away the dancing spots in his vision, and raised his arm. With shock, he noticed that the demonic army seemed to come to a halt. For a brief moment, they gaped in the direction of the flare, and then cowered away from it. He had no idea what it was, but it gave him a moment to regroup.

He glanced down at the wound on his side and held his breath. Thin, dark rivulets were running between his fingers, coloring his hand red, but the pain wasn't as sharp as he expected. The look of his own blood made him slightly lightheaded—or perhaps it was the blood loss that made him feel this way. There was no time to contemplate it, no time to think or strategize. As soon as the light subsided, submerging the battlefield back under the blanket of darkness, the demons attacked with new strength.

Avoiding the strikes of demonic swords, slashes of their talons and claws, and punches of their massive fists, he spun around, setting ablaze as many enemies as he could. He heard

Mrak Delar, Yaroslav and Lucan fighting by his side, but he couldn't take his eyes off his attackers.

"Zane!"

A familiar voice sounded somewhere on his right, and he glanced toward the sound, not daring to believe his ears.

"Aidan!" he shouted, running a demon in front of him through with his flaming blade.

"We're here! Hold on!" Aidan's voice rose above the battlefield, magnified by his magic.

The second voice—a gruff male voice—followed Aidan's, and the sound of it made Gunz's blood run cold.

"You know the drill, boys! Let's send these Hell spawns back to the hellhole they crawled out from!"

"Commander Moore?" hissed Lucan without stopping what he was doing. He crossed his daggers at a giant monster's neck and moved them sharply into opposite directions, cutting the head off the demon's shoulders in one move. "What the hell is he doing here?"

Bright flares of light ignited at the rear of the demonic army. The tight mass of monsters that separated them from the castle shuddered, and their attention wavered, giving Gunz and his friends a chance to regroup and double their effort. Gunz couldn't see what was going on there, but knowing how the Commander and his team worked, he could imagine.

Demons howled and roared in rage, more of them turning around to face the new adversaries. The flares of light got brighter, and the even lines of the demonic army started to separate. The monsters were falling left and right like trees under the axe of a woodsman. A moment later, Kal made his way through and halted in front of Gunz, his igneous eyes burning with the excitement of the fight. In his hands, he held a massive hammer dripping with black slime.

"Father!" yelled Gunz, thrusting his sword forward into a

monster next to Kal. "There is no elemental energy here. What are—"

"You didn't think I'd abandon you when you needed help, son?" roared Kal as he swept his huge hammer through the demonic mass, destroying the bodies of a few demons in one move.

The flares and bursts of the white light became brighter. The yells and screeches of demons became louder. The air was heavy with the reek of demonic essence and stench of black goo. But through all that, Gunz could sense Aidan's energy signature loud and clear, and it seemed to be ten times stronger than it normally was.

He easily recognized the presence of Commander Moore's fighters, but besides all that, he isolated a new magical energy type he didn't recognize. It was extremely powerful and completely unfamiliar. Whoever this being of magic was, Gunz was positive he had never met them before.

As the unfamiliar magic grew stronger, the situation became quite chaotic. The demonic lines shuddered and fell apart. The monsters scattered all over the valley in an attempt to retreat from the white light which seemed to burn through them just as easy as the flames of War Gunz was wielding.

Kal, Lucan and Yaroslav stopped fighting, lowering their weapons. They stood next to Gunz, breathing laboriously, covered in so much disgusting slime and blood that it was hard to see their faces. Mrak Delar approached him and pointed at the demons deserting the battlefield.

"It's over...," he exhaled, lowering his demonic blade.

Aidan, Gwyn ap Nudd and Commander Moore's team slowly headed toward them across the field coated in slime and bodies of disintegrating demons. The presence of the King of the Otherworld explained the white light and Aidan's magnified magical energy. However, it was the man walking behind them who drew Gunz's attention, making his eyes widen in awe.

Commander Moore walked behind his team, his entire body emitting a brilliant white light that could rival that of Gwyn ap Nudd. A set of silvery wings was folded behind his back, and as he progressed forward, they slowly started to dissipate. In his hands, he held two long, thin daggers, their blades shining just as bright as he was. All this time, Gunz had been positive that the Commander was human. He had never sensed even a smidge of magic in him. Watching him now, he couldn't believe his eyes.

The man approached Gunz and stared down at him, an uneven smirk lingering on his face.

"Well, hello, Burns," he said as he wiped his daggers on his sleeves and sheathed them. "Finally, you showed me what you're good for, boy." He winked at Lucan and laughed, the sound of his laughter echoing through the darkness of the valley.

A dangerous growl rumbled in Kal's chest at his words, and the Great Salamander stepped between the Commander and Gunz. Moore raised both arms, still chuckling.

"Relax, Great Salamander," he said, his grin growing wider. "I mean no harm to your son."

"What are you?" asked Gunz, stepping from behind Kal. "All this time I thought you were the only human on your team." He glanced at Lucan, noticing that his black eyes widened as he gave him a barely visible shake of his head.

"Doctor Harris was right," muttered Moore, staring down at him, not without curiosity in his eyes. "You are a powerful fighter, but when it comes to the World of Magic, you're still an inexperienced child."

"Gunz, this jackass is a Destiny Enforcer," huffed Mrak Delar, and if he could sound any colder, snow would've started falling. He turned to face Moore, cocking his head slightly. "The young Salamander is many things, but an inexperienced child is not one of them, Moore. He just got lucky that he never had to face the likes of you."

He took a step closer to the Commander, and the ground shook, responding to his emotions. The Commander's team shifted a step closer, raising their weapons.

"Whoa!" Moore raised his hands again, gesturing for his team to stand down.

Mrak Delar ignored him, turning back to Gunz.

"There are hundreds of Destiny Enforcers, if not thousands, roaming the human realm," he explained. "Some of them are there on the Destiny Council's orders. Some of them decided to abandon their duty and clipped their wings, returning to live among humans. All of them are powerful wizards and witches enhanced with special powers only the Destiny Council can bestow upon their warriors. One of their powers allows them to conceal their magical energy to such a degree that neither human nor supernatural can ever detect it. Unless they want to make it known who they are, that is." Mrak threw an icy glance at the Commander. "Am I right, Moore?"

"Right you are, Master." The Commander rubbed his forehead, smearing some of the black slime over his face. "Anyway, Burns, I'm sorry about what happened..." He fell silent, a vibe of discomfort lingering around him. "I was just..." He sighed and his forehead creased. "You're a soldier... You know what the chain of command means. I was just doing my job. I had no idea that the Destiny Council... all of us, actually, were under some kind of dark spell. None of us knew..."

He threw a glance back at Aidan and Gwyn ap Nudd as though searching for their support. Both remained silent, their faces showing no emotions. The Commander turned back to Gunz and sighed.

"Anyway, what I said... all that is not a good enough excuse for everything you've been put through, but that's all I have," he said, meeting Gunz's eyes calmly. "I *am* deeply sorry, and I hope you'll find it in your heart to forgive me. And if you ever wish to join my team as an equal, I'd be happy to have you."

A deep shudder ran through Gunz's body, and he took a step back involuntarily. "No," he said, his voice barely above a whisper. "I can live my entire life without ever coming back to that place."

"You're immortal." The Commander smirked.

"Exactly." A lopsided grin appeared on Gunz's face but died down almost immediately, and he sighed, noticing that Moore's eyes moved to Lucan. The elf paled and backed away, shrinking under his heavy gaze.

"Lucan, you, on the other hand, have no choice," said the Commander firmly. "You're coming back with me."

Lucan glanced at Gunz, silently pleading for help, then his eyes darted to Mrak Delar and Aidan. Mrak Delar frowned and approached the elf, seizing his elbow.

The Commander sighed, carefully observing the Master of Power, but came closer to Lucan, placing his hand in a thick leather glove on the elf's shoulder. "You know that you can't live in the human realm," he said peacefully, his voice almost pleading. "Unlike the rest of them"—he waved his hand around—"your appearance cannot be hidden. You will expose the World of Magic, and I can't allow it."

"I will conceal my appearance," whispered the elf, not raising his eyes. "I can create a powerful illusion—"

"You can't conjure an illusion every time you need to go grocery shopping and sustaining an illusion spell twenty-four-seven is impossible," objected the Commander, interrupting him. "You know it. You have nowhere to go. The Elzara clan was destroyed years ago, and I don't know if any of your kind are still alive in the far forests of Kendral. You have no choice, Lucan."

"Hold on a second," said Mrak Delar, raising his hand. "You're right, Commander. Lucan can't live in the realm of humans. But I can take him back to Kendral with me."

"You?" A smirk appeared on Moore's face as his eyes traveled up and down Mrak's body, as if he were measuring him. "With all due respect, Master. You're no longer the King of Kendral. Only the Master of Kendral can make this decision, and Lucan here knows very well why he can't go back to Kendral without a special invitation."

Lucan dropped his head, his long black hair covering his face, and his shoulders slumped. Gunz turned to him, but suddenly stilled as something inside him snapped, raising alarms in his mind. It wasn't an energy of magic or a demonic presence. It was something entirely different. Something on the level of intuition.

He snapped around. Like a dark sinister shadow, a demon rose silently from beneath a thick layer of sticky goo, broken weapons, and demonic body parts that hadn't yet disintegrated. Holding a heavy iron spear, the monster raised his arm. With unbelievable speed, he pulled his arm back and propelled the spear through the air, aiming at Mrak Delar who stood a few steps away from him.

"Mrak, watch out!" Gunz shouted, reaching for his magic. Time slowed down. The sound of his own voice—desperate and filled with fear—rang through his mind, resonating with pain. Turning his head, he saw Aidan, Gwyn ap Nudd and Kal springing into motion, shouting something, but their movements were torturously slow, and he couldn't hear their voices.

Mrak Delar turned around and his eyes flew wide open. His lips moved as he said the words of a protection spell—a split second too late. The spear went through his shield before it fully formed, heading directly for his heart. Before anyone could react, Lucan, who stood next to the Master of Power, threw himself in front of the deadly weapon.

The spear penetrated his chest, and he cried out, falling to Mrak's feet, his fingers clasping the piece of iron protruding from his chest with both hands. Dropping to his knees, the

Master of Power quickly explored the wound and raised his eyes at Gunz, remorse clouding his features.

Gunz roared, fury spiking the flames of War. In two strides, he reached the monster and decapitated him with one swing of his sword, setting the demon's disintegrating body ablaze. He turned around, taking enraged breaths, and shook his head, pressing his lips into a painful straight line.

"Lucan..." He approached the elf and lowered down by his side. His eyes stopped on the spear and with his military training, he knew that the injury was fatal.

"It's okay...," whispered the elf, a thin stream of scarlet liquid trickling from the corner of his mouth. "Death is better than going back... to the Destiny Council compound... I'm tired of fighting... Gunz..."

Gunz didn't listen to him. His eyes met Mrak Delar's. "Mrak, please..."

"I don't think I can," moaned the Master of Power, despair making his voice sound shaky and raspy. "There is no elemental power in this realm, and I need the Power of Earth to perform the healing magic. Besides... I'm drained and the healing magic requires a lot of energy."

"Yaroslav!" yelled Gunz, twisting around, searching for the vampire. His own wound responded with a sharp pain in his side, and he groaned, leaning to the side slightly.

The vampire kneeled next to him and shook his head. Lucan's lips, smeared with bubbled blood, twitched a little.

"Stop, Gunz...," Lucan whispered, his chest shuddering with short, uneven breaths. He raised his eyes at the vampire and the darkness of Famine's power vanished, revealing their emerald glow. "I never thought... I could call a vampire... a friend..." He swallowed weakly. "But we both know... the vampire's blood can't heal an elf..."

Yaroslav nodded, and Gunz sat back on his heels, holding Lucan's fading gaze.

"Lucan, listen to me." The Commander's voice sounded too harsh in the dreadful silence. "I am willing to offer you the mantle of a Destiny Enforcer. I'm sure the Destiny Council will accept my decision." He took one knee next to the elf, gazing at him intently. "Accept it, and you will ascend to immortality. You'll live… Lucan."

"I'd rather die…," the elf whispered and turned away, his eyes fixed on Gunz.

"Lucan, please, listen to him." Mrak Delar gently touched his shoulder. "Not all Destiny Enforcers are like the Commander here. I've met quite a few decent people among their kind. Some of them left the Destiny Council services after a while. It's your life… the only way to save you… please…"

A tear ran down the Ancient Master's cheek, dropping into the thick mass of Lucan's white hair. He leaned forward slightly, covering his face with his hands.

"No… my life for yours, Master… fair trade…" His eyes rolled back, and he exhaled. His fingers unlocked, and his hands fell to the ground with a soft thud.

Gunz shook his head and got up. "No," he said, with shock noticing how firm and self-assured he sounded. "He's not dead. I can sense his heart beating. And there is one more way to save him."

He channeled his magic and drew a rune in the air, infusing it with the magic of the Dark Codex.

CHAPTER 40

~ ZANE BURNS, A.K.A. GUNZ ~

"What is this magic?" hissed the Commander. "It's not the magic of a Great Fire Salamander..."

Gunz threw an indifferent glance at him, his eyes shining white, and touched the rune with his fingers. "Master Alliandr, I summon thee," he whispered the summoning spell and dropped his arm powerlessly.

"How dare you summon the Master of Kendral into this mess!" hissed Moore, but Kal put his hand on the Commander's shoulder and slowly shook his head.

A moment later, the Master of Kendral manifested next to Gunz and immediately bent forward, clutching his chest, as if someone just punched him in the gut. When the initial reaction to the absence of elemental powers was over, the young Master of Power straightened, and his attentive black eyes swept from one person to the next, halting on Mrak Delar.

"Mrak...," he whispered and kneeled next to him, an expression of concern crossing his face. "Are you okay, Master?"

"I am... not really," replied the Ancient Master, raising his eyes at the young man, who looked like a younger version of him.

"Master Alliandr," said Gunz, approaching him. "I'm sorry I had to summon you into a realm with no elemental powers, but my friend is dying, and you're the only one who has the power to save him."

"I need the Power of Earth to perform the healing magic," said Alliandr, shaking his head. "It doesn't exist—" He cut himself off as his gaze stopped on Lucan, lingering a moment too long on his elongated ear exposed by his hair. "An elf? I thought…" His voice trailed off, and he glanced at Mrak Delar, a question in his eyes.

"Master, meet Lucárion, the last of the Elzara clan," said Mrak Delar. "He saved my life…"

"Elzara…," echoed the young man, and a deep frown settled on his face. "I recall something that I've read in the Riders' history archives. They were all destroyed. How did he survive the massacre?"

"Long story," replied Gunz. "He can tell you all about it later. Alliandr, can you take him back to Kendral and heal him there?"

Alliandr gently probed the edges of the elf's wound, moving his fingers around the spear. "He's still alive. It's not easy to kill an elf."

He touched Lucan's forehead with two fingers and whispered a spell. Lucan's eyes flew wide open, and he gasped for air like a person who was submerged under water too long. His eyes stopped on the Master of Kendral, and his pale face became blue.

"Master—," he croaked.

"Lucárion, if I don't take care of your wound soon, you'll die," said the Master of Kendral, interrupting him. "I can't do it here. I must take you back to my realm, and I have to do it now, before it's too late."

"Back to Kendral?" whispered Lucan, and a warm, wistful expression suffused his features.

"Would you like to go back with me?" asked the young Master and then repeated, "If you don't, you'll die."

"Would you allow me back in your realm?" asked Lucan breathlessly.

"Why wouldn't I?" Alliandr shrugged, his eyebrows rising.

"I submitted to my captors," whispered Lucan, swallowing hard. "I betrayed my clan and my kind by doing so. I broke a sacred oath... An elf should never allow himself to become enslaved... I was too weak... I have no right to come back—"

For a moment the Master of Kendral met Mrak Delar's eyes. A deep shudder ran through his body. A haunted look settled on Mrak's face. Then Alliandr shook his head, and a sad smile touched his full lips.

"Lucárion, there was a time when I had to kneel before my enemy," he said softly. "There was a time, when Master Mrak Delar wore a brand of a slave and a collar. Those who live in glass houses shouldn't throw stones..." He glanced at Gunz over his shoulder, giving him a curt nod, and switched his attention back to the elf. "Would you allow me to take you back and heal you?"

Lucan's ashen face lit up with a light of hope as his eyes settled on the young Master of Kendral. "Yes, my lord... Oh God... Home... I never thought it would be possible..." Then he glanced up at Gunz. "Will I ever see you again, Burns?"

"Sooner than you think." Gunz chuckled.

Lucan pulled Famine's ring off his finger and sighed with relief, offering it to him. "Wearing this ring felt worse than anything I've ever experienced. Can you please give it back to her?"

"I will." Gunz took the ring and put it in his pocket.

Master Alliandr lifted the elf with a grunt and nodded at Mrak Delar. "When it's all over, please come see me, Master," he said softly, but there was no doubt—it was an order. Holding Lucan in his arms, he snapped his fingers and both vanished.

***

They crossed the dark valley and stopped in front of the drawbridge into the castle. The bridge was down, and the gates were wide open, but no one was waiting for them—neither by the wall nor inside, as far as Gunz could see. He opened his other sight and explored the area just to confirm his suspicion. The building seemed to be abandoned, and he couldn't detect any hostile presence.

With Lucan gone, they no longer had the power of Four, but he could still sense Death somewhere within these walls. His energy signature was weak and barely detectible, but he had no doubt, Angel was still here. For the first time since they arrived in this lifeless realm, he felt the presence of light. It was feeble, disappearing and rising again like an uneven pulse, yet Gunz recognized it right away—the power of knowledge and light— the energy of Archangel Uriel.

He waved for his friends to follow him and crossed the bridge, walking through the gate. By looking from outside the walls, he couldn't get a full picture of how large the building truly was. The shadowy fortress was looming over him, exuding a silent threat from every brick. Built of rough, black stonework, its walls were rising high, melting into the infinite darkness of the sky. As far as he could see, there were no windows in the lower levels. Only at the top corner towers, tiny windows crossed by iron bars gaped like the blind eye sockets of a skull.

The main door was wide open, just like the gates in the outside wall, and it looked like the black mouth of a beast, ready to swallow them whole. Gunz shuddered, halting in front of it. He scanned the castle again, searching for Angel, and then crossed the threshold without looking back.

As he expected, the spacious lobby was dark. A musty, unclean odor hung heavily in the air, and Gunz cringed inwardly as he detected barely noticeable scents of blood, smoke and burnt flesh mixed into it. He also noticed a weak residue of the Black Fire energy but that didn't stop him since he had no doubt the actual flames were gone by now. Commander Moore whispered something and held out his hand. A large orb lit up with a bright white light in his palm, and he threw it in the air. The shadow shied away from the light, hiding grudgingly in the far corners.

Two dark hallways and a narrow wooden staircase led away from the lobby. Gunz sharpened his hearing, but the silence of this place seemed to be disturbed only by the slow and even dripping of water somewhere far in the distance. The location of the sound coincided with the location of Angel's energy, and he pointed at the stairway.

"Are you sure?" whispered Mrak Delar. "I can't sense anything."

Gunz nodded and carefully moved up the stairs. The wooden steps were old and partially rotten, and his every step produced a mournful squeak that sounded piercing in the surrounding silence. He passed a few flights of stairs, and when he finally stepped on the hard floor of the top level, he exhaled, just now realizing that he had been holding his breath all this time.

Following the dark hallway, he halted in front of the last door and glanced back at his friends and the Commander with his team. All of them were staring at him quizzically, as if asking why they were here.

They can't sense them... A thought materialized in his mind, but he shook it off. *It's impossible... Aidan, Kal and Gwyn are a lot more sensitive than I am, and the Commander seems to possess powers I've never heard of...*

"Angel and Uri are here," he whispered. "Can't you feel their presence?"

He didn't know why he was whispering. There was no one

in the castle. Besides, even the words said in the softest of whispers reverberated from the low ceilings and stone walls, becoming a hissing echo. But for some reason, he couldn't bring himself to speak out loud.

Since no one said anything, he pushed the door carefully. It opened with a rusty squeak that made his teeth ache. A cloud of smoke puffed through the doorway even though there was no fire, and the suffocating stench of burnt flesh invaded his senses, making his stomach turn. Gunz coughed, hiding his face into the crook of his elbow.

"*Ventius...,*" whispered Aidan from behind his back, sending a light gust of wind through the room.

When the smoke dissipated, Gunz crossed the threshold and stilled. Everything inside this stone chamber was blackened by flames, and he was sure that it hadn't been a regular fire.

"Black Fire," whispered Kal, placing his hand on Gunz's shoulder protectively. "What the hell happened here?"

Gunz raised his eyes, and everything inside him twisted in pain. In the shimmering light of the orb, he saw two men sprawled helplessly in midair. Their eyes were closed, and their long hair hung in limp, lifeless strands. Deep shadows lay under their eyes and cheekbones, making their faces look like skulls with bluish-gray skin stretched over them. They didn't move. Even their chests remained motionless.

Both Angel and Uri were in their true form, but their wings were broken, hanging at an unnatural angle. Black and golden feathers were scattered all over the floor under them. The golden feathers were covered in dark brown stains of dried out blood. Large drops of thick silvery liquid were trickling slowly from a terrible gash on Angel's chest, falling to the floor and onto the heap of black feathers beneath him with a ringing splatter.

The essence of Death... Gunz stiffened, a painful memory of Rasputin's lab materializing in his mind. The essence of Death and the Black Fire. He turned around to see the identical expression of horror on Yaroslav's, Mrak Delar's and Aidan's faces, making obvious that the same memory crossed their thoughts as well.

"Someone was trying to conjure the Living-Dead Flame," said the Master of Power.

"Maybe," agreed Kal. He squatted and picked up a black feather coated in a silvery liquid, rolling it between his fingers. "If they tried, they failed. To create the Living-Dead Flame, you need to sacrifice a Fire Salamander. As far as I know, there are only two of them in this world, and we both are here, alive and well."

"Let's assume, you're right," muttered the Commander. He halted next to Kal, his troubled eyes surveying Uri. "But why did they need an Archangel? They took his blood and some of his grace." He moved his hand under Uri, muttering something under his breath, and a faint golden glow ignited around his fingers, following his every move. "I wonder what they were *really* cooking in this Hell's kitchen."

Commander Moore turned around and flicked his eyebrow at his team. Two men separated from the crowd, and Gunz recognized the wizards. They approached Angel and Uri and started to chant. Turning in the air, their motionless bodies slowly lowered down, until their backs touched the floor softly.

Gunz stared down at his friends, sprawled on the floor next to his feet, and a blinding fury spiraled through him. The flames —scarlet, bloody flames of War—broke through his skin, and a dangerous growl rumbled deep in his throat. The energy of War permeated the air. The walls trembled and a deep crack crossed it, running up to the stone ceiling. Kal gasped, reaching him in two steps.

"Son, I don't know how you're still connected to the power of Four with Lucan gone. It's probably the Codex that allows you to do it… But you need to let it go," he whispered into his ear so no one else could hear his words and squeezed his shoulder. "Take a deep breath and release whatever it is your anger has summoned."

Gunz took a deep breath, getting the fire in him to dissipate and sighed, his shoulders slumped. "I'm in control," he said, his voice unnaturally calm and emotionless. "Are they dead? Is it even possible?"

"This is Death and an Archangel," said the King of the Otherworld. "They can't die. Ever. They're in an enchanted sleep. The Destiny Council can revive them. They'll be fine. Just like Commander Moore, I'm more concerned with what kind of dark spell was performed here. Black Fire, essence of Death and blood of an Archangel."

He frowned and his eyes moved up and to the left, getting slightly fogged. For a moment he remained silent, his fingers fidgeting with a loose strand of his black hair.

"Maybe it's because I'm not an expert in Dark Arts, but I can't come up with anything that would require these ingredients." Gwyn shrugged and arched his brow at Mrak Delar. "Perhaps you can suggest something, Master? Among all of us, you're the only one who has hands-on experience with Dark Magic."

"Thank you, Gwyn," muttered Mrak Delar sarcastically. But by the way he folded his arms, Gunz knew that the Master of Power was deeply hurt. "What would I do if you didn't remind me of my past once in a while? Anyway, I know nothing of the sort." He turned to Moore. "Commander, you need to take them to the Destiny Council as soon as possible. Hopefully, once they're back to normal, they can shed some light on everything that's happened here."

The Commander inclined his head in an unmistakable bow. Gunz eyebrows climbed up at the display of respect he never thought this man was capable of.

"Yes, my lord," Moore said, addressing the Ancient Master. "I will summon you all as soon as they're able to talk."

He waved at this team, and two large vampires separated from the rest. They walked to Uri and Angel and lifted them, draping them over their shoulders without any sign of strain.

Commander Moore waved his hand, and a door shining with a brilliant white light materialized in front of him. Once his team disappeared through the portal, he made a step toward it, but before he could walk through, Aidan stopped him. He glanced at the Commander, his gaze as cold as the desert night.

"I'm coming with you," he said in a tone of voice that even the Destiny Enforcer didn't dare object to. "Someone has to make sure that Angel and Uri are well taken care of."

"But of course, my lord," said Moore, his lips stretching into a semblance of a smile. "After you."

He waved at the door and bowed mockingly. Aidan frowned but didn't say anything. Throwing a quick glance at his friends, he waved his hand and walked through the shining doorway.

The Commander followed him but halted next to the threshold and turned around. His eyes halted on Gunz, and he smirked, giving him a sharp military salute.

"See you soon, Burns." He turned around and disappeared through the portal, closing it.

"Sure," growled Gunz, cringing inwardly. "As soon as never."

CHAPTER 41

~ ZANE BURNS, A.K.A. GUNZ ~

By the time Mrak Delar finally managed to open the portal back to the human realm, the sun was already up, caressing the rocky land of Mount Vottovaara with its warm touch. The soft morning rays reflected in the surface of the swamp and multiple puddles, throwing playful flairs of light.

The Master of Power was so drained that he could barely keep an upright position, but he was the only one who could open the portal. Neither Gwyn ap Nudd nor Kal knew the exact location of their final destination, and Gunz wasn't sure he had enough strength in him left to protect Yaroslav while traveling through the Fire Salamander portal.

It took Mrak a few tries to open the portal, and when they finally made it to the rocky plateau, he sat down, resting his back against a boulder, and closed his eyes, his hands lying limply on his lap. Kal squatted next to him and placed his hand over Mrak's heart, channeling some of the fire energy through him to give him a tiny boost of strength.

"Master, you look like you're on the verge of shutting down," he said softly, rising. "Do you want me to take you back to the wolf's ranch? Or maybe home, to Kendral?"

The Ancient Master chuckled and cracked his eyelids half open. "Just look?" he mumbled, his speech slightly slurred. "I wish I could go home now, but Gunz, Yaroslav and I are not done yet." He sighed, moving his head from left to right and winced, a grimace of pain distorting his features. "I think I don't have a single cell in my body that doesn't hurt…"

Kal got up and waved his hand, unfolding the flaming curtain of his portal. Gunz stared at the fire—normal elemental flames—and his heart ached with the desire to leave with Kal and be done with all of this.

"Father," he called. The Great Salamander turned around and looked down at him. Even though he didn't smile, his deeply set eyes got warmer. "Thank you…" Gunz inclined his head slightly, putting all the gratitude he felt into this tiny gesture.

Kal smirked with a slight shake of his head. "You don't need to thank me for taking care of you. Ever. You *are* my son, Gunz. What did you expect?"

Kal stepped closer and brushed his cheek with his fingers in such a fatherly manner that Gunz's heart expanded with warmth. Then he glanced down at Gunz's side where he held his hand pressed over his wound.

"Revert and heal yourself, my child. Actually, you're better of asking your *Russkij* Blondie to heal you. Safer for humans that could be in this area." Kal shrugged indifferently, as though he couldn't care less about the humans and their realm. "Anyway, don't do anything until you take care of your wound."

"Yes, Father." Gunz smiled as the Great Salamander nodded and walked through his portal, pulling Gwyn ap Nudd with him.

Now that the fight was over and the adrenalin was no longer charging through his system, the pain in his side became unbearable. He groaned and leaned to the left slightly, watching fresh blood staining his fingers.

Awkwardly, he lowered down next to the Master of Power. To his amusement, Mrak scooted over, giving him his place, and Gunz couldn't help but chuckle—there was so much free space by the giant boulder, yet Mrak moved for him. Yaroslav sat down in front of them, crossing his legs and put his katana by his side.

"Ready?" he asked, tucking his disheveled hair behind his ear.

Gunz shuddered. "Ugh, no offense, Slavik, but I'm never ready for that."

"Tough." Yaroslav snickered and bit his wrist. Gunz watched the vampire as he lifted his face. With his lips parted, his fangs covered in blood looked like deadly blades. His glowing eyes widened for a split second as he met Gunz's gaze, but he didn't say anything and extended his bleeding arm to him.

Gunz grimaced at the taste and smell of the vampire's blood. He let go of Yaroslav's arm a few seconds later and looked down. The wound stopped bleeding and its edges pulled together, forming an ugly scar. But most importantly, the pain was gone.

"Thank you," he said quietly and leaned back against the boulder. Even though the injury was healed, he felt so sore and exhausted that he couldn't even think about moving, let alone walking down the mountain hill or—oh horror—riding a horse.

Yaroslav just nodded and lay down, folding his arms over his face, shielding his eyes from the sunlight. "We should go soon," he murmured. "I don't think I can stay much longer in the sun."

"Yeah... you're right," said Mrak Delar. "We should get the hell off of this cursed mountain and get the horses back to the Horsemen so they can send them..." He shrugged tiredly, an exhausted smirk appearing on his face. "Wherever they summoned them from."

Yaroslav and Gunz nodded, but none of them moved.

"I can't imagine spending another twenty-four hours in the saddle," moaned Gunz. "But we should go anyway."

Mrak and Yaroslav hummed in agreement, but all three of them remained motionless.

"Maybe I can make our journey back a little easier. I don't think we need to walk all the way down Vottovaara," said Gunz a few minutes later, probing the area with his other sight. He got up and swayed slightly on his feet, bracing himself against the boulder. "I think I can summon the red stallion here."

"I don't think you can…," objected Mrak Delar. "Didn't they say that the mountain was blocked for them?"

"Not anymore. Something tells me we broke that spell when we freed Angel and Uri." Gunz squeezed his fingers into a fist, staring down at the red jewel of War's ring and channeled some of his power through it, calling to his fiery steed. The air around him shimmered and his entire body got engulfed in scarlet flames. A portal swirling with the energy of War opened up in front of him, and Gunz staggered back involuntarily.

"Come…," he whispered, fire rising in his eyes. The ground trembled, and Gunz exhaled, enjoying the unexpected wave of power that spread through him.

Both Mrak Delar and Yaroslav jumped to their feet, pressing their backs against the rock. A flaming red stallion stepped out of the portal and halted next to Gunz, lowering his head to his shoulder. Gunz wrapped his arms around the horse's hot neck and pressed his cheek against it.

"You came," he whispered, not daring to believe that his magic worked.

"Of course, young Master." The stallion's voice sounded in Gunz's mind. The horse neighed as if he was laughing, and shook his head, his fiery mane brushing over Gunz's face. *"You called—I came. Isn't it the way it works?"*

The beautiful black mare and the tall black stallion, followed by Siv, emerged from the portal.

"Oh, hello there," neighed Siv, his purple eyes stopping on Yaroslav. He leaned back and then forward, stretching like a house cat, and a wide grin showed off his massive choppers. "I think I was starting to miss you."

"You were?" asked Yaroslav cautiously, not sure what to expect next.

"Of course," replied Siv with a sly wink. "You know how it is... We get used to our pets, and they become like members of the family or something."

"A pet," repeated Yaroslav, his fangs expanding to full length as he bent down and picked up his katana.

Siv eyes rounded, and he pressed his ears down, stepping behind the mare. "Hey, hey!" he neighed warningly. "You touch me, defective vamp, and I'll show you what a magical horse can do. I'll get her to deal with you." He jerked his head at the black mare.

Yaroslav exchanged a look with Gunz and they both burst out laughing. Sheathing his katana beneath his half-destroyed leather coat, Yaroslav mounted Siv, patting his neck. It took a few tries for Gunz to get on his tall red horse as he could barely pull himself up into the saddle. Mrak approached the giant white stallion and patted his back, whispering something into his ear. The stallion bent his front legs and slowly lowered down to the ground, allowing the Master of Power to get into the saddle easier.

When I get back to Kendral, I'm going to ask Mrak to give me a few lessons in horseback riding, Gunz thought, grabbing the pommel of the saddle as the red horse shifted beneath him. *And teach me how to deal with horses too...*

"You don't need to 'deal' with me, young Master," said the red stallion and there were unmistakable tones of humor in his voice. "All you had to do was tell me that you were tired, and you needed my help to get in the saddle. I would do as you command."

The horse pushed off the ground, quickly gaining height,

and Gunz leaned forward, grasping at the saddle with both hands.

Fire Almighty... never again...

* * *

GUNZ WASN'T sure how long it took for them to get back to Hawk's ranch. When the horses touched the ground softly, halting by the fence, the sun started creeping down to the horizon, throwing the last pink rays across the desert. The front yard was empty, but the look of it made his chest tighten with dread.

The wards and protection spells were gone, and Hawk's house stood unprotected. The ground was blackened by fire, and he could still feel the energy of his element permeating the air. Even though the entire territory in front of the ranch house seemed to be recently cleaned, he noticed a few dark spots staining the light gray asphalt and the beige desert sand.

It's blood... A thought rushed through his mind, and his stomach knotted. *What happened here while we were gone?*

The door of the house opened, and the three Horsemen walked out, heading toward him. The stallions neighed happily, greeting their masters. Holding the pommel of the saddle with his stiff fingers, Gunz swung his leg and slid down the horse's side. His knees gave in, and he fell to all fours, breathing laboriously. Every square inch of his body was sore and aching, and the ground under him felt unsteady.

Two strong hands grabbed him under his arms and yanked him to his feet. He grunted and raised his eyes to see Viggo Warrington standing by his side, a lopsided grin playing on his lips.

"Not much of a horseman, are you?" he asked, sarcastic twinkles in his eyes.

"No," replied Gunz, wishing that the world would stop spinning around him. "Never claimed to be."

He pulled the ring off and gave it to War. Viggo took it and put it back on his finger. Spreading his wide shoulders, he stretched, an expression of pure bliss suffusing his features as if the ring gave him an energy boost. Then he gently ran his fingers over the red stallion's back and whispered, "You can go, my friend. Until it's time for us to ride again." He waved his hand and his portal opened up, breathing with the energy of War.

"Farewell, young Master..." The stallion neighed softly. He touched Gunz's shoulder and walked through the portal, disappearing in the rotating flames.

With a sigh of relief, Gunz turned around, searching for Yaroslav and Mrak Delar. Yaroslav was talking to Siv, standing in front of the magical stallion with his arms folded. Judging by the expression on the vampire's face and by Siv's impatient dancing, they were playing on each other's nerves again.

Mrak Delar was still on his horse. He was lying on the stallion's neck, his arms hanging limply, his eyes closed.

"Dammit," whispered Gunz and bolted toward him.

As fast as Gunz moved, he didn't reach him in time. The Master of Power slowly slid off the horse's side, plummeting down to the hard desert land. Luckily, Yaroslav was closer. Reacting with vampiric speed, he caught the Ancient Master before he hit the ground and gently lowered him to the warm pavement of the driveway.

Mrak Delar opened his eyes, and a groan of pain escaped his lips. His hand moved down, halting over his stomach where a large brown stain was growing bigger with the redness of fresh blood. Even though his white clothes were dark and stiff from demonic slime, blood and dirt, and it was hard to notice that he was wounded, Gunz cursed himself for not paying attention to his friend's condition. He lowered down to his knees, watching scarlet rivulets spilling between Mrak's fingers.

"Mrak," he said softly, "why didn't you say something? Can you heal yourself?"

Mrak Delar shook his head faintly and closed his eyes. "I thought I could handle it," he whispered barely audibly.

"He's drained. He can't heal himself. But if he doesn't get help right away, he'll die within a few hours." A cold voice sounded above Gunz's head. He looked up and saw Pestilence standing behind him, his dark eyes observing the Master of Power with unconcerned interest.

The infamous Horseman squatted next to the Master and carefully pulled the ring off his finger. Mrak sighed and relaxed, his body going limp in Yaroslav's arms.

"I'll take care of your wounds," said Yaroslav.

"Vampire blood?" muttered Mrak Delar breathlessly. "I think not..."

"We'll see...," murmured Yaroslav. "At a minimum, let's check out your wounds and clean them. If not magical, at least medical precautions?" He pulled the Master of Power to his feet, supporting him with his shoulder. "You know what they say about an ounce of prevention and the pound of a cure. Trust me —it's worth it."

"What do *you* know?" objected Mrak Delar weakly. "You're a goddamn vamp... your wounds heal faster than you can say *ouch*."

As soon as they made their first step, Mrak Delar cried out and stopped, leaning heavily on Yaroslav.

"I'll carry you," offered the vampire.

"Not unless you're ready for the *ashes to ashes* part of your life journey," growled Mrak Delar, taking a careful step forward.

Listening to his friends bickering, Gunz smirked and shook his head. He followed Yaroslav with his eyes all the way to the porch. The door opened, and he saw Tessa and Missi meeting them, ushering them inside. He couldn't see their faces clearly from this distance, but something in the way they both moved and looked gave him an unpleasant jolt.

"Mr. Burns." He heard Famine's voice and flinched, turning around.

"Yes, ma'am, what can I—," he started to say, but then remembered that he had her ring and reached for it in his pocket.

She took it from him, and a cold smile lifted the corners of her thin-lipped mouth. "So, what happened to your elf?" she asked, but her voice, flat and indifferent, showed just how little she cared.

"He had to return to Kendral," replied Gunz dryly.

Famine opened her portal, sending her beautiful black mare on her way, and turned back to Gunz. "Well, if you ever see him, tell him to visit me in South Florida. There are enough swamps and jungles there. He'll feel right at home. Besides—" She didn't finish her statement and winked at him. Her playfulness made Gunz's skin crawl, and he exhaled with relief when she finally snapped her fingers and vanished from the ranch.

Pestilence released his steed and threw an arrogant smirk at Gunz. "I wasted too much of my precious time here with all of you. I have places to be, infections to spread," he muttered with a nonchalant twirl of his hand. "Give my love and prayers to the Ancient Master."

He laughed, and vanished without waiting for Gunz's reply, leaving him alone with War. Viggo Warrington strolled casually to him and smiled as though they were old friends.

"Zane," he said, and cleared his throat, an unusual vibe of discomfort gathering around him. "I hope you don't mind me calling you that."

Gunz shrugged, resting his back against the fence. "I believe you already called me every name possible." He glanced at War, who leaned against the railing next to him. "What can I do for you, sir? I believe our mission is over. Death is safe, the veil is still intact, and the last three seals are not broken. You can safely return to your gaming business in California."

Viggo Warrington chuckled, and there was so much bitterness in the sound of his laughter that Gunz did a double take.

"Oh, child...," whispered War, shaking his head. "It's true what they say... Ignorance is bliss."

"What are you talking about?" Gunz met War's steel eyes and shuddered. His gaze wasn't cold and indifferent like Pestilence's, or Famine's. Something in the way he behaved reminded him of Angel, and for some reason, that sent a wave of shivers down his back.

"Think back," said War. "From the moment you fought Skiper-Zmey to the moment you freed Death."

"A lot has happened between now and then." Gunz shrugged. "What exactly—" He cut himself off, staring at Viggo.

War flicked his eyebrow at him. "You have to think, son. Being one of the Horsemen, I'm gifted—or perhaps burdened—with the gift of sight. However, the rules are strict, and I have no right to reveal to you what I see. No matter what, I must remain neutral. Taking sides would trigger the kind of consequences no one here wants to see. So, think, Zane."

"But you already helped us by letting us use your horses to find Death," objected Gunz. "Why can't you tell me what's going on?"

"But we didn't help *you*," said Viggo Warrington, running his fingers over his unshaved chin. "We helped one of us—Death. So, think." He tapped him on his shoulder and added, "Think out loud."

Gunz swallowed and rubbed his forehead.

"Okay... Like I said... A lot has happened since our fight with the Lord of Chaos. We were under constant pressure—all of us... running all over the realm and the Land of Dreams. All the evil Morena had released from the Dark Nav—Rasputin,

Ivan the Terrible, hundreds of phantoms, and God only knows what else—they kept us busy. And then Chernobog's scamming didn't help either..."

He stopped talking, his mind racing with all the thoughts, images of the past few years flashing before his eyes.

"It was a nonstop roller coaster with no time to stop and think," he continued, rubbing the back of his neck. "Then some Master of the Dark Arts managed to compromise the Destiny Council and all their organizations... They pushed all of us into a corner, making me..." His voice trailed off, and he stared at War as understanding washed over him like an icy wave.

"They made you what?"

"They broke me, Viggo," said Gunz quietly, averting his gaze. "I had no fight left in me. All I wanted to do was drop everything and leave the realm of humans. I still do..." He took a sharp breath that sounded almost like a gasp.

"So?"

"A while ago, Aidan told me that it was my destiny to face the Lord of Chaos in the final battle. Something about my destiny being set in motion? So, if I leave—"

"Say it, child."

"Oh God, I can't leave," whispered Gunz, a painful realization making his heart sink to his knees. He raised his eyes at the Horseman. "I can never stop fighting, can I... And I don't even know if Skiper-Zmey is the only evil I have to face... The enchantment that required the Living-Dead Flame and the blood of an Archangel. Was that... please no..."

"Say what's on your mind, Salamander!"

"Are you saying that Skiper-Zmey was just a decoy?" Gunz hid his face in his hands for a moment, a dreadful feeling turning his muscles into weak mush. Then he lifted his head and cleared his throat. "Morena, Zmey, the followers of Chaos... All this time we were busy fighting shadows? While the real evil was free to—" He fell silent, staring at War in horror, all his muscles laden with fear.

"I said nothing of the sorts." Viggo's lips stretched into a short-lived, lopsided grin. "You said it, Fire Salamander. And you were right, but not entirely."

"Viggo, please, I can't deal with riddles," said Gunz, bowing his head, "I'm too tired."

"I know you are." Viggo Warrington pushed off the fence and turned to face Gunz. A strange shadow crossed his features as he raked his hand through his hair, pushing it off his face. He put both his hands on Gunz's shoulders and squeezed slightly. "In a few minutes, a man whom you despise will come to summon you and your friends. You will not argue with him. You will not fight him. You will go with him willingly. All I want you to do is open your mind and listen, son. Do you understand me?"

"Yes, sir."

Viggo Warrington sighed and lowered his arms, his mouth set in a hard line. "Don't just listen, hear… And stand by Kalidus. He loves you as only a true Father can love his son."

"Yes, sir," whispered Gunz, barely moving his lips, thousands of chaotic thoughts swirling through his mind, spiking the fire energy around him, making his eyes glow with the magic of the Dark Codex.

"I must go now," said War. "If you ever need my help, you know how to find me. After all, you're a Child of War just as much as you are a Child of Fire." He flashed his lopsided smirk at Gunz and vanished with a light pop.

CHAPTER 42

~ ZANE BURNS, A.K.A. GUNZ ~

"Gunz!" Tessa ran up to him, throwing her arms around his shoulders. He grunted as every cell in his body responded to her light touch with nagging soreness.

"I'm a little dirty," mumbled Gunz, holding his hands up awkwardly.

"I'm so glad to see you here and in one piece," she said, ignoring his words. "Mrak said Aidan is with the Destiny Council... I wish he were here too." She whispered the last words, unlocking her arms and dropping her head low.

Gunz gently lifted her face and searched her red-rimmed eyes. "What happened here?"

He observed everyone in the kitchen and frowned. Mrak Delar sat on the table with his shirt off while Hawk and Missi were taking care of his injuries, applying a dressing and some ointment with a sharp, unpleasant odor. Theron and two large men stood by the window, their faces gray from exhaustion and grief. Yaroslav wasn't in the room, and Gunz assumed that with his thirst getting worse, the vampire didn't want to be around bleeding wounds.

"Where are Karma and Raoul?" he asked, his throat dry.

Tessa didn't answer, but her eyes filled with tears.

"Raoul is fine," replied Theron. "More or less. He had to leave. I don't know if Kal told you, but the Grand Master of the Wardens Order is dead." He fell silent, staring uncomfortably at his hands clenched together.

"Karma is dead. I'm sorry," said Hawk quietly without raising his head as he kept applying bandages over Mrak's injuries. "Last night, when the Guardians attacked the ranch, she was killed and so were three members of my pack. I'm surprised neither Aidan nor Kal told you."

"We were a little preoccupied..." Gunz dropped his head, sorrow shredding his insides. "I'm sorry too..." His throat closed up and he fell silent, leaning his shoulder against the doorframe powerlessly.

"We buried them right away in the pack's cemetery," continued Hawk. His voice was void of emotions and lifeless, and even though he didn't lift his face, his hand with the bandages shook. "You know, werewolves' traditions. We don't keep our dead in funeral homes and morgues. What's dead shouldn't be in the realm of the living. If you want to say your goodbyes, Theron can show you the way. It's not far."

Before Gunz could answer, a sound of a short struggle on the outside interrupted him. He snapped around and stilled, ready to spring into action. The entrance door hit the wall as someone kicked it open with considerable force, and a moment later, Commander Moore walked into the kitchen, holding Yaroslav by the scruff of his neck. The vampire didn't fight him, but an expression of utter misery shadowed his features.

A deep growl rumbled in Gunz's chest, and without thinking twice, he pulled his Swiss army knife out of his pocket, turning it into the sword. *A man whom you despise will come to summon you and your friends. You will not argue with him. You will not fight him.* Viggo Warrington's words flashed through his mind, and he lowered his sword.

"Let. Yaroslav. Go," he said quietly through gritted teeth, pronouncing one word at a time, everything inside him shaking with anger.

Moore snickered and shoved the vampire at Gunz strong enough to unbalance both of them. Yaroslav staggered forward but managed to keep his footing. He spun around with a loud hiss, his fangs expanded, katana in his hand.

The Commander didn't blink an eye. He pointed at Gunz, Yaroslav, Mrak Delar and said in a businesslike tone of voice, "You, you and you"—his eyes stopped on Missi and Tessa and he pointed at them too—"and you two are summoned. Follow me."

He waved his hand, muttering something under his breath, and a door blazing with a white light materialized in front of him. "I suggest going willingly, without fighting, Burns," he added mockingly, pointing at the portal.

"Wasn't going to," muttered Gunz as he converted his sword into the knife and put it away in his pocket. He watched Mrak Delar pulling a fresh shirt over his battered body awkwardly and then helped him off the table. The Master of Power winced but didn't say anything and headed toward the door.

Gunz waited until Yaroslav, Missi and Tessa crossed the threshold, and then turned to the Commander, who was waiting for him with a patronizing smirk on his face.

"Just curious." Gunz tilted his head slightly, returning the smirk. "Are all Destiny Enforcers such perverted assholes, or are you a special case?"

"A special case." Moore burst into a loud guffaw, slapping his thighs with his hands as if Gunz just told him the best joke. He cut his laughter abruptly, seized Gunz's neck and pushed him through the door.

* * *

THE MAIN CHAMBER of the Destiny Council's building was barely illuminated by the flickering light of the magical orbs. They danced around the perimeter of the room, moving slowly in a clockwise motion. The heavy desk at the far end of the room was empty, and the head of the Destiny Council stood by it, quietly conversing with Kal and Aidan who sat in the first row of the stadium seating. Angel sat in the massive armchair on their right, and Uri perched on the wide arm of the chair. Both looked like they were at the end of their ropes, but at least they weren't bleeding or unconscious.

While all that looked peaceful enough, everything inside Gunz was stretched like a bowstring. He expanded his Salamander senses, checking the chamber and everyone present, but didn't register anything out of the ordinary.

The Commander walked down the steps and bowed to the Councilman. "My lord," he said. "The Fire Salamander and his team are here." He pointed in Gunz's direction.

"Thank you, Commander," said Magnus, giving Moore a quick tap on his shoulder. "You may leave now."

Moore bowed again and snapped his fingers, vanishing from the room. Magnus looked up and gestured at them to approach. "Please, come here and take a seat," he said, pointing at the first row of empty chairs. "I think it's time we all had a friendly conversation."

Gunz exchanged a quick look with Mrak Delar and walked down, his steps echoing against the tall ceiling. He halted in front of the Councilman, glancing at Kal over his shoulder. The Great Salamander gave him a tiny nod and frowned, and Gunz knew exactly what it meant.

He inclined his head in the smallest bow he could muster and greeted him dryly, "My lord."

Mrak Delar, Missi and Tessa also bowed and sat down next to Kal and Aidan, but Yaroslav remained standing, exuding discomfort from his every pore.

Magnus approached the vampire, giving him a quick once-over, and then extended his hand to him. Yaroslav looked down at his hand but didn't move. Magnus smiled wider and lowered his hand.

"I know, it's quite unusual for a member of the undead supernatural community to be invited into the Trial Chamber and survive the invitation," he said, sounding calm and friendly. "I assure you, Prince Potemkin, you're not in any danger today. None of you are. On the contrary, we summoned all of you here to extend our deepest and sincerest gratitude…" He cleared his throat and his heavy gaze halted on Gunz. "And to offer our apologies."

"That won't be necessary," said Gunz icily.

Magnus sighed, sounding crestfallen. "I understand how you feel, young Salamander—"

A fury, dark and fierce, spiraled through Gunz. For a moment he stood with his jaw set, his chest shuddering with strained breaths as he endeavored to suppress his rising fire. "You"—he took another breath, clenching his fists—"have no idea what you are talking about."

Kal, Aidan and Mrak Delar rose from their seats, ready to interfere if needed, but Yaroslav didn't move a muscle. He crossed his arms over his chest, and a deadly smirk appeared on his face.

Backing away, Gunz raised both his hands and chuckled darkly. "My lord, you are not in any danger either, but it would be a lot healthier for you if you left your apologies to yourself."

He seized Yaroslav's elbow and pulled him around the Councilman toward the seats. He sat down and took a deep breath, everything inside him still shaking.

Magnus swallowed, fear hiding in his eyes. "We'll get back to this conversation later," he said, throwing a side glance at Gunz. "Prince Potemkin, first of all, we wanted to extend our gratitude to you. You were the first person who suspected that something was wrong with our organization and were brave enough to approach the Sisterhood of the Sun—"

"I was stupid and reckless," Yaroslav cut him off. "If Aidan didn't interfere…" He shook his head. "I don't know what would have happened. Yes, I did suspect that something was off, and I wanted to find out, but there was also another reason… a personal one…" He bowed his head, a deep line etched between his eyebrows.

"I know your reason," said Magnus. "My condolences, Prince. Please tell your maker, Akira Ida, that we'll meet with her in a few days."

Yaroslav nodded but said nothing, and Magnus switched his attention to Tessa and Missi.

"Melissa and Therasia," he said, approaching the young women, "you need to go back to the Guardians Order. The situation has been restored to normal, and the Order has resumed their daily operations."

He held out his hand and two round pendants materialized in his palm—one was attached to a long gold chain and the other one was hanging on a key ring.

"My pendant?" whispered Tessa, and despite everything, happiness reflected in her eyes.

Aidan glanced at her and cringed visibly. "I didn't realize you wanted to go back to the Guardians HQ."

Magnus walked up to Tessa and put the chain around her neck. She ran her fingers over the design and glanced back at Aidan, her eyes begging him to understand.

In the meantime, Magnus approached Missi and gave her the key ring with the pendant. "If you two are ready to resume your duties in the Guardians Order, I will open the portal for you."

As Tessa and Missi got up, he waved his hand and a portal rotating with white shimmering light opened up in front of them.

"Tessa—," Aidan started.

She approached him and encircled his waist with her arms, placing her head on his chest. "I love you, my ancient god, but I need to finish what I started. Now that the Archmage is no longer controlled by the dark spell, everything is going to be different. I have to do it, my love."

He lifted her slightly, pressing her to his chest and kissed her, feeling her lips parting under his. A moment later, he pulled away and gently lowered her to the floor, his eyes slightly foggy.

"I love you...," he whispered, his lips touching her hair. "I will miss you every moment of every day, but I understand."

Tessa hugged him one more time and walked through the door, followed by Missi.

"You don't have to miss her. You can visit Therasia any time you wish, Aidan." The head of the Destiny Council closed the portal and approached him, touching his chest with two fingers.

"No!" Aidan jumped aside like from a poisonous snake, but it was too late. A pendant with a Triskele engraved on it materialized on his chest. His hand went up of its own accord, grasping at the chain. "I'm done with it! You owe me that much!"

Kal got up, putting his massive hand on Aidan's shoulder. "Magnus, Gwyn ap Nudd is not here to speak for his son, but I am," he growled, dangerous flames igniting on the bottom of his eyes. "If you were sincere in your apologies, you will release Aidan from his servitude."

"Great Salamander, please," said Magnus, "you both didn't let me finish." He turned to Aidan. "We're just the Destiny Council and there are powers in this world that are mightier than ours. You swore your loyalty, Aodh mac Lir, and you broke your oath. You've been around long enough to know the consequences of that."

Aidan bowed his head, a painful smirk curving his lips.

"So, you have a choice, god of the Otherworld," continued Magnus. "We are authorized to clear all charges against you if you agree to honor your oath. Just one year and no more extensions. Your other option is to run your entire life, branded as an oath-breaker."

"No," growled Kal. "No more servitude. You will clear all the charges and let him live in peace."

"I wish I could." Magnus threw his hands in the air. "I am just a messenger here. But, Aidan, if you let me finish, there is a chance you're not going to hate the idea of working with us that much."

"Go on," said Aidan, stopping Kal.

"Just one year—no extensions, no conditions, no gimmicks," continued Magnus, speaking faster. "You will no longer report to the Guardians Order. We need you to assist the Wardens. Actually, one Warden in particular. And you're not going to be working for him, but with him."

"Who?" asked Aidan.

"Father Raoul de Beaumont," said the head of the Destiny Council. "As you are all well aware, the Grand Master of the Order is dead. Father Collins is going to take his place in Paris. It means Raoul will have to handle all the affairs of the Order in Florida on his own. With everything that's going on, we can't reallocate another member of the Order to help him, and he needs someone who's more powerful than he is. We must preserve the knowledge he's guarding. Raoul gave up a lot to help you all, from what I understand. So, Aodh mac Lir, will you help him?"

Aidan rubbed his forehead tiredly. "You don't need this." He pointed at the pendant on his chest. "Remove it, and I will help Raoul willingly. I am sure I speak for everyone here when I say that if Raoul will ever need our assistance, we are all going to be there for him."

"I can't. You don't' understand... I don't have such power," said Magnus. He sounded so tired and dejected that Gunz actually started to believe him against his better judgement. "I swear on my power. This pendant is just a key that will open all the Destiny Council's doors for you. It's not a collar, not a leash, and not a symbol of servitude. Just one year, and your oath is cleared. After that, you can either keep the pendant or melt it."

Aidan glanced at Kal, and the Great Salamander nodded, throwing his hands up in resignation. He wasn't pleased, and he didn't even try to hide it. Magnus sighed and turned to Gunz, his heavy gaze pinning him in place.

"Young Salamander," said Magnus, but Gunz shook his head, raising his hand up.

"I already told you," he said quietly. "I don't want your apologies. I don't want to hear that you have been controlled by some spell and how sorry you are for…" He shook his head again, swallowing the thick lump in his throat. "Just let it be."

"Fine, fine." Magnus backed away from him and walked to the side of the room. "I'm not going to say anything, but I want to show you something… someone…"

He moved his fingers, drawing invisible symbols in the air, and a tall cage materialized on his left. Gunz cringed inwardly as the memory of Mrak's trial flashed in his mind. Slowly, he got up and walked toward the cage, all his muscles stiff. A man lay on the cold marble tiles. His wrists, locked by Destiny cuffs, were attached to a thick iron ring embedded into the floor. Gunz stared at him, everything inside him wound up like a tight spring.

"What is this?" he croaked, his fingers wrapping around the bars. "What the hell is this?"

Magnus approached him and stared down at the prisoner. "This is Liam Porter—the man who tortured you, Mr. Burns," he explained, tones of regret in his voice. "And if you think he was controlled by the spell, I assure you, he wasn't. He wasn't affected by the dark magic, so everything he put you through, he did of his own volition."

Magnus touched the bars, and they disappeared. Liam

flinched like a person waking up from a heavy sleep and lifted his head. As his eyes settled on Gunz's face, he roared like a caged animal and launched at him. Stopped by the length of his chain, he dropped to his knees, breathing heavily.

Gunz looked down at the prisoner and anger slowly boiled up in him, threatening to spill. "Why, Liam?" he whispered, fighting to stay in control.

"Why?" Liam raised his head, staring directly in his eyes, and laughed. "I guess I didn't beat you enough, fireworm. You still don't get it!"

Torturously slow, Gunz turned toward Magnus but couldn't say a word. His power and magic bubbled up inside him, creating an explosive concoction.

"Mr. Burns, this wizard is no longer employed by the Destiny Council," said Magnus, inching away from him. "He's yours to do as you wish."

"I don't... understand...," Gunz muttered, the semi dark room flowing around him in a slow nauseating manner.

Liam chuckled. "Aw, my lord, you need to explain yourself better. For a Fire Salamander, this one is not that fast on the uptake." Liam winked at the Councilman, a grimace of disdain on his youthful face. Then he switched his attention to Gunz, and his blue eyes darkened with so much hatred that Gunz shuddered. "Too bad I don't have my belt on me. I think before that long-haired mongrel interrupted us, I was getting some points across quite nicely, don't you think? We were just getting to the third base of our wonderful relationship."

Gunz froze. Even his heart stopped beating. Everything around him ceased to exist. All he could feel was unadulterated rage expanding within him to the level he could no longer control. All he could hear was the pounding of his pulse in his ears. Before he could think about what he was doing, his sword was in his hands. He raised it above his head and plummeted it down at the young man.

Liam didn't move, staring at him without blinking. The blade struck the iron ring, breaking the chain that connected the cuffs to the floor. Shaking from head to toe, Gunz screamed, raising his sword again.

"Go ahead," hissed Liam, "do it. You have already taken everything from me. My life is the only thing you can take now…"

Breathing hard, Gunz lowered his sword—a move that was more painful than he was ready to admit. He stared down at the young man and shook his head, feeling the anger simmering down in him.

"No, Liam, I'm not going to kill you," he said, every word taking a significant effort. "You're not that lucky. Besides, I do feel responsible for the monster you have become."

He turned around and looked at his mentor. Kal got up, staring at him intently, his shoulders tensed. Aidan, Yaroslav and Mrak were already standing, but none of them made a move to stop him.

"Father, I don't know anyone who can instill manners as well as you do," he said softly. "Do you think you can teach this sorry excuse of a human being what it means to be a wizard and a man? I don't think his parents ever succeeded in doing that…" He thought for a moment, his eyes returning to Liam, and added with a cold smile. "And Father? If you ever feel compelled to apply some of your *special* medieval methods of education, feel free to do anything you think is right."

Kal approached Gunz, placing his hand on his shoulder, and stared down at Liam with the kind of smirk that promised the young man nothing good.

"I think I can do that, son, and maybe more." He turned to the head of the Destiny Council. "Magnus, do you mind taking his cuffs off?"

"Not at all," mumbled Magnus, cold sweat glistening on his

face. He touched the cuffs with his finger, and they unlocked with a soft metallic click.

Kal grabbed Liam by the scruff of his neck and waved his hand, opening his portal.

"I'll be back in ten minutes," he promised and disappeared behind the wall of fire, pulling Liam along.

CHAPTER 43

~ ZANE BURNS, A.K.A. GUNZ ~

Gunz sat down and leaned forward slightly, lowering his face into his hands. No one tried talking to him, and he was grateful for the few minutes of silence. As promised, Kal returned ten minutes later and sat down on a seat next to Gunz, tapping him on his knee.

Gunz lifted his face and saw Uri and Angel standing next to Magnus. They didn't talk, but Angel's gaze directed at Aidan triggered a few warning bells in Gunz's mind, and the expression of sympathy in his eyes didn't make him feel any better. He was about to get up and approach Angel when Magnus raised his hand, asking for attention.

"As unpleasant as it was for most of us, the official part of our meeting is over, but there is something else we must discuss." While his voice was calm and soft, there was something about his overall appearance that just reinforced Gunz's feeling of dread. "Grim Horseman, you may proceed."

Angel gave a start, rubbing the back of his neck. For a moment, he looked a little lost, like a person who didn't know where to start.

"Angel, who held you imprisoned?" asked Mrak Delar.

"We don't know," replied Angel, throwing a sideway glance at Uri. "Whoever this man was, the Followers of Chaos assisted him and obeyed his every command as if he were the Zmey himself. He appeared and disappeared as he pleased. Always surrounded by a veil of dark mist, we could never see his face or distinguish his energy signature. He didn't seem corporeal either... More like a shadow or a ghost."

"I believe he is a god," interjected Uri. "One of the ancient ones. He never spoke a word to us except for a few incantations and spells he needed to cast, and while we couldn't recognize his energy signature, I'm positive he's not a Master of the Dark Arts but an evil deity. Even in his incorporeal state, he was more powerful than any dark wizard I'd ever met."

Kal exchanged a quick look with Aidan and nodded. "Gwyn ap Nudd and I suspected as much. So, what did he want from you?"

Angel lowered his head, his hands squeezing into fists. "Unfortunately, he got from both of us everything he wanted," he whispered so softly that even Gunz with his sharp Salamander's hearing could barely make out his words. "From me, he needed the essence of Death to create the Living-Dead Flame. But since I refused to comply with his demands and open the void, he needed the blood of an Archangel to do it—"

"Hold it right there, Angel," said Kal, raising his hand. "To create the Living-Dead Flame, they need a Fire Salamander. I'm the Fire Elemental and I assure you, there are only two Fire Salamanders and both of them are here." He jerked his thumb toward Gunz. "He couldn't complete the incantation."

Angel raised his dark eyes, and a pained expression crossed his strong face. "I still can't believe it's real...," he whispered with a barely visible shake of his head. "There was one more Fire Salamander, Kal, and you had no idea he existed. No one knew..." He fell silent, observing every person in the room. "This man was in his late twenties when he was captured. He didn't even know what he was…"

Angel looked away, a muscle twitching in his jaw, and his shoulders sagged. Normally lighthearted and cheerful in his human form, now he looked like he had aged twenty years in one minute.

"To make a long story short…," he continued at length. "They have kept him imprisoned, torturing him, since nineteen-forty-two. I can only guess what kind of enchantment they placed on the castle—the entire realm even—that neither the Fire Elemental nor Semargl could sense the presence of a Child of Fire."

"Impossible," Kal exhaled, throwing a quick glance at Gunz.

"Yet it is the truth," said Angel. "This man was so tortured that he was willing to die just to stop it all. Besides, I don't think he knew the consequences of what he was doing… He walked through the Black Fire and completed the spell, creating and stabilizing the Living-Dead Flame."

"Dammit." Mrak Delar got up sharply and winced, bending forward slightly. "Now they can break Veles' curse and free Skiper-Zmey at any time. There is absolutely nothing we can do to stop them."

"You're right, Master," agreed Uri, "but unfortunately this is not the worst news."

"What could be worse than the Lord of Chaos rising again?" asked Gunz, memories of the fight for Mount Karasova flashing before his eyes. "The last time, we threw everything we had at him and we barely made it. If not for Angelique's sacrifice—" He cut himself off and clenched his jaw.

"What could be worse?" A painful laughter broke through Uri's tightly pressed lips. "The Lord of Chaos times three." He took a deep breath, rubbing his scarred knuckles with his thumb. "I believe we're dealing with a dark triple."

"Can I die now?" murmured Gunz, covering his eyes with his hand.

"Who?" asked Mrak Delar and Kal at the same time.

"Angel, you said they opened the void." Aidan got up, his pale face covered in small droplets of sweat. "Why? What did they bring out from the void?" His voice trembled and disappeared into the heavy silence that enveloped the chamber.

Angel and Uri exchange a heavy look. "I'm sorry, Aidan," said Uri softly, "but the answer to this question will affect you more than anyone else."

"Say it," hissed Aidan, his fingers clutching at his throat as if he couldn't breathe.

"Aidan." Angel approached him, putting his hand on his arm. "I'm sorry, my friend, but your stepmother walks the realm of the living again."

Aidan let out a harsh breath, as though Angel's words somehow gave him relief. "I knew it... I could feel her foul presence from the moment we destroyed the dark spell here, in the Destiny Council realm..."

"We think that these three—Aoife, Skiper-Zmey through his close followers, and the unknown dark entity—had a plan, and it has been put in motion years ago," continued Uri. "Everything that's been going on in the last few years is just a part of their elaborate design, and unless we learn what it is, we can't stop them."

"I was right," mumbled Gunz more to himself than to anyone else. "The Lord of Chaos was nothing but a decoy to keep us all busy and our attention away from the real problem."

"Yes and no," said Magnus. "Skiper-Zmey did what he was supposed to do and so did Aoife, but they weren't just a diversion. Darkness is rising, and I'm sure both the Lord of Chaos and the immortal air demon still have a part to play."

"You're probably right, Magnus. At least it makes sense,"

agreed Mrak Delar. "Here is what doesn't. All this time, I believed no one except Death could open the void."

"That's exactly what gave me the idea that the head of this unholy triple is an ancient god." Uri leaned against the desk, folding his arms. "Only ancient beings of tremendous power are privy to this knowledge."

"Like Chernobog?" supplied Gunz, cringing at the thought that the god of Destruction could have played them all.

Uri glanced at him with interest but shook his head. "Chernobog or his twin brother, or any of the oldest gods of any pantheon would know something about it. But as dark and twisted as Chernobog is, I'm positive it's not him. Believe it or not, the energy of this deity felt a lot darker than that of the god of Destruction."

A heavy blanket of silence enveloped the chamber again, and no one dared say a word. Every person in the room was drained by the overuse of their magic, barely keeping an upright position from physical exhaustion, and there wasn't much to say anyway. Gunz glanced at Aidan. The news about the air demon rising seemed to have taken the life out of the god of the Otherworld. With his shoulders slumped and his head bowed down, he looked like a shadow of his former self.

"I need to go back to the Otherworld and speak with my father," said Aidan flatly. "He is in danger too. I don't know what's coming, but we must be ready to defend Gwyn's domain and the magical nexus that lies beneath the Otherworld."

"Aidan—" Gunz got up but cut himself short, not sure what he was going to say.

"I'm glad Tessa is with the Guardians again." Aidan glanced down at him but averted his gaze almost immediately. "I hate to put more pressure on you, Zane, but I must help Gwyn. The veil, the Otherworld, and the Isle of Legends cannot fall to the dark forces. Can I count on you in case Tessa needs help?"

"Why is it even a question?" Gunz smirked tiredly and waved

his hand around. "You can always count on any of us, Aidan. And so can Tessa."

Aidan nodded, extending his hand to him, and Gunz squeezed it in a firm handshake. There was something so despondent and gloomy in his friend's eyes that his heart gave a painful jolt.

"We fought them before and won," Gunz said quietly. "We can do it again. You're not going to face this immortal air-bitch alone."

Aidan smiled weakly. "I know. I just need a little rest, probably. Maybe twenty-four hours of uninterrupted sleep or so."

"I wouldn't mind that either," replied Gunz with a lopsided smirk.

Aidan waved his hand, opening a blazing white door, but before he could walk through it, Magnus stopped him.

"Aidan, I would like you to take Prince Potemkin with you," he said, and Yaroslav got up, his eyebrows slowly rising. "Gwyn ap Nudd believes Yaroslav needs to see something, and quite frankly, I agree with him."

Yaroslav turned to Gunz. "I'll return to the human realm as soon as I can," he said softly, his blue eyes filled with sadness. "I'll find you."

"Shouldn't be hard, considering our blood bond. You can probably sense me no matter which world or nexus I am in?"

"True. I can also sense when you're in distress." Yaroslav threw a scorching stare at Magnus. He bowed to Mrak Delar and Kal and followed Aidan through his blazing door.

Magnus waited until the door closed and shivered like from a cold wind. "The vampires give me the heebie-jeebies," he muttered, rubbing his arms with his hands.

"Well, I don't know about the rest of the vampires, but this one should," growled Mrak Delar, rising with visible effort. "After all, he's the only remaining descendant of Dracula, is he not?" His full lips stretched into a deadly smile, and Gunz knew that the Master of Power was slowly shifting toward his dark side. "Listen, Magnus, with everything that's coming, I believe we all have our hands full now. But there is one thing I wanted to warn you about."

"Of course, Master, what is it?"

Mrak Delar draped his arm around the Councilman's shoulder, and his smile grew considerably wider and more sinister.

"You know me well enough. I'm not big on playing by the rules. So, consider what I'm about to say with full seriousness." He chuckled, directing him toward Gunz. "You see this young man?" He jerked his chin at Gunz, and his fingers dug deeper into Magnus' shoulder while his voice got colder, morphing into a dangerous growl. "He's my friend. Just like Aidan and Yaroslav and Tessa and the rest of our little team. So, hear me well... If I catch you just look the wrong way at him..."

Mrak Delar closed his eyes, and when he opened them again, they were flooded with darkness. He turned Magnus to face him and then spread his arms. Blinding lightning spliced the air, forking into the floor between them, and he laughed—the sound of his laughter so ominous and grim that Gunz couldn't help but shudder.

"Master, what are you—," Magnus whimpered, unable to move.

"What I am trying to say, Magnus, is that if I hear that you mistreated him in any way, there will be no place in this world, or any other world, where you'll be able to hide from my wrath!" boomed Mrak Delar, and mighty thunder rumbled through the chamber, making its walls tremble.

"I second that," murmured Kal with a light twirl of his hand, flames rising on the tips of his fingers.

Mrak Delar laughed again and released his power. "Your Destiny Enforcers won't be able to save you either. I promise." He winked at the mortified Councilman in a most friendly manner. "Well, now that we settled that, I'll be going back to

Kendral. I want to discuss the situation with Master Alliandr and do some light reading in the Riders' Library. After all, we still don't know who that dark entity is."

"That's a wonderful idea, Master." Magnus smiled, but his eyes remained wide and terrified, large drops of sweat sliding down his cheeks. "You're known as the wisest and most knowledgeable Master of Power since Master Azor himself."

"Am I now?" purred Mrak Delar, winking at Gunz. "Then please allow me to bid my farewell." He bowed to Magnus, but his elegant bow was filled with mockery to the brim. Then he looked up at Kal and raised his eyebrow. "Great Salamander?"

Kal smirked, putting his hand on Gunz's shoulder. "I believe my son and I will join you, Master."

Gunz gaped at Kal, unable to speak coherently. He'd never doubted that if push came to shove, both his mentor and the Ancient Master would stand by his side, but he'd never seen them openly rebel against the higher power like the Destiny Council just to protect him. He bit his lip, his heart expanding with warmth.

"But Great Salamander?" squeaked Magnus, his eyes darting between Gunz, Kal and Mrak Delar. "I'm sorry, but the young Salamander cannot leave with you. He is the Great Fire Salamander, the protector of the human realm. He is the only one who—"

"Correct me if I am wrong, Councilman," said Kal with a light bow. "Just a short while ago, the Destiny Council abducted my son and kept him imprisoned. Who was protecting the realm of humans then?"

"We were under a spell!" Magnus shouted, slamming his hand against the side of the desk. "We can't be held responsible for that."

"I don't care," said Kal with an indifferent shrug. "My son needs time and rest to recover after everything that has been done to him. Period. I'm taking him home whether you like it or not."

"My lord," said Gunz, trying to sound as respectfully as he could muster. "Since the evil trio has the Living-Dead Flame already, there is nothing we can do to stop them from raising the Lord of Chaos. Am I right?"

"Yes," grumbled the Councilman, dropping into a chair.

"But here is what we can and should do," continued Gunz. "Neither Aoife nor the dark god made their presence known yet. It means they're still not ready for the final chapter of their plan. It's the calmness before the storm, and we don't know how long it will last. We must use this time wisely. We need to get ready to protect our realms—human and magical—and prepare for a war. We must learn as much as possible about our adversary and see what we can do to stop them." He glanced at Kal, noticing warm sparkles in his mentor's flaming eyes. "It's not about me needing some rest, Father... although to be honest, I desperately need it."

Gunz sighed, running his hand over his cheeks, feeling the roughness of his stubble under his fingers.

"The young Salamander is right, Magnus," said Mrak Delar. "We need to use this time to regroup and get ready. Aidan and Gwyn ap Nudd will reinforce the defenses of the Otherworld and the Isle of Legends. Master Alliandr and I must get ready to defend Kendral. Gunz is coming with us. He'll work with the Lady Gatekeeper on getting the Land of Dreams ready for the attack. Get your Guardians to keep an eye on Mount Karasova day and night and have all of your Enforcers at the highest alert."

Magnus pursed his lips, his eyes narrowing at the Master of Power. "All that sounds wonderful, Master, but your plan has a hole the size of Texas."

"How so?" Mrak Delar shoved his hands into the pocket of his pants, staring back at the Councilman with a cold smirk.

"The same question I asked earlier. If the Great Fire Salamander, the protector of the human realm, is gone, who is going to protect it?" Magnus pulled a small handkerchief out of his pocket and blotted his sweaty forehead.

"We will," said Angel, stepping forward. "I believe an Archangel, the Slavic god of Nature, and Death can provide enough fire power to hold on for a few minutes so you can summon the Fire Salamander from Kendral. Besides, as soon as Yaroslav comes back from the Otherworld, I'm sure he and the Scarlet Queen will stand by our side, as they usually do."

"Assuming, you will extend your personal apologies to Ms. Ida, that is," added Uri snidely.

"My lord, I just need..." Gunz lowered his eyes for a moment, and sighed. "It doesn't matter what I need. But here is what you need, sir. You need to either support us or get the hell out of our way. Because given the circumstances, we are the only people who stand between the light and the darkness. We are the first and the last lines of defense."

Magnus stiffened. Anger clouded his features for a split second, but he quickly got in control of his emotions and plastered a fake smile on his face.

"You're right," he said softly. "If everyone is in agreement, then we have a plan. So, let's use this temporary peace to get ready." He waved his hand dismissively and somehow his fake smile got brighter, or perhaps it was the shine of magic in his eyes. "That'll be all. You may go."

Angel rolled his eyes and then winked at Gunz. "See you soon, Fire Gecko." He grabbed Uri's elbow and snapped his fingers, vanishing in a cloud of dark smoke.

Coming from Death, it sounded promising. Gunz chuckled and unfolded the fiery curtain of his portal, allowing Kal and Mrak Delar to walk through it first.

EPILOGUE

* * *

~ Yaroslav ~
The Otherworld

Yaroslav glanced down at his own reflection in Gwyn's polished floor and shuddered. His leather coat was shredded and torn. His clothes and skin were covered in a thick layer of dirt, slime and brown stains of dried blood. He raked his fingers through his disheveled hair and sighed. It would take him an hour in a shower just to get his hair back to normal.

"Slavik." Aidan's voice sounded on his left, breaking his train of thought, and he glanced up.

Gwyn ap Nudd stood in front of them, his arms dangling tiredly along his sides. Seemingly, the King of the Otherworld looked the same, but there was something in the set of his shoulders and in the hard lines around his mouth that betrayed his internal turmoil and his concern.

"My lord," said Yaroslav, bowing to him.

"Yaroslav," said Gwyn quietly, his voice tired and raspy. "How are you?"

The question wasn't what he expected, and his eyebrows slowly rose. "I'm fine, my lord," he replied, shifting from foot to foot. "Thanks to your son, I'm still alive and free."

Gwyn ap Nudd nodded, his fingers running over the thin line of his mustache absentmindedly. "Listen, Yaroslav," he continued, discomfort palpable around him, "Aidan and I need to have a quick discussion. After that, my son will take you anywhere you need to go. But in the meantime, there is something I want you to see."

He paused, and Yaroslav threw a puzzled glance at Aidan, but the god of the Otherworld just shrugged, shaking his head.

"Please follow me," said Gwyn ap Nudd, gesturing at the door into the kitchen.

Yaroslav walked through the living room and into the kitchen. Even though Gwyn exhibited signs of discomfort and doubts, he wasn't concerned. He didn't feel anything, his mind blank. Despite his vampiric nature, his muscles were buzzing with exhaustion, and he wasn't sure if it was the result of the long battle he just went through, or something entirely different.

He stopped, leaning against the middle island, and looked up at the King of the Otherworld.

"Please don't hate me, my friend. I'm just trying to help you," murmured Gwyn.

He channeled the magic of the Otherworld and raised his arms, his long fingers moving as if he were playing an invisible musical instrument. As his deep voice filled every corner of the spacious room, a large portal rotating with a shimmering white light opened between him and Yaroslav. A chilly wind spun around them, ruffling Yaroslav's long hair, throwing it into his face. The light of the portal became too bright for him to handle, and he grunted, raising his arm.

As Gwyn's voice blended with the howling of the wind, Yaroslav could no longer hear anything. Blinded and deaf, he stood motionless like a statute, and when he felt a soft touch to his shoulder, he flinched and jumped aside, his hand reaching for his katana automatically.

"Yaroslav..." A familiar, soft voice touched his ears, and everything inside him crashed.

He opened his eyes and froze in place. His unbeating heart pulsed, and a thick lump stuck somewhere in his throat.

"Peyton..."

His voice, just a whisper, melted into the silence that enveloped them. He wanted to look around to see where Gwyn was, but he couldn't take his eyes off of her. She was just as beautiful as he remembered her, and those amazing blue lakes of her eyes gazed at him with so much love that everything inside him twisted with pain.

She smiled, her puffy coral lips quirking up at the corners. He wanted to reach forward and touch those luscious lips, run his fingers over her amazing copper hair that made her look like a little sunshine. But he was afraid... He was terrified of the idea that his fingers would slip through her, afraid that it was some kind of mirage or illusion created by Gwyn's magic.

"That's all I wanted," she said. "To see you just one more time. To feel the coldness of your skin under my fingers..."

Reaching forward, she brushed her fingers over his cheek, and he gasped, feeling her skin against his. She was real. Corporeal.

How is it possible? How...

With a soft moan, he pulled her into his embrace, resting his cheek atop her head. She encircled his waist, hiding her face into the crook of his neck, and held her breath.

"Are you back? Alive? How are you back?" He voiced his questions, but he wasn't sure he was ready to hear the answers.

"No. I'm dead."

The finality and sadness in her voice twisted his soul, and he wrapped his arms tighter around her. She shifted slightly and then pulled away from him.

"Yaroslav, listen to me," she said, gazing up at him. "The Destiny Council and Gwyn ap Nudd gave us this time because there is something I have to... Something you need to know, and you have to hear it from me."

He put his hands on her waist and gently lifted her, lowering her on top of the kitchen island. Bracing his arms against the countertop on either side of her, he leaned forward, dropping his head. His dirty hair cascaded down, falling on her lap, and he was glad she couldn't see his face at this moment.

"Speak," he said softly without looking at her. Her scent—so familiar, so real—invaded his senses, and his head swam with desire, his fangs expanding.

"Yaroslav, you're blaming yourself for what happened to me," she said, her fingers playing with his hair. "You must stop doing it. My death was not your doing. The woman who killed me was infected by the dark spell, and she received her orders from the Grand Master of the Sisterhood who was affected by the same spell."

She stopped threading through his hair and cupped his cheeks, forcing him to look up. He met her eyes and tears, hot scarlet drops, slid down his face, leaving red paths in dirt and dust.

"I'm sorry," he croaked, swallowing his pain. "I couldn't protect you."

"No, you couldn't." She took a napkin from the table and gently wiped the traces of blood off his face. "No one could. As long as the Destiny Council and all their organizations were controlled by the dark spell, no one was safe."

"Peyton—"

"You must stop blaming yourself. Guilt is a heavy burden, but you, my prince, have nothing to feel guilty about." She lowered her face and planted a tender kiss on his forehead. "Our relationship was doomed from the very beginning. You were a vampire, and I was a slayer. I broke the most sacred oath of the Sisterhood. I fell in love with a vampire prince... And I would do it all over again if I could."

Unable to speak, he nodded, his hands settling on her hips. She felt so real. He could hear her heartbeat, the sound of blood rushing through her veins. He had a hard time believing that she was dead.

"You must be ready for what's coming," she continued. "You must be strong and at your full power. And this guilt you're carrying around just holds you down. So, promise me, Yaroslav—"

"Anything..."

"Promise me you'll stop blaming yourself and you'll work with Zane and Aidan to stop those who are responsible for my death. Swear to me, Prince Yaroslav Potemkin."

He didn't move, everything inside him turning into cold stone. With a low growl, he pushed off the counter and unsheathed his katana. Lowering down to one knee, he placed the tip of the blade to the floor, holding its grip with both hands.

"I swear," he whispered, gazing up at her. His eyes lit up with an angry scarlet glow and his last words came out in a low hiss. "I swear, I'm not going to stop, and I'm not going to rest until all three of them are put down like rabid dogs."

Peyton jumped off the counter and kneeled before him. Softly, she took the katana from his hands and lowered it to the floor by his side. He dropped his arms powerlessly, keeping his kneeling position, unable to move. She cupped his face, tilted his head down slightly, and pressed her lips to his. He moaned softly, his entire body responding to her touch, but she pulled away almost immediately, gazing into his eyes.

"I love you, my royal pain," she whispered, a sad smile playing on her lips.

He swallowed and broke their eye contact for a moment. "I love you too."

"No, you don't." She chuckled, caressing his cold cheek. "And it's okay. I always dreamed about hearing those words from you... So, thank you for saying it."

Her voice got distant and hollow. White sparkles surrounded her body as it became transparent and slowly, she disappeared. Yaroslav sat back on his heels, his fingers fidgeting with the edge of his torn shirt. With his mind blank and hollow, he didn't think. He couldn't. He just sat there, unmoving and tired.

"Slavik?"

He raised his head and saw Aidan, his face shadowed by concern.

"I'm okay." Yaroslav picked up his katana and sheathed it as he rose to his feet.

"Do you want to stay here and get some rest first?" asked Aidan.

"No," he replied evenly. "I need to go back to Arizona and then home. I believe we all have a job to do. Can you take me to Hawk's ranch, please?"

* * *

AIDAN DROPPED YAROSLAV off just outside the border of Hawk's property. Ignoring the discomfort of being under the bright Arizona sun, the vampire slowly walked to the fence. Leaning on the railing, he observed the property and smirked. He knew what he needed to do next. Placing two fingers in his mouth, he whistled.

"Sivka-Burka, come!" he shouted, hoping that Siv was still

hanging around the ranch and hadn't returned to the Land of Dreams.

Before he finished the summoning call, the magical stallion materialized next to him. "You called?" he neighed, hitting the ground with his hoof.

Yaroslav nodded. Approaching the horse, he patted his neck, threading his fingers through his golden mane. Siv moved his ears, his purple eyes darting to Yaroslav, and then snorted.

"What's with the unusual public display of affection, defective vamp?" he asked, pushing him with his shoulder playfully. "I know you want something. So, spit it out."

Yaroslav chuckled. "How fast can you move?"

"Faster than you can fly as a bird or run as a vampire," replied the stallion, a light touch of arrogance in his voice.

"Perfect," Yaroslav whispered to himself and added louder, "That's exactly what I need now. Speed…"

"Why?"

"Speed lets me think better."

"Think? I had no idea you knew how to do that," neighed Siv, baring his white choppers. Yaroslav growled, displaying his fangs, and the stallion backed away, snickering. "Never mind that. Hop on, if you know how to ride without a saddle, that is."

In one fluid move, he flew on top of Siv's back and grabbed his mane. The magical stallion pushed off the ground, rising high in the air.

"Where to?"

"I have a few things I need to take care of, but before I go anywhere, I need to get some rest and clean up. How do you feel about visiting Fort Lauderdale, Florida?"

"Oh, yeah… I'm a 'hooves in the sand' kind of horse," neighed Siv, dancing in the air. "I feel good!"

Everything around him blurred as the stallion took off at an incredible speed. Yaroslav leaned forward, pressing his chest against the horse's neck, and closed his eyes, enjoying the speed and the feeling of weightlessness.

* * *

~ Zane Burns, a.k.a. Gunz ~
Kendral
One month later.

THE CLANGING of metal on metal and wild bursts of laughter carried far through the forest. Gunz sat on top of a small hill, watching Kal and Mrak Delar sparring against Lucan in a small clearing below. For the first time since he had met Kal, his mentor was suppressing his deadly fire energy. Mrak Delar, on the other hand, was cheating a little, using the power of Earth to unbalance the elf slightly.

Lucan, dressed in the Master of Kendral's personal guard uniform, was deflecting the strikes of Mrak's black sword as easily as he was avoiding the blows of Kal's massive hammer. Mishka kept circling above the fighters, shouting at them and spitting tiny fireballs, and it was hard to say who he was cheering for.

Everything looked so peaceful that for a few minutes, Gunz allowed himself to relax and not think about anything else. He lay on his back, folded his hands behind his head and closed his eyes, enjoying the warm touch of Kendral's sun to his face.

When he felt a touch to his shoulder, his lips stretched into a wide smile. "Hello, Slavik," he said without opening his eyes. "How did you get here?"

Yaroslav chuckled, and the soft rustling sound of his leather coat suggested that he sat down. "The Master of Kendral gave me permission to enter, and then Siv carried me over."

Gunz opened his eyes and pushed himself into a sitting position. Yaroslav sat next to him, his long legs bent, his arms resting atop his bent knees. His fingers were playing with a blade of grass absentmindedly as his eyes followed the fighters below. A few yards away, Siv was nibbling on the wildflowers, his golden mane sparkling with the reflected sunlight.

Gunz glanced sideways at the vampire. On one hand, he wanted to ask him a few questions, but on the other, he wasn't sure he was ready to hear the answers.

"When are you planning to go back home?" asked Yaroslav without looking at him.

Gunz sighed. "I am home."

"You know what I mean." Yaroslav turned his head to look at him.

"I don't know, Slavik," replied Gunz. "Guardians and Wardens are keeping an eye on Mount Karasova and the veil as we speak. Every day, we receive reports from them and the Destiny Council, and every day it is the same—nothing is going on. Everything is quiet in Kendral and in the Land of Dreams. If the evil-triple is up to something, they are not making their presence or intentions known."

"No, they are not," agreed Yaroslav, his voice light and distant. "But there are a few things I think you should know. I'm sure the Guardians and Wardens don't talk about it."

Gunz didn't say anything, a heavy knot twisting in the pit of his stomach. Since he discovered the Fire and was brought to Kendral to learn how to control his power, all he had wanted was to go back home, to the human realm.

Now everything felt different. Perhaps being imprisoned by the Destiny Council and everything that had been done to him changed him. Or maybe he was tired, but all he wanted was to stay here, in Kendral. He started to understand why Kal didn't want to be anywhere around humans and their affairs.

Here, in Kendral, he didn't have to live under the constant pressure of controlling his power. He didn't have to fight and bleed, deal with pain and loss. He didn't have to worry about the

Destiny Council, or about the next set of supernatural assholes who believed they had the right to rule the world.

"What's going on, Slavik?" he asked, barely able to utter the words. "If you went through the trouble of contacting the Master of Kendral and convincing this four-legged troublemaker to carry you between the two realms, it has to be important. Besides, you're sitting under the direct exposure of the sun and not complaining. Go on... tell me."

Yaroslav chuckled. "The sun here is not as bad as in the human realm." For a split second, he fell silent, gazing at him, his blue eyes filled with sadness. "You have to come back with me, Zane. We need you there. Just like you said, it's quiet around Mount Karasova and the other magical realms, but the streets of the city are turbulent.

"All sorts of supernatural scams reared their heads now. Maybe they sense that the balance between the light and the darkness is tipping toward the darkness, and that makes them believe they can do whatever they want. Or maybe they know that the Fire Salamander has left the city... But it's a bit on the hectic side. My mother's company lost quite a few fighters, as you know, and she didn't get a chance to hire new ones yet. But she is trying to assist Agent Andrews and his team as much as she can. Uri, Angel and Svyatobor are helping them too, but we still need you, my friend. Jim asked me to tell you that your position as an FBI Consultant is still available if you want to come back."

Gunz nodded and bit his lip, dropping his head.

"There is another reason I came here," said Yaroslav, and there was so much concern in his voice that Gunz lifted his head to look at him.

"What is it?"

"It's Aidan." Yaroslav rubbed his face, readjusting his position to face him. "He didn't take the news about the air demon rising well. He doesn't leave the Otherworld, and he talks only to

Tessa. But even she can't talk him into coming back to the human realm."

"I can't blame him," muttered Gunz. "I don't want to go back there either."

"Gunz," said Yaroslav, touching his knee. "You must come back, my friend. You must talk to Aidan and get him out of hiding."

"I know," murmured Gunz, a bitter smirk making a quick appearance. "When it comes to me, there is always some kind of *'must'*. No one ever tells me that I *must* relax, or I *must* have some fun."

Yaroslav chuckled and tapped him on his shoulder. "Why not?"

He rose to his feet, unsheathed his katana, and offered him his hand. Gunz took it and got up, brushing dry grass off his pants.

"Why not have some fun before we go back to the human realm?" asked Yaroslav, pointing down with his sword. "Let's show these three jokers how to use their swords properly. Besides, your brain functions better while you're fighting anyway."

Gunz laughed and manifested his sword, starting on his way down. Mrak Delar noticed their approach and spun around, a wide smile lighting up his features. His black blade met Gunz's sword with a loud bang, sending a few sparks into the air.

"I didn't say that I'll go back with you, Slavik," growled Gunz, pushing the Master of Power back.

"You didn't have to," yelled Yaroslav, easily sidestepping Lucan's strike. "You are the Great Fire Salamander, the protector of the human realm. It's in your nature."

* * *

~ Kalidus, The Great Salamander ~

Kendral
One hour later.

DEEP IN THOUGHTS, Kal walked toward his smithy. The visit of Yaroslav Potemkin, and everything the vampire had told them, gave him food for thought. He had no doubt that Gunz would return to the realm of humans with the vampire, most likely taking the Ancient Master with him, but he wasn't sure how he felt about it.

The events of the last few months rushed before his eyes, and he shivered as if suddenly he could feel cold. Gunz's lifeless, haunted eyes and the way he had dropped his humanity—that wasn't something he ever wanted his son to go through again. Not, if he could help it.

He reached the small meadow and halted at the edge of the forest, expanding his Salamander senses. The door of his hut was closed, just the way he left it, but something seemed to be different. He closed his eyes and opened his other sight, detecting a slight touch of a foreign magical energy signature. As weak as it was, he recognized it right away, and a low growl rumbled in his chest.

Crossing the clearing in two long strides, he swung the door of his smithy open and walked inside. The fire in the forge burned weakly, and in the flickering light of the flames, he saw a man sitting by the small table at the far end of the room. As soon as he noticed Kal, he got up and closed the top button of his elegant human-style business suit. His steel-gray eyes reflected the red flares of the fire, or perhaps it was his own flames dancing in his eyes.

Kal frowned, putting his massive hammer on top of the anvil. "War," he said flatly, "what are you doing here? It's not every day a Horseman of the Apocalypse visits the realm of magic."

Viggo Warrington smiled, his lips curving into a lopsided grin, and then bowed a formal Kendral bow.

"Great Salamander," he greeted him calmly, "please sit down, we need to talk."

"About?" Kal walked around the anvil and pulled the chair out, sitting down across from the Horseman.

Viggo reached into his pocket and produced a small jewelry box, pushing it across the table toward the Fire Elemental. Kal caught the box and opened it. A large, red jewel lay on the black, silk lining. He touched its smooth surface and held his breath as a powerful wave of magical energy emitted by the stone rushed through him.

"What is it?" he asked, exhaling.

Viggo raised his right hand and pointed at his ring. "The jewel of War," he explained, lowering his hand. "I need you to make a ring out of *Ardenium* steel and embed this stone into it."

"Why?" asked Kal, leaning forward slightly.

"Because *Ardenium* steel looks so-o-o pretty," murmured War sarcastically, lowering down into his chair. "You know why, Kal. *Ardenium* steel can counteract the negative forces of the Apocalypse, making the use of my power safer without the need to worry about bringing forth doomsday."

Kal rolled his eyes, pursing his thin lips. "I know that, dumb-ass," he grumbled. "Why now and why do you need the second ring?"

"Why now? You really have to ask that?" Viggo leaned forward, slamming his hand on the table. "The Darkness is here. It's not rising or coming! It is here! And you know that! My ring will give a lot more firepower to the one who wears it. Harnessing the power of War could be exactly what you need now to face the unknown dark deity and his two demented sidekicks, don't you think?"

Kal laughed coldly, leaning back in his chair, and the fire burned brighter in the forge. "Why do you care? You are the

Horseman of the Apocalypse, for fire's sake—the ultimate power of destruction. Besides, no one except you can control the energy of War anyway. So what's the point?"

"I care!" War got up sharply, and his chair fell back with a loud thud. "I care because it is deeply personal for me," he added quietly, burning Kal with his heavy gaze. "And you're right. Only my descendants and I can harness the power of War." He paused and took in a deep breath. "This is why I need you to make this ring and give it to my—"

"Gunz...," Kal exhaled, dropping his hand with the jewel on the table. "How could I miss all the signs? This is why he was able to merge with the Dark Codex. He is... the son of War... He should be more powerful than any demigod walking the human realm."

Viggo bent down and grabbed his chair, positioning it closer to Kal. "Great Salamander," he said softly, sadness curving his lips into a lopsided smile that looked so much like Gunz's. "Gunz is your son in everything that matters. Even though I've been watching him since the moment of his birth, you are his father more than I can ever be. He is a Child of Fire and the Great Fire Salamander. Knowing that his destiny was set in motion..." His voice trailed off and he averted his gaze. "I could no longer sit back and observe. He will need all the help he can get."

"Agreed." Kal got up, placing the jewel back into the box. "I will make the ring, Viggo. But now, I need to have a talk with my son... Gunz. He must know what he is."

"Wait, Kal." Viggo seized Kal's arm above his shoulder. "I don't think it's wise. It'll turn his world upside down. Right now, it's not a good time for this kind of revelation. He must focus on the war ahead, not on his genetics. We must keep it a secret, at least for a while."

Kal folded his arms, shaking War's grip off, and bent down

slightly. "You're as old as creation, Viggo, and you still haven't learned it."

"Learned what?"

"You can't keep the truth hidden forever. It doesn't matter how hard you guard your secrets. The truth will always come out. At the worst possible time, and in the worst possible manner." Kal sighed and bit his lip, frowning. "I lied to the Ancient Master, Viggo. No, I didn't lie to him, but I didn't tell him the full truth either. I made a mistake. And my boy... Gunz paid for my mistake. If only I told Mrak the truth..." He shook his head, pressing his fingers to his eyes. "Anyway, I will never lie to those I love. Keeping secrets doesn't protect them. It puts everyone in danger."

"You're right." Viggo nodded, his steel eyes flooding with sadness.

Kal waved his hand and unfolded the fiery curtain of his portal.

"Farewell, Horseman," he said softly. Then he smirked tiredly and lifted the hand with the little jewelry box. "And thank you. For everything."

Viggo Warrington raised his hand and snapped his finger, vanishing from the smithy. Kal shook his head and stepped through his portal.

Fire Salamander—go, he thought as the smoldering flames engulfed him. *Gunz, my son, I'm sorry, but you must know the truth...*

BOOK SIX: EXCERPT

Read on for an excerpt from
N.M. Thorn's new book:
The Fire Salamander Chronicles. Book 6

* * *

~ Zane Burns, a.k.a. Gunz ~
Coral Springs, Florida
Six month later...

A lonely rider moved slowly along a dark street, the sound of his horse's hooves echoing through the silence of midnight suburbia. His pale face looked almost translucent in the silvery light of the full moon, and his eyes shone with a soft, reddish glow. A light, warm breeze ruffled his long, blond hair, brushing it off his face and throwing it to his back.

Despite the warmth of the South Florida weather, he wore a long leather coat, and his tall riding boots seemed to be out of place in combination with his modern jeans and tight, black shirt. His stallion was just as unusual as the rider, its thick mane and long tail sparkling gold with the reflected glimmer of the streetlights. All in all, the pair of them didn't fit into the contemporary surroundings, looking strangely archaic and outlandish.

Crouching on the flat roof of a single-story building at the edge of a large corner plaza, Gunz watched as the rider slowly promenaded back and forth along Coral Ridge Drive. He shook his head, pursing his lips. *"Slavik, what the hell are you doing, man?"* he asked, using their blood bond. *"You and Siv stand out like a sore thumb here."*

A wide grin split Yaroslav's face, and even from this distance Gunz could see the tips of his fangs showing from under his parted lips.

"That's the idea," murmured the vampire, patting Siv's neck. *"Just keep an eye on things and be ready when the time comes. They're still far, but I can sense them already. Can you?"*

Gunz nodded, forgetting that Yaroslav most likely couldn't see him. He inhaled, detecting the barely noticeable salty odor of the ocean and the delicate scents of grass and earth. But together with the freshness of the evening, the reek of demonic essence invaded his senses, and he grunted as his stomach twitched. Sharpening his hearing, he registered the guttural roar of engines somewhere in the distance.

"I can sense them, alright." He stared in the direction of the sound, but the street remained as dark as ever. *"Demons on motorcycles."* He rolled his eyes. *"What a cliché."*

"Yeah, well..." Yaroslav's hand slowly moved down toward the hilt of his katana as he rose slightly on the stirrups. *"Just because they are a 'cliché', it doesn't make them any less dangerous."*

Yaroslav was right. It'd been a few weeks since the motorcycle gang, calling themselves *Night's Angels,* arrived seemingly out of nowhere. One day, everything was fine, and the next day, all hell broke loose. The Night's Angels invaded the streets, robbing people, burning houses, abusing and raping residents without much care for their victims' age or gender. They were equal opportunity destroyers, and since they showed up, people were afraid to sleep at night or step out of their homes after sunset.

The gang had spread around the area like a plague, and the police and national guard were helpless, all their efforts ineffective against the powerful supernatural assailants. The demons, even though they weren't pureblood abominations of Hell, seemed to be impervious to modern fire weapons. Besides, some members of the gang were rogue vampires, upirs, and even werewolves, which was quite uncommon since lycanthropes preferred to keep the company of their own kind, obeying no one but their Alphas.

Reports about similar problems flooded Jim's desk, and FBI Headquarters turned to him, expecting him to find a silver bullet solution to the quickly spreading wave of violence and chaos. Soon, it became clear that there were only two ways of killing the members of the demonic gangs—decapitation and fire. Since neither police nor national guard walked around armed with swords and incendiary devices, and exposing the World of Magic to humans wasn't an option, Akira's company had to step in.

At first, Akira refused to let Yaroslav get involved in the situation on the streets. His last disappearance had awakened motherly instincts in the ancient vampire with new strength, and like a true helicopter parent, she spread her wings over him, afraid to let him out of her sight. Unable to disobey his maker, Yaroslav stuck in the *EverSafe Security* building and no amount of begging and pleading from his side could convince Akira to change her mind.

However, after Gunz and Agent Andrews cornered her in her office, explaining why they needed Yaroslav's help, she had no choice but to agree. Reluctantly, she allowed her son to leave the building with them, but not without some stipulations—Gunz was supposed to be Yaroslav's personal bodyguard.

It'd been a while since Gunz and Yaroslav began fighting on the same side, facing the followers of Chaos and other supernatural creeps. They knew each other's strengths and weaknesses; they had the blood bond, which allowed them to communicate telepathically, and they trusted each other with their lives and beyond.

As far as Gunz was concerned, agreeing to be Yaroslav's bodyguard wasn't going to change much in their normal dynamics, and if his promise would give Akira peace of mind and Yaroslav his freedom, it was worth it.

Angel, Uri and Svyatobor came and went, showing up only when Gunz summoned them in extreme situations. However, they couldn't remain in South Florida on a constant basis, trying to contain outbursts of chaos all over the world. Aidan had never come back from the Otherworld, helping Gwyn ap Nudd reinforce the defenses around his realm and the Isle of Legends—one of four magical nexuses on Earth. Tessa had returned to the Guardians Order, and Mrak Delar remained in Kendral. So, it was up to Gunz and Yaroslav to deal with the Night's Angels and protect the city.

The short blast of a police siren ripped Gunz from his thoughts, and he leaned forward slightly, ready to jump off the roof and get involved if needed. The red and blue lights sliced through the darkness, reflecting in the windows of the vacant units of the plaza as a single police cruiser approached Yaroslav, signaling him to stop.

He halted and inclined his head respectfully, giving the police officer a tightlipped smile. "What can I do for you, sir?" he asked softly, carefully covering his katana with the side of his coat.

The policeman, a stout man in his late fifties, walked out of his vehicle, his right hand trembling slightly over his gun holster in the best traditions of western movies. Gunz snickered. He knew perfectly well that Yaroslav could rip this man apart with his bare hands before he could even think about pulling his gun out.

"Sir," said the policeman sternly, "step out of your—" He cut himself off and cleared his throat uncomfortably. "Just, um"—he twirled his hand in Siv's direction—"get off your horse. Hold your hands where I can see them."

Yaroslav dismounted and raised his arms up. "License and registration for my vehicle?" he asked in all seriousness, but the wild twinkles of suppressed laughter danced in his eyes. Siv snorted loudly in a very much un-horse-like manner. Gunz made a move to get off the roof, but as if sensing his intentions, Yaroslav glanced in his direction and gave him a tiny shake no.

"Don't get smart with me, son," grumbled the policeman, his face red from either annoyance or the reflected lights of his car. He lowered his hand on the handle of his gun, ready to give another command, when Yaroslav tensed and looked to his left, his hand reaching under his coat for his sword automatically.

"*Yaroslav, get ready. They're coming... Many of them,*" said Gunz as a wave of demonic essence assailed his senses with the new strength. "*You need to get rid of this cop.*"

"Officer," said Yaroslav, turning back to the policeman, his voice friendly but firm, "I'm sorry to cut the entertainment short, but I need you to get back into your car and leave. It's not safe for you to be here."

The older man's jaw dropped, and he all but hopped in place. Pulling his gun out, he pointed it at Yaroslav's chest and shouted, "Turn around slowly. Hands behind your head. Let's see what you're gonna sing after a night in jail, smartass punk."

Yaroslav sighed. Still holding his arms up, he reached with his right hand and pulled the sleeve of his coat down, exposing a thick, leather bracelet on his left wrist. It was bright red, and the black logo of *EverSafe Security* was clearly visible even in the unsteady light of the surroundings.

The officer's eyes widened, and his eyebrows climbed up as he stared at the red bracelet. "Are you an employee of Ms. Ida's company?" he managed to say finally, putting his gun away.

"I'm Yaroslav Potemkin, part-owner of *EverSafe Security*, sir," replied the vampire, lowering his arms. "I'm sorry, but the shit is about to hit the fan here, and you're not equipped to handle what's coming. Please, allow me and my team to do what has to be done without endangering human lives. I need you to leave."

The policeman stared at him, flabbergasted. "But you're alone. Where is your backup, your team?" he mumbled, staring around wildly. "You're just a boy…"

The bright headlights of the upcoming motorcycles lit up the air at the far end of the street and the roar of their engines became louder. In one swift motion, Yaroslav mounted Siv and pulled his katana out.

"I'm a dangerous boy," he hissed, pointing the blade in the direction of the police cruiser. "I'll be all right if you let me do my job. Leave now, sir."

As the policeman hopped into his car, shut down the lights and left, Gunz switched his attention to the approaching gang. Being in the middle of South Florida suburbia, he couldn't use his elemental energy, and knowing what was coming, he needed all the help he could get. He channeled his magic and connected with the Dark Codex. As the instant headache blinded him for a split second, he grunted, planting his fist against the warm metal roof.

"Slavik, I'm ready," he growled. *"I can see them."*

Before he finished his statement, the silence exploded with the thundering of engines, and the darkness shied away from the blazing beams of the motorcycles' headlights. Gunz couldn't quite count how many gangsters were in the group. They barged into the area, laughing and screaming profanities, but as soon as they saw Yaroslav and Siv, they slowed down and surrounded them, swarming around them like a bunch of vultures.

"Gunz, stand down and watch the road," hissed Yaroslav. "There are less than thirty of them here. But judging by the amount of negative energy I can sense, there should be a lot more. Something is not right. Once I get them off their bikes, I can deal with them on my own."

"I know. Try to get them off the road and into the plaza," murmured Gunz, an intense feeling of unease spreading through him, making his shoulders ache. Both Akira and Jim had directed them here. Each of them stated that they received intel placing Night's Angels in this neighborhood at this time. They wanted Yaroslav and Gunz not only to protect the residents and vanquish the demons, but also learn what they were searching for.

The bikers came to a screeching halt, and the demonic energy spiked around them to a new high, permeating the air with its suffocating stench. Brandishing their chains, clubs infested with metal spikes, swords and knives, they got off their bikes and moved closer to Yaroslav. The vampire didn't blink an eye, staring down at them calmly.

"What can I do for you, gentlemen?" he asked softly, relaxing his posture as he lowered his sword arm down.

A large demon, dressed in leather pants and a vest with the gang's name on the back, stepped forward, planting his feet wide apart. With his long, overly muscled arms, and massive chest and shoulders, he was living proof of Darwin's theory of evolution. His narrow forehead with a low hairline just added to his resemblance to an ape.

He halted next to Siv, taking in Yaroslav's appearance, and his thick lips stretched into an ugly sneer. Tapping his metal club on the palm of his hand, he turned to his gang, flicking his bushy eyebrow.

"This one is a vamp, yah know?" He jerked his chin at Yaroslav and pointed his club at one of the gangsters. "Your kind, Dick. Wanna have a word with him before I tear him a new one?"

A vampire, presumably Dick, stepped forward, followed by at least ten more vampiric members of the gang. He cocked his head, his uneven smirk exposing his dangerous blade-like fangs.

"Long, blond hair," he hissed, his eyes shining scarlet. "Katana. I bet you anything, this is Yaroslav Potemkin. If I'm right, he stopped being my kind when his maker, the Scarlet Queen, sided with humans, fighting against us."

Yaroslav smirked and waved his hand at the vampire lazily. "Bell bottom jeans, obnoxious polyester shirt... Hmmm, let me guess?" He tapped his finger against his lips. "In the beginning of the seventies, you were turned accidentally by a drunk vampire who was getting high on your LSD-spiced blood?"

The vamp howled in anger and launched himself at Yaroslav. The katana swooshed through the air, and flakes of gray ash fell to the ground in the place where the vampire Dick had been standing just a second ago. The rest of the gang shouted and shifted closer, their weapons at the ready.

"Slavik, if you and Siv step away, I can turn them all into ashes before they know it," projected Gunz, ready to spring into action.

"Something is not right, Gunz. I was expecting a lot more of them. Keep your strength. I'll deal with them on my own," replied Yaroslav, switching his attention back to the gang.

The rest happened so fast that Gunz could barely follow their movements. Yaroslav laughed and gave Siv a light kick on his sides. The horse reared and neighed angrily, smoke and fire coming out of his ears and nostrils. He pushed off the ground and jumped over the heads of the monsters, landing onto the pavement of the empty plaza. The demons shouted all at once and followed them, surrounding the vampire.

One moment, Yaroslav was still on his horse, and the next

BOOK SIX: EXCERPT

moment, he had vanished. The vampiric gang members followed him, becoming nothing more than a blur. The sound of metal on metal, cries of pain and curses rose in the air, but all that lasted no longer than a few seconds. The remaining group of gangsters stood back to back in the center of the plaza, staring around with wide eyes as they searched for Yaroslav, the weapons in their hands trembling. Both the horse and the rider were gone, leaving behind piles of dust and ashes.

Straightening to his full height, Gunz scanned the plaza but couldn't see his friend anywhere. Bright flares of light a few blocks away attracted his attention, and he sharpened his senses. Closing his eyes, he opened himself to the flow of magical energy and used his other sight to investigate the area.

"Slavik, where the hell are you?" he yelled through their blood bond. *"Something is going down a few blocks north. We need to get moving."*

The ground trembled under the even beat of Siv's hooves, and the rider, terrifying in his fury, materialized in front of the demons. Without slowing Siv down, he flew off the horse and landed on the pavement softly, graceful and dangerous like a nocturnal predator. Before the gangsters could react, he went through their lines, leaving piles of dead bodies behind. Siv neighed, crashing the remaining demons with his hooves, showering them with smoke and flames.

Once the last demon fell, Yaroslav swung up into the saddle and waved for Gunz to come down. Gunz jumped off the roof and grabbed Yaroslav's hand, getting behind him on the horse. Moving at a fast gallop, Siv passed through a couple of city blocks and came to a sharp halt, remaining under the cover of the shadows on the side of the road.

Past the intersection, a dark wall of demons stretched across the street, blocking their way. All of them were dressed in the Night's Angels getups, armed to the teeth, and looked even more ferocious than the previous group. Their motorcycles were parked behind the front line, barricading the road. Spread from the fence on the left side of the road to the fence on the right side, they made sure that there was no way around them. The only way to pass them was through.

"Dammit," exhaled Gunz, probing the new obstacle with his Salamander senses. "Why do I have the feeling that someone knows we are here and—"

"Doesn't want to be disturbed," Yaroslav finished his statement.

"I can carry you over them before they would even know what happened," suggested Siv, observing the motorcycle gang with his eyes narrowed. "No biggie."

"And leave behind at least a hundred of supernatural hostiles?" asked Gunz, shaking his head. "We can't do it. Thousands of innocent humans live around here."

He dismounted and tapped Yaroslav on his knee, pointing at the wall of demons.

"Slavik, I'll take the friendly bunch on the right," he said, manifesting his sword. "You and Siv can take the ones on the left. Just stay as far away from me as possible."

"Sounds like a grand plan. Let's not keep their bosses waiting."

Yaroslav winked at Gunz, a mischievous grin on his face seeming out of place in combination with the dangerous glow of his eyes. Gunz chuckled, shaking his head—taking things seriously wasn't in his friend's nature.

"Fire Salamander—go!" Yaroslav murmured and urged the dancing stallion toward the left side of the street.

DEAR READER

Thank you so much for reading The Burns Enigma. I hope you enjoyed the book and will join Zane Burns' next adventure in the sixth book of the series.

If you would like to stay up-to-date on the latest information about new releases, special offers, and more, sign up for my mailing list and get a FREE novella. Click here to join.

For more information follow me on Facebook and Instagram.

www.facebook.com/nmthornauthor
www.instagram.com/nmthornauthor/

Join N.M. Thorn's Facebook Fan Group to meet other readers, discuss the novels and the characters, get updates and do anything else related to the series.

BEFORE YOU GO...

Your reviews mean the world to me and are greatly appreciated. If you enjoyed the Burns Fire, please take a few minutes to leave a review. It doesn't have to be long. It can be just a few words or stars rating.

Please help spread the word by taking this small extra step and leave your review on Amazon and/or Goodreads.

ALSO BY N. M. THORN

The Fire Salamander Chronicles

The Burns Path (Prequel Novella Book 0 - for my subscribers)
The Burns Fire - Book 1
The Burns War - Book 2
The Burns Defiance - Book 3
The Burns Codex - Book 4

ABOUT THE AUTHOR

N.M. Thorn currently lives in South Florida with her husband and son. Owner of a digital marketing agency by day and a writer by night, she loves spending her times creating new worlds, paranormal planes of existence and anything that could be described as supernatural.

When she is not busy working with everything digital or exploring fantasy worlds, she enjoys spending time with her family, reading, painting and martial arts.

If you would like to share your thoughts, ideas or just send N.M. Thorn a message about the Fire Salamander world, feel free to contact her at: https://www.nmthorn.com/

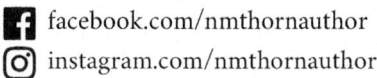

facebook.com/nmthornauthor

instagram.com/nmthornauthor

Printed in Great Britain
by Amazon